THE GRAND GAME
BOOK 9: DREAMS OF POWER

THE GRAND GAME
BOOK 9: DREAMS OF POWER

TOM ELLIOT

COPYRIGHT

THE GRAND GAME

The Forerunners have achieved the impossible. Or have they?

Michael has been playing the Game. Growing in strength. Slaying his foes. And avoiding entanglement with the Powers. But the time is fast coming when that will no longer be possible. Almost a Power himself, Michael must answer the question: is he ready? Are his people?
And what will they do if the truth is uncovered?

Join Michael on his epic journey and find out!

PRAISE FOR THE GRAND GAME:

"Interesting portal litrpg. Well-paced and the start of a new series. Curious to see where it goes..." —**Tao Wong on goodreads.com.**

"... Great action, great storyline and I honestly binge read it, start to end..." —**Alex Kozlowski on goodreads.com.**

"Smart MC. Great Tension. Full of Action." —**CookieCrumble on RoyalRoad.com.**

"Everything I look for in a LitRPG." —**CosmereCradleChris on RoyalRoad.com.**

"Oh I liked this very much!" —**The Enlightened Beard on amazon.com.**

"One of the best in this category this year." —**kindle customer on amazon.com.**

Author's Note

Dear Readers,

Thank you for reading the Grand Game. This is a self-published book. Even though care has been given to the review and editing of this novel, some mistakes may have slipped through. If you spot any grammatical errors or typos, please get in touch with me via email.

This book also contains game-like elements. They are generally unintrusive and integrated into the story, but beware, they exist. Otherwise, I hope you enjoy Michael's story.

Happy reading!
Tom (**TomLitRPG.com**)
Support me on PATREON

CONTENTS

MICHAEL'S EVOLUTION

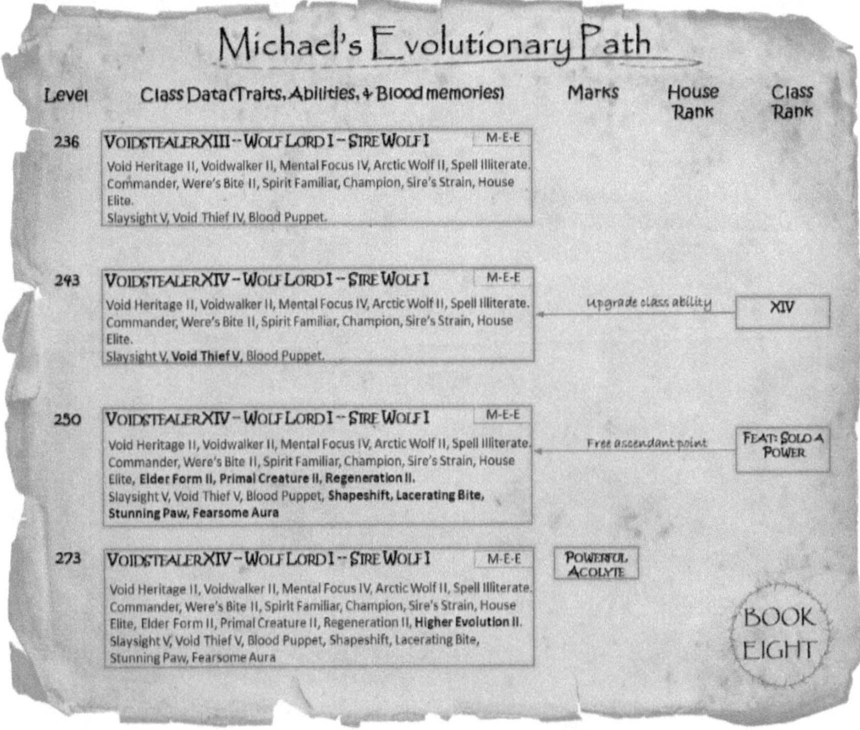

As always, Michael continues to grow during his adventures in the Forever Kingdom. The chart above only illustrates his latest achievements (as accomplished over the course of the last book). If you wish to view Michael's earlier evolutionary charts, please visit my site at the link below.

tomlitrpg.com/michael

The System of the Grand Game

The universe of the Grand Game continues to expand with every book in the series, and at this point, it no longer makes sense to include all the maps, charts, and diagrams in each new book.

If you wish to learn more about the world of the Forever Kingdom or understand the system of the Grand Game better, please visit my site at one of the links below.

tomlitrpg.com/game-lore
tomlitrpg.com/world-lore
tomlitrpg.com/glossary

Michael at the End of Book 8

Player Profile: Michael

Level: 273. **Rank:** 27. **Current Health:** 100%.
Species: Human. **Lives Remaining:** 4. **Ghost's Lives Remaining:** 4.
Active Pacts: 7 / 20.
True Marks: Powerful Acolyte.
True Marks (hidden): Worthy Adversary, Wolf Protector, Wolf Progenitor.
False Marks (fabricated): Lesser Shadow, Lesser Light, Lesser Dark.

Faction Data: Forerunners

Faction officers appointed: 2. **Sectors claimed:** 0 / 3 (+1 from Safyre).
Faction Leaders: Michael, Safyre. **Faction Custodian:** Adriel.
Players pledged: Nyra, Ceruvax, Terence, Teresa, Anriq, Shael, Keros, Sedgwick, +10 forsworn mages.
Non-players pledged: Adriel, Pack of the Reach (500), Bane Wolves warband (2,000), arctic wolves (200), dire wolves (130), nagians (100).

House Data

Governing bloodline: Wolf.
Core Tenet: Just Retribution.
Second Tenet: Protector of the Ancients.
Affinities: Renegades, outcasts, and criminals.
Followers: 2 / 200 (Nyra and Ceruvax).

Active Buffs

** denotes boosts affected by items.*
Damage reduction (DR) (reduces damage incurred only):
Life: 20%. Death: 25%. Air: 55%. Earth: 55%. Fire: 55%. Water: 55%.
Shadow: 40%. Light: 40%. Dark: 40%. Nether: 120%. Physical: 62%*.

Resistances (RES) (negates damage and/or rebuffs spell effects):
Life: 10%. Death: 12.5%. Air: 27.5%. Earth: 27.5%. Fire: 47.5%*. Water: 27.5%. Shadow: 20%. Light: 20%. Dark: 20%. Nether: 80%*. Physical: 0%.

Ghost (DR / RES): Fire: 85% / 102.5%. Nether: 85% / 102.5%. Physical: 91%* / 42.5%.

Stolen spells (3 / 3)

oblivion (tier 6), noxious vapors (tier 6), seeping shadows (tier 6): expires in 1.5 days.

Other Benefits derived from Items

Damage: +30% damage (ebonheart), +40% damage (faithful).
Abilities: perceive tier 6 spelled wards (sorcerer's coif), move soundlessly (wayfarer's boots), hands immune to hazardous substances (wayfarer's

gloves), spellhold: furious storm (mage's surprise), psi-feed (psi bracelet), penetrate tier 5 illusions (true-seer ring).
Traits: +20% aoe evasion (tiamaten vest).
Skills: +5 ranks in thieving (scoundrel's wristband).

Attributes

Available: 13 points.
Strength: 48 (40)*. **Constitution**: 56 (44)*. **Dexterity**: 166 (142)*.
Perception: 132 (127)*. **Mind**: 200 (188)*. **Magic**: 106 (85)*. **Faith**: 20.

Classes

Available (Michael): **1 point. 0 ascendant points.**
Available (Ghost): **1 point.**

Primary-Secondary-Tertiary tri-blend: voidstalker (fabricated). **voidstealer XIV (hidden).**
Ascendant Class: wolf lord (rank I, hidden), sire wolf (rank I, hidden).
Familiar: stygian pyre wolf XV (unique, hidden).

Traits

HFO: *denotes human-form-only benefits.*
WFO: *denotes wolf-form-only benefits.*

void heritage II (wolf, hidden): +4 Dexterity, +4 Strength, +8 Mind, +8 Perception, +12 Magic.
voidwalker II (wolf, hidden): improved senses in all conditions, nethersight, immunity to blindness.
arctic wolf II (wolf, hidden): +10 Constitution, +4 Mind, +6 Strength.
were's bite II (wolf, hidden, ascendant): 0 to 30% chance of granting another player the were-trait.
sire's strain (wolf, hidden, ascendant): boosts your other wolf traits by +1 tier.
elder form II (wolf, hidden, ascendant): +20 to all attributes, shapeshift.

house elite (bloodline, hidden): bound to House Wolf, detect dormant wolf bloodline strains.
secret blood (bloodline, hidden): conceals the wolf blood of yourself, your followers, and your familiar.
blood puppet (bloodline, hidden): grants you the enslave ability.

beast tongue: can speak to beastkin.
Marked: can see spirit signatures.
inscrutable mind: +8 Mind.
mental focus IV: increases effectiveness of Mind skills by 40%.
intrepid explorer: logs all locations in first-discovered sectors, and safe zone location in any visited sector.
spell illiterate: cannot cast mana-based spells.
potion resistance II: potency of potions reduced by 2 ranks.

spirit talker: can speak to spirits.
bold blood: +1 attribute per level.
higher evolution II: can evolve your Class to ascendant rank 2.
commander (ascendant): can share bloodline traits or blood memories with your followers.
champion (ascendant): increases the strength of blood memories.
spirit familiar: can bind a willing spirit as your familiar.
mage-host: +10 Mind, +10 Magic.
slip-through-shadows*: 20% chance to evade aoe damage.

spirit familiar (Ghost): mirrors player attributes and level, and shares ability slots with them.
psionic being (Ghost): retains telepathic skills and abilities from her former incarnation as a dire wolf.
free spirit (Ghost): can roam an unlimited distance from her host, but only within the same sector.
born again II (Ghost): grants your familiar 2 additional lives, will resurrect in spirit vessel.
pyreborn II (Ghost): +60% fire magic resistance and +60% fire damage.
voidborn II (Ghost): +60% nether resistance and +60% necrotic damage.
mirrored jewelry*: gains benefits of rank 7 rings, bracelets, and necklaces.

primal creature II (WFO, legendary): 18 feet long, +30% resistance, 3 attack types (physical, fire, poison).
regeneration II (WFO, legendary): health regeneration of +2% per second.

Skills

Available skill slots: 0.
light / hide armor (current: 180. Constitution, basic).

dodging (current: 232. Dexterity, basic).
sneaking (current: 249. Dexterity, basic).
shortswords / tooth and claw (current: 237. Dexterity & Strength (WFO), basic).
two weapon fighting (current: 213. Dexterity, advanced).
thieving (current: 180. Dexterity, basic).

chi (current: 208. Mind, advanced).
meditation (current: 240. Mind, basic).
telekinesis (current: 211. Mind, advanced).
telepathy (current: 237. Mind, advanced).

insight (current: 265. Perception, basic).
deception (current: 258. Perception, master).

channeling (current: 236. Magic, basic).
elemental absorption (current: 116. Magic, master).
null force (current: 82. Magic, master).

null life (current: 44. Magic, master).
null death (current: 53. Magic, master).
nether absorption (current: 244. Magic, master).

magma maw (Ghost) (current: 156. Magic, master).
stygian claws (Ghost) (current: 164. Strength, master).
ash armor (Ghost) (current: 171. Constitution, master).
telepathy (Ghost) (current: 137. Mind, advanced).
death magic (Ghost) (current: 141. Magic, advanced).
nether manipulation (Ghost) (current: 131. Magic, master).

Abilities

Constitution ability slots used: 15 / 44.
greater load controller (HFO) (15 Constitution, master, light armor).

Dexterity ability slots used: 141 / 142.
crippling blow (HFO) (Dexterity, basic, shortswords).
minor piercing strike (HFO) (5 Dexterity, advanced, shortswords).
deadly backstab (30 Dexterity, elite, sneaking).
superior trap disarm (HFO) (15 Dexterity, master, thieving).
superior lockpicking (HFO) (15 Dexterity, master, thieving).
greater set trap (HFO) (15 Dexterity, master, thieving).
wind daemon (30 Dexterity, elite, two weapon fighting).
vanish (30 Dexterity, elite, sneaking).

Mind ability slots used: 186 / 188.
mass puppet (15 Mind, master, telepathy).
stunning slap (HFO) (Mind, basic, chi).
improved windborne (15 Mind, master, telekinesis).
lesser engine of war (30 Mind, elite, chi).
sentient shurikens (HFO) (30 Elite, master, telepathy).
shadow jump (30 Mind, elite, telekinesis).
greater quick mend (30 Mind, elite, chi).
impregnable mind (30 Mind, elite, meditation).
astral bite (Ghost) (5 Mind, advanced, telepathy).

Perception ability slots used: 126 / 127.
powerful analyze (30 Perception, elite, insight).
greater trap detect (15 Perception, master, thieving).
conceal small weapon (HFO) (Perception, basic, deception).
mimic (HFO) (30 Perception, elite, deception).
superior ventro (5 Perception, advanced, deception).
doppelganger (45 Perception, grandmaster, deception).

Magic ability slots used: 20 / 85.
superior draining bite (Ghost) (10 Magic, expert, death magic).
mist-thin (Ghost) (10 Magic, expert, nether manipulation).

<u>Strength ability slots used:</u> 32 / 40.
charge (WFO) (1 Strength, basic, tooth and claw).
overpowering blow (WFO) (1 Strength, basic, tooth and claw).
ponderous steps (WFO) (30 Strength, elite, tooth and claw).

<u>Other abilities:</u>
adept slaysight (hidden) (Class, elite, telepathy): paralyze, shatter, sleep, terrify, blind.
void thief extraordinaire (hidden) (Class, elite, any void skill and telepathy): 3x steal, siphon, negate, redirect on direct-damage, channeled, damage over time, aoe, wards).
manifest (Ghost) (Class, master): explosive entry II, necrotic wake II.
diresight (Ghost) (Class, advanced, telepathy).
direshield (Ghost) (Class, expert, telepathy).
enslave (hidden) (blood memory, greater): dominate 2 subjects per day.
shapeshift (hidden) (ascendant Class, legendary): twice per day, greater elder wolf.
lacerating bite (WFO) (ascendant Class, epic, tooth and claw).
stunning paw (WFO) (ascendant Class, legendary, tooth and claw).
fearsome aura (WFO) (ascendant Class, legendary, telepathy).

Known Key Points

Kingdom Sector 1 (Nexus) safe zone.
Kingdom Sector 12,560 (wolves' valley) nether portal and safe zone.
Kingdom Sector 18,240 nether portal 1 (guardian tower), and nether portal 2 (Draven's reach).
Kingdom Sector 75,172 nether portal 1 (Draven's Reach) and safe zone.
Kingdom Sector 65,231 (Korg Minor) safe zone and nether portals to Korg Deep.
Kingdom Sector 65,232 (Korg Major) safe zone and nether portals from Korg Deep.
Kingdom Sector 45,104 (Brotherhood sector) safe zone.

Dungeon Sector 101 (scorching dunes) exit portal and safe zone.
Dungeon Sectors 102, 103, and 104 (haunted catacombs) exit portals and safe zones.
Dungeon Sector 105, 106, 107, 108, and 109 (guardian tower) exit portals.
Dungeon Sector 14,913 (candidate's dungeon) exit portal and safe zone.
Dungeon Sector 73,102 (Draven's Reach) one-way entrance portal, safe zone, and exit portal.

Nether Sector 30,199 nether portal 1 (dead) and Rift-X.

Aetherstone Bracelet Stored Points

sector 24,401 safe zone.

Netherstone Stored Point

sector 30,199 (Rift-X: somewhere in dunes).

<u>Equipped</u> (30 / 30 Game items)
<u>Weapons</u> (2 equipped)
ebonheart (+30% damage) (soulbound).
faithful (+40% damage).

<u>Armor & Clothes</u> (12 equipped)
tiamaten scalemail vest (+32%, +4 Constitution, slip-through-shadows).
sorcerer's coif (perceive tier 6 wards).
ranger's kit (+24% damage reduction, 4 pieces).
bomber's belt (5 x acid bombs, 5 x smoke bombs, 5 x ice bombs, and 5 x fire bombs).
belt of the chameleon (8 x rank 4 nether protection crystals, 9 x rank 4 disease protection crystals, 6 scent concealment crystals, 5 x mental concealment crystals, 4 x rank 6 disease protection crystals, 2 x rank 5 poison protection crystals, 1 x rank 4 strength enhancement crystals, 0 x rank 4 dexterity enhancement crystals, and 2 x rank 4 magic enhancement crystals).
wayfarer's boots (legendary item, +8 Dexterity, move soundlessly).
wayfarer's gloves (legendary item, +8 Dexterity, hands immune to hazardous substances).
cloak of the Reach (legendary soulbound item, +10 Magic, +20% fire magic resistance, +20% nether magic resistance).
scoundrel's wristband (+5 ranks thieving, 0 / 300 trap-making crystals) (<u>triggers</u>: pressure plates, sound glasses, tripwires, motion pins, remote control, spell detector, psi detector. <u>elements</u>: lightning, poison clouds, fire, spring-coiled daggers, bear-trap clamps, small explosives, blots of darkness, ice, spiked-pit, hallucinogenic mist. <u>guides</u>: reflect, split, and funnel. <u>keys</u>: remote, timed.)

<u>Rings & Accessories</u> (13 equipped)
goliath's ring (+8 Strength).
acrobat's ring (+8 Dexterity).
sharpshooter's band (+4 Perception).
hale stone (+8 Constitution).
savant's ring (+4 Mind).
troll's talisman bracelet (+6% damage reduction).
mage's surprise (+10 Magic, spellhold: trigger-cast tier 5 spells).
psi bracelet (legendary item, +8 Mind, psi-feed).
simple potion bracelet (3 / 3 full heal potions).
aetherstone bracelet (1 / 5 stored locations, 2 stone charged).
jeweled pet (grants Ghost: mirrored jewelry trait).
true-seer ring (true-seeing: penetrate tier 5 illusions).
Forerunner bracelet (council set, 1 of 30).
Brotherhood bracelet (set F05, 1 of 10).

<u>Other</u> (2 equipped)
large bag of holding (200 slots).

seeking eye of sylvana (legendary item, +invisible, 4 hours use, track & scout).

<u>Ghost (1 equipped)</u>
Forerunner collar (council set, 2 of 30).

<u>Backpack Contents (key items only)</u>

<u>Money</u>: 223 golds, 5 silvers, and 3 coppers.
1 x coil of rope.
cat claws.
20 x acid bombs, 20 x smoke bombs, 20 x ice bombs, and 20 x fire bombs.
small bag of hiding (tier 6 concealment ward).
a simple shovel.
stygian shortsword, +3.
stygian shortsword.
netherstone.
19 x greater portal scrolls.
packet of unrefined cynacilin powder.
farspeaker bracelet (Tyelin set, 1 of 15).
farspeaker bracelet (Safyre set, 1 of 4).

<u>Upgrade Items</u>
8 x upgrade gems.
piercing strike tier III, IV, & V.
ventro tier III & IV.
load controller V,
whirlwind V,
trap disarm V,
lockpicking tier V,
set trap V,
mass puppet V,
windborne V,
enhanced reflexes V,
trap detect V,
ventro V,
lesser imitate V,
charge II, III, IV & V,
overpowering blow II, III, IV & V,
stomp V.
2 x aetherstones (etched).

<u>Soulbound Items</u>
Tartan token.
Vivane token.
Kesh Emporium access card.
tavern bill of ownership.
BHG ID (junior member, 1 / 10 active jobs).
journeyman rogue's underworld token.

pioneer's compass (soulbound, attuned to safe zone).
unmarked chest key card (from Nicola).
Forerunner faction token (ID: 0001).

Miscellaneous Loot

None.

Alchemy Stone Contents

(500 / 500 ingredients stored).
310 x lumps of necrotic plasma, and 190 x vials of nether residue.

Bank Contents

Money: 655 gold, 0 silvers, and 0 coppers.
2 x full healing potions.
2 x full mana potions.

Tavern Money: 300 gold, 0 silvers, and 0 coppers.

Open Tasks

Heist in the Dark (steal chalice from the Power, Paya).
A Perverted Trial (stop the Triumvirate abuse of the Combat Trial).
Brokering Peace (establish peace in sector 12,560 within 4 months).
Brotherhood Obligations (join the brotherhood on three nether expeditions).
Revive the Guardians (awaken Draven's brethren).
Locate the Lost Prime (find the hidden Prime).
Resurrecting Death (make Adriel a scion again).
Found a new House (persuade two non-Wolf Powers to join your House).
A Place to Call Home (claim sector 18,240 within 9 days).
Rescue the lost Pup (rescue Saya).

Open Pacts

Deliver cynacilin. Status: pact obligations fulfilled. Blythe owes you a favor equivalent to the worth of sector 75,172.
Inner Council Pacts with Safyre, Anriq, Teresa, Terence, and Shael.
Guardian Tower Access Pact with Bacheus (deliver a tithe once a month for access).

Feats Accomplished (by book)

Solo your First Boss, Play the Game.
Novice Dungeoneer, Realize your Lineage.
Rift Defender, Pioneer of the Realms, Solo your First Dungeon.
(none).
Master Dungeoneer, The Bigger they Are, A Mighty Player.
Ascending to New Heights, Charging Headlong into Power, First of Many.
Apprentice Dungeoneer.
Solo a Power, Realm Explorer.

If you wish to view Michael's earlier player profiles, please visit my site at the links below.

tomlitrpg.com/michael

CHAPTER 580: HARBINGER AND TREE

...

...

Passage completed.
You have entered sector 30,199 of the Nethersphere.
Warning: The rift you traversed is closing! The void tree that created the ley line between sectors 30,199 and 18,240 is no longer anchoring the rift.

Estimated time until the ley line is no longer navigable: 4 minutes, 59 seconds. Return to the Kingdom before then or risk being stranded in the Nethersphere.

I entered the Nethersphere 'dressed' like a harbinger and riding on the back of a flying void tree. It was no wonder then that my entrance elicited cries of alarm and fear from the brotherhood. But they wouldn't stay scared for long, I knew.

Lowering my dog-like head, I surveyed the scene before me.

The battle between the brotherhood and stygians was still raging across the desert sands. To the west, I spied the orc Duskar leading his cavalry division of five hundred in a charge. Thundering across the sands, the players and their nightmare mounts ploughed straight through the horde of hydras attempting to stop them.

Far to the south and east, I spotted a few lone figures dotting the dune tops. Those had to be the brotherhood scouts tasked with keeping watch for fresh threats from the nest in this sector.

The thousand-strong division of spellcasters, led by the nether witch Cait, occupied a line of dunes to the north. Instead of using individual shields, the mages had erected an enormous silver dome to protect the entire division. It was a major working, impressive not just for its size but for the coordination it must have required. The air above the dome itself shimmered and sang as the spellcasters launched a veritable storm of magic on the stygian swarm south of them.

And swarm it was.

Of the ten thousand odd nether creatures that had started the battle, some two thousand were already slain. But it was mostly the lesser stygians that made up the dead. More than half of the seventy elite nagas that led them were still alive. All were shielded, and all were launching deadly voidballs at the silver dome protecting the brotherhood's spellcasters.

But the nagas concerned me little, and the lesser stygians even less.

It was the harbinger I searched for. The colossal creature—a hideous blend of bull, mammoth, and scorpion—was unmissable, and it didn't take me long to spot its corpse decorating the sands.

Ah, good, it's dead already. Relief sang through me. It was only the void tree that needed dealing with then.

My gaze flickered back to the brotherhood army, and specifically, the thin line of foot soldiers that was the only thing separating the spellcaster's shield dome from the swarm. I was searching for one person in particular—a tall woman with two curved swords and dressed in purple scale mail. Kartara.

There she is.

The huntmistress was staring up at me, or rather, at the young void tree in whose branches I sat, and even though a few hundred yards separated us, I could see her face clearly.

It was expressionless.

No matter that a void tree, a powerful psionic against which her people had few defenses, hovered in the air above her like a vengeful demigod. This situation had to be akin to her worst fears.

Yet, she showed no fear.

Betrayed no hesitation.

Which was dangerous—for me. Soon, she was going to order her people to attack the new threat. Or *threats*. Because from her perspective, I was one too.

You have crossed through a tier 5 barrier dome spell. This shield prevents entities of tier 5 and below from crossing through.

My gaze flickered to the right—to the shimmering haze of purple curving off into the distance and around the rift behind me. It was the brotherhood spell stopping the lesser stygians and nagas from re-entering sector 18,240. What the void tree had called a 'lock.'

My neck craned further back. The rift was there, ever-present. It was shrinking certainly, but still open and, according to the sector welcome message, would remain so for the next five minutes. Still, I didn't think the rift was a factor anymore. The stygians on the other side were a spent force, especially now that the young void tree had abandoned them.

Almost as if the thought had summoned him, the void tree spoke anew.

"WOLFLING..."

At the same time, Kartara projected her voice forcefully through the farspeaker bracelet on my wrist.

"Dusk, break off your attack. Retreat all the way to the mages. I want your people on standby but under cover and protected. Be ready to rush the new harbinger on my order. Cait, reassign seven companies to defense. The silver dome must be expanded. It will have to shield the entire army now."

"What about the rift?" the nether witch protested. *"If I have to re-task that many mages, we won't be able to keep it sealed."*

"Forget the rift!" the huntmistress snapped. *"It's not a priority anymore."* Not bothering to wait for Cait's response, she went on. *"Heg, order the foot soldiers back. The line is to retreat. I want the infantry reformed under the silver dome as well. Senzo, have your people disappear into the sands. They are to avoid the tree's notice, at all costs. But find out what the hell is happening out there! Is a second swarm heading our way?"*

She fears an ambush, I realized. Because from the huntmistress' perspective, it would make no sense for the tree to emerge from the rift alone and unaccompanied.

The tree's branches rustled.

I eyed them warily. Only seconds had passed since our transition through the rift. Still, I found it surprising that the tree had not attacked yet. It was the only reason I'd not resumed my own assault.

Well, that, and the fact that I would be at a distinct disadvantage in an airborne fight.

Dodging the tree's stygian thorns while having only his branches to rely on for solid footing would not be easy. Not to mention, there were also the few hundred flying serpents winging their way to me to consider. Had the tree summoned them? Was that why it had not attacked yet? Was it waiting for its reinforcements?

"WOLFLING... YOU... DID... THIS."

Interestingly enough, the tree made no reference to Kartara's rapid-fire commands across the farspeaker network, nor to the still ongoing discussions between the huntmistress and her subordinates. Could he not hear them? And did I dare contact her?

"WOLFLING..." the tree thundered, all his branches quivering in anger now. *"TELL... THEM... TO... STOP."*

"Stop what? I whispered, projecting my voice with ventro.

"STOP... KILLING... MY... CREATIONS."

I blinked. He meant the nagas. The void tree seemed fixated with them and wanted them protected. That meant we had leverage against him. But I rather doubted I would be able to get the huntmistress to call off the assault on the nagas—and in the middle of a battle, no less—especially since she was likely to be doubly wary about the messenger.

I looked like a harbinger, after all, and I'd come through the rift accompanied by the tree. Then, too, Kartara was already suspicious of my previous persona, Havick. No, speaking to the huntmistress now was not going to get me far.

But perhaps there was another way I could use the tree's obsession with the nagas.

"And if I don't?" I taunted.

"THEN... YOU... WILL... DIE... HORRIBLY."

My lips curled into a contented snarl. It was better for the tree to focus his ire on me than on the brotherhood army below. "Do your best, then," I growled and began my assault.

＊　＊　＊

You have cast wind daemon, multiplying your speed by 2x for 1 minute.

You have cast seeping shadows (modifying your attacks to deal shadow damage and increase your foe's shadow affliction by +5%). Duration: 1 minute.

My paws brimming with Ceruvax's seeping shadow buff, I raked my claws into the branch underfoot.

You have failed to stun a young void tree with stunning paw.
You have grazed your target, afflicting him with shadow. Current affliction: 5%.

My foe responded instantly. Whipping forward a few of his branches, he flung four separate streams of black thorns my way. Worse yet, the volleys were all launched from different directions.

But the tree could not match me for speed, and as widespread as the thorn barrage was, with wind daemon empowering my limbs, I was faster. Ducking, leaping, twisting, and contorting my body, I managed to avoid being hit.

You have evaded a stygian thorn.
You have evaded a stygian thorn.
...
...

More of the tree's limbs quivered—at least a dozen this time. *Hells*, I thought, my pulse quickening. *Is he going to expend his entire load of thorns in a bid to get me?*

It seemed that way.

The stygian thorns were a strange—and perhaps unique—psionic construct that I had not encountered elsewhere in the Game. Alike, yet different from my own astral blades, they were not created through a casting. Instead, they *grew* on the tree's branches, replenishing slowly over time.

On the one hand, this left the void tree with a huge arsenal of the psionic constructs—somewhere in the region of a few thousand projectiles—but on the other hand, it also meant the tree's thorn ammunition was limited—at least in the short term.

Once my foe stripped his branches of the thorns, he would have no more projectiles to throw at me. And worse yet—from the tree's perspective, anyway—he had already wasted many of his thorns in the first half of the battle on the other side of the rift.

This, though, didn't mean as much as I would have liked it to.

The void tree still had more than a thousand thorns to throw at me, and from the looks of it, he seemed intent on expending all of them in the space of a few seconds.

Twelve tree branches whipped forward, saturating the air with the ebon slivers.

Knowing I had no choice, I played my trump card—and shadow jumped.

You have teleported into a level 230 stygian naga's shadow.

I wasn't fleeing, not exactly.

Rather, I was changing the nature of the contest. If there was one thing I was sure would rile the tree further—and perhaps even force him to ground—it would be me attacking his creations.

Emerging from the aether, I found myself in the middle of the nagas' formation and surrounded by thousands of lesser stygians. I was in the very heart of the swarm—a swarm still under magical assault from the brotherhood.

I didn't let any of that bother me, though. Lunging forward, I struck at the naga in front of me with tooth and claw.

You have cast overpowering blow.
You have hit a stygian naga for 1.5x more damage.
A stygian naga's shield has blocked your attacks.
You have critically hit a stygian naga.
You have critically hit a stygian naga.
Your target's shield has been destroyed!

The naga's defenses, already weakened by the brotherhood mages' spells, wasn't able to withstand my onslaught and collapsed before the hapless creature even realized it was under fresh assault.

Leaping forward, I wrapped my jaws around the nape of the elite's neck and bit down—anchoring myself in place—while I beat at it with both my paws.

A stygian naga has failed to resist lacerating bite.
Your target is <u>bleeding</u>. Duration: 23 seconds.
You have stunned a stygian naga for 5 seconds with stunning paw.
You have backstabbed a stygian naga for 5x more damage.
You have backstabbed a stygian naga for 5x more damage.
A level 230 stygian naga has been killed.

The giant snake collapsed bonelessly beneath me, its slaying the work of mere seconds. Lifting my bloody muzzle, I took stock of the surroundings.

Every naga in range was staring at me. I had their attention for sure. And not only theirs.

"WOLFLING... STOP!"

"MAKE ME," I roared, not caring whether the void tree heard me or not. Launching off the corpse underfoot, I rushed towards the next naga.

It was time to wreak havoc.

Chapter 581: Killing Machine

My plan was simple. To kill as many nagas as I could and in as short a space of time as I could manage. And the best way to go about that was using my telepathic abilities.

So, weaving psi, I cast.

You have activated fearsome aura.
You have failed to petrify any hostiles.
Your targets are shielded from mental manipulation by the protective aura of a level 340 young void tree.

I grimaced. The spell's failure would only make what I had to do harder.

But the outcome of my casting was not entirely unexpected. I'd been hoping that being airborne would weaken some of the stygian Power's abilities—or perhaps even remove them entirely. Alas, it seemed this would not be the case.

Still, I had other weapons in my arsenal. Drawing stamina, I cast anew.

You have cast vanish. You have failed to conceal yourself.
Multiple hostile entities have detected you.

"Damn spores," I growled. Sector 30,199 was obviously still rife with them. I didn't dare stand idle long enough to cast oblivion and get rid of the tiny creatures, though.

A pack of hydras was pounding toward me from the right, while from above, two dozen flying serpents had reversed course and were diving down. Then there were the nagas. Nearly all of them had broken off their attacks against the brotherhood and, instead, were turning their attention inward.

To me.

Even as powerful as I was as an elder wolf—which was the true form I wore beneath the doppelganger disguise—there was no way I would survive a concentrated assault from forty-odd elites. *Right then, I guess that means it's time to split the enemy's attention.*

"Ghost, you'd better join me."

The pyre wolf had been eagerly awaiting the instruction. *"My pleasure, Prime,"* she replied with bloodthirsty glee.

My familiar exploded onto the battlefield—literally.

She emerged fifty yards to my right, in almost the exact center of the incoming hydras and wreathed in flames. Billowing out, they consumed everything in a ten yard radius.

Ghost has cast explosive manifest, taking the form of a level 273 stygian pyre wolf.
27 hostile entities have been critically injured.
6 hostile entities have been killed.
2 hostile entities have blocked your familiar's attack.

The hydras shrieked as, all of a sudden, they were subjected to searing flames. Their skin charred, their eyes melted, and their insides smoldered.

"Excellent work, Ghost," I murmured. Leaving the pyre wolf to her mayhem, I swung to face the opposite direction. Six nagas were bearing down on me, their eyes gleaming with righteous fury and their shields brimming with energy.

As if that will protect them.

I didn't turn to run. I didn't use shadow jump to flee. Instead, I charged headlong across the dunes to meet the six, drawing stamina as I went.

You have cast ponderous step. You are now <u>heavy</u> (causing the ground to shake with each step). Duration: 1 minute.

New energy coursed through me, giving my body new weight as the spell took effect. The ground underfoot heaved, trembling at each strike of my paw, and all about me in a ten yard radius, the sand rippled and the dunes shook.

The six nagas slowed.

Perhaps they finally realized what threat they faced, or perhaps the void tree was in their ear, telling them to flee. Whatever the case, it didn't matter. It was already too late for them.

Flying across the ground at breakneck speed, I rushed into the nagas' midst.

2 of 6 stygian nagas have passed a physical resistance check.

You have knocked down 4 stygian nagas, disrupting their concentration for 1 second.

A snaking head snapped down. Altering course nimbly, I evaded the attack.

A tail whipped through the air. Dropping to my belly, I let the slashing appendage pass harmlessly by.

Two nagas opened their mouths, spewing out a malign mix of noxious bile, hissing black fumes, and who knows what else. But I was done with dodging. Trusting my void armor to fend off the attack, I leaped upward and straight at the closest.

2 x sprays of cloying death have hit you. Nether and death magic damage repelled!

A level 241 naga's shield has blocked your attacks.

Using my lupine skull like a battering ram, I struck the stygian elite I targeted head-on. My attack failed to penetrate my foe's shield, of course, but it *did* send the black bubble encasing it tumbling backward—and away from the rest of the naga pack. Which was what I'd been aiming for.

I didn't drop back down to the ground either.

Instead, using three of my clawed paws to cling to the naga's shield as tenaciously as any cat, I lashed at it with my final paw.

Five strikes.

That was all it took. After five daemon-fast strikes empowered with overpowering blow, the naga's shield burst like an overripe fruit.

It should have come as no surprise, really. Many of the buffs the forerunners' elites had cast upon me in sector 18,240 continued to bolster my attacks. Still, I was almost caught off guard as the black bubble collapsed beneath me before the thing had completed so much as a quarter turn.

But only almost.

Dropping down on the naga—which, needless to say, was even more astonished than I was—I locked my teeth around its neck. This time around, I didn't bother with using my jaw to keep it subdued while I raked at it with my paws. There was no need for such. It had taken me this long, but I finally realized, courtesy of my allies' buffs and my elder form, I was a veritable killing machine.

So, I did what I should have with the previous naga I'd killed.

I closed my jaws tight around my foe's neck and yanked.

Scales compressed. Flesh tore. Bones shattered. And a split-second later, I found my mouth full of revolting meat.

You have killed a level 241 stygian naga with a fatal blow.

Urgh. Turning my head to the side, I spat, ejecting the stygian's foul remains. In a single bite, I'd ripped away the greater part of the creature's neck, leaving its head clinging to a strip of flesh too meager to hold it up.

Damn, this may be easier than I'd—

A voidball has hit you.
A voidball has hit you.
A voidball has hit you.
Nether damage repelled! Void armor charge remaining: 85%.
Void thief triggered!
Warning: you have reached the limit of your stolen spells. Do you wish to replace any of your 3 tier 6 stolen spells with the tier 5 voidball spell? If you refuse, knowledge of the new spell will be lost.

I didn't bother stealing the voidball spell. There was no point. I was already immune to nether damage, and besides, the naga's spell was less powerful than those I'd acquired from my allies.

Still, I couldn't afford to be needlessly struck. Whipping around, I spied another dozen orbs of churning dark energy sailing toward me. They could be easily dodged, though. My gaze darted back to the remaining five nagas in the pack. The three voidballs had come from them.

They've had their shot. My turn now.

Rushing forward, I threw myself into the fray again.

✳ ✳ ✳

You have killed a level 241 stygian naga with a fatal blow.
You have killed a level 220 stygian naga with a fatal blow.
You have killed a level 233 stygian naga with a fatal blow.
...
...

I killed the five other nagas as easily as I had the first. The entire time, I had the void tree screaming in my ear. He railed, ordered, threatened, and even begged me to stop.

I ignored him, of course.

The stygian Power was doing exactly what I wanted—rushing groundward. And if it was my killing of his creations that was spurring him on—and it seemed it was—I saw no reason to stop what I was doing.

The six elites' deaths affected the battle in other ways, too.

The nagas' response was the most noticeable. Not only did the three dozen remaining elites stop converging on me, they reversed course with pleasing alacrity and rushed south through the rest of the swarm.

The nagas, it seemed, had decided to flee the battlefield.

On the young void tree's orders, no doubt. Content to let them go, I turned my attention to Ghost. The pyre wolf was inflicting her own brand of mayhem on the swarm. Exploding in and out of the battle, she left a swath of mangled and twisted lesser stygian corpses in her wake.

Recognizing the pyre wolf for the threat she was, much of the swarm had refocused their attention on her. I was not concerned, though. Ghost's nether and fire magic resistance had improved to the extent that she was immune to both, and even the nagas would have a hard time hurting her now.

Besides, if the pyre wolf did get into any serious trouble, she could simply unmanifest and escape with impunity. No, Ghost was not in any danger, not from the lesser stygians, anyway.

My gaze drifted upward. The void tree, on the other hand, was another matter.

"Will you flee too?" I shouted. *"Are you as craven as your creations?"*

The stygian Power was not, in fact, fleeing. He was descending toward me at what I suspected was the fastest rate he could manage, but I didn't let the truth dissuade me.

"I... WILL... KILL... YOU... SLOWLY... FOR... THIS... WOLFLING!"

I eyed the void tree speculatively. The wormlike mass of fleshy white appendages that hung below the Power—his roots—were writhing violently.

By all appearances, my foe was furious—so furious, he was behaving irrationally and rushing heedlessly into danger. But could I trust to that? Or was this all some sort of ploy?

In my gut, I knew it wasn't.

For all his power and mental strength, my foe was no tactician. During my week-long probe of the void tree's nest—former nest now, I supposed—he had erred in too many ways for all of it to have been an act. The two overlords he'd sent away, the two he had kept dormant, the lesser stygians whose lives he'd spent so frivolously, and even the harbingers who had walked into a trap on his orders, all pointed to one thing.

The young void tree was arrogant.

So convinced was he of his own invincibility that even now, after being forced to flee sector 18,240, he didn't seem to truly comprehend the danger he was in. It was a mistake for which I would make sure he paid the ultimate price. But before that—I glanced back over my shoulder at the brotherhood army—there was the small matter of allies to attend to.

The single glance I cast over my rear was enough to assure me that things were faring as well as they could with the brotherhood. Duskar's cavalry company was already sheltering behind the much-expanded silver dome, and even the infantry was nearly within its reach.

The brotherhood's farspeaker communication network was ablaze with chatter and had been so ever since the first communication I'd overheard. And even though I listened with only half an ear, I could not fail to hear the furious questions being lobbed back and forth as the huntmistress and her subordinates tried to make sense of what they were seeing.

A hydra roared.

The sound rose from so shockingly close I felt the ground beneath vibrate. Swinging my head back around, I found myself face-to-face with a large stygian. There was no time to dodge or weave psi, so I did the only thing I could. I ducked my head, protecting my eyes.

Six gargantuan jaws locked down on the scruff of my neck and tugged—hard.

I did not budge. Not an inch.

Even the hydra's prodigious strength was no match for my elder form's defenses. Raising my head and baring my teeth in a vicious snarl, I battered the creature away with a massive paw.

You have stunned a level 147 stygian hydra for 5 seconds.

With a startled hiss, the nether creature's jaws unlocked as it sagged senselessly beside me. Paying the hydra no further heed, I studied the vicinity anew. Despite the ease with which I'd defeated the stygian, its attack was a timely reminder. Notwithstanding the nagas' flight, I was still inside a stygian swarm—one bent on killing me.

I could not afford to grow careless.

Stepping over the downed stygian, I fixed my gaze southward. I needed to contact Kartara, but I also needed to draw the void tree as far away as possible from the more vulnerable brotherhood, and the best way to do that was to pursue the fleeing elites.

"I'm going after the nagas," I told Ghost as I broke out in a run.

"Alright," she said uncertainly. *"But what about the void tree?"*

"He will follow me," I replied confidently. *"But if, for some reason, he doesn't, unmanifest. Don't risk entangling with the thing. Clear?"*

"Clear," she acknowledged.

"And don't engage the brotherhood either," I warned. *"They don't know we are on their side yet, and I don't want to risk antagonizing them further."*

"I won't," she promised. *"Good hunting, Prime."*

"Thanks, Ghost," I murmured, and shadow jumped.

You have teleported into a level 234 stygian naga's shadow.

* * *

You have killed a level 234 stygian naga with a fatal blow.

"NO... YOU... WRETCHED... CREATURE. STOP!"

Raising my head from the bloody corpse at my feet, I stared skyward. Just as I had expected, the young void tree had altered his course and was flying southward as fast as he could. Still, I judged it would take the stygian Power at least another minute to catch up to the fleeing nagas and me.

Plenty of time to thin their numbers further.

Slinking forward, I went in search of my next victim. While I did, I listened more fully to the babble of voices on the farspeaker link.

"...telling you. This is our chance," Duskar was saying. *"We have to act now, while it's still distracted."*

"There's no reason to attack the harbinger just yet," Cait protested. *"Just look at what it's doing. It's killing the nagas faster than we can. By the Powers, it has already slain eight!"*

"It's a trick," Duskar scoffed.

You have killed a level 227 stygian naga.

"Make that nine!" Cait crowed.

"I hate to disagree, Dusk," Senzo said quietly, *"but whatever is going on is no trick. Fiona and I have analyzed the corpses, and there can be no doubt: those nagas are truly dead."*

"Then something has driven the damnable thing mad," Duskar growled. *"And anyhow, the harbinger is still dangerous. We should kill it while we still have the chance."*

"On the contrary, we should capture and study it," Cait objected. *"I highly doubt that the harbinger is mad. But if it were, imagine what we could learn from it!"*

"Capture it?" Duskar laughed. *"That's insane."*

You have killed a level 233 stygian naga.

"Insane?" Cait asked sharply. *"Are you sure you want to—"*

"We will not try to capture the harbinger," Kartara said, cutting across the chatter. *"Duskar is right. Attempting to do so will be too dangerous."*

"But—" the nether witch began in protest.

"Enough, Cait," the huntmistress snapped. *"Heg, an update, please."*

"We're in position," a voice I didn't recognize said. *"The last infantry squad is now safely under the dome."*

"Excellent," Kartara murmured. *"Now, people, enough about the harbinger. We know what it is doing. But what about the void tree? Anyone care to hazard a guess as to what it has in mind?"*

Momentary silence.

You have killed a level 230 stygian naga.

"It appears to be fleeing south," Senzo ventured finally.

"Or it's trying to lure us into an ambush that way," Duskar muttered.

"Why bother, though?" Cait asked. *"Even with the dome, our mental defenses are not strong enough to resist the tree's influence. It should be able to break through before we can do more than scratch it."*

"True," Kartara mused. *"Unless..."* I could almost sense her frown. *"Unless it's injured,"* she finished. *"Senzo?"*

"Checking with Fiona now," he replied.

Another drawn-out pause.

"Fiona has managed to analyze it," the spymaster reported back eventually.

"And?" Duskar demanded impatiently.

You have killed a level 218 stygian naga.

"It's definitely injured," Senzo said. *"But nowhere near enough for it to be fleeing. It still has around half its health."*

"Only half?" Kartara wondered. *"Did Fiona manage to get an exact read?"*

A pause, then, *"Yes. The young void tree's health is at sixty-three percent."*

That number caught even my attention. Pausing in my rampage through the nagas, I raised my eyes skyward once more and inspected the floating Power anew.

A young void tree's health is at 63%.

Well, well, I mused as my own analysis confirmed the brotherhood diviner's results. At the end of our initial skirmish in sector 18,240, the stygian Power's health had been at fifty-seven percent. I had *assumed* he would have restored himself in the interim and had not bothered reanalyzing him since.

So, why hadn't he?

"Why hasn't it healed itself?" Duskar asked, unconsciously echoing my own question.

"It can't," Cait pronounced, *"not while it is floating, anyway. A void tree's roots must be grounded in order for it to feed off the mists."*

Thank you, Cait, I whispered to myself.

The nether witch's words, however, called into question my own strategy and left me wondering if it was wise to let the void tree land. If my foe couldn't heal himself until he was grounded, what else couldn't he do while airborne?

Was it time to change tack?

"Then Havick wasn't entirely full of nonsense," Kartara said in a contemplative tone. *"He was able to harm the void tree—and appreciably."*

"Too bad he isn't here," Duskar growled.

I couldn't have asked for a better cue to join the conversation. *"Oh, but I am,"* I said, speaking into the farspeaker bracelet for the first time.

Stark silence followed my pronouncement.

I waited patiently, having anticipated their reaction. Using the farspeaker bracelet was a risk, but not an appreciable one anymore, considering the new distance between me and the void tree.

Despite his rapid approach, the stygian Power was still hundreds of yards away. That distance was the only reason I had risked the earlier telepathic communication with Ghost—or let her manifest in the first place—and now it should also serve to keep the void tree from eavesdropping on my conversation with the brotherhood.

"Who is this?" the huntmistress demanded sharply.

"Come, Kartara," I said gently. *"You know who it is."*

"Havick?"

"Yes."

"Where are you hiding?"

"I'm not."

I could have told her where I was, of course, but it was better if the brotherhood worked it out for themselves.

"Kartara," the spymaster called abruptly. *"I didn't mention it earlier, not thinking it pertinent, but now..."*

"Just spit it out, Senzo," the huntmistress snapped.

"Fiona thinks there is something amiss about the harbinger," he reported.

"Amiss how?" Kartara asked testily. Clearly, events were moving fast enough that even the huntmistress' temper was fraying.

"She isn't sure," Senzo replied. Then, as if sensing his leader's growing impatience, he added hastily, *"There is nothing wrong with its analyze data. It's perfect. But it has not used any death spells or its tail to attack. Not once."*

I chuckled. *"My tail. I will have to remember that. Note to self: use it more, or pretend to."* Unlike a real basilisk's tail, my wolf form tail was not an offensive weapon.

Kartara inhaled sharply. *"You are the harbinger,"* she stated flatly.

"I am."

"Nonsense," Duskar declared. *"Havick can't be the harbinger. It's a trick—and we all know what sort of tricks the void trees can play. This must be another one."*

"This is no trick," I replied adamantly. *"If you don't believe me, have a look at the rift."*

"What about it?" he growled.

"It's closing."

"Another lie," he snarled.

"It's not," I insisted. *"Check your Game messages, you'll see. According to my own alerts, the rift will seal in exactly one minute, fifty-three seconds."*

"By damn," Senzo murmured. *"He's not lying. It is closing."*

"See? I told you. The rift is closing—courtesy of the work my allies and I performed on the other side. Now, is that enough to allay your suspicions, Duskar? Or can you imagine a scenario where the void will go to all the trouble of killing its own creatures and abandoning its claim on an entire sector just to deceive you?"

It was not Duskar who answered, however, but the huntmistress. *"We believe you,"* she said with a finality that the others did not fail to miss.

"You've shapeshifted into a harbinger?" Cait asked in awe. *"How is that possible?"*

"Well, I haven't, not really. I'm a doppelganger." I was fairly certain Kartara had already worked out this bit for herself, given the discrepancies Fiona

had observed now and during my previous incarnations as Havick, and I saw no reason not to reveal the truth anymore.

"The doppelganger ability is a tier six one," Kartara said evenly.

"It is."

"Then you are a Powerful Initiate," the huntmistress said.

Her pronouncement set her subordinates muttering in consternation again, but the brotherhood leader didn't sound all that surprised herself. But then again, I'd given her plenty of clues: my use of vanish, my ability to confound their diviner Fiona, and last but not least, the netherstone—an artifact that could only be obtained by slaying a stygian Power.

"I'm guessing you worked out that much before today," I murmured.

"I did, but it's a matter for discussion at a more opportune time." A pause. *"Right now, I'm more interested in what you intend on doing about the void tree."*

"Kill it," I said succinctly. *"Are you with me?"*

The huntmistress didn't reply immediately, but when she did, the eagerness—and hunger—in her voice was undisguised.

"Oh, we are. We definitely are."

Kartara's words sent a ripple of excitement coursing through me. I'd half-feared her cynicism and distrust would get the better of her, but I'd not misjudged the huntmistress. She knew as well as I did that this was not an opportunity she could let slip by.

The first real chance the brotherhood had in years—or was that decades or centuries?—to slay a void tree. They could not let it go abegging.

I jerked my muzzle upward. But time was short, and we didn't have much of it to decide on how to go about killing the stygian Power. Already, the void tree had descended to three hundred feet. He was still screaming in my metaphorical ear, but I'd long since stopped listening.

"What do you need us to do?" Kartara asked.

If I were in human form, I would have smiled. The huntmistress was not trying to take charge. When it came to tackling the void tree, *I* was the expert, and the tactics we would employ were mine to decide—rightfully so.

"I'm going to teleport onto the tree again," I replied. *"I will be more effective if I am up close. Unfortunately, entering melee range is also going to help the tree's own attacks. Dodging all his thorns is going to be nearly impossible. Any way you could help with that?"*

"Did he just refer to the void tree as a 'he'?" Cait muttered.

Ignoring the nether witch's interjection, the huntmistress asked a question of her own. *"Hmm. Can you survive one of its—his—thorn salvos?"*

"Yes," I said simply.

"Then don't bother dodging. My people will handle it."

"Excellent," I replied, not questioning her confidence. *"Another thing. Can you stop him from rooting himself again?"*

"I assume you want to prevent him from healing anew?"

"That's the idea," I agreed.

"Cait will see to it. And don't worry about the flying serpents. We'll keep them off your back, too."

"Thank you," I murmured. I wasn't worried about winged snakes, but I didn't bother explaining.

It seemed that while the void tree was dead set on protecting the nagas— all of whom were still fleeing southwards—he had no compunctions about sacrificing the lesser stygians in a bid to delay my slaughter of his creations, and the creatures had already attacked me multiple times during my conversation with the brotherhood.

None of the flying serpents had come close to harming me, though, nor, for that matter, had any of their landbound fellows. The creatures simply lacked the raw power or speed to harm me. I'd grown too strong for them.

Drawing mana, stamina, and psi, I saw to my preparation. *"One last thing,"* I said to Kartara.

"Yes?"

You have cast seeping shadows.

"The stygian wolf—make sure she stays alive."

"You summoned her?" the huntmistress guessed.

You have cast wind daemon.

"I did," I replied, again choosing not to elaborate. There would be time aplenty to discuss Ghost's true nature later if it became necessary. *"Keep her safe."* I drew psi, preparing to shadow jump. *"I'm good to go. Are your people ready?"*

"They are."

The psi spell thrummed in my mind, waiting for release. *"Good. Then, you won't hear from me again—not until the void tree is dead. I won't risk using the farspeaker link while in melee range."*

"That's probably wise," Kartara agreed, then added more softly, *"Good luck, Havick."*

"Thanks. Let's hope I won't need it." Not waiting for her response, I released the spell weave I held and blinked out.

✳   ✳   ✳

You have teleported onto a level 340 young void tree.

"YOU... AGAIN!" the tree bellowed.

"That's right, I'm back," I agreed, running lithely along one of the Power's larger branches until I reached his trunk.

It was hard to imagine where the tree's consciousness lay, but at a guess, it was either within his solid center or the mass of roots beneath, and if I wanted to inflict fatal damage, it was against either of these areas that I had to strike. "It's time we finished this."

"GLADLY!"

Not deigning to reply, I dug my clawed hind quarters into the hard bark beneath and anchored myself in place. With any luck, if the brotherhood did as they promised, this round, the fourth and final round of my skirmish with the tree—*or was that fifth?*—would go much quicker. Raising a paw, I got to it.

You have grazed your target, afflicting him with shadow. Current affliction: 5%.

My right forelimb a blur, I raked my claws down the trunk before me, barely scuffing the bark's surface. But that was alright. I was only just getting started.

My left paw flashed out. My right again. Then left. And right once more.

You have stunned a young void tree for 1 second (partially resisted).
You have grazed your target.
You have grazed your target.
You have grazed your target.
A level 340 young void tree's shadow affliction has increased to 25%.

Of course, my foe did not stand idly by while I laid into him with my paws. Eight of his branches quivering in outrage, the void tree, launched a formidable salvo of thorns.

Steeling myself for what was to come, I ignored the onrushing missiles and kept slashing at the tree's bark.

You have grazed your target.

…

…

Fortunately for me, my foe had not concentrated his attack. No doubt, expecting me to dodge, he had decided to saturate the area and make evasion impossible. As it was, he only weakened the effectiveness of his assault. I smiled grimly. It would be a good test case of the brotherhood's capabilities.

The tree's salvo was almost on me. *How are they going to stop it?*

But the brotherhood didn't stop it.

And the deluge of ebon black slivers descended upon me unimpeded.

A stygian thorn has failed to injure you. The attack has been blocked by your impregnable mind, consuming 0.1% psi in the process.

…

I reeled under the psychic assault, and as the seconds ticked by, and one after the other, the black thorns struck, each eating away a tiny percentage of my psi, I couldn't help but wonder if I'd been betrayed.

A stygian thorn has failed to injure you.
A stygian thorn has failed to injure you.

…

I didn't forgo my own attacks, though. If I had been betrayed, I would deal with it *after*. And there would be an after, that much I was certain of. As deadly as this thorn barrage was, it was not enough to stop me.

Your psi is now at 63%.
A level 340 young void tree's shadow affliction has increased to 55%.

The black shower ended, leaving me scathed, but far from defeated. My face contorting in a snarl, I broke off my attacks and drew psi. I'd weathered one salvo. But I was not so sure I would survive another, especially not if the void tree concentrated his next attack and launched many times more—

Haskil has cast time lapse, restoring any health, mana, stamina, and psi you lost during the last 5 seconds. Your psi is now at 92%.

I blinked. *Haskil.* That had to be a brotherhood mage. And that spell… Now, I understood why the huntmistress asked the question she had.

A voice came through the farspeaker bracelet. It was Kartara. She was not speaking to me, but I suspected she meant for me to overhear. *"Cait, is your spell ready?"*

"Yes."

"Good. Release it."

There was no answering response from the nether witch, but it was only a moment later that I found out what spell the huntmistress had in mind.

Cait has activated a witching eye's <u>transference</u> buff.
Cait wishes to add you to a transference circle. Do you accept?

Even though I had no idea what a transference circle was, any doubts I had about the brotherhood's motives had been assuaged, and I wasted no time in responding in the affirmative.

You have been designated as the <u>center of a transference circle</u>. As its focus, your mana, psi, stamina, and health will constantly be replenished by the other transference participants, draining them in turn. Current number of participants: 12. Duration: unlimited; this buff will remain in effect as long as transference participants continue to channel their energy into the circle.

The connection was instantaneous. One second, I was a single man—or wolf as the case may be—fighting on my lonesome, the next, I was at the center of an enormous confluence of energy as twelve conduits of spirit sprang into being to connect me to the other participants.

A transference circle has fully restored you.

Stamina, mana, psi, and even health gushed into me. It was as if a seemingly never-ending ocean of strength stood by, waiting to replenish my energy wells the moment they dipped in the slightest.

My lips lifted in a wolfish smile. The brotherhood's aid simplified things greatly. Forgoing all thought of defense, ignoring the winged snakes circling overhead, and even my foe's sustained and ongoing psi attacks, I stood tall on my hind legs and raked at his trunk like a cat.

The void tree's fate was sealed. And this time around, there would be no escaping.

✳ ✳ ✳

Transference circle still active. Remaining number of participants: 5.
Cait has cast lava pool.
A young void tree is 100% <u>shadow afflicted</u>, and its health is at 42%.

My foe's health dropped quicker than I expected.

In hindsight, I realized that a large part of the toughness the void tree had exhibited previously was a result of the mists' restoring touch. But now, unrooted and bereft of outside aid, the stygian Power was having a much harder time coping.

Which naturally led him to harangue me again.

"FILTHY... DOG!"

"YOU... WILL... NOT WIN!"

"CALL... OFF... YOUR... HOUNDS... WOLFLING!"

"FIGHT... ME... FAIRLY."

I ignored my foe's feeble attempts at distraction, of course. But given how well things were going, I did take the time to assess the rest of the battle.

We were winning—soundly and on all fronts.

The nagas were still fleeing southwards—and wisely Kartara let them go. If the brotherhood had opted to pursue them, the tree would likely have tried to intervene.

The army of lesser stygians, meanwhile, had lost all cohesiveness. Thanks to Ghost and the brotherhood mages' efforts, they were largely a spent force.

The flying snakes were also losing the battle raging in the air. Kartara, it turned out, was a prolific summoner. During the course of my battle with the void tree, she'd unleashed a small army of her own into the sky—mostly flying wind elementals. Individually, each was more than a match for one of the winged serpents. And better yet, the huntmistress saw to it that her summons' numbers were constantly replenished.

I, too, had made significant inroads.

My claws had stripped away all the ash-colored bark from the patch of trunk I assaulted, exposing the stark-white wood beneath. The wood wasn't any softer, but with my forelimbs brimming with shadow and the tree fully shadow afflicted, each swipe of my paws dealt more damage than previously.

A young void tree's health is at 36%.

Better yet, Cait had forced my foe to reverse his downward trajectory. Time and again, the stygian Power attempted to land. But each time he neared the ground, the nether witch transformed the area into a pit of boiling lava that the void tree was none too keen to dip his roots into.

Eventually, realizing he would not be allowed to anchor his roots anew, the void tree changed tactics and shot skyward. Perhaps that was in a bid to break the transference circle. But I didn't think he was going to succeed. From what I understand of Cait's witching eye spell, it was based on line of sight. And the stygian Power simply didn't have enough time to escape sight range.

It didn't stop him from trying, though.

A young void tree's health is at 25%.

Victory is a foregone conclusion, I thought in satisfaction.

Despite my confidence, I remained wary.

The void tree had more than a few powerful spells in his arsenal that could turn the tide—psychic scream, psi drain, and nether sacrifice, not the least amongst them.

Yet, he used none of those spells.

A young void tree's health is at 13%.

Despite teetering on death, my foe attempted no desperate gamble, tried no last-minute surprise, and executed no last-gasp maneuver.

Which led me to conclude he couldn't.

Going airborne, it seemed, had done more than stop the void tree from holding the rift open and regenerating from the mist. It had also stopped him from using his most devastating abilities.

No wonder it took him so long to make the decision to uproot himself.

A young void tree's health is at 9%.

My muzzle dropped open into a smile as my foe's health dropped into single digits for the first time. Even the stygian Power had to realize by now that he was not going to survive. *What will he do?* I wondered idly. *Plead for mercy? Or bluster on?*

A faint buzzing tickled the edge of my consciousness. Having experienced the sensation before, I immediately recognized it for what it was—the spillover from a telepathic communication.

You have passed a Perception check!
Mental sendings detected.

Given that we were in a largely empty sky, with the closest winged serpent more than a hundred yards away, there could be no question as to the source: the young void tree.

And this time around he was not speaking to me. *Is he even speaking? Or was something more nefarious going on?*

My eyes narrowing in concentration, I attempted to identify the underlying pattern in the sendings.

You have passed a Mind check. Communication link identified.
A young void tree is engaged in a telepathic conversation with an unknown entity.

Ah, I knew it. My foe *was* talking.

But who was the unknown entity? And why was the stygian Power trying to speak to them now of all times?

I should ignore the sendings, I knew. The fight was all but won, and there was no need to attempt snooping in on the conversation of a being as powerful as the void tree. But despite myself, I was intrigued—and who knew what bearing it would have on the battle—and so, I focused harder.

Eavesdropping successful!

The buzzing resolved itself into words, and with no little trepidation, I listened in. Eavesdropping on a Power's conversation was no small thing and a far cry from snooping on the mental sendings of a pair of low-level thieves. The chances of getting caught were significantly higher.

You have passed a mental resistance check! A level 340 young void tree has failed to detect your mental intrusion.

The Game's confirmation eased my mind. My presence had gone unnoticed—for now, anyway. My doubts quelled, I focused on the ongoing conversation.

"... FATHER... YOU... MUST... HELP... ME."

"WHY? I WARNED YOU, DID I NOT?"

The second sending—shot back from where I couldn't immediately tell—was smoother and more controlled than that of the stygian Power I fought. It was obviously coming from another void tree, but was it from the mature one in this sector or... something more dangerous?

Both prospects were equally frightening.

"YOU... DID."

Even as unfamiliar as I was with my foe, I could tell the admission was difficult for him to make.

"BUT... NOW... I... AM... DYING. HELP... ME... PLEASE."

A moment of stark silence.

Despite my rising concern, I kept my emotions locked down. I couldn't afford either tree to sense my eavesdropping. Doing my best to keep my thoughts small, I kept beating at my foe.

A young void tree's health is at 6%.

"NO."

The pronouncement rang with finality, leaving me elated, even while it had the opposite effect on the young tree.

"WHY?" my foe asked forlornly.

"THE FACT THAT YOU ASK THAT IS REASON ENOUGH. DO YOU UNDERSTAND NOTHING AT ALL?"

The younger tree did not respond, but his misery grew in leaps and bounds.

"YOU CREATED RECKLESSLY," the other tree responded, driving the point home, *"GIVING OUR ENEMIES A VALUABLE RESOURCE THEY SHOULD NEVER HAVE BEEN ALLOWED TO POSSESS."*

"BUT... THE... NAGAS... ARE—"

"YOU IGNORED MY ADVICE," the second tree went on, speaking over my foe. *"YOU LET MY HARBINGERS—MINE, NOT YOURS—BE FOOLISHLY SLAIN. AND THEN YOU LOST THE SECTOR THE FATHERS ASSIGNED TO YOU."*

The reference to the harbingers clinched it: my foe was speaking to the other void tree in this sector. That eased my worries further. While the rank forty-two mature tree was certainly not to be trifled with, he at least was a known quantity and nowhere near as powerful as the void fathers were rumored to be.

I listened on.

"BUT YOUR BIGGEST CRIME BY FAR? THAT WAS STRENGTHENING THE WOLFLING. YOU HAVE MADE HIM STRONGER."

"THEN... DON'T... LET... HIM... KILL... ME. IT... WILL... ONLY—"

"IGNORANT, CHOSEN. DON'T YOU REALIZE IT IS ALREADY TOO LATE FOR ME TO SAVE YOU?"

"BUT—"

"YOU LACK EVEN THE SENSE TO PROTECT YOUR SENDINGS. THE WOLFLING IS LISTENING."

I stilled. I'd been found out. Somehow, I'd done something to trip myself up and reveal my presence to the mature tree. Or....

Frantically, I parsed the earlier Game message.

....and realized something I should have picked up earlier. It only made mention of the young void tree! The Adjudicator had not confirmed that I'd gone undetected by the telepathic conversation's second participant.

Idiot, I berated myself.

My thoughts churning faster, I rechecked the walls around my mind. But they were unbreached and strong as ever. Discovering that was not as comforting as it should have been, though.

The mature tree was a *major* Power. Who knew what it was capable of?

"NOTHING TO SAY, WOLFLING?" the older tree asked, almost coyly.

I stayed quiet. It was one thing to engage in conversation with a foe I knew I matched in telepathic strength; it was another thing entirely to do the same with a Power who had just decisively demonstrated his telepathic abilities far outstripped my own.

The mature void tree laughed uproariously in my mind. "DO NOT THINK YOUR SILENCE WILL PROTECT YOU, PRIMAL SCUM. I SEE YOU. I KNOW WHAT YOU ARE. YOU MAY SAVOR YOUR VICTORY HERE TODAY. BUT DO NOT LET THAT DELUDE YOU INTO THINKING ME AND THE REST OF MY BRETHREN WILL BE AS EASY TO SLAY. WHEN I—"

I broke off the connection.

I'd heard enough, and with the mature tree aware of my spying, it was unlikely I was going to hear anything of value anymore.

Eavesdropping stopped. Telepathic link broken.

A level 421 mature void tree's subliminal command has failed to take root.

My eyes widened in alarm. Hells, just listening to the mature void tree appeared dangerous. I hadn't even been aware of his subversive touch. The Adjudicator hadn't warned me, nor had I felt the least brush against my mental walls. How had the bloody tree penetrated them?

I had no idea.

Still, I could only be grateful to the impulse that had spurred me to break off from the mental link when I did. No doubt, it had saved me.

But just as an added precaution, I poured the entirety of my psi into the mental walls protecting my consciousness, completely severing all links between myself and the outside world. There was no point in taking any more chances.

No further alerts from the Adjudicator dropped into my mind, as I half-expected.

I exhaled explosively. The lack of Game messages was a good sign. It had to be. *Now, it's time to be done with this damnable battle.* Shifting my focus back to the 'real,' I attacked my foe with renewed vigor.

It was past time he died.

A young void tree's health is at 3%.
A young void tree's health is at 2%.
A young void tree's health is at 1%.
...

✳ ✳ ✳

Transference circle still active. Remaining number of participants: 2.

The final stretch of my tussle with the void tree was all one-way. Yes, he railed at me, yes, he peppered me with thorns, and yes, he struck at me with his etheric lashes.

But none of the things the stygian Power attempted were able to change the course of the battle, and his demise, when it came, was sudden and dramatic.

You have killed a level 340 young void tree!

All about me, the tree withered. The few black thorns remaining fell free, branches rotted before my eyes, and the rancid stench of death filled my nostrils.

Wrinkling my nose in disgust, I studied my paws. Dirt and soft bits of bark clung to them, but even as I watched, they began to shrink. My foe was dissolving before my eyes.

No, not dissolving. Decaying.

It was as if the only thing that had been keeping the tree's physical shell alive was his strength of will. And now that it was gone, the rest of him was collapsing.

The branch underfoot cracked.

Then broke.

And in a split second, I went from being comfortably perched to plummeting downward. But despite my being over a thousand feet above ground, my situation was not as problematic as it seemed. I had multiple ways to see myself to safety.

But before I did that, it was time to share the good news.

"Kartara," I called over the farspeaker link, "*it's done.*"

Her reply was immediate. "*Truly?*" she asked, her voice more than a little breathless.

"*Truly,*" I replied gravely. "*The void tree is dead, and his corpse is dissolving.*"

"*I can't... It's almost too—*" She broke off abruptly. "*You're falling,*" she said in sudden realization. "*Hold on. I'll get Cait to—*"

"No need," I interjected. Contorting my neck, I focused on Ghost's distant, but still visible form, and shadow jumped.

You have teleported into Ghost's shadow.

I emerged from the aether in a jumble. The momentum of my freefall had not abated, and I crashed headlong into the ground, breaking multiple bones in the process.

Only for them all to heal a moment later, thanks to the transference circle. Rolling back to my feet, I shook myself free of dirt. Immediately, Ghost brushed up against me. *"You did it, Prime!"* she congratulated.

My mouth dropped open into a smile. *"We did it,"* I corrected. *"The brotherhood played their part, as did you."* Not to mention, everything the forerunners in sector 18,240 had done to get us here. *"Taking down the void tree and its nest was a team effort."*

Before she could respond, another voice intruded. *"Havick?"* Kartara called, her voice neutral and in control once more.

I was not surprised by how quickly the huntmistress had regained her composure. I'd come to expect no less from her. *"I'm down and safe,"* I replied to her yet unvoiced question.

"Good." A pause. *"We must talk."*

"We must," I agreed, and looking around, finally took stock of the surroundings. The brotherhood was still arrayed along the line of dunes to the north, beneath their silver dome. But already, I could see a few emerging.

The immediate area was free of threat as well. The few lesser stygians that remained were scattering. Some headed south after the nagas, but most just fled mindlessly into the desert. The battle was decidedly over. Still, the brotherhood had some mopping up to do.

"I'll wait here," I added, not deeming it necessary to define where exactly 'here' was. I was sure Senzo and his scouts already had a fix on my position. *"Come, find me when you can."*

"I'll do that," was the terse response.

Closing down the farspeaker link, I turned back to my familiar. *"Keep watch, Ghost. I don't expect the brotherhood to try moving against us, but better safe than sorry."*

"You're going to check your Game alerts?" she guessed.

I nodded. *"There's a whole host of them vying for my attention."*

She sat down on her haunches. *"Go ahead, Prime. I'll make sure we're safe."*

"Thank you, Ghost," I murmured, and turning my focus inward, I opened up the first waiting message.

Unsurprisingly, the first Game alert was the one describing my level gains.

You and Ghost have reached level 282!
For achieving rank 28, you have been awarded 1 additional attribute point and 1 Class point.

I whistled softly. Ghost and I had advanced *appreciably*. We'd gained a whole nine levels. And while I expected that some of the gains were a result of the nagas I had killed and the lesser stygians Ghost had slaughtered, slaying the void tree itself likely accounted for six of our new levels.

A worthy reward on its own, I thought in satisfaction as I opened the next message.

Your tooth and claw (shortswords) has reached rank 24, your two weapon fighting rank 22, your chi rank 21, and your deception rank 26.
Ghost's magma maw has reached rank 16, her stygian claws rank 17, and her telepathy rank 14.

My skill gains were as expected. I was slightly disappointed that I'd not managed to raise my nether absorption to tier six, though. Since I'd hit rank twenty-eight, I had acquired another Class point, leaving me with a grand total of two. But I was loath to spend either of them on anything except advancing slaysight and void thief.

However, neither of my Class abilities was ready for upgrade—and they wouldn't be until I took one, or both, requisite skills, namely telepathy and nether absorption, to tier six.

I sighed. Advancing my Class abilities would just have to wait. In the meantime, though, I could do something about my unspent attribute points—all *thirty-two* of them.

Turning my attention inward, I checked my player status and, specifically, my current attribute ranks.

Strength: 40. Constitution: 44. Dexterity: 142. Perception: 127. Mind: 188. Magic: 85. Faith: 20.
Total Attributes invested (ignoring benefits from items): 646.

I sucked in a breath through my teeth. I hadn't considered my attribute progression in a long time, and to see how far I'd come was shocking. I had started the Game with two attribute points—two!—and now I had six hundred and forty-six.

But it was not just that.

The truly staggering part was how... different I was. Most players at my level would have three hundred and twenty attributes—ignoring any feats or traits they may have acquired along the way, that is.

I had more than twice that.

From the perspective of attributes alone, there was no doubt I was overpowered. And with my elder form, I'd gained the abilities to match. Which, I suppose, accounted for the relative ease with which I'd rampaged through the stygian Powers.

But I could not forget that the stygians were not players. They didn't have the same advantages. And amongst other players—and Powers—I was certain to find some who were also overpowered, if hopefully, not to the same extent I was.

My drive to get stronger had not—and could not—wane, I knew. Especially not when considering my next probable destination after this.

Still shaking my head in rueful disbelief at my player growth, I left off further musings and focused on the attributes themselves. The question now was which to upgrade.

Not Perception. I'd taken it as far as I needed to for the time being. And not Dexterity either. Most of its abilities were not ready for upgrade yet.

Which left Mind.

I had two Mind abilities ready for upgrade to the elite tier. And then too, I had enough points to take the attribute itself to rank two hundred—which was something I'd been keen to do for some time now.

Mind it is.

Reaching out to the Adjudicator, I willed my intent to the Game.

Your Mind has increased to rank 220. Other modifiers: +12 from items. Available ability slots: 34.

Congratulations, Michael! You have accomplished the feat: <u>Mentalist</u>. Requirements: advance your Mind attribute to rank 200.

As a reward for your achievement, you have gained the trait: <u>Mentalist</u>. This is a generic trait all players receive upon attaining this milestone. Tier one of the mentalist trait boosts your most-used mental skill in a small but effective way. You can now also use your telepathy to communicate mind-to-mind with those who lack the skill, dropping words directly into their minds and reading their responses the same way.

I smiled. From Ceruvax and Adriel's tutelage, I'd known to expect the feat. The exact breakdown of the resulting trait had been more in doubt. Still, I couldn't complain about what I had received.

While the changes to my telepathy skill appeared almost insignificant, they were anything but. Courtesy of the mentalist trait, I could now use my mindvoice to speak directly to any non-player—something that I was sure would come in handy in the future.

Alright, that's that. Time to peruse the next alert.

Banishing the hovering Game message, I opened the subsequent set of notices.

The ley line between Kingdom sector 18,240 and Nethersphere sector 30,199 has been closed. You have sealed your second rift. To obtain the next rank of the Rift Defender feat, close 8 more rifts.

Sector 18,240 is no longer under assault by the nether!

With the destruction of the ley line between sector 18,240 and the Nethersphere, the sector's safe zone has been reestablished, and the nether toxicity in the region has stopped rising. Note that the existing free-floating mists in the sector will not automatically be dispersed. Appropriate steps must be taken to see it banished.

Your task, <u>A Place to Call Home,</u> has been updated. You have forced the void to retreat from sector 18,240, thereby allowing its safe zone to reform. You now have 31 hours remaining to claim the sector.

Objective: Secure sector 18,240's safe zone before your allotted time runs out to establish control of the sector.

Mission success, I thought, grinning in pleasure. *Or almost, anyway.* With the void vanquished and the safe zone reformed, I had no doubt that Safyre was already seeing to the sector's claiming.

Just twenty-four more hours. That's all the time the Forerunners would need to establish a hold on the sector, and then...

And then, my people would truly have a home to call their own.

Still smiling, I opened the next message.

Congratulations, Michael! The Forerunners have accomplished the feat: <u>Rift Redeemers</u>. Requirements: close a tier 7 rift.

Thanks to your efforts and those of your faction, a tier 7 rift has been sealed. A tier 7 rift is one stable enough for even stygian Powers to traverse. Your faction is the first in millennia to have closed a rift of this magnitude, and as such, all present and future members of the faction will gain the trait: <u>rift sense</u>.

Rift sense is a factional trait that is similar to the explorer trait but is geared specifically towards rifts. It immediately makes a faction member aware of any rifts in the sector they are in. Both the rift's location and its tier are revealed to the player. In addition, when in the sector, the locations always shine bright in the faction member's mind, ensuring they are never lost.

Note, factional traits are highly prized and are only awarded for historic achievements. Like faction membership itself, factional traits are not discernible using analyze or any other similar ability. Factional traits are not permanent. In the event that a player leaves a faction, they will lose access to the benefits derived from a factional trait.

"Factional traits," I murmured to myself. Now, those were a surprise. Neither Ceruvax nor Adriel had made mention of them in our prior discussions, which likely meant they were exceedingly rare. As for the trait itself, its benefits were obvious, especially considering that—

An insistent buzzing interrupted my thoughts.

It was coming from another Game alert, I realized, one seemingly prompted by my acknowledgment of the factional trait message. Intrigued as to why that may be the case, I let the new message unfold in my mind.

Warning! There are currently 3 open rifts in sector 30,199.

The first rift is a tier 3 rift designated Rift-W, the second is a tier 5 rift designated Rift-Y, and the third is a tier 6 rift designated Rift-Z. The destinations of all 3 rifts are unknown.

The locations of Rift-W, Rift-Y, and Rift-Z have been added to your Logs.

Concern shot through me. There were three more rifts in this sector? And *all* three were active?

Damnation! That leaves us wide open to an ambush!

We could be assaulted from any direction—and not just from the mature tree's nest in the south. The shock of that realization was almost enough to force me to my feet to sound the alarm.

But before I could do so, another Game message, unbidden, opened in my mind.

Rift sense activated.

Your mind has been attuned to the locations of the newly-discovered rifts.

I settled back down as a trio of pulses impinged on my awareness. They were coming from the three rifts, and from the sense I got of them, they were even farther away than the mature nest.

"What's wrong, Prime?" Ghost asked.

She'd noticed my momentary tension, I realized. *"Nothing,"* I mumbled back, *"or nothing urgent, anyway. I just found out there are three more rifts in the sector."*

Concern washed through our bond. *"Oh? Should we—"*

"There's no immediate danger," I assured her. *"The rifts are too far. Just stay vigilant."*

Turning my attention inward again, I pondered the Game's warning further. As I did, I realized that the rifts in question were also smaller than the one we had just closed. That meant none of the three could discharge a stygian Power.

Well, there's that to be grateful for.

My eyes narrowing, I worked through the rest of the implications. Given its tier, Rift-W had to have been formed by a stygian seed, whereas Rift-Y and Rift-Z were likely the work of a pair of stygian saplings. *Interesting*, I mused. Now that I had time to consider the matter more calmly, I realized the three rifts were actually not of any real threat to me or the nearby brotherhood army.

If anything, *we* were a threat to *them*.

Particularly if the mature tree didn't suspect I knew the three rifts' exact whereabouts. And I couldn't see any reason why he would suspect that. I'd not gone anywhere near the other rifts, and they were all clear across the sector.

Exploring those rifts will be interesting, I decided, even as I wondered what lay on the other side of them. *More* undiscovered sectors?

Sadly, though, uncovering the rifts' mysteries would have to wait. Focusing on the Adjudicator's messages anew, I opened the next Game alert.

Congratulations, Michael! You've slain your 4th tier 7 creature, deepening your Power Mark. Slay further Powers to evolve your Mark further.

You have accomplished the feat: <u>Fell a Tree!</u> Requirement: Vanquish a full-grown tree.

A young void tree has fallen—the first to do so in centuries. That you managed to orchestrate his defeat is a feat unto itself. Yet, you did it while a mere Initiate and without the aid of any Powers. As a result, you have been offered a choice in the matter of your reward.

Option 1: The rank 7 soulbound artifact, the <u>nightstalker's talisman</u>. This item will grant you the tier 7 Class ability, <u>shroud of darkness.</u> This spell will envelop you in billowing black clouds that are resistant to dispersing and will nourish any wolf or player of Wolf blood within its area of effect. In addition, the artifact will increase your physical damage resistance.

Option 2: The rank 7 soulbound artifact, the <u>mindslayer's torc</u>. This item will grant you the tier 7 Class ability, <u>awakened slayer.</u> This spell will create an astral simulacrum of yourself that can be used either in defense of your own consciousness or to attack the mind of another. In addition, the artifact will increase your mental resistance.

Option 3: The rank 7 soulbound artifact, the <u>void mage's signet</u>. This item will grant you the tier 7 Class ability, <u>spell immunity.</u> The spell hardens your void armor into an impenetrable shell, granting you complete spell immunity for 10 seconds. In addition, the artifact will increase your magic resistance.

Make your choice now.

I smiled. I'd finally come to my true reward for slaying the void tree. I'd half expected a trait, Class points, or even another ascendant point.

What I had not anticipated was a soulbound item.

Not that I could fault the Adjudicator's chosen form of reward. All three artifacts on offer would provide me with another Class ability—only my third such, actually. And the fact that each artifact was soulbound meant the new ability would become a permanent addition to my arsenal. I could never lose it. For all intents and purposes, it would function like an ordinary Class ability.

Except in two crucial aspects.

One, I wouldn't be able to upgrade the new ability—which was disappointing. But on the other hand, not having to do so also saved me seven Class points because the abilities on offer were *already* at tier seven.

Tier seven, I repeated, still slightly awed by the fact.

That was a Power-level ability. Not elite-level. Not envoy-level. *Power-level.* Ordinarily, I wouldn't gain such an ability until my skills exceeded level three hundred, and the early accrual was only made possible by the fact that I was acquiring it via a soulbound item. So, despite the resulting disadvantages, I was more than glad the Adjudicator was offering me such an artifact.

There was another consideration, too—Ghost.

Courtesy of the jeweled pet item I'd looted from Leafbright, Ghost would *also* be able to use the ability provided by the soulbound artifact—making me doubly grateful for the Game's choice of reward. Now, though, it was time to make a decision.

A nightstalker's talisman.

A mindslayer's torc.

Or the void mage's signet.

Those were the choices on offer. The significance of the artifacts' descriptors did not escape my notice either. They matched exactly with the three constituent Classes of my melded voidstealer Class—which, of course, could be no accident. Clearly, the Adjudicator had created the items specifically for my use, and that alone left me in no doubt as to their potential usefulness.

Yet, I could choose only one.

So which will it be? I mused.

Each of the three artifacts appeared to focus on a different aspect: the nightstalker's talisman on physical combat, the mindslayer's torc on psi usage, and the void mage's signet on magic—or rather, on magic negation.

The shroud of darkness ability sounded nice. As both a form of crowd control and buff, it would incapacitate my foes—by blinding them—even as it healed my wolven allies. The ability would be most effective in a large-scale skirmish like the one I'd just fought. But outside of that? It would be... less useful. Then too, the core of what the shroud did—hiding me—was little different from what vanish did.

The nightstalker's talisman is not an option, I decided.

Awakened Slayer was definitely intriguing. At the same time, though, its Game description was the vaguest.

An astral simulacrum... what was that?

And what did the Adjudicator mean by a simulacrum 'of myself'? It almost sounded as if the simulacrum would be akin to the demonic aspects of Mammon I'd encountered in the Eastern Marches. That would make the simulacrum a construct.

But not a spell construct—a psi one.

Would the simulacrum be autonomous? The way Mammon's constructs had been? Would it manifest in the physical plane the way my astral shurikens did? But if that was the case, how would it defend my consciousness, or for that matter, attack my foes' minds?

I sighed. I had no idea. But at least the Game was clear on the simulacrum's purpose. It was a tool for mental warfare, both offensive and defensive. And for now, that was all I could say for certain about it.

I turned to the last artifact.

Thankfully, there was nothing ambiguous about the spell immunity ability. What it did and how it did it was self-evident. The capability to nullify magic damage for a whole ten seconds was not to be underestimated either. With such an ability, I could confidently face even the strongest spellcasters.

Yet...

The ability was only defensive in nature. And it only worked against spell damage. *And* in many ways, what spell immunity did was no different from what my void armor already did, even if the tier seven ability promised to do it better.

No, I decided, *I don't need more defensive or crowd control options.*

I had a plethora of those already. What I truly needed—especially from my first tier seven ability—was more attacking options. And as vaguely worded as its ability's description was, only one of the three artifacts offered me that.

The mindslayer's torc.

On the brink of making my choice, I hesitated. Selecting the torc would be a gamble. It might not live up to my expectations as an offensive tool. Still, even if awakened slayer served only to strengthen my mental defenses, it would not go to waste—particularly seeing as how I was likely to run across more void trees in the near future.

The mindslayer's torc it is, I decided resolutely and willed my choice to the Game.

Your choice has been made. Artifact construction commencing...

...

...

I lowered my dog-like head downward in expectant anticipation. It seemed to take an eternity, but in reality, it was no more than a few seconds before the item crystallized between my pawed feet.

A rank 7 mindslayer's torc has been created.

A gleaming hoop materialized on the bare earth. The torc was made from a thin strip of flattened silver and had been bent to form a perfect circle that would sit snugly around my neck—were I in human form, that is. The artifact also lacked any embellishments, and had I spied it in a merchant's stall, I would not have spared it a second look.

Still, I knew the thing to be priceless.

But despite my eagerness to snatch up the item, I schooled myself to patience and reached out to inspect it with my will instead.

The target is the rank 7 artifact: the <u>mindslayer's torc</u>. This item increases your mental resistance by 25% and grants you the Class ability, <u>awakened slayer</u>.

Ah. Twenty-five percent mental resistance was nothing to scoff at. It would make an appreciable difference to my psi defenses—and Ghost's as well. Sadly, though, analyzing the artifact had yielded no further insights as to the ability it unlocked.

Extending a foreleg, I brushed my paw against the torc's surface.

You have acquired the mindslayer's torc. This rank 7 artifact is only usable by the player Michael. Do you wish to soul-bind this item?

I replied in the affirmative and felt new bonds slip into place between the torc and me.

You have soulbound the <u>mindslayer's torc</u>. From this point onwards, this artifact cannot be stolen, lost, or kept from your hands except by the strongest of enchantments.
Warning: You cannot equip this item while in wolf form. Since the mindslayer's torc is soulbound, it has been automatically stored in your backpack. Note, no benefits may be derived from the artifact until it has been equipped.

I snorted in annoyance. I'd known I wouldn't be able to put on the torc. Not only was I in wolf form, but I also had the maximum allowable items equipped already. Still, I had hoped to at least learn what the thing did!

I guess learning more about awakened slayer will just have to wait until I can shift again.

Meanwhile, there were more Game alerts demanding my attention. Impatient now to complete my review of the messages, I let the last set of notices unfurl in my mind.

You have completed the hidden task: <u>Ancient Resurgence</u>. For millennia, no player or Power has seen fit to seriously challenge the void trees' supremacy.
Until today.
You are the first player in centuries to have slain a full-grown tree, albeit one who was amongst the youngest and weakest of his kind. Well done, scion. Your victory has rekindled a war long since thought lost and has given the nether fresh cause for concern. But not only did you slay a young void tree, you orchestrated the destruction of 4 harbingers and 4 overlords. You also saw to the destruction of an entire stygian nest and closed a tier 7 rift, forcing the void to retreat and relinquish its hold on sector 18,240.
By your actions, you have shown yourself to be a <u>Stygian Nemesis</u>. This has become the third and final tenet of your burgeoning House. Staying true to your House's tenets will deepen your Wolf Mark in the future. Straying from it will see your Mark weaken.

Congratulations, Michael, you've defined all 3 tenets of your new House, thereby establishing the strictures to which the bloodlines of your new House must conform. As such, you may begin deepening your Wolf Mark once more.

Your task, <u>Found a new House!</u> has been updated.
A House is a nebulous thing. Some consider it to be merely a dressed-up faction. Others conceive of it as something more, as something that resonates with who they are. But what your House is, and what it will be, is

for you alone to determine. If your House survives, its actions may very well echo through eternity. Choose well, Progenitor.

You have defined the doctrine of your new House, thereby fulfilling one of the requirements necessary for its founding. The central objective of this task remains unchanged, though.

Objective: Convince 1 other Power not of Wolf blood to join your House.

I sighed.

The new Game messages confirmed something I'd long suspected—my Wolf Mark had stopped changing. In fact, it had stopped doing so weeks ago—ever since I'd left Draven's Reach, to be precise. And this, despite me completing numerous tasks in the interim. My Mark was *supposed* to change with every task completed. Yet it had not.

So, why had it not?

At first, I had been at a loss to explain the change. Then, I'd begun to suspect the cause. However, until this point, I'd had no concrete evidence to support my supposition. Now, though, I could say with near certainty when the change had occurred—and why.

The shift had happened five tasks ago—when I'd acquired the Wolf Progenitor Mark.

At first, I'd thought nothing of the timing, considering it to be coincidence only. The Progenitor Mark had served its purpose, after all— granting me the ability to undergo a second higher evolution—and there had been no hint whatsoever that it could, or would, do more. Adriel had known nothing about the Mark. And neither had Ceruvax and Farren. And so, I'd all but forgotten about it.

But then I received a task to establish the tenets of Wolf. And *after* that, I'd gotten one to found a new House. And, finally, there was the last Game message and the not-so-inconsequential reference to me being a 'Progenitor.' They all suggested the same thing.

The new House and my Progenitor Mark were inextricably linked.

In fact, I thought it safe to assume it was only *because* of the Progenitor Mark that I was able to found a new House at all!

Sadly, though, the realization didn't give me any greater insight into what needed to be done to *actually* create the House. The latest task update was no help. I would even go so far as to call it maddeningly vague.

And my most knowledgeable allies—Ceruvax, Adriel, and Farren— didn't have any insights to offer on the matter either. They knew nothing about how to go about *founding* a new House, and not unexpectedly—given the strength of their ties to their former Houses—they seemed largely disinterested in the idea.

I would just have to figure it out myself—somehow.

But at least, I can deepen my Wolf Mark again from here on out, I groused. Doing so was crucial to achieving the next ascendant rank.

Still so much to do, I thought, half-despairingly. *How am I—*

"Prime," Ghost called out in warning. "*We have incoming. The brotherhood is on its way.*"

CHAPTER 587: QUESTIONING

Breaking off from my musings, I raised my head to scan the sands ahead. Kartara and her subordinates were approaching. My deliberations about the new House would have to wait until later. Now, it was time to deal with the brotherhood.

Sitting down on my haunches, I observed the six advancing brotherhood members. Kartara was in the middle. The other five players—Cait, Senzo, Duskar, Fiona, and a dwarf named Heglin—formed a tight circle around her, almost as if they were seeking to protect the huntmistress from the big bad harbinger.

I snorted. *As if Kartara needs protection.*

Lidding my eyes, I focused on the only brotherhood player I'd not yet met—Heglin. Given the dwarf's steel-clad form and the bits of conversation I'd overheard through the farspeaker link earlier, I assumed Heglin to be the brotherhood's infantry commander.

The dwarf's gray eyes were stony, and he walked almost in Kartara's shadow, shielding her back. More than anything else, it signaled his loyalty to the huntmistress.

"Ghost, it's time you got going," I ordered as the brotherhood officers drew closer.

The pyre wolf, seated on her haunches beside me, turned her head my way. *"Why? They've seen me already."*

"That may be," I allowed, *"but I'd rather they don't get a close look at you."* My eyes alighted on the diviner, Fiona. *"Especially that one. She is far too astute for my liking."*

Ghost tracked the direction of my gaze. *"Oh, alright."* Her head turned left and right, examining the multitude of corpses scattered across the dunes. *"It was a good hunt,"* she pronounced.

"It was," I agreed.

"They will make for good Pack."

My lips twitched. Was Ghost subtly prompting me to recruit the brotherhood? It seemed so. *"You think I should invite them to join the Forerunners?"*

"I do," she replied immediately. *"Are you going to?"*

"I'm not sure yet," I admitted. The brotherhood had not survived as long as it had by being incautious. There would be questions aplenty—and lots of suspicion.

And I was not certain yet how far I was willing to go to allay their concerns.

Banding together with Brotherhood for a single mission was one thing; tying the Forerunners permanently to them, and them to us, was another thing entirely. Especially since the Brotherhood was a dominant and widespread presence in the Kingdom. If we joined forces, word would get out about the Forerunners, and I was not sure I was ready for that yet.

"Well, do what you think best," Ghost said, sensing my ambivalence.

Still preoccupied by the question she'd posed, I only nodded vaguely in response.

My gaze drifted back to the huntmistress. I would have to share some truths with Kartara, I knew. Common courtesy demanded at least that much. And it was more than common courtesy that I owed the brotherhood.

But how much truth is enough truth? I wondered.

＊　＊　＊

Ghost has unmanifested.

The pyre wolf vanished before the brotherhood officers closed to within fifty yards. Her disappearance gave them pause, but only momentarily, and when they resumed walking again, it was with stiffer strides and tighter expressions.

I nearly rolled my eyes. *Right, they think I am up to something.*

"Where'd it go?" Duskar demanded as the six came to a stop twenty yards from me.

I ignored the orc. "Should I be flattered or insulted?" I asked Kartara, measuring the distance between me and the brotherhood officers.

The huntmistress shrugged. "Both if you wish." Angling herself to the left, she walked a slow, measured circle around me with Heglin her silent shadow.

Duskar's lower jaw jutted out. "How is he speaking?"

"He's using ventro," Fiona said faintly.

The orc scratched his head. "Ventro? Never heard of it."

"It's a deception ability," Senzo answered. Following on the huntmistress' heels, he, too, began circling me. "I've never witnessed a doppelganger's transformation before. The change is... remarkable."

"Thank you," I said with quiet amusement.

Scowling, Duskar spun to face the huntmistress. "Are we sure this is him? The one called Havick?"

"Havick doesn't exist," Fiona muttered before Kartara could respond. "He was a persona, no more." She waved her hand disparagingly in my direction. "As is this."

Cait advanced forward. "What I'd like to know," she said, coming straight at me, "is how he grew so big. The doppelganger spell does not add mass." The elf came to a halt beside me, her hand raised and poised to touch, but stopping just short of doing so. "May I?" she asked, her eyes shining brightly.

I thought of refusing, but the truth was that, of all Kartara's subordinates, I liked the nether witch best. Her curiosity was undisguised and unabashed, and her requests, when she made them, were always direct and to the point. And besides, I needed to allay their fears.

And I had no doubt the brotherhood was scared.

I'd just killed a young void tree after all, something their entire organization had failed to do in centuries. All their talk and all their

47

questions—even Duskar's—was just a mask, one that poorly concealed their uncertainty.

"Go ahead," I said, inclining my head in permission.

The elf needed no further encouragement. Lowering her hand, she ran impersonal fingers through my splotchy dog coat. "It feels real," she stated.

I laughed. "Of course it's real. That's my—" I broke off at a sharp tug. "Ow! That hurt."

"Huh," the elf remarked, dispassionately studying the bits of fur in her hand. "Interesting." Stepping back, she looked over her shoulder at the huntmistress who had completed her circle and was watching Cait's inspection with an inscrutable expression.

"He's no stygian," the nether witch pronounced.

"You're sure?" the huntmistress asked.

Cait nodded. "I am. It's a disguise. Has to be."

Fiona stepped forward eagerly. "Let me inspect him. I'll be able to—"

"No," the huntmistress and I shot back simultaneously.

Kartara turned to me, one eyebrow raised. "I know why I said no. Why did you?"

I scowled—although in my present form, they likely took it for a snarl, which I was fine with. "I still remember her last inspection, even if you don't. Your diviner will not be inspecting me again," I said firmly. "Not now. Not *ever*."

Kartara nodded equably, not contesting the point, and Fiona stepped back, her shoulders sagging. "Have it your way," the huntmistress said. "But you didn't answer Cait's earlier question."

I cocked my head to the side. "Oh?"

"What are you beneath that skin?" Kartara asked. "Not human, obviously. No human doppelganger has the mass to impersonate a harbinger. So, what are you?"

"That's a good question."

She waited for me to go on, but when I didn't, she pressed further, "An answer would be even better."

I sighed. "I'm human."

"Really?" Cait asked, stepping farther back and eyeing my large and visibly inhuman frame.

"Really," I repeated, ignoring her obvious skepticism. "But I won't tell you how I managed to transform into a harbinger."

Duskar growled. "How can we trust him if he insists on leaving us in the dark?" he demanded, directing the question at the huntmistress, not me.

I turned the orc's way. "I made no bones of the fact that I keep secrets. You knew before we began all this that I would not share my identity, nor the location of the sector on the other side of the rift. Nothing has changed since."

Senzo chuckled. "Come, 'Havick.' Do not take us for fools. You just killed a void tree, the first in millennia! At the very least, that makes you a Powerful Initiate—or an envoy. That changes *everything*. Tell us why we shouldn't believe this is some twisted ploy to win our favor?"

"An envoy?" I mused, glancing at Kartara. "You think I am an envoy?"

She shrugged. "I don't, but Senzo thinks it's a possibility."

I turned back to the spymaster. "Interesting. I get why you think I'm at least tier six. But why are you so sure I am just that? What's to say I am not higher leveled and a full Power already?"

He snorted. "No one becomes a Power by taking the risks we've seen you take. The rise to the top is long and hard. The foolhardy do not often survive."

I ignored the implied insult. "What risks?"

He ticked off points on his fingers. "You walked willfully into our castle, the heart of our domain, alone and unaccompanied. The brotherhood may want for any Powers of its own, but that doesn't mean we lack teeth. It would've cost us dearly, but even if you were Tartar himself, we could have slain you then and there."

I chose not to dispute the point. "Go on."

"Then you gave us your netherstone. I don't care who or what you are, or how powerful you think you may be, but that was a damn fool thing to do. We could have stranded you here for eternity."

I nodded. "And is that all?"

"Of course not," he rejoined. "Then there is the tree. Who in their right mind tackles a young void tree—alone and without any guarantees of help? Not a Power who has had to fight every step of the way to get where he is, certainly."

"As interesting as everything you said is, it's only conjecture," I pointed out. "Hardly what I'd call conclusive proof."

"That's true enough," Kartara agreed. "But there is something else Senzo hasn't mentioned yet."

I swung her way. "And that is?"

"Technically, Cait just attacked you," she replied.

I stared at her blankly for a moment. "By attack, I suppose you mean her tugging free a clump of my fur?"

The huntmistress nodded. "If you truly were a Power, you would've realized the significance of her doing that." She paused. "*And* the significance of Cait not receiving a warning from the Adjudicator when she did."

Realization dawned. "The Game warns players when they are about to earn the wrath of a Power," I guessed. The nether witch had attacked me and had not received any such warning—leading her and the huntmistress to conclude I was not a full Power.

Kartara nodded solemnly. "Correct."

I sighed. Once again, I'd run afoul of one of the huntmistress' tests, only seeing the trap after it had been sprung. "Alright, I guess you worked all that out neatly enough." My gaze found the spymaster again. "But what leads you to suspect me of being an envoy?"

Senzo glanced at Kartara, who nodded almost imperceptibly, before continuing, "The brotherhood is the single most powerful non-Power group in the Game. The factions have been trying for centuries to recruit us—and many are not opposed to using force or guile to do it."

I swished my tail idly. "I see. Then the theory is what...? I went through the trouble of all of this—putting my own life and those of your own people in very real danger, I may add—for what? To simply win your trust?"

Senzo nodded. "The notion is not as far-fetched as you make out."

If I had hands, I would have thrown them up in irritation. "How does appearing to you as a harbinger help me win your trust? And if your 'trust' was all I was truly interested in, why did I insist your people fight the stygians here and not on the other side of the rift?"

Duskar snickered. "Who knows? No one said you weren't a stupid envoy."

Before I could retort, Kartara held up a hand. "It's unlikely you're an envoy. Senzo knows that, as does Dusk." Her lips quirked. "No matter how much he might want to pretend otherwise. Too many things don't add up for that to be a real possibility." Her look grew serious again. "However, the idea that this is all the machinations of a Power is not as absurd as you think. I've witnessed firsthand the lengths some Powers will go to co-opt the brotherhood to their cause. We need assurances that whatever you are, and whoever you say you are, that you are not trying to manipulate us."

"Was keeping my word not enough?" I asked softly.

"Your word?" Duskar laughed. "What does your word matter when—"

"He didn't have to come through," Heglin said suddenly.

Breaking off, Duskar turned to face him. "What does that mean?"

Shrugging, the dwarf pointed to the spot so recently occupied by the rift. "There was no reason for Havick—or whatever his name is—to come through the rift. He could have stayed safely on the other side and still gotten everything he wanted—a sector scoured clean of stygians. The fact that he is here must count for something."

"It does." Kantara turned to face me again. "So, why did you come through? Why did you abandon your allies on the other side and come here to face a stygian Power?"

"If those allies even exist," Duskar muttered.

Ignoring him, the huntmistress leaned forward. "Be honest, Havick. Give us a reason to believe."

"I came because I made a promise," I said quietly. "A promise that you and your people would not have to face the void tree." I held her gaze. "And my promises are never made lightly."

The huntmistress studied me measuringly for a moment, weighing my answer. "You kept your word," she said finally. "And more importantly, you did what you said you could. And for that I'm more grateful than you can imagine."

She inhaled deeply. "But it is not enough."

I inclined my head. "I didn't think it would be."

Kantara sighed, a sound replete with exasperation. "What do you want from us, Havick?" she asked tiredly.

I looked up. "Truthfully? I want your help fighting the stygians."

"That's it?" she asked with barely concealed incredulity.

"That's it," I repeated. "I am willing to seal a Pact to confirm the veracity of my words."

The suggestion did not catch the huntmistress unawares. "And is that all you are willing to attest to via Pact?"

"It is."

Senzo raised one eyebrow. "You will not swear with the Adjudicator as your witness that you have no intention of recruiting the brotherhood for your faction?"

"I will not," I replied evenly. I couldn't swear to such, because I *did* intend on recruiting the brotherhood—if not today, then sometime in the future. I might not be willing to trust them with the full truth just yet, but there was no doubt our interests were aligned when it came to the stygians.

Senzo rubbed his chin. "Will you promise then that by associating with you, the brotherhood will not be drawn into a conflict between Powers?"

"I will not," I repeated—because, of course, that was exactly what might happen.

The spymaster laughed bitterly. "Then this—" he waved his hand in my direction—"whatever this is, it's exactly what we feared: a plot to entangle us in the Grand Game."

"It's not," I refuted sharply. I inhaled, then continued more calmly, "But I will not deny that I am embroiled in Game—albeit unwillingly. The brotherhood may be tainted by association."

"Then why should we have anything to do with you?" Duskar demanded.

Help came from an unexpected source.

"Hello?" Cait asked loudly. "Did no one notice the dead tree? We couldn't have killed it without him. Hells, we didn't even do it! He did." The nether witch swung to face the huntmistress. "How can we turn away the first player in brotherhood history to ever slay a young void tree and still claim to hold true to our mission?"

Kartara did not reply to the elf, but it was clear that the question perturbed her.

"Truly, Cait?" Senzo asked softly. "You would ally with a Power—one we know little about? And risk destroying the brotherhood in the process?"

"We face that risk every time we enter the nether," Cait declared fiercely.

"We do not," Senzo contradicted. "The brotherhood has only managed to survive as long as it has because we've stayed out of the Game. You're right, we confront danger in the nether on a daily basis, but we don't do so in Nexus and the other sectors our bases are located in. And for good reason—they are our safe zones. Our safety nets. Remaining neutral and staying out of the Powers' eternal conflicts is what has allowed us to rebuild time and again despite our losses against the stygians." He stabbed a finger in my direction. "If we ally with him, and he falls afoul of the Triumvirate— or any major Power for that matter—then our bases themselves will be under threat, and *that* will spell the end of the brotherhood."

Cait fell silent, having no response.

And truly, there was none to be had. Unless ...

The nether witch raised her chin. "We should at least hear Havick out, then. We might not go so far as to ally with him—" glancing over her shoulder, she threw me an apologetic glance—"but we don't even know what he wants. Let's listen to what he has to say before we wipe our hands of the matter."

Is that what the brotherhood intended? To break ties with me? Listening to Senzo's explanation, I could not fault their impulse to do so. In the long run, I was perhaps a bigger threat to their organization than the stygians.

But Cait had a point, too.

The brotherhood was unlikely to advance its mission without the help of someone like me. Survival or mission success. Those were the conflicting goals the brotherhood was grappling with.

"I suppose we can do that much," the huntmistress said finally, drawing me out of my thoughts. Her gaze came to rest on mine. "So, Havick, what is it that you desire from the brotherhood? Tell us plainly, please."

I exhaled slowly. Kartara was tackling the problem head-on, and the time had come to share some dangerous truths. "Plainly? I will do that," I promised. "It may be a long talk, though." I glanced down at my pawed feet. "And I'll need some privacy first."

"Why?" Duskar demanded brusquely.

"To shift," I replied, letting my mouth drop open in a gruesome smile. "I'm getting drearily tired of wearing this harbinger's skin."

The huntmistress waved her hand in the direction of the barren desert dunes to the north. "Go then, shift. We'll be waiting here when you're done."

✳ ✳ ✳

Kartara had no reason to fear I wouldn't return, of course. The brotherhood still held my netherstone, and without it, I wasn't going anywhere.

Well, there are those other rifts in the sector.

Given the nature of the ley lines, I knew for certain that the sectors on the other side had to be in the Kingdom. So, I wasn't as trapped without my netherstone as the brotherhood thought I was.

I didn't fear betrayal, though. At this point, the brotherhood had every reason to want to hear what I said. But what they would do after I shared my truths was another matter entirely.

"You will tell them everything?" Ghost asked from the dune top where she was keeping watch.

We were a few miles north of the battlefield, much further out than I thought even Senzo's scouts would range on their own. I was at the bottom of a hill, and out of sight of any prying eyes, getting ready to shift.

"*I won't,*" I replied. "*But I will need to tell them enough to make them aware of the dangers they'll be facing.*" I would not accept the brotherhood—or anyone else, for that matter—into the forerunners without them understanding what they were getting into.

Ghost frowned. "*How will you do that?*"

I laughed. "*That's the tricky bit. And to be honest, I haven't quite worked out that part yet.*" I glanced up at her. "*You ready?*"

She nodded. "*I am. It's all clear up here.*"

"*One more thing, Ghost. While I'm shifting... scan my thoughts.*"

For a heartbeat, the pyre wolf didn't say anything. "*You're worried that the tree may have done something to your mind?*"

"*Not really,*" I replied. "*I think I cut him off in time. But it can't hurt to make doubly certain.*"

"*Then don't worry about it, Prime. Go ahead and shift. I'll check your mind and alert you if anything is amiss.*"

Not needing further encouragement, I lay down flat and began casting.

✳   ✳   ✳

You have cast vanish. You are hidden.

You have dispelled your doppelganger spell, returning to the elder wolf form.

You have shapeshifted, taking the form of a level 282 human.

You have cast doppelganger, transforming into Havick.

Returning to human form and assuming my Havick disguise was a lengthy process—one requiring multiple spells—which was why I'd asked the brotherhood for privacy and had Ghost keep watch while I went about it.

But finally, it was done, and I walked upon two legs once more.

"*Your mind's clean,*" Ghost reported immediately.

"*Thanks, Ghost,*" I replied. "*That's a relief to know.*"

"*You're welcome. How does it feel to be human again?*"

I grinned. Today's transformation into a wolf wasn't my longest by any means. Yet, undoubtedly, it had been the most eventful. So much had happened, it felt like I'd spent a lifetime on four legs. "*Like I'm missing half of myself,*" I replied.

The pyre wolf snorted. "*You should spend more time as a wolf. It suits you.*"

"*I will,*" I assured her. "*But my human form is just as necessary.*" I drew the mindslayer's torc out of my inventory. "*Especially for things like this.*"

Her ears flickered up. "*You're going to put it on now?*"

I nodded. "*It's about time we found out what awakened slayer does, don't you think?*"

The eagerness I sensed through our bond was answer enough. Smiling at her anticipation—and my own—I clasped the torc around my neck.

You have unequipped a savant's ring (+4 Mind). Equipped items: 29 / 30.

You have equipped the tier 7 artifact, the <u>mindslayer's torc</u>, gaining +25% mental resistance and the <u>awakened slayer</u> ability. Note, this artifact's full properties can only be seen by you, its true owner.

Awakened slayer is a Class ability that is linked to your telepathy skill. It allows you to create a fully autonomous astral simulacrum of yourself to <u>guard</u> your own consciousness or to attack the minds of your foes. The construct will reside in your mind and will be a faithful replica of you in terms of size, shape, attributes, and skills.

Note, however, that the simulacrum will only have access to your telepathic abilities, and unless directed otherwise, it will automatically defend your consciousness from all forms of mental assaults, direct or subversive. You can take direct control of your simulacrum at any time you desire, but doing so will leave your body in the physical plane defenseless.

If you <u>project</u> your simulacrum into the mind of another, the target's subconsciousness will instinctively create its own astral constructs to protect itself and ward off your assault. The mental fortitude of the target will determine the strength of these constructs. Note, your simulacrum must still overcome the target's mental defenses.

A full day of meditation is required to constitute your simulacrum. Once formed, the astral construct will reside permanently in your consciousness until slain. Sheltering your simulacrum in your mind requires no energy, but projecting it into the minds of others is a channeled variant that will consume psi on an ongoing basis. If the simulacrum is destroyed, it may be reconstituted.

This spell cannot be upgraded.

Your secret blood trait has been triggered! To conceal your bloodline, your <u>awakened slayer</u> ability will be hidden in its entirety.

Ghost's mirrored jewelry trait has been activated, granting her +25% mental resistance and the <u>awakened slayer</u> ability. Note, in order for your familiar to create her own simulacrum, she must spend a full day meditating in her spirit vessel.

"Ah," I exhaled, rocking back on my heels. There was far more to the awakened slayer ability than I'd first suspected. The construct would live in my mind—permanently—something I found both intriguing and disturbing.

Even more fascinating was that I would be able to send it—*him? me? what was the right term here?*—into the mind of my foes.

And Ghost could do the same.

"What do you think of the new spell?" I asked my familiar.

"I want to try it," she shot back immediately.

I laughed. *"I do too. But sadly, that's going to have to wait. I don't have a full day to spare and won't for a while yet."* I paused. *"You could get started on your own meditations, though."*

"Are you sure?" she asked, not able to suppress the quiver of excitement this prospect induced.

I smiled. *"Of course. Go ahead."*

"Thank you, Prime!" Ghost replied, unraveling her form.

Ghost has unmanifested.

Ghost has begun casting <u>awakened slayer</u>. Time remaining until the spell is complete: 23 hours, 59 minutes, and 57 seconds.

Your familiar has entered a deep meditative state. While in this state, she will be unresponsive and unaware of her surroundings.

I took my time rejoining the brotherhood, my thoughts largely preoccupied with how to approach the forthcoming conversation. It was not going to be easy, especially when it came to making sure I didn't reveal too much.

I found Kartara and her officers waiting exactly where I'd left them.

"Welcome back, Havick," Duskar said with only the faintest trace of sarcasm.

Nodding absently, I scanned the battlefield. There were no longer any stygians in sight, or at least none that were free. All those that remained had either been slain, fled, or captured.

The rest of the brotherhood army was not standing idly by either. Except for the four officers waiting for me—Fiona and Heglin were not with them anymore—every other player had been pressed into service looting the dead stygians or corralling the captured ones—presumably with the intent of taking them back to the brotherhood's castle so that they could be shackled with obedience collars.

My gaze focused on the six dozen mages crawling over the harbinger's corpse. "How long is it going to take them to retrieve its netherstone?"

Cait shrugged. "They're nearly done, but I will supervise the final stage myself."

"Which reminds me," Kartara said. "What do you want us to do with the nagas you killed?"

My brows rose. "You're offering me their loot?"

She shrugged. "It's yours by right. They're your kills."

I shook my head. "No, they're not. I promised your people the spoils from the nagas. It doesn't matter that I killed them. They're yours." Besides, it was largely my fault that many of the nagas had fled. Then, too, the forerunners already had a tidy haul of scales from the nagas I'd slain on the other side of the rift.

"Thank you," Kartara said simply.

Nodding in acknowledgment, I glanced at Senzo. "Any sign of movement from the south?" The four hours I'd allocated for this mission were about up, and if the mature tree had sent any reinforcements—besides the three dead harbingers—they would be showing up soon.

The spymaster shook his head. "None."

"Good," I said, relieved, and turned back to the huntmistress.

"You ready to begin?" she prompted.

"Almost." I took a second look at the surrounding dunes but failed to spot any brotherhood corpses amongst the dead. Kartara's people must have recovered the bodies already. "How many did you lose?"

"Eighty-three," she replied.

I sucked in a breath. The number was low, fantastically low. Still, their sacrifice had been real. That was eighty-three players who would not be coming back—ever.

I ducked my head in respect before meeting Kartara's gaze again. "I am honored by their sacrifice. Without your people's help, without the sacrifice of the eighty-three fallen, my people and I would never have succeeded in doing what we set out to. No matter what happens from here on out, I promise I will not forget what the brotherhood has done for us."

For a long moment, Kartara said nothing. "I can say the same, Havick," she said finally and with equal gravity. "We have lost fewer people on this expedition than we have on any previous major rift dive, and that is due in no small part to your own intervention." She inclined her head. "You have my thanks, Havick."

On the tail end of the huntmistress' words, a surprising Game message unfurled in my mind.

Your task, <u>Brotherhood Obligations</u>, has been updated. By the huntmistress' own words, you have completed your first expedition with the brotherhood, albeit under the guise of Havick. Revised objective: Join the brotherhood on 2 more nether expeditions.

"Well, the Adjudicator has spoken, it seems," Kartara said lightly, breaking the solemnity of the moment. "I guess that is one less expedition you owe us."

I smiled. "I will not begrudge you the remaining two I owe you." I paused. "Although I am not so certain you will want my help after you hear what I have to say."

Kartara's smile faded. "Then, shall we get down to business?"

"Yes, but before we do—" I glanced at Cait—"can you cast a shield of silence spell?"

"I can," the elf replied. "Why?"

"What I have to say shouldn't be discussed out in the open."

Duskar's brows drew down. "Why the hell not? There is no one here but us!"

"That's not quite true," I murmured. "There are spores aplenty in the vicinity."

He blinked.

The cause of the orc's surprise was not what I assumed it to be, though— as I soon learned when Cait shook her head. "The spores have been dealt with," the nether witch pronounced.

It was my turn to evince surprise. "You're sure?"

She nodded. "I am. Go ahead and check for yourself if you wish."

Not quite willing to take her word for it, I drew stamina. "I'll do that," I said and released the casting I wove.

You have cast vanish. You are <u>invisible</u>. Duration: 5 minutes.

"Huh, fancy that," I said as the spell activated without a hitch, and without any telltale notices from the Game that I'd been detected either.

"So?" Duskar demanded impatiently when I reappeared after letting the buff lapse. "Tell us what you came to say."

"One moment." I turned to Cait. "I'd still like you to raise that shield of silence."

Rolling her eyes, the nether witch glanced at the huntmistress.

"Do it," Kartara replied. "I don't think Havick is going to talk otherwise."

The elf closed her eyes, and a moment later, another Game message opened before me.

You have been enclosed in a ward of silence. This is a sound barrier and will prevent any noise from intruding or escaping.

"Satisfied?" Cait asked.

I nodded. "Very." I sank down to the ground, sitting cross-legged on the naked sand. "Sit, everyone. This is probably going to take a while."

✳   ✳   ✳

You have sealed a Pact with Kartara, Duskar, Senzo, and Cait. For the next hour, you will not speak any falsehoods to them.

A quiet sigh went around the circle formed by me and the four brotherhood officers as the Pact I'd decided to enact went into effect. More than anything else, it would convince them of the truthfulness of my words.

"So," Senzo exhaled. "It's true then. You *are* a Powerful Initiate."

I understood the reason for his remark. Pacts were the domain of Powers, and even the least amongst them could form one.

"Technically, I'm a Powerful Acolyte," I replied. "But I haven't advanced my ascendant Class to rank two, so I'm not yet a minor Power."

"Not yet he says," Senzo muttered, shaking his head in rueful amazement.

"What level are you?" Duskar asked quickly.

"Level two hundred and eighty-two," I answered. That made me higher leveled than their huntmistress. I stole a glance in her direction, but Kartara's face was devoid of expression.

"What ascendant Class did you adopt?" Cait asked curiously.

"I won't answer that," I said evenly.

Duskar's brows drew down. "Why not?"

"Because not only will it endanger me, it will endanger your lives as well."

"Nonsense," the orc scoffed. "How can just knowing your Class be dangerous?"

"I won't answer that either," I replied equably.

Duskar's face devolved into a scowl, but before he could retort, Kartara raised a hand, stopping him. "What about your other Classes? Will you tell us what they are?"

"No."

She nodded, seemingly unperturbed by my refusal. "Because it will be dangerous too?"

"Correct."

"What about your name?" Kartara asked. "Can you tell us that?"

"There is nothing inherently dangerous about knowing my true name—" I began slowly.

"Well, thank the Powers for that," Duskar muttered.

"—but I prefer not to share it all the same."

The orc gnashed his teeth in frustration. "Goddamn."

Ignoring him, I addressed Kartara again. "Knowing who I am may lead you to figure out things about myself that I prefer to remain secret for now. However, knowing my true name is not necessary and will have no bearing on the other truths I have to share."

"I see," the huntmistress murmured. Sitting back, she drummed her fingers on her leg. "Then perhaps it's best if you tell us what you deem necessary before we question you further."

I inclined my head in acknowledgment, then, inhaling deeply, began, "So, obviously, my name is not Havick."

"Obviously," Senzo murmured.

I threw him a wry look. "What you need to know is as follows." Holding up my right hand, I raised one finger. "I am a *human* Powerful Acolyte, and belong to a faction with only one other Power. She, too, has not ascended to the rank of minor Power. We are not allied with any of the Game's other Powers. Our faction has discovered a hidden sector, one already cloaked by a shield generator, and which I fully expect to see claimed by tomorrow."

I paused, scanning their faces. But none of the four evinced more than mild surprise. They had guessed or surmised for themselves much of what I'd just said.

I raised another finger. "When I said earlier that it would be dangerous, I was not being precise. Let me rectify that now. If knowledge of what I am spreads, I believe *every* Power in the Game would bestir themselves to see me and those allied with me dead. That includes Loken, Arinna, Tartar, and the Triumvirate."

Cait gasped, Senzo's eyes widened in alarm, and even Duskar paled. Only Kartara showed minimal reaction. But for the slight tightening of her lips, her expression remained unchanged.

I ticked off another point on my fingers. "Thirdly: I am committed to fighting the void. As is my faction. We believe them to be one of the biggest threats facing the Kingdom. If they are not stopped, they will consume the whole world."

My pledge and heartfelt words seemed to please the brotherhood players, and I could almost see the tension ease from their shoulders.

"Fourth: there is more to the void than you think." I paused, deliberating silently with myself on whether it was really necessary to reveal the next bit. But the brotherhood had a right to know the nature of the threat they were facing.

"The trees are sentient," I stated badly.

The four said nothing, waiting for me to go on, but when I didn't, frowns creased their faces.

"Uhm, we knew that already," Cait said delicately.

"Then perhaps you mistake my meaning. What I'm getting at is that the trees can talk."

Palpable silence.

"What do you mean, they can talk?" the huntmistress asked carefully.

"Just that. The young void tree spoke to me in my mind."

Alarm shot across the faces of Senzo, Duskar, and Kartara. Only Cait appeared unperturbed by the news. "What did it have to say?" she asked eagerly.

I smiled. "He, not 'it'," I corrected. "That's how the tree perceived himself. As for what he had to say: surprisingly little of value, actually. But I did manage to gather he was the one to have created the nagas."

"Oh my." The elf sat back, biting her lip. "Are you sure about that?"

I nodded. "As sure as I can be under the circumstances. It was why he got so angry at their destruction."

"And it is also why you attacked the nagas in the first place, isn't it?" Kartara guessed, composed once more. "You were trying to attract the tree's attention."

"Correct. It worked too."

"That explains a lot," Senzo whispered.

"It does indeed," Kartara murmured. She focused on me again. "What else can you tell us about the trees?"

I hesitated again, wondering if I should go on.

"What is it?" the huntmistress asked, watching the play of emotions across my face intently.

"The young tree wasn't the only one to speak to me. The mature tree did as well."

More silence, and this time, there was a profound and dangerous quality to it.

"Relax, he did not subvert my mind."

Duskar inhaled sharply. How can you be so—"

"—sure he didn't?" I finished for him grimly.

He nodded warily, looking more than a little worried.

"Because if he had, I would be dead," I said bluntly. "I shut down the mental link between us before he could complete his spell. And my familiar has since scoured my mind. She is certain nothing is amiss."

"Your familiar..." Kartara began. "That would be the stygian wolf?"

I nodded.

"How did you manage to acquire a stygian for a familiar?" Cait demanded.

I smiled tightly. "That's another one of those questions I won't answer."

She sighed. "Can we see her at least?"

"Not right now. She's... busy." I raised my right hand anew, splaying all my fingers again. "But back to my list. There's one more thing you all need to know. The fifth and most important." I paused, leaving my words hanging there.

"What's that?" Senzo prompted.

I drew in a deep breath. They would not like what I had to say next, I was sure.

"Half of the Endless Dungeon has already fallen to the void."

CHAPTER 590: AN OUTSTRETCHED HAND

For a drawn-out moment, no one said anything.

Finally, though, Kartara broke the silence. "That makes no sense," she said slowly.

Duskar nodded emphatically. "It can't be true. It can't."

"He must be mistaken," Senzo agreed.

"The huntmistress is right, what you say makes no sense," Cait added, biting her lip. "No one—not even the Triumvirate—can claim to know the exact size of the Endless Dungeon. Yet, here you are stating half of it has fallen? It's nonsense, that's what it is."

"It is not," I refuted implacably. "It's the truth."

I understood and even sympathized with their struggle to digest what I was telling them. I'd seen the huntmistress' map of the Nethersphere in the brotherhood castle, after all. As far as I could tell, there had been no dungeon sectors marked on it.

And indeed, from every discussion I'd ever had with Kartara and the others, there had been nothing to suggest they were even aware of the void's presence in the Endless Dungeon.

Which was part of the reason why my statement had left them undone.

The other part, of course, was learning that half of the Endless Dungeon had *already* fallen.

Today, the brotherhood had just learned that the war they'd been waging all their lives had another front—one they were totally ignorant of. So, of course, the news hit hard.

Pressing her hands together, the huntmistress leaned forward. "Who told you this? The Adjudicator?"

I shook my head. "He did not. Someone else did."

Some of the tightness around the huntmistress' eyes vanished. "Then you could've been lied to. You have no direct evidence of what you've been told."

"On the contrary, I do. My allies and I were instrumental in stopping the nether's invasion in a dungeon." I paused. "That's where I killed my first Power—a harbinger—and gained the netherstone. That's where I learned the stygian seeds are dangerous to handle. And that's where I found out that it's not just the Kingdom, but the Endless Dungeon, that's under assault by the void."

"What's the name of the dungeon?" Duskar asked.

"I cannot say."

"And what about the one who shared this information with you?" Senzo queried. "Can you tell us his name?"

"I cannot."

Neither Senzo nor Duskar looked happy with my refusals, but before they could make much of it, Cait rejoined the conversation. "What you say still does not make sense," she protested. "The Endless Dungeon is *already* part of the Nethersphere. Why would the void bother invading it?"

I turned her way. "Perhaps because the Game has cut off their access to those sectors, and they want back in? Or perhaps because the void fathers have realized that if you rob players of their dungeons, they will be weaker and easier to kill?"

"But that would imply—" She broke off.

"It would imply the void is not nearly as mindless as we've been assuming," the huntmistress finished for her. Her gaze found mine. "They have a strategy in mind."

I nodded. "I think so too." I leaned forward. "And I think it goes beyond reclaiming territory they've lost to the Endless Dungeon."

Kartara's brows creased. "Explain."

"I and my, uhm… associates believe the void's expansion is not random, that there is a reason they appear in the Kingdom sectors they do, and that reason is the ley lines."

Kartara's eyes narrowed. "You believe they are using the portals between dungeon and Kingdom sectors to identify their targets," she surmised.

I smiled. The huntmistress caught on quickly. "Yes."

"That would mean if we identified the fallen dungeons, we can predict which Kingdom sectors are in peril!" Cait exclaimed.

"Also correct."

Kartara scrutinized me carefully. "Things are still not adding up. If as many dungeons have fallen to the void as you're claiming, why haven't we heard anything of it? The factions must be aware of what's going on. They control most of the dungeons in the Game. So, why haven't they told anyone?"

I tilted my head to the side. "That's the question, isn't it?"

The huntmistress' gaze sharpened. "Are you suggesting—"

"There have been rumors," Senzo said abruptly.

Kartara stared at him. "What rumors?" she rasped.

"Nothing about the void," the spymaster replied hastily. "But…" He pressed his closed fist against his mouth and bit down worriedly. "There has been talk of dungeons being temporarily sealed, of others being permanently closed to the public, and of portals not working." He met the huntmistress' gaze. "The usual stuff, and nothing we'd ordinarily concern ourselves with."

She nodded slowly.

"The rumors are sporadic," Senzo went on, "and on their own, they are not enough to conclude that dungeons are being lost to the void—and certainly not on the scale Havick is implying." He sighed. "But admittedly, the gossip does lend credence to his tale. We will have to dig further for confirmation."

"You should do that," I said emphatically. "As for why this has remained unnoticed for so long, I have some theories…" I rubbed my chin, wondering how much to say. "This is conjecture only, but my own feeling is that the void has been at this for centuries—eating away at the Endless Dungeon bit by bit—and so slowly most wouldn't notice."

"The Powers would have, though," Cait pointed out. "Some have been around for longer than that."

"They should've," I agreed grimly and left it at that. Everyone around the circle knew what I was implying.

"I see," Kartara murmured, glancing at Senzo. "Whatever you do, do it carefully, but I agree: this must be verified."

Nodding, the spymaster turned back to me. "Do you know which dungeons have fallen?"

I shook my head. "I don't have that level of detailed information, sorry."

He sighed in disappointment.

"But I know who does."

"And let me guess," Duskar growled, only half-sarcastically, "you're not willing to name them."

I eyed the orc. "I might be, but... it will require you binding yourself to secrecy."

He shrank back. "Binding, as in...?"

"Becoming my follower and agreeing to obey me," I said mildly. "Are you willing to do that?"

Duskar's glare was answer enough.

"I didn't think so," I murmured. Turning back to the huntmistress, I found her studying me quizzically.

"You are much more than you appear to be, Havick," she said softly.

I shrugged. "Aren't we all?"

My flippant response did not faze her. "It is obvious that you have access to knowledge and things we don't. It is obvious, too, that you could play a pivotal role in our fight against the void. We would be foolish to reject any arrangement you suggest. However—" steepling her fingers, she peered intently into my eyes, as if trying to divine my secrets—"I still don't understand what you want from us. And until I do, I can't risk tying the brotherhood to you or your faction."

"I told you," I said evenly, "I want your help fighting the void."

"I'll need more than that," she replied. "Give me the specifics."

I fell silent, considering my next words carefully. "I want the brotherhood to join my faction," I said, finally acknowledging the issue we'd been dancing around.

"I knew it," Duskar muttered.

"How does joining your faction help us fight the void?" the huntmistress asked, her gaze locked on mine.

"Well, for one, you'll gain unfettered access to the knowledge you just mentioned. And as you know, information is power. Armed with such information, I have no doubt, the brotherhood can make greater inroads into the nether than you have previously—and figure out what's truly going on in the Endless Dungeon."

Kartara's expression did not change. "Are you saying you will withhold the information if we don't join your faction?"

"No," I admitted. "I will not. I will share what I know regardless, but if the brotherhood chooses to remain separate, you and your people will have to accept that I will not—cannot—share everything. Doing so may jeopardize my own people, and I will not do that. You will also have to accept what I tell you at face value, and accept not knowing the source of the information."

Kartara nodded. "I see. And what else will we gain by joining your faction?"

"A base."

"A base?" the huntmistress echoed.

"Yes. A base hidden away in a sector that no one will likely ever find. From such a base, you will be free to focus your efforts against the stygians unhindered by the machinations of the Game."

Senzo's brows creased. "That will also isolate us—something we can ill-afford."

I stared at the spymaster. "Why's that?"

"As much as we may loathe the Grand Game, we are dependent on it too," he explained. "Without the customers who buy our wares, we'll lack the funding necessary to pursue our war against the void. The players themselves are essential, too. Without them, we won't have the recruits we desperately need to replenish our ranks."

I frowned. "I imagine my own people could alleviate some of the shortfall, but you're right, joining my faction will significantly curtail your recruitment efforts and income." I turned back to the huntmistress. "That is something you will have to consider."

She nodded. "So, knowledge and a base. That's two things you have to offer. What else?"

I held out my hand, palm up. "There is also this."

Leaning over, Cait scrutinized my outstretched arm. "Your hand's empty," she said, stating the obvious.

I chuckled. "It is. But that's not why I'm holding it out. This next bit is better seen than told." I waved my arm in the huntmistress' direction. "Take it."

Kartara studied my palm leerily. "What is it you intend on doing?"

"Adding you to my faction," I replied. "But only for a minute," I added loudly over the other's protestations.

Katara's brows creased. "What good will that do?"

"You'll see."

She still didn't take my hand.

"Trust me," I said gently. "And besides, what's the worst that could happen? There are no consequences to abandoning a faction. You can leave any time you desire. But I'm betting you won't want to."

The huntmistress eyed me for a second longer, then, moving decisively, clasped her hand to mine.

You have accepted Kartara, a player, into the Forerunners faction. Kartara is free to break her pledge of loyalty to the faction at any time and without consequences. As are you. However, until such time as the Forerunners disavow the dread summoner—or vice versa—she will be considered the faction's sworn woman, and her actions will reflect on it.

As a result of her new status, Kartara has gained the factional trait: rift sense!

CHAPTER 591: A DECLARATION OF INTENT

Kartara gasped.

The others, already on edge, half-rose, hands on weapons.

The huntmistress raised a hand, only slightly shaky. "It's alright. I'm fine."

"What is?" Duskar asked. "What did he do?"

"He gave me a trait," Kartara murmured absently while she craned her head left and right. She was trying to get a fix on the other rifts, I imagined.

Senzo frowned. "What sort of trait?"

The huntmistress' attention snapped back to her subordinates. "Rift sense. It has revealed the presence of three other rifts in the sector."

That bald statement only renewed the trio's anxiety.

"They pose no danger," I assured them. "The rifts are even farther away than the mature tree's nest, *and* lower leveled than the one we just closed."

"Are you sure?" Duskar demanded at the same time as Cait asked, "How can you tell?"

"I can tell," I said, addressing both of them, "because of rift sense." Seeing from their mystified expressions that they still remained unenlightened, I added, "Thanks to the trait, the three rifts shine like beacons in my awareness. I can tell exactly where they are and how far away—" I tapped the side of my head—"in here."

"That's exactly how rift sense works," Kartara agreed before anyone could argue with my assessment. "It's a remarkable trait. How did your faction get it?"

She deliberately did not call the Forerunners by name, I noted, for which fact I was glad. "The trait is newly acquired," I admitted. "The Adjudicator awarded it to us after the tree's fall."

Senzo whistled softly. "Damn, that's a nice reward."

"Why didn't we get anything like that?" Duskar complained.

Cait rolled her eyes. "Perhaps, because we didn't do anything except kill a few nagas."

"The brotherhood did more than that," I countered. "And assuming you are willing to join my faction, this trait can be yours too."

Cait did not reply, nor did Senzo or Duskar, but as one, their gazes found Kartara.

"It's a remarkable trait," the huntmistress repeated, feeling the regard of the others. "And there is no doubt it will be of immense help in any future rift dives we attempt." She inhaled. "But—"

I closed my eyes, realizing what her decision was going to be.

"—we cannot join your faction," Kartara finished.

I didn't let any of my disappointment show. "Why?"

"For all the reasons Senzo gave earlier," she stated forthrightly. "The brotherhood cannot afford to disappear from the minds of the Game's players. Our role is not just to fight the void, but to be *seen* fighting the void. That way, we can serve as an example that will hopefully encourage some of them to do the right thing and take up the fight as well."

The huntmistress paused. "Then, too, there is yourself to consider. I cannot claim to know what you are or why the Game's Powers want you dead, but it would be remiss of me not to consider the implications of your earlier pronouncements. You claimed the truth would make you a pariah—and any allied with you—and I believe you."

She blew out a troubled breath. "The Kingdom cannot afford for the brotherhood to become refugees, Havick. We have to be able to operate in sectors where the Powers rule. We cannot risk being actively hunted by them." She stared at me searchingly. "Do you understand?"

I wanted to say I didn't, but I did. I sighed. "I do. So, where does that leave us?"

"As allies?" she offered.

My brows furrowed. "How would allying with me be any different from joining my faction? The brotherhood will still be tainted by association."

Kartara leaned forward. "You're right. The brotherhood cannot openly join forces with you, nor can we support your faction in any conflict it engages in, but that's not to say we cannot come to an understanding of sorts."

"An 'understanding'," I murmured. "Then it's a secret alliance you're proposing?"

She nodded. "I am."

I rubbed my chin. "Go on, then. I'm listening."

She shrugged. "There is not much more to it. What I'm proposing is simple. The brotherhood will arm and fund your people. From our prior discussions, I gather your faction is short on money, supplies, and weapons. We can provide all that."

I nodded slowly. All those were things the Forerunners required. But we needed more, too. "What about manpower—players?"

She shook her head. "Regrettably, we can't provide that. The brotherhood will not lend your faction direct military aid again."

"Why not?" I objected. "I get the brotherhood not wanting to get involved in a factional war, but surely you can—and should—join forces with us against the void?"

"We can't," she reiterated. "As it is, after today alone, there will be many unanswerable questions."

I frowned. "What does that mean?"

Her look turned wry. "Have you forgotten? You entered the battle as a harbinger and were seen battling a flying void tree. What's worse, you won, and in full view of all two thousand of my people."

My frown deepened. "Are you saying—"

"No one will deliberately betray you," Kartara interjected. "And in fact, except for the four of us, there are only a handful of others who know Havick and the harbinger are one and the same." She shook her head. "But a harbinger fighting a void tree? And defeating it? That tale is too fantastic not to get out. People will talk. It's inevitable. And eventually, the factions will send their spies to find out how the brotherhood managed to slay a void tree and to learn more about the harbinger who betrayed the void."

I bowed my head. The huntmistress was right, and if I'd had time to think through the matter myself, I'd likely have come to the same conclusion. After today, the brotherhood was bound to attract significant attention from the new Powers.

And once the Game's factions started digging, sooner or later, my own involvement would come to light.

"It's not all bad, though," Kartara added. "Senzo has a plan."

I looked up. "A plan?"

The spymaster nodded. "Yes. We can't hide the truth of what happened here today, but we can obfuscate it, piling lies atop lies. When I'm done, there will be so many rumors flying through the rank and file, it will take someone weeks—or months, if we're lucky—to separate the truth from fiction."

"Weeks," I repeated, not liking the estimate one bit. "That still implies that the truth will get out."

Senzo grimaced. "Unfortunately, the truth usually does. There is no way we can hide what happened indefinitely. Eventually, one of the Game's factions will realize the brotherhood had help from an outside Power, and that will only further their curiosity as to what occurred."

My lips thinned. As much as I wanted to dispute the spymaster's assessment, I couldn't. I turned back to the huntmistress. "And what does the brotherhood get out of a secret alliance?"

"Knowledge for one," she replied promptly. "Your help for another—with you by our side, I foresee more victories for the brotherhood in the near future. And finally, there is rift sense."

My brows rose. "You will stay in my faction, then?"

"If we can come to an agreement, yes. And assuming we do, I will also select a few more of my people to join your faction—in secret, of course—so that they too can gain access to its factional trait."

I nodded. What the huntmistress was proposing made sense and would benefit both the Forerunners and the brotherhood in the long run. There were still a few more issues to iron out, though. "What sort of help are you expecting from me? Personally, I mean. Given that you can't afford any more rumors to spread, I gather you will not want me openly slaying void trees again."

"Definitely not," she said firmly. "We will have to take more care in our future battles to keep your involvement secret."

My lips turned down.

"It's an unnecessary complication, I agree," Kartara said, noticing my expression, "but it's not something that can be helped. One dead void tree is difficult enough to explain. Multiple slain void trees would be impossible."

She was right. Even leaving my bloodline out of the equation, openly killing the void trees would attract too much attention—and of the wrong sort.

"So, do we have a deal?" Kartara asked.

Clasping my hands together, I bit gently down on my knuckles while I thought the matter through. The huntmistress' proposal was a good one and would give me nearly everything I wanted—in the short term, anyway.

The sticking point was the gossip that was already circulating among the brotherhood ranks. Senzo's plan for dealing with it was far from ideal and meant that eventually, the brotherhood—and the Power who had aided them—would eventually become of significant interest to the new Powers.

But perhaps there was a better way to stop the rumors from spreading.

"I have an alternative to propose," I said.

The huntmistress tilted her head to the side. "Oh?"

"You said the army will talk, and I get that. But that only becomes a problem if they rejoin the Game."

Kartara's brows creased. "I'm not sure what you're—"

"What if the official version of the battle is that the brotherhood lost?"

Kartara blinked. "Lost?"

"Yes, what if none of your people return—except for you and a few carefully selected individuals to carry back the tale of the brotherhood's defeat, of course."

"Where would they go?" Cait asked, confused.

"To his faction, obviously," Duskar growled, his face growing heated. "The bastard is asking us to gift him our entire army!"

"That's one possibility, certainly," I said blandly. "And naturally, I am not unopposed to the notion."

Duskar's face grew more incensed.

Chuckling, I went on. "In fact, they could even—"

"Stop toying with Dusk, Havick," Kartara instructed, looking far less amused than I was. "You must know I will not surrender my people to you. No matter how well intentioned you appear, the players you are talking about are brotherhood soldiers and my responsibility—and will remain so."

"I was fairly certain you'd feel that way." I smiled. "But you have to admit, leaving your army in my care *would* make things easier."

"Enough," the huntmistress said tersely. "That's not an option, and you know it. So, out with it. What are you really proposing?"

I shrugged. "That they stay here."

Senzo's brows drew down. "Here?"

"Yes, here," I said, my face growing serious again as I turned back to the huntmistress. "I think it's high time the Brotherhood establishes a base in the Nethersphere, don't you?"

"You want us to strand two thousand of our people in the nether?" Duskar spat. "How is that any better than letting them join you?"

I rolled my eyes. "Oh, don't be so dramatic. They won't be stranded. They'll be isolated, I agree—which is what we need them to be—but they will also be doing valuable work."

"Such as?" Senzo asked.

"Investigating the other rifts in the sector, for one. Seeing how the mature tree reacts to a protracted player-presence for another. As far as I know, no one has actually tried to live in the Nethersphere before. How would the void trees react to such an incursion? And is it even possible?"

"Who cares?" Duskar protested. "Why would anyone want to live here?"

My eyes flickered to him. "Because like it or not, the brotherhood's present tactics are not working."

"What do you mean by that?" the orc demanded hotly.

"Come, I've seen the map of the fallen sectors in the brotherhood's castle. It's grown, hasn't it? I imagine a hundred years ago—or even fifty years ago—it wasn't as large."

Duskar jutted out his jaw stubbornly. "So?"

"So," I said, drawing out the word, "that map alone is a clear indication that your strategy is failing. Your rift dives are not working. Face facts: the brotherhood is losing the war and the nether is expanding."

"That's unfair," Senzo objected. "We lack the resources to take the fight properly to the void. If—"

"If what?" I interjected. "If the Powers suddenly had a change of heart and joined your cause? If you managed to recruit more players? Neither of those things is going to happen. You all know that."

Silence fell over the brotherhood officers, and it fell to the huntmistress to break it. "What are you getting at, Havick?"

I leaned forward. "It's time for a change," I said softly. "It's time to stop fighting this war on the nether's terms, and start fighting it on your own."

CHAPTER 592: A CHANGE OF STRATEGY

My pronouncement elicited only a single terse word in response from the huntmistress.

"Explain," she ordered.

"Gladly," I said. Sitting back, I took the time to gather my thoughts. "From everything you've told me, and from everything I've learned of the void from... other sources, I think it's fair to say that the initiative is squarely with the enemy at the moment. The void fathers are the ones making all the moves. They are the ones determining which sectors to attack and which new fronts to open. *They* are the ones choosing the battlefields. You and the brotherhood are in reactive mode, only attacking the positions the stygians expect you to."

Kartara nodded, her expression shuttered. "A fair assessment. We are the Kingdom's protectors. We defend against what the void attacks. But what other alternatives do we have?"

Spreading my arms, I took in the surroundings. "This sector, for one."

The huntmistress raised one eyebrow. "You're suggesting we try to reclaim sector 30,199?"

"I am," I said, ignoring her disbelieving tone. "This sector is as good a place as any to begin a counter-offensive. By all indications, it is deep within the void's territory and important to the nether. There is a mature tree here, three other rifts, and what, by all appearances, is a harbinger creche. Why *not* start here?"

Senzo scratched his head in bemusement. "For all the reasons you just laid out. If we did as you suggested and established a base here, how long do you think it would last against a concerted attack?"

Duskar scanned the barren desert dunes. "The terrain is indefensible," he agreed. "Even if the mature tree leaves us with enough time to fortify a camp, the ground underfoot will not support proper earthworks. Any walls we erect will not be worthy of the name."

I shook my head. "I'm not suggesting you establish your base in this exact spot. There is a mountain range to the north. The terrain there is more conducive to building a fort, and additionally, if you delve underground, the stone itself will help keep the nether mists out."

"But your netherstone is tied to this location," Cait pointed out. "Our people will require constant and ready access to a portal if they are to remain in the sector. For obvious reasons, they can't be miles away from one."

I shrugged. "True. But you'll have a new netherstone soon," I said, gesturing at the dead harbinger.

"It's an interesting suggestion, Havick," Kartara said, "but not workable, I think. Or have you forgotten the three other harbingers under the mature tree's control? Marching the army across miles of barren sand while under constant assault by the mist will be difficult enough, but to do it while under threat of no less than three stygian Powers? That would be foolhardy."

I smiled. "Oh, did I forget to mention? Those three are dead."

Senzo, Duskar, and Cait stilled, their eyes widening in shock. Kartara's expression was more controlled as she exhaled carefully in a bid to hide her reaction.

She was only partially successful.

"You did forget," the huntmistress said. "When—and how—did this happen?"

"The three harbingers died on the other side of the rift," I replied. "They attacked the cloaking shield my people erected around the sector. Their assault was not wholly unexpected, though, and in response, we lowered the shield, lured them in, and dispatched them." I paused. "Their deaths were what prompted the void tree to flee to this side."

Senzo eyed me askance, but he didn't question the veracity of my words. The Pact I'd made earlier still compelled me to speak only truth, after all.

"You make it sound so easy," the spymaster muttered.

"I don't mean to," I replied. "And I assure you, we didn't take the threat lightly. In the end, though, slaying the three harbinger *was* easier than we anticipated, but that was largely the result of a mix of bad judgment on the young tree's part and careful planning on our own."

"So.... your faction now has four netherstones?" Cait asked, sounding both impressed and a little jealous by that fact.

My smile widened. "I expect so."

"That does frame things differently," the huntmistress murmured. She'd barely paid my exchange with Cait any heed, and her thoughts had clearly been elsewhere since I'd reported the deaths of the three harbingers.

I glanced at her. "It does, doesn't it?"

She nodded. "The loss of all four harbingers explains the mature tree's inaction. No wonder he hasn't sent any reinforcements. He likely doesn't have any powerful minions left to call on."

"The mature tree could come himself," Duskar pointed out.

"That would mean uprooting himself," Cait objected, "and he won't risk doing that."

I nodded, agreeing with her assessment.

"But he could bring up reinforcements from elsewhere in the void," Senzo warned.

"He can, and surely will," the huntmistress agreed, "but it will take time for the nether to gather and dispatch aid—and it is not just any aid the mature tree requires. It's Powers he needs. After his losses to date, nothing less will suffice." Her gaze found mine. "That gives us time to safely reach the mountains."

I clasped my hands together in suppressed excitement. "Then you agree to my proposition?"

Kartara pursed her lips. "Not so fast. I agree that establishing a base in the sector appears feasible, but that is still a long way from expelling the void from it."

"But it's the first step to doing so," I argued. "Like I said earlier, while rift diving may work against a stygian seed or even a sapling, your own experiences have already shown they are not nearly as effective against a full-grown tree. Take the young void tree we just killed, for instance. It took a whole series of battles for my faction to dislodge the thing. Over the course of a few days, we steadily weakened its defenses, killing two overlords, dozens of nagas, and thousands of lesser stygians—and yet he was still no pushover during the final confrontation." I shook my head. "I'm convinced it's going to take more than a single battle to defeat the mature tree."

Kartara frowned. "It's a campaign you have in mind, then?"

"That's exactly right," I replied. "We, or rather you and the brotherhood, have to stay entrenched in this sector, and bit by bit, weaken the mature tree's defenses, until we are ready to strike the final blow."

"A mature tree is not a young tree," Duskar objected. "What you are asking could take months or even years."

"It could," I said bluntly, "which is why establishing an impregnable base is an important first step."

"But aren't you forgetting something?" Senzo asked. "Your faction fought the young tree in a sector that was still nominally part of the Kingdom. The void was constrained in what reinforcements it could send. Not so here. What's stopping the void from sending ten harbingers against us—or twenty?"

"The same thing that stops any expanding empire from concentrating its forces too much—the need to defend the territory it already holds," I retorted. "Any reinforcements the void brings to bear in this sector will have to be taken from elsewhere, weakening *that* sector's defenses. Now, granted, the void can still choose to do that, but will it do so recklessly? Will it expose other void trees in order to protect this one? I am not so certain it will. The mature tree already made that mistake, and look where it is now."

Senzo frowned. "And if you are wrong?"

I shrugged. "Then we abandon the sector, retreat—and try elsewhere."

The spymaster still didn't look convinced.

"Also, think of the benefits," I encouraged.

"What benefits?" he asked.

Instead of answering the question directly, I replied with one of my own. "Who landed the final blow against the harbinger your people killed?"

"I did," Kartara replied.

I suspected that might have been the case. "And I'm guessing you did so because you *don't* possess an evolved Class and thus cannot acquire the Powerful Initiate Mark?"

The huntmistress' lips tightened fractionally, but she replied evenly enough. "Correct."

I nodded. "You did it to protect the rest of your people, of course—because anyone in the Kingdom sporting a Powerful Initiate Mark will become fair game for the Powers there." I ran my gaze slowly across the four. "But all of you have grown so used to the status quo, you've not realized a core truth: the Game's factions and your fear of them have tied your hands."

The brotherhood players stiffened, feeling the sting of my criticism, but none of them interrupted.

"Imagine, the brotherhood didn't have to fear letting its people become Powers," I went on. "Imagine that for every stygian Power your people slew, you gained a new Powerful Initiate. Imagine that you had a stronghold in sector 30,199—a sector so isolated that nearly no one could get to it. Imagine you could nurture your newly-made Powers there, safe from the machinations of the Game. Now, tell me, what would the brotherhood be able to achieve then?"

Awed silence.

"That's..." Duskar sputtered. "That's..."

"Ambitious," Kartara finished for him, her gaze resting on me.

I didn't look away. I knew she understood the implications of what I was asking. If the picture I painted came to fruition, then many of her subordinates would surpass her in level and power—because she, of course, could not become a Power herself.

Asking anyone to permit such would be a bitter pill to swallow. How much harder would it be for Kartara, who had likely been in command of the brotherhood for years?

If she wanted to, there were a dozen different excuses the huntmistress could use to dismiss my suggestion, and as loyal as her people were to her, they would undoubtedly go along with whatever she decided.

"Ambitious and intriguing," Kartara continued, her face still inscrutable. "And a notion worth exploring further. I agree to your proposal."

My shoulders sagged in relief, even as my respect for the huntmistress grew.

"However, there is still the matter of provisions to consider," she went on as if there was nothing momentous about her decision. "If the goal is to keep the brotherhood stronghold in sector 30,199 isolated, I cannot supply them directly from our stores."

"Agreed," I said. "My faction will keep your people fed."

Duskar shot Kartara a look. "We are really doing this?"

She nodded. "We are. If the outcome of today's battle has shown anything, it's what can be achieved with Powers fighting by our side. This is not an opportunity we can afford to ignore." She paused. "Besides which, Havick is right, the brotherhood has been on the defensive for too long. It's time we took the fight to the void."

She inhaled, then issued a series of pronouncements in rapid succession. "The army we leave behind in sector 30,199 will be the genesis of something new: the brotherhood's first Nethersphere chapter. It will function autonomously and will be charged with making inroads into the territory held by the void.

"The chapter will operate under a veil of secrecy, and its members will make a Pact sworn oath never to return to the Kingdom until the void has been fully defeated. I'll remain in charge of the public-facing part of the organization—the Kingdom chapter—and will use it to funnel suitable candidates to the Nethersphere group.

"Unfortunately, necessity and circumstances dictate that the entire army be conscripted into the new chapter. None of the players we brought here today will be afforded an opportunity to return to the Kingdom. But I want to be clear, all future enrollment in the Nethersphere chapter will be voluntary." She exhaled. "Now, are there any questions?"

Silence fell again as Kartara's subordinates digested her words, but if the others were perturbed by Kartara's emphatic adoption of my suggestion, they did not show it.

I, too, ruminated over the huntmistress' words. Once again, Kartara had surprised me. She had not only heard and understood what I had said, she had wholeheartedly grabbed hold of the notion and developed it into something that, in the long run, had every chance of success.

Assuming, of course, we managed to establish and maintain a foothold in sector 30,199 in the first place.

"Who are you putting in charge of the new chapter?" Duskar asked finally.

"You," Kartara replied.

The orc straightened. "Me?"

"Yes, you." She smiled. "I have no doubt you are up to the task."

"But..." The orc licked his lips as, almost involuntarily, his gaze slid sideways to me. "You want *me* to work with him?"

Kartara laughed. "No doubt you will give Havick no end of trouble, but you are our best war leader, Dusk. Heglin and Cait will also stay with you and serve as your seconds."

The nether witch straightened. "I will?"

Kartara's lips turned upward again. It was as if her decision had buoyed her, and much of the tension she'd been carrying had vanished in its wake. "Of course," she said lightly. "You are one of our foremost nether experts. Who better to study the creche here?"

Cait's eyes brightened, and she nodded decisively. "I will not let you down."

"I know you won't," Kartara replied. "Now, are there any other questions?" Although she fielded the question to the group at large, it was to me she looked.

I said nothing for a moment, still meditating over her choice of commander. It was fair to say Duskar didn't like me—nor me him, for that matter—and I couldn't help but feel that had factored in the huntmistress' decision.

Did Kartara fear for the new chapter's continued loyalty?

I thought so.

The Nethersphere chapter would be operating independently from the Kingdom one, and like it or not, would be heavily dependent on my faction for its survival, at least initially. Which, of course, was problematic from the huntmistress' perspective. Such dependence might sway their loyalties, leading them to trade their allegiance to the brotherhood for me. But by appointing Duskar their commander significantly, she'd significantly reduced the chances of that happening.

A calculated decision, then, I mused.

Still, I could not fault it. And for all my dislike of the orc, I did not doubt his competence.

Turning my focus outward again, I found Kartara and the others watching me intently. "I have just one question," I said, ignoring their stares. "Two, actually."

"Go on," the huntmistress.

"Who will be returning to the Kingdom with you?"

"Just Senzo," Kartara replied. She threw the spymaster an apologetic look. "His expertise I cannot spare, and truthfully, he will be more useful in the Game than here in the nether."

I nodded. "Makes sense."

"And your other question?" Kartara asked.

"What's Duskar's new title?" I paused. "And please don't tell me I have to call him huntmaster!"

Just as I hoped, my question set the others chuckling.

Kartara smiled at me knowingly. My intention had been to set the others at ease—and it had worked—but not without the huntmistress realizing what I was about. Not that she seemed to mind.

"Alright, now that we have all settled—" Kartara glanced at Duskar— "tell me how you want to do this."

The orc leaned forward. "Well, first, we need to..."

Your Pact to speak no falsehoods to Kartara, Duskar, Senzo, and Cait has expired.
You have accepted Duskar, Cait, and Senzo into the Forerunners faction.

The four brotherhood officers and I did not deliberate long over what needed to be done or how to go about doing it. Feeling the press of time, and the not-insignificant threat from the mature tree to the south, we formalized our alliance through four separate Pacts.

You have sealed a Pact with Senzo and Kartara. Both players have agreed to never reveal their membership status in the Forerunners. In addition, Kartara will see your faction supplied with weapons and money. In exchange, you will share any information gathered about the stygians that does not compromise the source.
These Pacts will only terminate when the void has been fully vanquished.
You have 9 / 20 active Pacts.

You have sealed a Pact with Cait and Duskar. Both players have agreed to never reveal their membership status in the Forerunners. In addition, Duskar and Cait will never return to the Kingdom again and will also ensure no other member of the brotherhood's Nethersphere chapter does so either. In exchange, you will see the brotherhood's Nethersphere chapter supplied with food and will provide them with any military assistance they require.
This Pact will only terminate when the void has been fully vanquished.
You have 11 / 20 active Pacts.

The Pacts I formed with Senzo and Kartara were identical and, of necessity, did not cover every eventuality. Doing so would have been impossible, and in the end, it was not the Pacts themselves, but trust and shared goals that underpinned our alliance.

Likewise, the Pacts sealed between me and the two members of the newly dubbed Nethersphere chapter were also identical. Many of the details—like when and how often we'd provision them, what sort of military aid we would provide, and so on—still needed to be hashed out, but that could only happen once the new chapter had established a base of operations.

And it was finding such a base that was the focus of most of our deliberations.

"Then we are agreed," Kartara said, rising to her feet as our discussions drew to a close. "Dusk and Cait, you will head north into the mountains."

The pair nodded.

I'd inducted the duo into the Forerunners, which meant that they, too, now had rift sense, which was all to the good. The factional trait, it turned out, was going to prove its worth sooner than any of us had anticipated.

It just so happened that Rift-W, the smallest of the sector's remaining rifts, was also in the north, and by my best estimate, also somewhere in the region's northern mountains. As such, Cait and Duskar would navigate by the rift itself and use it to lead the army unerringly north across the desert—at least until they reached the mountain range. Thereafter, they would deviate course and hopefully find somewhere suitable to settle in.

Duskar's gaze slid in my direction. "If all goes well, we should reach the mountains in two days."

I knew the reason for the orc's stare. For the moment, the brotherhood was wholly dependent on my understanding of the sector's geography—which admittedly was incomplete—and it was clear to see that it did not sit well with the Duskar.

"After which," Cait continued, unaware of the dark looks her new commander was throwing me, "we will kick off our sector 30,199 campaign in earnest and start probing the rifts and the creche."

I nodded. "With the eventual goal of destroying the mature tree."

"The tree must fall," Kartara agreed, echoing the sentiment. The huntmistress paused, looking uncharacteristically unsure for the first time. Finally, she stuck out an arm in Duskar's direction. "Well, then, I guess this is—"

She broke off, her gaze turning inward.

I knew what that portended—a Game alert. I'd received one too, and it was flashing urgently for attention. Letting the message unfurl in my mind, I scanned its contents.

The Adjudicator has allocated you a new task: <u>Campaign 30,199</u>. In keeping with your recent declaration and the alliance you formed with the brotherhood, you are charged with seeing sector 30,199 freed from the void's clutches.
Objective 1: Close Rift-W.
Objective 2: Close Rift-Y.
Objective 3: Close Rift-Z.
Objective 4: Defeat the mature void tree.

"Well," Kartara murmured. "Isn't that interesting?" Noticing my preoccupied expression, her gaze sharpened. "You got a task too?"

"I did," I replied, seeing no reason to hide the fact.

She glanced at the others. "You three did as well?"

"I got *two*," Cait said, sounding shocked.

My brows rose. "Two?"

She nodded mutely.

"Recite it," the huntmistress instructed.

The nether witch did just that.

Her first task turned out to be identical to the one given to me, Senzo, and Duskar. Her second task was one she shared only with Duskar and charged the pair to establish a brotherhood stronghold in sector 30,199.

"Well," Senzo remarked, rubbing his chin thoughtfully, "if we didn't already know, we now know: the Adjudicator is keenly following what we do here."

Kartara nodded. "And as we all know already, doing what the Game wants can prove highly beneficial. Let's not disappoint the Adjudicator."

The others nodded in agreement.

Extending her arm again, the huntmistress clasped hands with first Duskar, then Cait. "Good luck, you two."

"Thank you, ma'am," Duskar replied.

The huntmistress smiled. "It's just Kartara. We're equals now, remember? And if everything goes well, it will not be long before you surpass me."

Duskar shifted uncomfortably.

Sensing his discomfort, Kartara laid a reassuring hand on his shoulder. "You'll do fine." Her gaze swapped to Cait. "You both will."

Stepping back, her eyes found me. "Ready to go?"

I glanced at Senzo.

Understanding my unspoken question, he fielded the huntmistress' question instead. "We've just the final preparations to see to."

"Then go get it done," Kartara ordered. Turning away, she headed towards the dead harbinger. "In the meantime, I'll help Cait finish harvesting the netherstone."

* * *

"This here is Eccleston."

I inclined my head in acknowledgment to the player Senzo had picked out. Eccleston was posted on sentry duty on the top of a tall dune about a mile out from the main body of brotherhood soldiers, and except for the three of us, no one else was nearby.

"Eccleston is one of my best people," the spymaster continued as the player in question and I shook hands silently. "He is also a loner. And even though he served in the brotherhood for more than half a century, he had no friends within our order."

My brows rose at that. "That true?" I asked Eccleston.

"It's true," he replied in a voice that sounded rough and unused.

"Eccleston spends more time on scouting missions than he does back at home base," Senzo explains. "And given his expertise and the sensitive nature of his missions, he reports directly to me."

I grunted. "Useful that."

Senzo smiled. "It's one of the main reasons I picked him. Given Eccleston's seniority and erratic routine, no one will question your comings and goings into the brotherhood keep."

Saying nothing, I studied the player, who weathered my regard stoically.

Eccleston was taller than I was and had broader shoulders than I did, but the differences were nothing that doppelganger couldn't compensate for. But there was more to successfully impersonating someone than appearances alone. And if I was going to 'become' Eccleston, there was a lot I needed to know.

And time was in short supply.

"Tell me about yourself, please," I said. "Start with a rundown of your skills and..."

✳   ✳   ✳

You have cast doppelganger, transforming your form into that of Eccleston, a level 192 half-elf phantom assassin, and concealing your Powerful Initiate Mark. Duration: infinite.

Less than an hour later, Eccleston and I were done. Leaving the real phantom assassin behind, and dressed in both his clothes *and* skin, I made my way back to where the huntmistress awaited, surrounded by a small group of officers.

As I strode across the sands, I noted that the brotherhood army was already in motion. Forming a long, snaking line and protected by cavalry formations both at the front and the rear, the players were making steady progress northward.

Pausing on a dune top, I took a moment to scan the horizon in all directions. But no matter where I looked, I spotted no sign of any stygians. I pursed my lips thoughtfully. It seemed the mature void tree had truly decided to cut his losses and let us leave unimpeded.

Little does he know that's not what we intend.

The collared stygians had been slaughtered too, I saw. The brotherhood obviously didn't care to risk keeping the creatures captive in a sector containing a tree that was still very much of a threat. Descending the dune, I came to a stop before the huntmistress.

"Eccleston," she greeted neutrally.

My gaze flickered over those accompanying her. Duskar had already left—presumably to lead the army in its march north. Cait, Heglin, Fiona, and of course, Senzo still remained behind, though.

Staying in character, I inclined my head. "Huntmistress."

A small smile played at the corner of Kartara's mouth. "Heg and Fiona have been let in on the plan. Your deception is unnecessary."

I grimaced. "Why?" We'd agreed beforehand that, irrespective of the Pacts we'd sworn, the less everyone knew about me, the better.

She shrugged. "Bringing them in was necessary. They, too, will be serving as Duskar's seconds."

The dwarf, Heglin, I'd already known about. Fiona, though...

I shot Senzo a dark look. "You left *her* in charge of your scouts?"

The spymaster chuckled. "I know there is some bad blood between you two, but trust me, Fiona is more than capable of doing the job."

"I can speak for myself, too!" the blonde woman snapped. She spun to face Kartara. "This is a mistake."

"Your objections have been noted, Fiona," the huntmistress replied evenly. "Nonetheless, the decision has been made. You *will* comply with your orders." She paused. "Unless you wish to forsake your oath?"

The diviner ground her teeth audibly. "No. I do not." Turning around, she glared at me. "Let's get this over with then."

79

I frowned. "Get what over with?"

"Their Pact-binding," Cait supplied. "Heg and Fi will make the same oath Duskar and I did."

I sighed, but didn't demur. Seeing as how Kartara had already brought the pair into the loop, forming a Pact with them was necessary—no matter how much I disliked the notion.

"Alright," I grumbled. "Let's do it."

*　　*　　*

You have accepted Heglin and Fiona into the Forerunners faction.
You have sealed a Pact with Fiona and Heglin.
You have 13 / 20 active Pacts.

Taking Heglin and Fiona's oaths was only the work of a few minutes, and Kartara, Senzo, and I soon saw the backs of the pair as they and Cait rejoined the northbound brotherhood column.

"Here," Kartara said, tossing me something, "this is yours."

You have acquired a netherstone etched with the coordinates of Rift-X.

"Thanks," I muttered, holding the black stone loosely in my hand. "I assume Cait was successful in harvesting the other stone from the harbinger?"

Kartara nodded. "She was."

I glanced at the spot where the void tree would've landed—assuming any part of it had survived to do so. "Any other notable loot?"

Following the direction of my gaze, the huntmistress shook her head. "I had my people go over the area with a fine-tooth comb, but nothing of the tree remains."

"Ah, well," I said, disappointed. I hefted the stone in my palm. "So, where should I drop you two off?"

"Sango..." Senzo replied, and when we get there, let's try to make a good show of it."

Chapter 594: Barging About

You have entered the safe zone of sector 45,104 of the Forever Kingdom, an open sector forming part of the region known as the Coral Islands. It is currently neutral territory, unclaimed by any faction or Force.

Note, a shield generator is in place around the sector, preventing portals from opening anywhere except in the designated teleportation areas.

I stumbled theatrically out of the gateway and into the brotherhood port town of Sango. Kartara followed in my wake, and then Senzo.

The reaction from those watching was instantaneous.

"Huntmistress!" a customs official exclaimed, bounding onto the teleportation platform. "You're back!"

The portal winked out behind us.

The official's excitement faded. "Where are the others?" he asked, perplexed.

"Dead," Kartara answered, her face pale and scrubbed of emotion.

"Dead?" the official yelped, his face whitening. "Surely not—"

"They're gone, Mack," Senzo said, his own face grief-stricken. "All of them." He gestured to Kartara and me. "Only we three managed to get out."

Mack licked his lips. "B-but... but..."

Kartara clamped a hand down on his shoulder. "It's a disaster, no doubt about it, Mack. But the brotherhood will survive. We always do." Not waiting for the official's response, she spun around. "Senzo, hurry to the castle. I wanted a meeting of every surviving senior officer convened forthright!"

Stiffening, the spymaster saluted. "Yes, ma'am," he barked, before dashing off.

Kartara turned to me. "Eccl, you know what to do."

Throwing her a sloppier salute than Senzo, I reached into my pocket and withdrew the portal scroll I held ready.

"What—? Who..." the official sputtered.

Placing her arm around Mack, Kartara carefully, but firmly, drew him away, giving me space to cast my spell.

Channeling mana into the scroll, I opened a portal.

Kartara and Senzo had things well in hand. They didn't need me, and it was well past time I returned home.

∗ ∗ ∗

You have entered the safe zone of sector 12,560.

Between one step and the next, I transitioned from the teleportation platform in Sango to the Roost in sector 12,560.

And once more, I found a reception committee waiting for me.

"He's back!"

"Is he?" a second voice hissed back. "I don't recognize the face. Who's that?"

My skin tingled as the two forsworn posted in the Roost cast a series of analyzes over me—to no avail.

"It has to be him," the first voice replied. "Saf said he may look different. And who else but a forerunner is going to teleport directly into the Roost?"

"Relax, you two," I said, with amusement tracing my voice. "It *is* me." Reaching into my pocket, I tossed a small stone chip in the pair's direction. "That proves it."

Studying the faction token I'd given them, Mariam and Deryn relaxed immediately.

"Welcome back, Wolf Lord," Mariam said formally.

I waved her greeting aside. "None of that now. How are things back home?"

"Progressing rapidly," Deryn replied, his excitement shining through. "The safe zone has reappeared!"

"Excellent," I murmured. "I assume our claim has already begun?"

Mariam nodded. "It has. The sector will be ours soon." She paused. "Safyre asked us to watch for your return. Should we inform her you're back?"

I shook my head. "No, I'll do that myself. Open a portal to sector 18,240 for me, please."

Mariam inclined her head. "Of course." Closing her eyes, she began whispering.

"Err... you might want to fix your face," Deryn suggested as he returned my token. "If you enter the cave looking like that, Keros might skewer you before you have time to identify yourself."

I laughed. "A valid point. I'll do that."

✱　✱　✱

You have dispelled your doppelganger spell, returning to your original form.

You have entered sector 18,240 of the Forever Kingdom. It is currently neutral territory, unclaimed by any faction or Force. Note, a shield generator is in place around the sector.

Intrepid explorer activated. Sector 18,240 has gained a new location: <u>sector safe zone</u>. As the discoverer of the sector, the new location has automatically been added to your Log. Additionally, it will always shine bright in your mind, ensuring you are never lost.

Rift sense activated. There are no open rifts in this sector.

Game messages bombarded me on my re-entry into sector 18,240. I didn't mind, though. This time around, they had nothing but good news to share.

A grin spreading on my face, I waved to the windknight standing guard nearby and already fast approaching. "Afternoon, Keros," I greeted. "It's me. I'm back."

Ignoring my cheerful demeanor entirely, the windknight drew to a halt before me, his poleaxe at the ready. "Token," he demanded tersely.

"Come, Keros," I admonished, "We accomplished the impossible today. Surely, that deserves a smile? Or, if not that, a warmer greeting at least."

The scowl did not leave the forsworn's face.

I sighed. "Have it your way," I muttered and placed my faction chip in his waiting hand.

Keros grunted as he read the soulbound item's data. "You're clear to proceed."

"Why, thank you," I murmured, retrieving the stone chit.

Striding past the windknight, I took in the rest of the cave. It was starkly empty. Not even the wolves had returned. "Where is everyone?"

"At the lake," was the laconic response.

"Ah. The safe zone reappeared there then?" I surmised.

The windknight gave a clipped nod. "Yes. The others are busy securing it." He shifted slightly. "You did well," he added abruptly.

My eyebrows rose. As begrudging as Keros's praise was, it was heartfelt, nonetheless. *Today seems like a day for miracles.* "Thank you," I said, choosing not to comment further.

"Is the tree dead?" he asked.

"It is," I replied. "The brotherhood helped with its slaying."

A smile finally flickered across the stern knight's face. "Good." That was all he had to say on the matter, though. Swinging about, Keros returned to watching the teleportation zone.

It was the only allowed arrival point in the sector. Anyone portaling in from outside the sector—even other forerunners—would have to go through the windknight first.

And he was a much tougher 'customs official' than the ones the brotherhood employed.

The smile slipped back onto my face at the comparison. For all of Keros' dislike for me and his generally frosty demeanor, I was grateful for his vigilance and steadfast duty. He was doing his part to keep the sector safe.

Still, we'll have to change the arrival point soon, I mused.

It would be more practical—not to mention, safer—to relocate the sector's arrival point closer to the new safe zone where the bulk of our forces would be encamped from now on.

I drew a portal scroll from my backpack. For now, though, my journey was not quite done. Another short hop across the sector was required.

Drawing mana, I fed it into the item in my hand.

Portal scroll consumed.
You have opened a greater portal within sector 18,240.

✳   ✳   ✳

The nether toxicity at your current location is at tier 8.

I chose the riverside gully as my exit point—and specifically the basin Safyre had dubbed as her command post during the battle—figuring that it was the most likely place I'd find her and the others.

But the basin, like the cave, was abandoned.

"Huh," I muttered, turning about in a full circle as I studied the stark surroundings. Except for the ubiquitous mists, I was alone. The forerunner army was close by, though, I knew that much. I could hear them, not to mention feel their mindglows.

Not unexpectedly, most of those I sensed were massed around the region my explorer trait told me was the safe zone. That was at least a few hundred yards northwest of my current position. Given that we had flooded the void tree's former valley, that would put the safe nest in...

...the newly created lake.

I frowned. Had the Adjudicator really manifested the safe zone there? And if he had, how in hells were we supposed to fortify a body of water that occupied an area larger than one square mile?

Damn. That could spell trouble.

Worried now that securing the safe zone might be trickier than I'd anticipated, I dashed forward. The basin's sidewalls were steep and high, but they were no match for my speed and agility, and I bounded up without trouble.

A strange sight greeted me when I topped the basin.

The safe zone *was* in the lake.

In the exact center, to be precise.

It sat right atop the hill the void tree had so recently occupied. The hill had expanded, too, I noticed—or the water had receded—and now it was a small island about a hundred yards in diameter.

The island was not the strange part, though.

The flat, elongated barges surrounding it were.

There were dozens of the large contraptions drifting across the lake. Each bobbed up and down, and while water lapped at their sides, they appeared in no danger of sinking.

The barges can't be as flat as they appear, I thought. Leaning forward unconsciously, I scrutinized the contraptions anew.

And indeed, as I looked closer, I noticed the barges' hulls curved upward, but the curvature was so slight as to be nearly imperceptible. I spotted other things, too.

The start of a spidery crack on the underside of one barge. The distinctive red-hued tone of another. And the solidness of a third. The short glimpse I caught of that barge's edge suggested that its hull was at least six feet thick.

I blinked in sudden realization. The barges were actually solid chunks cut off from the overlord's shell!

Sliced off, rather, I amended.

Because as thick as the hull I'd noted was, I knew the overlord's shell was thicker. Still, somehow, my allies had managed to harvest the remains of the two overlords we'd slain during the battle.

My gaze darted across the lake to where the two stygian Powers had been anchored. And sure enough, their bodies were nowhere to be seen. Unlike the previous overlords we'd destroyed, the pair had not been airborne when we'd killed them, which meant Safyre and the others had managed to recover their shells intact.

And no doubt, foreseeing the same difficulties I had with securing a water-locked safe zone, they had come up with an ingenious solution.

Barges made from the overlords' shells.

Each was at least thirty yards long and six yards wide, and even as I watched, ropes were being strung between them. Tugging on the ropes, the soldiers aboard the barges drew them closer until they locked in place end to end.

Thus creating a floating wall atop the water.

Or rather, three walls. There were that many barges.

"By goddamn," I murmured, impressed. "They've built a floating fort."

Now, I understood why I'd received no Game message informing me of the forerunners' impending claim on the sector—it hadn't started yet.

Creating the fort was the reason for the delay. Until the three concentric barge circles around the island were complete and the more than one thousand soldiers aboard fully surrounded the island, the safe zone would still not be secured—technically anyway.

But by the looks of it, the work of building the fort was nearly done.

My eyes drifting further afield, I studied the thin translucent shield surrounding both the island and the inner half of the lake. All the barges lay inside the barrier, and given the absence of mist inside the dome-shaped magical construct, it was a safe bet to assume its purpose was to keep the mists out. Which I imagined was easier to do now that there wasn't a void tree and two overlords hanging around and polluting the area.

Next, my gaze skipped to the lake's shoreline. About half a mile of rocky open ground lay between me and the water's edge.

And nearly all of it was littered with stygian corpses.

The forerunners' nagians complement were working the area, piling and stacking the bodies—presumably for our players to loot later.

Speaking of which ...

Turning my head to the right, I spotted the 'command' barge. Safyre and the rest of the faction's players were aboard. They hadn't noticed me yet; none of the forerunners had.

Enough stalling, I thought with a small smile. *Time to go say hello.* Drawing psi, I shadow jumped.

Chapter 595: Claimants

You have teleported behind Safyre.

I stepped out of the aether and into Safyre's shadow, and for a split second went unnoticed.

"...must coordinate with Sedgwick," she was saying. "It's imperative that we—"

"He's back," Nyra blurted, the first to spot me. Unlike Safyre, she was facing me fully. The rest of the forerunners' command group—Adriel, Farren, Ceruvax, Shael, Anriq, Lucius, the twins, Regus, and Duggar—were also on the barge, along with some fifty other forerunners.

Breaking off, Safyre spun around, her eyes widening as she caught sight of my grinning face.

Before I could say anything, she threw herself forward and wrapped me in a hug. "Michael," she whispered into my chest. "I thought..."

I closed my arms around her. "It's done," I murmured soothingly, understanding her unspoken fears. "And I survived. As did most of the brotherhood."

Giving me one last squeeze, Safyre stepped back. She was as aware of our watching audience as I was. We'd talk again later—in private. For now, there was forerunner business to attend to.

"The void tree?" she asked.

"Dead," I confirmed.

That drew heartfelt sighs from everyone. "Then it is done," Teresa breathed.

"Mostly," I agreed.

Ceruvax's eyes narrowed. "Mostly?" he repeated, latching onto my qualification.

I waved aside his question. "There is a lot I must tell you all, but none of it is urgent. We can discuss the void tree and sector 30,199 later." I turned my head left and right, taking in the circle of barges and the island they ringed. "For now, let's concentrate on this sector. How are things going?"

"Slower than we hoped," Adriel replied. Stepping forward, she brushed her lips against the side of my face. "You did well, Wolf."

Surprised by her unexpectedly warm greeting, I shrugged uncomfortably. "I couldn't have done it without any of you."

The lich smiled. "I'm not so sure about that." Before I could respond, her tone turned more business-like. "But as for why things have been moving so slowly..." She gestured at the lake. "The water is the main reason for that."

I nodded. "You had to build the barges and maneuver them into position. I get that. But they all look to be in place now?"

"They are," Farren replied. "As always, you have impeccable timing." The corners of his mouth turned up. "If I didn't know better, I'd think you deliberately dodged the grunt work."

I chuckled. "The timing of my arrival is a coincidence, no more, I assure you." My amusement faded. "But tell me: how did the battle end? I didn't see any forerunner... bodies on the shore. How many did we lose?"

Somber faces and dark eyes greeted my question. *It's bad then*, I thought.

"Two hundred and ninety-seven," Safyre said softly.

I blanched. That was nearly ten percent of our total force. I'd known we would lose people, but I'd been hoping our losses would be more akin to the brotherhood's. "Why so many?" I whispered, my voice sounding half-strangled to my own ears.

Safyre squeezed my hand. "Six separate packs of hydras broke through the western cordon while we were busy dealing with the harbingers."

"It was my fault," Terence said, his eyes downcast.

"No, it was not," Ceruvax retorted sharply.

"I should have stopped them," the young knight persisted.

"And I've told you a dozen times already, boy, you could not have," the envoy replied, looking vexed. "None of us could." His eyes lifted to mine. "It was a pre-planned maneuver."

"The timing was suspicious," Lucius agreed. "The tree must have been preparing the offensive in secret, and the harbingers' arrival provided the perfect opening." He shrugged. "But as devastating as the lesser hydras' counterassault was, ultimately, it failed. Terence and the dwarves stopped them before they could shatter our lines."

Still looking unhappy, Terence opened his mouth to protest, but Teresa kicked him in the shins, silencing him.

I shook my head slowly, still unable to verbalize my own feelings on the matter. Three hundred and ninety-seven dead. It was a veritable butcher's bill.

So many.

The others had said the hydras had broken through while we were preoccupied with ambushing the harbingers. But how many had died after that? How many could I have saved if I'd not pursued the tree into sector 30,199?

"Michael?" Nyra prompted.

Raising my eyes, I found and held Shael's gaze. "Who did we lose?" As the forerunners' bard, it would've fallen to him to record the names of the dead.

He shifted uncomfortably under my stare. "Uhm... The Bane Wolves suffered the most grievous losses. A few wolfmen perished as well, and some wolves too..."

My gaze drifted in Duggar's direction.

"The Pack survives," the dire wolf alpha replied serenely. *"The fallen will be missed."* His eyes drove into mine, as if willing me to believe. *"But the Pack survives. And that is what counts the most."*

Neither disputing nor agreeing with Duggar's sentiment, I turned back to Shael. "Tell me the names of the dead."

"Huh..."

Safyre touched my arm gently. "Shael has everything written down and recorded," she assured me. "We can go over it all later and mourn them properly. But right now, we need to focus on—"

"No," I interjected. "I want to know now. Tell me."

Safyre flinched.

I was being unnecessarily harsh, I knew. And it was not even Safyre and the others I was angry with. Only myself. It was I who had insisted we claim the sector in nine days. It was I who had left to chase down the tree.

And in the end, it had cost two hundred and ninety-seven lives.

There was no running away from that fact. Two hundred and ninety-seven people whom I'd sworn to protect were dead, and it was all my fault.

Adriel stepped forward. "Go," she said gently to Safyre. "I will handle him."

"But—" Safyre protested.

"Go," the lich insisted. "You have important things to do. All of you do," she added, raising her voice. She turned back to Safyre, a wry twist to her lips. "And believe it or not, I've seen my fair share of death. This is something I know how to deal with."

Safyre hesitated a moment longer, then, with a decisive nod, stepped away.

"I'm sorry, Saf," I said, speaking to her privately through my telepathy. *"I shouldn't have snapped at you. It's just..."*

Midmotion, she paused and looked back over her shoulder, a sad smile on her face. *"I understand. It hit me hard, too. Speak to Adriel. We'll talk later."*

✳   ✳   ✳

Adriel wasted no time in sitting me down in what she termed the bow of the barge, which was empty but for the two of us. The barge's complement of soldiers congregated at the far end—the stern—and the forerunners' command group had dispersed to the other barges, no doubt to enact whatever final preparations remained.

"You know the dead are not your fault, right?" the lich asked once we were alone.

I sighed. "They were my responsibility."

She nodded. "They were, but not entirely."

I glanced up at her. "Meaning?"

She shrugged. "They had free will, the same as you do. They *chose* to follow you. They *chose* to fight here today."

My lips twisted. "So, what? You're saying they chose to die? That their fate is their fault?"

She didn't back down from my stare. "Yes, that's exactly what I'm saying. Mostly, anyway." She paused. "This is the first time you've commanded a battle, isn't it?"

I shook my head. "I've led others before."

"But this is the first time you have had so many die under your command, isn't it?" she persisted.

I sighed again. "Yes," I admitted.

Adriel nodded. "What you are feeling is normal."

"Normal?" I asked, a sour cast to my face.

"Normal," she repeated firmly. "As a scion, it is your duty to lead your people responsibly—to not spend their lives frivolously. It is *not* your duty to save everyone. Sadly, that is impossible to do."

I bowed my head. "Rationally, I understand what you're saying. I agree with it too. Hells, before the battle, I even warned myself something like this might happen." I exhaled. "I thought I was prepared."

"But the reality is different, isn't it?"

I laughed hollowly. "It sure is."

Adriel sat down beside me. "Have you spoken to Ghost? Sometimes the best remedy is simply sharing the burden."

I nodded, knowing she was right. "Ghost is asleep, creating her astral simulacrum."

"Ah," the lich exclaimed, and although she looked intrigued by my words, she didn't pursue the matter. "Well, when she awakes, I suggest you have a long discussion with her on the subject."

"I will. And with Safyre, too."

The lich smiled. "You should do that."

I patted her hand. "Thank you, Adriel."

"You're welcome, Wolf." She rose to her feet. "Now, if you're done moping, there's work to be done."

✳   ✳   ✳

It took another hour to finish our preparations, and I spent that time traveling from barge to barge, reacquainting myself with everyone. Despite our losses, the mood amongst the army was upbeat, jubilant even.

They had done the impossible and survived.

And they were justifiably ecstatic about the fact. In the face of such happiness, my own dourness evaporated. It would have been churlish to try to hold onto it, really. And Safyre, Adriel, and the others had the right of it.

While the dead should be mourned, the living came first—always.

Thus, when the moment we had all been waiting for arrived, I greeted it with as much excitement as the others.

A faction has staked a claim to sector 18,240!

The Forerunners have established a cordon of more than 1,000 soldiers around the sector's safe zone. If the cordon remains unbroken for another 24 hours, ownership of sector 18,240 will transfer to the Forerunners.

"We've done it!" Anriq exclaimed fiercely.

The command group had gathered anew on a single barge, and this time around, the various captains had also joined in.

"Not quite," Regus cautioned. But despite his words, the wolfman was grinning broadly. "We still have twenty-four hours to go."

"Bah, it's a done deal," Sedgwick retorted. "There's nothing that can stop our claim now."

I said nothing, but privately I agreed with the dwarven merchant's assessment.

"What now?" Nyra asked, voicing the question on everyone's minds, and perhaps unsurprisingly, it was not to me they turned to for answers, but Safyre.

The aetherist, standing shoulder to shoulder with me, glanced in my direction, fielding the question to me.

I shook my head minutely. *"You should answer,"* I told her privately.

She arched one eyebrow in silent query.

"You are as much their leader as I am, and you earned their trust during the battle. Let's not return to the previous status quo. Lead them." I inhaled. *"And besides, this sector will be yours. When it comes to matters relating to it, you are the ultimate authority."*

Safyre did not refuse the responsibility I thrust upon her. "We wait," she said aloud. Her gaze found mine again. "And while we do, perhaps we should hear Michael's tale."

Chapter 596: The Road to Ascension

I shook my head. "We'll get to my tale in a bit. But if you don't mind, I have some questions first."

Safyre smiled. "Of course you do," she murmured. "Go ahead. Ask."

I ducked my head in acknowledgment, then dove right into it. "Who slew Gray and Black?"

Safyre's brows furrowed.

"The other two harbingers," I amended.

"Ah," she replied, her expression clearing. "Is that what you've been calling them? Well, I did. The others let me land the final blow." She shrugged helplessly. "They insisted."

"And it is a good thing we did, too," Adriel chipped in. "Saf's a Powerful Acolyte now."

I nodded. I'd known that, of course. I'd recognized the change in Safyre's spirit signatures the moment I'd laid eyes upon her. What confused me, though, was that nothing about her Class appeared to have changed. To be sure, I called up her analyze data again.

The target is Safyre, a level 225 human aetherist and Bastion of Light. She bears a Mark of Supreme Light, a Mark of a Powerful Acolyte, and is Lightsworn.

Safyre had grown in level since the battle, but little else about her player data had changed. I scratched my head. "Are you a minor Power now? Because if you are, I can't tell from your—"

I broke off. Safyre was shaking her head.

"I'm not," she said.

I frowned. "Why not?"

It was not Safyre who answered, though, but Ceruvax. "Her Light Mark has not advanced enough."

I turned to the former envoy. "What does that mean?"

"Your... companion is on the second ascendancy path," he replied as if that were explanation enough.

It was not, though.

While Ceruvax, Adriel, and I had extensively spoken about the second route to Primehood in the past, the discussions had always centered around House Wolf. I'd not questioned the pair about how a Forcesworn would ascend and had assumed—erroneously, it turned out—that they would only be required to deepen the Power Mark to do so.

"Anyone care to expand on that?" I asked somewhat testily.

Farren chuckled. "The Old Wolf seems to have forgotten not everyone is as steeped in Game lore as he is. But to answer you, a Forcesworn's advancement through the second ascension path is similar to a scion's. To reach legendary rank—and become a minor Power—Safyre will have to increase her affinity for Light."

"Meaning, I will need to deepen my Light Mark to that of Light's Friend," Safyre added.

I glanced at her. "They've explained all this to you?"

She nodded. "They have."

"I see. Well, I won't belabor the point further then. We can talk more about it later. Back to the harbingers. Have we harvested their remains?"

Farren held out his arm, revealing the three shiny black stones sitting in the palm of his hand. "We have."

"Excellent." I rubbed my chin. "Well, that takes care of the harbingers. What about the overlords? Did everything go according to plan with them?"

The idea, when it came to the overlords, was for Adriel to do the killings. Farren would never be a player again, Ceruvax couldn't acquire a Power Mark, that had been established centuries ago, and Keros, the last member of the overlord strike team, was Safyre's follower and wasn't able to either.

That left only Adriel to consider.

While the lich was technically still a non-player like Farren, it was an open question what would happen when she reacquired her body and became a player anew. Her overall level had changed in the interim, which was indication enough that the Adjudicator was still tracking her progression.

And if her level was changing, why not her spirit signatures? Would her Marks—when she reacquired them—reflect her accomplishments while a non-player?

I thought so. As did Farren and Ceruvax.

Still, it was a bit of a gamble. But one, I and the others had adjudged worth taking.

"It did," Farren answered, satisfaction writ clear across his face. "Adriel slew both."

His sister rolled her eyes. "I'm not sure if it'll make any difference in the end."

"We'll find out soon enough," I promised. Or as soon as I could resolve the other pressing issues still left undone. And I had too many of those. But those were problems for another day, and I shoved them firmly aside to focus on the now. "What about the nagas?" I asked. "Where are they?"

"You mean my undead pets?" Farren asked.

I nodded. "And Ceruvax's enslaved one, too."

"They're in the hills," Safyre replied. "That's where we are storing all the stygians for now—dead, undead, and living."

"Got it." That answered all my questions regarding our defeated foes. There was only one more matter to consider. My gaze drifted in the direction of the new safe zone. "Anyone been there yet?"

"Nyra and I have," Anriq replied. "We explored the island from end to end. There's not much of it to speak of, and what little there is is just muddy soil." He paused. "Well, except for the rebirth well. There's that."

"I'll take mud over water any day," Shael quipped. "At least the damn thing is on solid ground."

I smiled in silent agreement with the bard. "We'll have ample opportunity to build it up," I assured Anriq. "As for the rebirth well... let's hope we don't have occasion to use it anytime soon."

"We shouldn't," Safyre said firmly. "There are no live stygians for miles."

Adriel nodded decisively. "And annoying as this mist is, our people are in little danger from it as long as we keep the barrier around the island up."

"Hmm, speaking of the mist... when will it dissipate?" I asked.

The others exchanged looks.

"What?" I asked, noticing.

"We were discussing the very topic before your arrival," Safyre explained. "It's been several hours since the void tree fled, but other than for the overlords' concentrated plumes dispersing, none of us have been able to detect any lessening in the nether toxicity."

I frowned. "You haven't?" Not waiting for her answer, I queried the Game directly.

The nether toxicity at your current location is at tier 8.

My lips twisted. "Urgh. You're right. It's not reducing."

"We can't conclude that," Ceruvax objected. "Not yet, anyhow. The mists *could* be dissipating, but the changes may be occurring too slowly for any of us to perceive. Give it time."

"I agree," Adriel added. "We'll have to wait a full day at least before we can know for certain if the mists will persist."

I nodded reluctantly, seeing the sense in their advice. "Well, in that case, I guess I'm all caught up with how things stand in the sector." I threw the group a questioning look. "Unless there is something I've forgotten to touch on?"

Safyre shook her head. "No, I think you've about covered everything."

I inhaled. "Good. Then, it's probably time I told you about how things panned out in sector 30,199."

Teresa leaned forward. "Do tell."

"You've kept us waiting long enough," Terence agreed. "I want to know how you slew that bloody tree!"

I chuckled at their eagerness. "I'll get there," I promised. "But let me start at the beginning. When I left this sector, I was perched in the void tree's branches. And when we exited the rift, the first thing I saw was..."

✳ ✳ ✳

23 hours remain until the ownership of sector 18,240 transfers to the Forerunners.

Over the course of the next hour, as the barges bobbed gently in the water all around us, I spun my tale of the void tree's final moments, my negotiations with the brotherhood, and the terms of the alliance we'd forged. And when I finally concluded, it was to find my audience had been left speechless.

"So…" Ceruvax ruminated, the first to break the silence, "the trees can talk."

I glanced across at the old wolf envoy. We were sitting in a tight-knit circle in the bow of the command barge. "You did not know?"

"No," he replied, looking troubled by the notion. "I did not."

I turned to Adriel. Noticing my questioning gaze, she shook her head. "It's news to me, too."

"And me," Farren confirmed. "But that does not mean the Primes didn't know," he added, sensing that was the thrust of my question.

"We should seek Draven's counsel on the matter," Lucius suggested.

I nodded noncommittally. There would be enough time later to speak of what came next, but for now, I wanted to make sure everyone comprehended what I'd told them. "Does everyone understand the implications?"

"Yes," Algar said, speaking up for the first time. "We'll have to assume the nether is a skilled adversary. For every move we make against the void fathers, we must presume they will counter."

I inclined my head in the high captain's direction. "You're right. We should expect retaliation—and not just in sector 30,199, but here too."

"Here?" Anriq asked, startled.

"Here," I confirmed.

"But how would the void even get in again?" Terence protested. "The sector is shielded!"

"Have you forgotten about the harbingers' attack on the Aether Cloak?" Safyre asked. "A sector shield is no guarantee of safety if the enemy has its aether coordinates. And if the harbingers knew where the sector was, we have to assume the mature tree who sent them does too."

Terence subsided. "I suppose so," he conceded.

"It's not only the shield we have to worry about, though," I said.

Safyre's gaze slid my way. "What do you mean?"

"I've been thinking about what the mature tree said about the nagas," I replied, not answering directly.

Adriel pursed her lips. "That they are a 'valuable resource' we 'should never have been allowed to possess'?"

"Yes, that."

Nyra shook her head in confusion. "I'm sorry, Michael, but I'm not following. What do the nagas have to do with what we were discussing?"

My apprentice was not the only one who appeared lost. Many of the others looked similarly bewildered.

"It's those portal infestations Adriel told me about," Farren guessed shrewdly. "That's what you're worried about, isn't it?"

I nodded mutely.

Shael's eyes widened. "You think the nagas may be able to subvert the nether portal from the guardian tower like they did the last time and enter this sector anew!"

"They could do that," I agreed, "or they could try using the one from Draven's Reach, too."

"Is that possible?" Anriq asked, aghast.

"I don't know," I replied. "We know from what they did to the guardian tower portal before that the nagas can suborn a ley line and use it for their own means. But do they need to be in physical contact with a nether portal to do so? Could they do it from afar?" I shook my head. "We just don't know. And that's a large part of the problem."

Ceruvax rubbed his chin. "Is that why you asked about the blood-bound naga earlier?"

"Yes," I replied. "We're fortunate to still have a live one captive. It's crucial we learn from it. We need to understand how its infestation ability works and what its limitations are."

The old wolf nodded grimly. "I will find out," he vowed.

"The implications are troubling," Farren mused. "And not just for this sector."

"They are," I agreed, my face just as bleak as Ceruvax's. "By the void trees' own admission, the nagas are new. But despite this, based on the little I overheard from the trees, they've already grasped the strategic significance of the nagas. Imagine what it would mean if the stygians didn't need to use rifts anymore to invade a sector? What if they could enter a sector using a dungeon portal? What chaos would reign then?"

My words sent shivers coursing through the others.

"It would spell disaster for the Kingdom," Safyre said softly.

"It would," I agreed. "But the nagas *are* new, and that means we are a long way from that point yet. Still, we should not ignore the danger they pose to this sector."

Safyre nodded. "I'll have sentries positioned around the Draven and Guardian portals."

Ceruvax shook his head. "That's not going far enough. We should establish a permanent outpost at both locations."

I rubbed the side of my face, considering the notion. "That's not a bad idea, especially seeing as how our people will be regularly travelling to the guardian tower from now on. An outpost at the portal would help facilitate their movements."

Safyre nodded in agreement. "I'll see to it."

"Thank you, Saf," I murmured. "Now, moving on, let's discuss sector 30,199 and the brotherhood. Is everyone comfortable with the terms of the deal I struck with the huntmistress? The brotherhood will need us to supply them with—"

"I'm not," Sedgwick interjected.

I stared at him in surprise. "Why not?"

"Your agreement hinges on the brotherhood's new Nethersphere chapter in sector 30,199," the dwarven merchant replied. "I'm not sure it's wise for them to remain in the sector or for us to help them expand their presence there. We have enough enemies already. Are you sure you want us also poking around a mature tree's backyard?"

"Why shouldn't we?" Teresa demanded, scowling.

"Because from everything the Wolf has just said," the dwarven merchant replied, his gaze still on me, "the void trees are *not* the minor irritant I always thought them to be. They seem to be as powerful a threat as the Game's Powers." He spread his arms to include everyone in the gesture. "And we all are already criminals in the eyes of those Powers. Do we truly want to become embroiled in a full-scale war with another powerful enemy, one whose true strength we still do not fully comprehend? Are we not biting off more than we can chew?"

"It is not a question of choice, Sedge," Safyre said before I could respond. "I, too, spared the void little thought before meeting Michael and the others. But since learning of what's happened to the Endless Dungeon, of the sectors that have fallen, and of the new Powers' inaction, I'm convinced the void is the greatest menace facing the Kingdom right now. We cannot ignore it."

The merchant sighed. "But do you understand the peril that puts us in?"

She nodded gravely. "I do." She scanned the faces of the others. "And I think everyone else does too."

"We do," Algar replied, speaking up for the New Haveners. "My people have lived for years in the void's shadow. It is relentless, let me tell you. If it is not opposed, it will consume everything."

"The Pack will not shy from the fight either," Duggar added.

"Opposing the void is our ancient duty," Ceruvax affirmed. "We cannot but do otherwise."

"We are built for it," Lucius said quietly.

And the nagians truly were.

"It gives us purpose," Anriq agreed.

"I see," Sedgwick said, seeming somewhat taken aback by the strength of his companions' resolve. "Everyone has already decided then: we'll do this thing. I only hope we don't come to regret our decision in the future."

"We might at that," I told the dwarf ruefully. "But we shouldn't let fear dictate our course."

"Who knew wolves were so wise?" he muttered.

I opened my mouth to respond, but before I could do so, Sedgwick waved aside his own words. "Don't mind me. It's sage advice, and I'm just a grumpy old dwarf. Go on. I will not object further."

I glanced at Safyre, who shrugged imperceptibly. *"He'll be fine,"* she assured me privately.

Letting the matter lie, I took a moment to re-gather my thoughts. The conversation had moved further along than I anticipated. I had not intended to broach the subject of our next steps, but now that the discussion had started, there was no avoiding it. "As I see it, moving forward, the forerunners have three key objectives."

"Only three?" Adriel asked, one eyebrow lifting disbelievingly.

"Only three," I replied firmly, and began ticking off points on the fingers of my left hand. "One: securing our home, sector 18,240. Two: expanding into sector 30,199. And three: gaining new strength."

Farren stroked his chin. "The first two I understand well enough, but what do you mean by the last?"

"Now that sector 18,240 is almost claimed, it's time to grow our numbers," I said. "And that means finding new recruits and acquiring more allies."

Anriq leaned forward. "Like Nexus' werewolf pack?" he asked eagerly.

"They're one group I intend on approaching," I agreed.

"What about the lost Prime?" Ceruvax asked.

"She is another I must meet," I replied. My gaze slid to Adriel. "Then there is Death to restore. There are also the under-dwellers to consider, the thieves guild, the bounty hunters, and so on."

"And the bloodlines?" Ceruvax asked. "How do you intend to go about restoring them?"

I grimaced. "Except for the lost Prime, I doubt any of the bloodlines still exist. I suspect we will have to start afresh."

The old wolf's eyes narrowed. "Start afresh, how?"

"The same way I did. The same way Nyra did. By finding new players and convincing them to awaken their blood instead of swearing themselves to the Forces."

"That could be challenging," Safyre murmured. "New players are a precious commodity in the Game, and the new Powers do not like sharing."

I nodded. "I am aware of that, but I have a plan—of sorts."

Terence rolled his eyes. "When do you not?" He pressed his hands together. "But you haven't mentioned Saya. When do we go after her?"

"*We* do not," I said quietly. I do."

Safyre stiffened, but I spoke on before she could protest. "Saya is not the forerunners' responsibility. Of everyone seated around this circle, only a handful of you have even met her. I will see to Saya's rescue on my own."

"No," Safyre objected.

"Yes," I stated flatly.

"You cannot," she reiterated.

I turned to face her. "We discussed this previously, remember? And we agreed it was best that I returned to the valley alone."

"That was before all this! When it was just the six of us. Now, we have so many more to help. We could send an entire army into—"

I shook my head. "No. Have you forgotten whose envoy is in sector 12,560? In whose clutches Saya rests? I will not expose the forerunners to Loken. Saya's rescue is best done quietly and by me alone."

Safyre threw up her hands. "It's a trap, and you know it, and you're going to walk into it blindly!"

I opened my mouth, a retort on the tip of my tongue, then stopped myself. The conversation was quickly devolving, and this was not a fight I wanted to have with Safyre, not here, not ever.

Inhaling deeply, I calmed myself before continuing. "What awaits in sector 12,560 is almost certainly a trap," I said softly. "But I will not be venturing into it blindly."

"Like that will make any difference," Safyre said. But despite her words, her tone was conciliatory. She, too, was trying to keep matters from escalating further than they already had.

"You're both right," Adriel said, entering the conversation. "To a point, anyhow."

Safyre and I turned to face the lich. While the rest of our companions were doing their best to look anywhere and at anything but me and Safyre, Adriel was not bothering with such pretenses.

"Michael, you're right," she continued, seeing that she had our attention. "Penetrating Loken's envoy's camp in the wyvern caves is a task best left to you, but Safyre is right, too. You cannot enter sector 12,560 alone. You should take a team with you."

"A team?" I shook my head. "I can't—"

"Let me finish," the lich interrupted. "There is no risk in assembling and stationing a team in the Roost. We already have people there, what's a few more? If you run into trouble, you can call on the team to help—or not. The choice will be yours. And just as importantly, you can check in regularly with them over a farspeaker link." Her gaze swapped to Safyre. "And if he misses a check-in, you can pull him out from whatever mess he has landed in with that new governor ability of yours—call to arms."

"That..." I rubbed my chin. "That actually makes sense."

Safyre nodded. "It does."

"Of course it does," Adriel said primly, "and if you two were thinking straight, you would have thought of it yourselves."

I ducked my head sheepishly. The lich was right, of course. Emotions had been clouding both my own judgment and Safyre's.

"I guess we don't have everything quite worked out just yet," Safyre said privately to me.

I chuckled in her mind. *"I guess we don't."* I dipped my head in Adriel's direction anew. "Thank you."

She smiled. "Only a pleasure."

Farren leaned forward. "Right, now that all that unpleasantness is out of the way, I take it you intend to leave immediately to rescue your friend?"

"As soon as the sector is claimed," I confirmed.

"I thought so," the archlich said. "In that case, we should decide now who will make up the team. Obviously, I cannot be on it. Nor Adriel. That tavern of yours is in a safe zone."

I nodded. "True. But there is more we must also decide."

Farren raised one eyebrow. "Such as?"

"The leader of any expedition force we send into sector 30,199 for one," I replied. "Who will act as our brotherhood liaison for another. Safyre will obviously be in charge of this sector, but she will need a support team as well, in case it's attacked. Then there is the matter of the guardian tower—we'll have to send a dungeon party there soon—and someone to command the outposts Ceruvax recommended."

Farren pressed his hands together. "We have a lot to decide, I see. Let's get to it, shall we?"

✳ ✳ ✳

You have created 6 new faction officer positions and 7 specialized faction groups.

<u>Forerunner Officers</u>

Faction Custodian: Adriel.
Nether Expeditionary Force Leader: archlich, Farren.
Brotherhood Liaison: dwarven merchant, Sedgwick.
Reach Outpost Commander: nagian psi knight, Zekiel.
Guardian Outpost Commander: nagian werefox, Elise.
Home Guard Captain: nagian mage hunter, Lucius.
Vault Guard Captain: windknight, Keros.

<u>Forerunner Groups (assigned members)</u>

Nether Force: Anriq, Regus, and the wolfmen.
Reach Outpost: 25 nagians, 1 company of Bane Wolves, 1 forsworn elite.
Guardian Outpost: 25 nagians, dire and arctic wolves, 1 forsworn elite.
Home Guard: 25 nagians, Adriel, 3 companies of Bane Wolves.
Vault Guard: 25 nagians, 5 forsworn rank 4 players.
Tower Dungeon Party: Nyra, Terence, and Teresa.
Support Team One: Shael, Ceruvax, and the forsworn elites: Mariam, Deryn, and Llewyn.

20 hours remain until the ownership of sector 18,240 transfers to the Forerunners.

It took another few hours to subdivide the forerunners and allocate everyone a suitable role. Not unexpectedly, the discussions proved contentious, and there were more than a few heated debates. But in the end, cooler heads prevailed, and matters were decided amicably enough.

Of necessity, the largest and most powerful elements of the forerunners—the bane wolves and nagians respectively—would remain in sector 18,240. Whatever happened going forward, we could not risk losing our home sector. In keeping with that strategy, both Adriel and Safyre would remain in the sector as well.

The composition of the nether expeditionary force had been a subject of intense debate. Some, like Sedgwick, thought we shouldn't send any forerunners into sector 30,199. Others, like Teresa and Anriq, argued for a much stronger force to be dispatched. Then, there were those like Safyre who believed sending the wolfmen and Farren would be too revealing.

She was correct on that point.

But the simple truth was that whether it was forsworn, nagians, or wolves we sent to the brotherhood's aid, something of the nature of the forerunners would be revealed. And in the long run, there would be no stopping the brotherhood from realizing who and what the forerunners truly were.

But seeing as the brotherhood's new nether chapter would forevermore be isolated in the Nethersphere, their learning the truth mattered little. And in the end, we decided to send the force best equipped to deal with the void, while at the same time ensuring we did not compromise the safety of our home sector.

And that force was the Pack of the Reach.

As former possessed, none of the wolfmen had the normal vulnerability a non-player had to the void's touch. Then, too, a wolfman had many of the same impressive regeneration traits a werewolf did. Even unshielded, one would be able to survive longer in the nether mists than most players. And with Farren leading them, they could prove to be a truly potent force.

But it was not the nether force assignments that were the most contentious; it was those to the dungeon party and my support team.

No one wanted to be the first, and everyone wanted to be in the second. Terence, Teresa, and even Nyra ferociously pleaded their case, but I steadfastly refused them.

For one, they were too low-levelled to face Loken's envoy, and for another, as our only other scions—or potential scions in the twins' case—they were too precious for the forerunners to risk losing.

In the end, I chose Ceruvax and Shael, backed up by three forsworn elites. Shael was already familiar with the wolves' valley, and even if he did leave the Roost, his presence should go largely unremarked.

The same could not be said for Ceruvax, of course.

If any of Loken's people spotted the former envoy, it would spell disaster. The trickster would immediately work out the implications and realize I'd awakened my blood. And then, I would be truly hunted.

But then again, if circumstances were so dire, I was forced to call on the support team for help, the worst had likely *already* befallen. And truly, when it came to combating Shadow's wiles, no one was more fit to do so than Ceruvax. I could count on him to rescue me should the situation warrant it.

The disposition of our forces complete, I stood up. "Right, now that that is all worked out, I will leave the finer details in your capable hands."

Teresa looked up. "Where are you going?"

I jerked my chin in the direction of the island. "There. I want to check out the safe zone. And after that, I need to meditate."

Terence frowned. "Meditate? Why would—" He broke off. "Oh, you're going to create your astral simulacrum."

"I am," I confirmed. "I suspect it will prove useful where I'm going. And since we have time to spare—" there was still more than twenty hours to go before our claim on the sector went through— "there is no better time than now to cast the spell," I finished with a glance in Safyre's direction.

Correctly interpreting my look, she rose smoothly to her feet and linked her arm with mine. "I'll join you for a bit if you don't mind."

I smiled. "Of course, I don't," I murmured and, arm in arm with her, strode off.

CHAPTER 598: SPLIT PERSONALITIES

Two hours later, after a quick jaunt around the new island—it was exactly as Anriq had described—and a more lengthy and intimate discussion with Safyre, we parted ways. She returned to the barges while I made my way to the hills bordering the eastern shore of the lake. Finding a comfortable crest on which to rest, I sank down into a cross-legged stance.

That's where Elise found me.

"There you are," the werefox said as she trotted up to me. *"I heard you were back."*

"Elise," I greeted the nagian druid. *"What are you doing out here alone?"*

"I could ask the same thing of you." Sitting down on her haunches, the werefox scratched at her right ear with a hind leg. *"But I'm not alone. There's a whole bunch of druids back there."*

I glanced where she pointed, but the others—nagians, too, I supposed—were beyond sight range. *"Oh? And why aren't all of you on the barges?"*

Elise shrugged. *"Safyre asked us to get started."*

"Get started at—" I broke off, realizing there was only one thing she could mean. *"With restoring the land? Already?"*

"What can I say, your fellow Power is a hard taskmaster." She laughed, robbing her words of their sting. *"But truly, we're all glad to do it. The lifelessness of the land is depressing."*

I nodded. *"And how is it going?"* Spreading my arms, I gestured to the pervasive mist still shrouding the sector. *"Is this not making your job tougher?"*

"The mists are problematic," she admitted. *"It's actually why I came to find you—well, not you, Ghost."*

"Ah. You want her to help you with her nether manipulation skill?"

"I do. But it's more than that. I miss her, too." She paused expectantly. *"So, where is she?"*

I pointed to my chest. *"Sleeping in her spirit vessel, I'm afraid. Ghost is also why I'm out here as well."*

"Oh?"

"Ghost is casting a spell—a long one," I said, not explaining further. *"I need to cast the same spell. Hers will finish before mine, though, so I chose to do it out here rather than in the safe zone."*

"Because the safe zone won't let her awaken when she is done," Elise said, understanding immediately. *"When will Ghost's spell be finished?"*

"In about sixteen hours, I'd say."

The werefox rose to her feet. *"Perfect. I'll be back then."* About to dash away, she paused. *"I heard you made me a commander of an outpost. Why's that?"*

I raised one brow. *"You don't want the job?"*

"I didn't say that, but I'd like to understand why you gave it to me."

I shrugged. *"You seem to have an affinity for the wolves. The guardian tower and the portal outpost are where they'll be spending most of their time from here on. The job should suit you."*

She bared her teeth in a foxlike smile. *"It will. Thank you, Wolf. And don't worry, we'll keep watch over you while you're busy."* Not waiting for my response, she ran off.

Shaking my head in wry amusement, I turned my attention inward.

It was time to begin.

You have begun casting <u>awakened slayer</u>. Time remaining until the spell is complete: 23 hours, 59 minutes, and 58 seconds.

You have entered a deep meditative state. While in this state, you will be unresponsive and unaware of your surroundings.

18 hours remain until the ownership of sector 18,240 transfers to the Forerunners.

✳   ✳   ✳

Spellcasting complete.

You have created a level 282 astral simulacrum of yourself.

A simulacrum, like an aspect, is a construct, but it differs in some striking ways. Where an aspect is a fully independent but impermanent construct that must be summoned on every occasion, a simulacrum is permanent and maintains its links to the host entity throughout its existence.

This means that while your simulacrum will have his own health, he will partake from the same energy pools you do. In addition, his skills, traits, attributes, and abilities will evolve as your own do.

Note, astral simulacrums are beings of pure psi. They have no body, nor access to any non-telepathic traits, skills, attributes, or abilities.

Your secret blood trait has been triggered! To conceal your bloodline, your astral simulacrum's Class will be hidden.

I returned to awareness surrounded by the murmur of voices speaking above me. I recognized the speakers immediately. It was Safyre and Ceruvax, both talking softly as they awaited my return, but for the time being, I ignored them.

Something else held my attention. Something wholly new... yet familiar. The simulacrum.

It—*no, he*—sat cross-legged in my mind, in a replica of my own pose. Seeing that he had my attention, the simulacrum folded himself in half until his head touched an imaginary floor. *"Wolf Lord,"* he greeted.

That the astral construct could talk did not surprise me. *"Where is this?"* I asked.

We were in my mind, I knew that much. But it was not my mind as I ordinarily perceived it. Usually, when I looked at my mindglow, I saw a nebulous ball of light surrounded by multiple layers of mental shielding. This time, I found myself looking down on solid ground, tall trees, and bright blue sky. My consciousness, it seemed, had been refashioned to mimic the real world.

"This is the dreamscape."

Even as the simulacrum answered me—in my own voice, no less—I found understanding of the concept entering my mind.

He was me, after all, and I, him, and what he knew, I did too.

That he had known something I did not—even if only for a few moments—was mildly surprising but only mildly. The knowledge had not come from within, but from the Game—spurred by the simulacrum's creation, no doubt—and he had accessed it quicker than I had.

I knew what the dreamscape was now, fully and completely.

In its most basic form, it was a manifestation of my dreaming mind. Most people—and this included players as well—had little conscious control over their dreams. Their subconscious dictated the direction they took.

I was not one of those people, not anymore.

My simulacrum—the dream-Michael—was my awakened subconsciousness. I—or he—had the power to reshape my mind, and from this point on, I knew I would never dream again, not the way most people did, anyway.

"Dream-Michael, I like that," the simulacrum pronounced.

At a thought, I entered the dreamscape fully. Coalescing into shape beside the construct, I let my gaze roam across the pristine forest that the simulacrum had imagined. Just looking upon it, I felt the urge to transform into a wolf and run wild through its depths. *"And I like what you've done with the place."*

He grinned. *"I thought you might."*

I smiled. *"What shall we call you?"*

He cocked his head to the side. *"I rather think dream-Michael has a nice ring to it."*

"We can't call you that," I disagreed. *"Too wordy."* Not to mention, confusing.

He sighed. *"You're right. Talking to ourselves like this, we might go crazy. Separate identities are a must."*

Saying nothing, I waited for him to volunteer a name.

The simulacrum deliberated for a drawn-out moment. I didn't rush him. This was important.

"How about... Decal?" he asked at last.

Decal.

Short for Decalthiya.

I sighed. Even after all this time, I'd clearly not forgotten the half-giant. Our initial meeting had been turbulent, and I'd known her for a short time only. Despite this, I'd grown to like her and had not forgotten the loyal warrior.

"A good name," I replied.

"Decal it is, then."

I nodded in acceptance, and as I did so, I felt a wall grow between us. Naming the simulacrum was more than a symbolic gesture. It was a deliberate separation of our personalities. While Decal and I still shared the same knowledge, we would no longer be reflections of the same person. He would not perceive my thoughts the moment I conceived them, nor I his.

It was a necessary separation, though, both for the simulacrum's benefit and my own sanity. He would have free will, if of a more limited variety than I did, and I would gain an added perspective—which, while not truly independent, was one I could trust wholeheartedly.

"What happens if you are slain?" I asked.

He shrugged. *"Then Decal dies. Whatever simulacrum you raise anew will be someone different."*

That made sense. *"And what are your limitations?"*

His expression turned somber. *"That depends on you, and how much autonomy you grant me."*

I thought for a moment, then spread my arms to take in the entirety of the dreamscape. *"This is your domain. To alter as you wish and to protect at all costs. I will not interfere. I promise, too, that I will not take direct control of you unless the need is dire. How you choose to guard the fortress of our mind, and how you attack our foes' consciousnesses, I will leave up to you. All that will fall to me is to direct you in your objectives."*

Decal bowed. *"You honor me with your trust, Wolf. I will not fail us."*

I smiled. *"See that you don't, Wolf."*

He bowed again. *"You'll want to know what I'm capable of."*

I nodded. *"I do at that."*

"Call up my profile," he suggested. *"It'll tell you everything you need to know."*

Reaching out to the Game, I did just that.

<u>Simulacrum Profile: Decal</u>

Level: 282. Rank: 28. Current Health: 100%.
Species: construct. Lives Remaining: 1.
Fabricated Class: astral projection.
True Class: astral aspect of the Power Michael.
Damage reduction (DR): none.
Resistances (RES): 25% mental resistance.
<u>Accessible Traits:</u> inscrutable mind, mental focus IV, mentalist I.
<u>Accessible Skills:</u> telepathy.
<u>Accessible Abilities:</u> guard, project, charm, shurikens, paralyze, shatter, sleep, terrify, blind.

I rocked back on my heels, justifiably surprised by Decal's capabilities — or lack thereof. *"Your abilities... they're different from my own."*

He nodded. *"Your abilities don't map directly onto me. But mine are still derived from yours."* He paused. *"There is something you should be aware of... I can only attack a single subject at a time."*

I frowned. *"Is that why you don't have mass puppet or some variation of it?"*

"Exactly. When I project myself, I will enter the target's dreamscape. I will quite literally be inside their mind. However, that limits what I can affect. I can charm, paralyze, or terrify the target, but only the target."

My frown deepened. *"What about their mental shields?"*

Decal spread his arms. *"Do you see any mental walls here?"*

I shook my head. *"I do not,"* I said, stating the obvious.

"That's because the dreamscape is different. Think of it as an alternative representation of the mindglows you normally visualize. Mental shields still exist here, but they manifest in other ways. If a hostile entity entered this dreamscape, he'd first have to find the kernel responsible for self-control, then overcome the defenses protecting it—including me—before he could charm you."

I chewed over that for a bit. *"Alright... That makes sense. But what about—"*

I broke off, my thoughts turning to the mature void tree and what he'd attempted. *"Everyone had a dreamscape, right?"* I asked slowly.

I knew this to be true already, but I asked the question anyway while I worked through what was troubling me.

"Of course. Like I said, it's just an alternate, if more advanced, representation of a mindglow. But far fewer can access the dreamscapes than can see mindglows." He cocked his head to the side. *"Why do you ask? What's bothering you?"*

"The mature void tree," I murmured. *"He almost subverted my mind. Did he—"*

"—enter your dreamscape to make the attempt? Yes, almost certainly a part of him did." He smiled. *"But the void trees will find it far harder to do so again with me around."*

My expression cleared. *"Then, it's a good thing you're here."*

My conversation with the simulacrum did not end there. We spoke at length about his nature and his capabilities.

Decal was an astral simulacrum, which meant he didn't—couldn't—exist in the real world. He would manifest only in my dreamscape—or that of my foes. It explained his lack of body and magic capabilities. He didn't need them. His only purpose was to guard my own mind or to attack the minds of those I deemed enemies.

But the astral simulacrum was far more than the simple offensive weapon I'd originally envisioned. Not quite a person—he lacked any consciousness of his own—Decal was nonetheless capable of both guile and subterfuge.

Just how effective Decal would be was yet to be seen, but I had a feeling he was going to prove as powerful as Mammon's demonic aspects—if in ways less obvious.

"You can't shift form, can you?" I asked as our conversation wound down.

"I can. While in your dreamscape, I can be anything I want. But for me, shifting is purely cosmetic. I won't acquire any of your elder form traits when I change, if that's what you're wondering." He grinned suddenly. *"But it was not just for you I created the forest. I look forward to exploring it as a wolf."*

I smiled, sharing in his happiness, despite the twinge of envy his words engendered. *"What happens to you when I change shape?"*

"Nothing. As Decal, my identity is separate from yours."

"And when you venture into another's dreamscape?"

Decal grimaced. *"Alas, I will lack definition when I do so. My form will still be humanoid."* He gestured down at himself. *"But all the details you see now will be absent. Instead, I will look more akin to a shadow."*

"Hmm. No face then?"

"No face," he confirmed.

I rubbed my chin considerately. *"That might not be a bad thing."*

He tilted his head to the side. *"You want to keep my nature secret?"*

"For as long as possible," I confirmed. *"Last question: what happens if you're analyzed?"*

"Go ahead and try it for yourself," he suggested.

Doing as the construct urged, I reached out with my will and inspected him.

The target is Decal, a level 282 astral projection.

"Well, well," I mused. *"That is certainly misleading."*

"It is, isn't it?" Decal said with a pleased smirk. *"No one, not even those who are able to perceive me, will know I am your construct."*

I nodded in satisfaction. He was right. Any enemy who became aware of the construct's presence would believe him to be a projection of someone called 'Decal.' They would have no reason to associate the simulacrum with me.

None whatsoever.

I smiled. *And that would make for some interesting possibilities...*

✳   ✳   ✳

A short while later, I opened my eyes to find Ceruvax and Safyre sitting patiently beside me.

"Did it work?" the old wolf asked the moment he noticed my return to awareness.

"It did," I replied, a tired smile lighting my face. For all that I had been meditating, my body still required real rest, and the day had gone on too long already. "The simulacrum is formed."

"That's great news," Safyre said warmly, squeezing my hand. "Tell us about it."

"Him," I corrected gently. "His name is Decal, and he will reside in my dreamscape from now on."

Ceruvax's eyes narrowed. "You've created a dreamscape?"

I shook my head. "Not me. Decal." Drawing a breath, I went on to explain everything I'd learned about the dreamscapes and Decal.

When I was done, I tilted my head to study the former envoy. From his expression, much of what I'd said was not news to him. "What do you know about the dreamscapes?"

"Not as much as I wish," Ceruvax grimaced. "Especially now that I've learned you have access to them." He exhaled. "The dreamscapes are a powerful tool that only psionic Powers have access to. A telepath employing one has a far greater arsenal of weapons to choose from than someone without."

I nodded. "That is my own impression as well. Do you think the void trees can use them?"

"The void trees?" Ceruvax echoed, appearing startled by the question. "Why would you ask that?"

"The mature tree almost subverted my thoughts," I reminded him grimly. I tapped the side of my head. "This, despite my mental walls."

Safyre leaned forward. "You think he did it by entering your dreamscape?"

"I do," I replied. "Decal does as well."

"You speak of him as if he is his own person," she said quietly.

"I do," I admitted, "and he is—sort of. But he is me too." I rubbed the back of my head. "It's not easy to explain."

She laughed. "I see that."

I smiled ruefully. "But enough of the dreamscapes. What's the news on the sector?"

Ceruvax's eyes glittered. "Check your alerts," he instructed.

My gaze darted to Safyre. A smile lit her face, and she was nodding encouragingly as well. "Alright," I murmured.

Turning my focus inward again, I found multiple Game messages clamoring for my attention.

The Forerunners have claimed sector 18,240!

This sector is no longer neutral territory. Modifying sector parameters...

...

...

Sector 18,240 is henceforth a closed sector under the control of the Forerunners, whose claim is yet <u>new</u>. The following restrictions apply to this region's safe zone: only Forerunner faction officers can assign ownership of buildings in the safe zone.

Note, if the Forerunners maintain control of the sector for another 29 days, the faction's claim will mature to <u>young</u>, thereby conferring upon you a greater degree of control over the sector.

Safyre has appointed herself the governor of sector 18,240.

Safyre has renamed sector 18,240 to <u>Sanctum</u>.

Safyre's <u>bastion of healing</u> trait has been triggered! A permanent sector-wide buff that increases the health regeneration of all faction members by +0.25% per second has been placed over Sanctum.

Congratulations, Michael, you have claimed your first sector and have accomplished the feat: <u>The Road to Power</u>! Requirement: secure your first sector. As reward, you and your familiar have been awarded 1 Class point each.

You have completed the task: <u>A Place to Call Home</u>! In doing so, you have stayed true to the tenets of your House, deepening your Wolf Mark.

Congratulations, Michael! You have accomplished the seemingly impossible task you set yourself and claimed sector 18,240 in 9 days. As a result, you've been awarded the feat: <u>Ambitious</u>.

Many consider power and ambition in the Game to be synonymous. And they are not far wrong. Those who seek to do great deeds—and succeed— are richly rewarded. You now number amongst their ranks. For setting yourself a truly audacious goal, and achieving it to boot, you have been granted the ascendant ability, <u>portal master</u>.

<u>Portal master</u> is a mythic ascendant ability that can be used to permanently alter the parameters of any Game portal in a neutral or faction-owned sector. Using this spell, one-way portals can be transformed into two-way portals or vice versa, dead portals may be reopened, and open portals may be closed. This spell does not occupy any ability slots, and its activation time is 7 days.

Note, mythic abilities are Classless ascendant abilities. They lack ascendant rank, cannot be upgraded, and are never offered during the course of a player's ascendancy. Instead, they can only be earned through the achievement of extraordinary deeds.

"Wow," I breathed as I opened my eyes again.

Safyre's lips turned up in a wry smile. "Wow, is about the size of it. We've done it. We've claimed the sector."

"I've *also* completed my task," I said.

"A place to call home?" Ceruvax asked. "Did the Adjudicator reward you?"

"He certainly has," I murmured, and read aloud the description of my new ability.

"A mythic ability," Ceruvax gasped, awestruck.

"You've heard of them before?" I asked.

He nodded slowly. "I have, but none of the scions I knew actually possessed one. And of the one you received... I've never heard the least whisper. It must be unique or exceedingly rare." He met my gaze. "It's a great boon," he finished gravely.

I couldn't disagree.

"But that cast time..." Safyre mused, biting her lip. "It'll prove troublesome."

"No doubt," I agreed. "Still, the spell's possibilities are intriguing."

Ceruvax nodded. "You could make the gateway to Draven's Reach two-way."

"And close the one at the Eastern Marches," Safyre added.

"Oh, I can do more than that," I murmured. "I can open the disabled nether portal in sector 30,199 and see where it goes. Or..." I paused. "Hmm, I wonder. Can I close the portal between the wolves' valley and Erebus' dungeon?"

Ceruvax stroked his chin thoughtfully. "That is certainly an interesting idea, but whether you could do it is less certain. As I understand it, the dungeon on the other side is owned by the Awakened Dead?"

I nodded. "It is. Which is wherein the problem lies."

According to the description of the portal master ability, the spell would not allow me to alter portals in sectors owned by other factions. But what about situations where one side of the portal was in neutral territory and the other side was not? The workings of the spell in such a scenario were less clear.

"But even if you could," Safyre mused, "what purpose would it serve?"

"I'm not sure," I admitted. "But it does give me more options to play with."

"Then you still intend on going ahead with your plan?" Ceruvax asked.

"I do."

Safyre held back a sigh and didn't try to dissuade me again. "When do you leave?"

I glanced upward. Even through the thick mists, I could still make out the darkness of the sky beyond. Full night had fallen, and like the Adjudicator had said, we'd just accomplished the impossible. Such an achievement should be celebrated. Not ignored.

I would allow myself one night, I decided. One night spent amongst friends and allies before I picked up my burdens and moved on.

To the next impossible task.

"I'll depart tomorrow," I finally pronounced. "At first light."

Ceruvax nodded. "Good. I'll make sure the rest of the team is ready and waiting." The old wolf rose to his feet. "I won't take up any more of your time. We can speak further tomorrow, and I'm sure the others also have matters they'll want to discuss before your departure." His head turned fractionally to the left. "Here comes the first one already."

Following the direction of his gaze, I spied Ghost in the far distance. From the sense I got of her mindglow, she was not alone either. It seemed my familiar's own casting had been as successful as mine, and her mind, too, now played host to a simulacrum.

CHAPTER 600: SPECTER

"So, Sanctum, huh?" I asked, turning to Safyre while we waited for Ghost to join us.

She smiled. "I thought it had a nice ring to it."

"It does." I looked out onto the horizon. "I truly hope that a sanctuary is what it becomes."

"We won't fail here," Safyre reassured me. "We've come too far for that."

I didn't have her confidence. For all that we'd accomplished, Safyre and I were still weak as Powers went, and Sanctum was still in its infancy. I shuddered to think of how we'd fare if Tartar, Arinna, or even Loken deployed their armies against us.

It would not be pretty.

"They won't find us," Safyre said, seeming to read my mind.

"I hope not," I muttered. I paused, deliberating going on, then rushed onward. "It's another reason why I must venture into the Shadow's den alone, you know."

Safyre turned to face me, her face somber, as I reopened a topic that I knew she'd been trying hard not to restart herself. She didn't say anything, though. Instead, her face still, she waited to hear what else I had to say.

"We can't risk any of our people falling into the hands of Loken or his envoy," I said quietly. "If the trickster puts them to the question, I'm not sure even Ceruvax will be able to hold out. And I don't need to tell you what a disaster it'll be if Loken learns of Sanctum's existence."

"We can't have that," she agreed. "But what makes you believe Loken won't be able to extract the knowledge from you?"

"I don't believe that." I laughed blackly. "I'm not so arrogant as to imagine I can withstand his power, not yet anyhow. But—" I inhaled deeply— "like I've told you and Adriel before, I don't think Loken is involved in whatever is going on. His envoy has to be acting alone. But even if I'm wrong, and even if Loken is at the center of things, I don't believe he will torture me for information."

"Why not?"

"Because he needs me for some or the other scheme he's running against the Awakened Dead," I said bluntly. "As yet, the trickster considers me no threat. But Erebus and his cronies? Them, I'm sure, Loken is worried about. Why, I don't know. Nonetheless, I can't see Loken risking his plans against the Dark right now by antagonizing me." My lips turned into a grim line. "After I've done what he wants, then, sure, Loken will have no compunctions about ridding the Game of me."

"That's a thin thread on which to hang your life," Safyre said softly.

Not to mention the rest of the forerunners.

But even though she had to be thinking it, Safyre refrained from voicing those words aloud.

I heard them, nevertheless.

"Don't I know it," I said. "But wishing things were otherwise will not change facts. And I have only two choices before me: move ahead or abandon Saya."

"But Saya is Pack," Safyre said.

"But Saya is Pack," I agreed. I could not—would not—abandon her.

Safyre laid her hand on mine. "I understand." She sighed. "I won't claim to like it, but I understand. Go and do what you must. And when you come back, you'll find Sanctum waiting for you."

"Thank you," I murmured gratefully.

"Phew," Ghost said, her mental sending intruding suddenly into both our minds, *"that took you two long enough. I'm glad you worked things out. Can I approach now?"*

I laughed, and Safyre smiled. *"Of course, you may,"* she said warmly.

✳　✳　✳

Ghost was not alone, physically, yes, mentally... no. Another rode her mind. The moment she stepped up to my side in the 'real', our dreamscapes merged, and almost involuntarily, I found myself pulled back in.

"You're back," Decal said, still sitting cross-legged in the same position I left him.

"I am," I agreed, materializing beside him.

"And we have visitors," he said, staring off into the distance.

"We do," I said, turning to look in the direction he gazed.

Two wolves were approaching. Jogging across the ground, they were a study in contrast. One was pitch black—Ghost—while the other was ice white. Her simulacrum.

Decal rose to his feet just as both wolves rushed to a stop before us.

"Prime," Ghost began without preamble, *"meet Specter."*

I turned to the second wolf. She was a pyre wolf, too, of course. Her eyes gleamed red, and she was just as large as Ghost. Stepping forward, I held out my hand for her to sniff. *"I'm Michael,"* I said, introducing myself, *"and it's a pleasure to meet you, Specter."*

"Specter," Decal mused, *"that's a lovely name."*

Ghost's gaze found mine.

"That's Decal, my simulacrum," I explained.

Ghost bobbed her head, likely having come to the same realization already, and greeted my alter ego.

"I like it here," Specter pronounced after the exchange of pleasantries was done. Her gaze roved over the tall trees and thick layer of leaves underfoot. *"It's much better than the caves we manifested."*

"I like the sun and space," Ghost agreed.

Specter ducked her head. *"I'll alter our dreamscape to match as soon as we get back."*

Ghost nodded. *"Do that, please."*

My familiar's simulacrum was clearly just as capable as Decal when it came to the dreamscape, but what about her other abilities? Curious, I pulled up her profile.

The target is Specter, a level 282 astral wolf.

<u>Simulacrum Profile: Specter</u>

Level: 282. Rank: 28. Current Health: 100%.
Species: construct. Lives Remaining: 1.
Fabricated Class: astral projection.
True Class: astral aspect of Ghost.
Damage reduction (DR): none.
Resistances (RES): 25% mental resistance.
<u>Accessible Traits:</u> psionic being.
<u>Accessible Skills:</u> telepathy.
<u>Accessible Abilities:</u> guard, project, astral bite, diresight.

My lips turned down. Just like Decal's had been, Specter's abilities were modeled after Ghost's, which unfortunately left her with only two real abilities—astral bite and diresight.

Still, astral bite alone would make the simulacrum a fearful foe. *"Well, now that we're all—"*

"M–M–ICHA–E–L–L–L...?"

I broke off as Safyre's voice intruded, echoing across the horizon.

I turned back to the others. *"We'll pick this up later,"* I promised. *"It seems I'm needed back in the real world."*

✳ ✳ ✳

"Where did you go?" Safyre asked as I opened my eyes. "You and Ghost have been sitting there, staring off into nothing for the last minute."

"Sorry," I said, shaking my head ruefully, "I got pulled into the dreamscape to meet Ghost's new simulacrum."

"Ah," Safyre exhaled. "That explains it." Her gaze swapped to the pyre wolf, who had similarly returned to the 'real.' "Have you told him yet?"

Ghost shook her head. *"Not yet."*

I frowned. "Told me what? What's going on?"

Instead of answering directly, Safyre held out her hand, allowing the yellowish smog to swirl around her fingers. "The mist, you've noticed it, of course."

I nodded. "Of course."

"It hasn't dissipated the entire time you've been meditating." She held my gaze, her own filled with concern. "More than a full day has passed, and there has been no change."

My frown deepened. "None?"

"None," she confirmed. "The toxicity at this spot is still at tier eight."

I grimaced. "That's going to be a problem."

"Definitely," she agreed.

114

As long as the nether mist pervaded the sector, it meant none of the non-players in our faction could move around without adequate safeguards—be it in the form of protection crystals or mage shields. Even most of our players would be constrained from moving freely.

Then, too, there was the effect the mists would have on morale and the sector itself. Until the yellow smog was banished, Elise and the other druids' efforts to restore the sector's vegetation would be badly hampered.

"Getting rid of the mist has to be a priority," I stated.

"You won't hear any arguments from me on that point," Safyre replied. "Unfortunately, our attempts to dispel the mists have failed."

I stared at her blankly. "What? As in completely?"

She nodded grimly. "Adriel, Ceruvax, the nagians, and I have tried every spell in our arsenal. They all work—up to a point. We can keep a region clear of nether, but only for a time, and only for as long as our spells remain active. Nothing we've done has managed to reduce the overall toxicity of the sector."

"Damn," I muttered, not liking the sound of that.

Safyre sighed. "Damn indeed. The way I see it, we have three choices. One: we erect permanent magic shields around all our settlements."

I shook my head. "I don't like it. Not only will maintaining the shields be a significant drain on our resources, but assuming the stygians ever return, we're effectively seeding the home ground advantage to them. The mists will nourish their forces while it hampers our own people. Not good."

"Agreed," Safyre said. "No one else likes option one any more than you do. Moving on, then. Option two: we seek help from the brotherhood."

I tugged at my lip. "That sounds more promising. Although... I'm not sure how much help they'll be. The brotherhood has never recaptured a sector like this from the void. Still, it's worth a try." My eyes darted back to Safyre. "But what's option three?"

Her own gaze slid in the pyre wolf's direction again. "Option three is Ghost."

I blinked, then realization dawned. "Her nether manipulation skill. You think Ghost will be able to disperse the mists."

"We do," Safyre replied. "No one in our faction has nether magic except for Ghost, and Adriel and I are both certain that in time, she will be able to destroy the mist."

"'In time'," I repeated slowly. "Because first, she has to raise the skill and get the requisite abilities."

The pyre wolf's nether manipulation skill was currently at rank thirteen. If she was going to do what Safyre wanted, it was a safe bet that Ghost would have to advance her skill to the elite tier, at the very least.

Safyre inclined her head. "Exactly."

I sighed, finally realizing where this conversation was going. "You want Ghost to stay."

Safyre nodded solemnly. "We do."

Because, of course, to train her nether manipulation, Ghost had to be in a nether-infested sector—and that meant either Sanctum or sector 30,199.

I turned to the pyre wolf. I'd promised Ghost never to leave her behind again, and yet here was Safyre asking me to do just that.

My familiar's mouth dropped open in a lupine smile. *"It's alright, Prime. Adriel, Saf, and I have already spoken. I'll stay if you can do without me."*

I blinked stupidly. The thought had crossed my mind that all this was a ploy by Saf and the others to keep me in Sanctum. Ghost's words were a clear refutation of the notion, and for a moment, I felt ashamed to have misjudged my companions so, however briefly.

"Are you sure?" I asked Ghost, keenly feeling Safyre's regard but keeping my attention focused on the pyre wolf.

"I am." She chuckled. *"And besides, I don't think you were going to allow me to manifest much in the valley. Were you?"*

"That would have been dangerous," I agreed. "If the wrong players spotted you..."

"Well, there you go. Better I stay here, then."

Despite the words and the manner in which they were uttered, there was a wistful undertone to Ghost's voice. She wanted to come, I realized, but she knew, too, that both she, I, and the faction would be better served if she remained in Sanctum.

I inclined my head. "Thank you, Ghost," respecting her decision. "You can stay."

You have slept 8 hours.
You have lost knowledge of 3 stolen spells.

I awoke early the next morning and saw to my preparations. Primarily, this consisted of rearranging my face—my whole identity, really—and addressing my loadout.

You have cast doppelganger, transforming your form into that of Linx, a level 230 elven blade dancer, and changing your Marks to those of Greater Shadow and Kalin. Duration: infinite.

You have unequipped the: Cloak of the Reach, ebonheart, tiameten scalemail vest, wayfarer boots, wayfarer gloves, psi bracelet, aetherstone bracelet, jeweled pet, forerunner bracelet, brotherhood bracelet, and a seeking eye of sylvana.

Ghost has lost the ability: <u>awakened slayer</u>. Note, your familiar's existing simulacrum is unaffected. However, in the event of its demise, Ghost will be unable to summon one anew.

You have equipped a ranger's kit vest.

"Morning," Safyre greeted as she walked into the cavern I'd retired to sleep in last night.

"Morning," I replied, looking up as I finished readjusting the last ties to my new vest—or rather, the old one.

Safyre's brows rose when she caught sight of my face, and a moment later, I felt a telltale tingle ripple across me. "Kalin," she mused. "That's the name of the minor Power leading the Marauder faction, isn't it? You're going to impersonate one of his Sworn?"

I grinned. "That's right, I am. It's as good an alias as any. And if I get caught, well then, it might misdirect suspicion."

"If you get caught..." Her gaze drifted to my discarded legendary gear. "Is that why you've removed all that?"

My amusement faded. "I can't ignore the possibility that I might be discovered, or worse yet, be caught, in which case I can't be carrying any revealing gear."

Safyre nodded slowly. "You've removed your forerunner farspeaker bracelet as well?"

"Yes. I'll get a clean, anonymous set for Ceruvax, the rest of the team, and me to use while we're in the valley." I jerked my chin in the direction of the bag of holding sitting innocuously beside my bedroll. "I'll store everything I won't be taking in there—including the Blood Talisman and the new netherstones—and leave them with you for safekeeping."

"You're taking this seriously," Safyre observed soberly.

I shrugged. "With Loken involved, either directly or indirectly, I can't afford not to. I have to be prepared for the worst."

Not saying anything further, Safyre waited patiently while I began packing away my unequipped gear.

✳ ✳ ✳

You have lost a bag of holding containing 44 items.
You have acquired the tier 5 spell, <u>disrupting ray</u> (stolen).
You have acquired the tier 5 spell, <u>mana strike</u> (stolen).
You have acquired the tier 6 spell, <u>noxious vapors</u> (stolen).

An hour later, I was ready to depart. But I was not the only one.

As Safyre and I entered the main cavern—it still served as our base and would continue to do so until the forts and the safe zone were ready for occupation—we found four other groups waiting to depart.

The first group consisted of Farren, Regus, and Anriq. They were heading into sector 30,199 and would follow in the brotherhood army's footsteps. After they joined Duskar's people and the brotherhood selected the site of their nether base, Anriq would etch one of our new netherstones, opening the way for direct and permanent communication between the brotherhood's nether chapter and the Forerunners.

Wishing the trio luck in their mission, I dropped a pair of netherstones in Anriq's hands—one marked, the other unmarked.

The second group was just as small as the first and was made up of Nyra, Terence, and Teresa. The trio was about to begin only their second dungeon dive together, but I could tell already that they were melding well as a team.

Stopping in front of them, I laid a hand on Terence's shoulder. "I'm sorry to say I have some bad news."

"Bad news?" the young knight asked, his face growing alarmed.

I nodded solemnly. "I'm afraid you three are going to have to delay your departure for the guardian tower until tomorrow."

"Why?" Teresa demanded. "What's happened?"

At my signal, Ceruvax stepped forward. "You two kittens have something more important to attend to today."

Teresa bristled. "Kittens? Don't call us that!"

"Well, I certainly can't call you pups," the old wolf growled.

Teresa's face grew redder, but before she could retort, Nyra cut in. "What's going on?"

Wordlessly, Ceruvax pulled an item free of his voluminous robe and set it on the ground before the others.

Terence skipped back, warily eyeing the yellowing wolf skull Ceruvax had placed on the floor. "What's that?"

"The Skull of Souls," I replied.

Terence backtracked further.

I smiled. "Relax. It's nothing to be afraid of. In fact, the day you two have been looking forward to for ages has finally come."

Teresa's gaze skipped from the skull to me, but she refrained from venturing any guesses as to its purpose.

"Today," I continued, ignoring her unexpected reticence, "is the day you infuse your blood with the spirits of your bloodline's fallen." Withdrawing the Blood Talisman, I set it down beside the Skull of Souls. "Today is the day you become true scions of Lion."

The twins finally began to catch on.

Halting his retreat, Terence advanced anew. "We're going to awaken our blood?" he asked eagerly.

Grinning, I nodded.

"B-but... but..." Teresa stammered, her eyes clouding in confusion. "How?"

"You remember the Ritual Combat Circle I told you about?" I asked. "And the possessed I fought in it?"

She nodded mutely.

"Well, I have Farren and Adriel's assurance that there were a few Lions amongst the possessed's number that day." I tapped the Skull of Souls. "And now their spirits reside in here—waiting for the right candidates to join with." My face grew serious. "I would prefer to witness your awakenings myself, but duty calls, and I can't delay my departure further. Ceruvax and Adriel are more than capable of helping you two through this, though."

Terence's gaze was still glued on the skull of souls. "We're really doing this?"

Adriel chuckled. "You really are."

Clasping the twins' hands, I turned to the next group, which was not really a group at all, but a single individual—Sedgwick. "You have the messages I penned for the huntmistress?"

He nodded. "I do." He held out his arm. "And these are the items you wanted."

I took the proffered bag, not bothering to inspect its contents. I would do that at a more opportune time. "Thank you," I said. "About the faction tokens—"

"Procured and stamped with the Forerunners' mark already," the dwarf cut in. "Adriel does quick work. Anriq has the set for Duskar's people." He tapped his breast pocket. "And I have those for Kartara's."

I whistled softly. "That was quick. Nicely done," I said, directing my praise at both Sedgwick and Adriel.

I inhaled deeply. There was nothing left to be done now, except to say my final goodbyes. "Open the portal," I said to the last group, which consisted of Shael, Mariam, Deryn, and Llewyn.

Ceruvax, the final member of our team, would join us later. Not only did he need to supervise the twins' blood awakening, but there were also his experiments with his blood-bound naga to consider. All in all, it would take the old wolf a few days to wrap up his work in Sanctum. Looking over my shoulder, I glanced his way.

"I'll join you in two days," he promised. "Stay out of trouble until then."

I grunted. "I'll try." Not waiting for his reply, I turned around and said farewell to Ghost, Safyre, and the others, then stepped into the portal Llewyn had opened. At long last, I was back on my way to the valley.

And this time, I didn't intend on leaving until Saya was safe amongst friends again.

✳   ✳   ✳

You have entered the safe zone of sector 12,560.
You have equipped a tier 7 concealed locator beacon and a farspeaker bracelet (1 of 6 in an unmarked set). Equipped items: 22 / 30.

"Can everyone hear me?" I asked over my newly equipped farspeaker bracelet.

"We can," came the chorus of replies from Shael, Mariam, Deryn, and Llewyn.

"Good," I said aloud. Glancing around the table, I took in the expressions of the other four seated alongside me in the common room of the Roost. Excitement and anxiety clouded their faces in equal measure. "Looks like we're all set to begin, then."

"What do you need us to do?" Llewyn asked a tad breathlessly.

For the three forsworn in particular, this mission was fraught with danger. They would be killed on sight as soon as they were spotted — regardless of whether or not they were in the safe zone. It was only the Roost's walls that protected them.

"Nothing for now," I assured him. "You will wait here."

"Oh," Deryn said. "That's it?" He, at least, sounded disappointed by the prospect of more waiting.

"That's it," I confirmed. "If I get into trouble I can't extricate myself from, I will call on you for help."

"What will you be doing?" Mariam asked.

"Scouting," I replied succinctly. Extracting the envoy's note Shael had given me in this very room over a week ago, I set it down on the table for them all to see.

The tavern keeper is not dead, but she will be soon.
If you want her back, meet me where you and she first met.

The reference to 'where you and she first met' was to Besina's cave, of course. That was less than a day's journey west from here. And while I was disinclined to believe anything the envoy said, in this instance, I suspected she did not lie.

According to the information I'd received from Saya the first time I'd returned to the sector, Loken's forces were encamped in the valley's western mountain slopes—the very same direction in which the dead wyvern mother's cave nest lay.

Loken had known about Besina's cave network, of course, and presumably, he'd told his envoy all about it. No doubt, she had jumped at the chance to base her forces there. The dark environs were ideal for Shadow's minions.

But not just for Shadow. For me too.

120

What the envoy perceived as a strength against Light and Dark was a weakness when it came to dealing with me.

It was the only thing, in fact, that gave me hope of successfully infiltrating Shadow's base. I did not kid myself, though. It would not be easy. And the chance of failure would be high.

Which is why I would need a contingency plan.

Muriel and Tartar.

If war was still raging in the valley, as I knew for a fact it had been when I met Shael here ten days ago, then both Powers likely still had significant forces concentrated in the sector. Their armies were the ammunition I needed.

But Captain Talon, the envoy in command of the tartan legions, had already fallen afoul of my machinations once. He would be doubly wary this time around. And of Muriel or her people, I knew nearly nothing.

Still, I would need to approach both groups.

Grimacing at the thought of what I would need to do, I expanded on my earlier statement. "As much as I'd like to head directly to the wyvern mother's caves and the envoy's base, doing so would be foolhardy. I need to get the lay of the land first. I need to find out which factions are still in the sector and where the balance of power lies."

"I can help with that," Shael offered.

"No," I said firmly. "The envoy's spies will be on the lookout for you. It's best that you, too, stay in the Roost, at least until Ceruvax joins us."

The bard sighed but didn't protest the order. "Have you equipped the tracking device?" he asked instead.

Lifting my left leg onto the table, I removed my boot, barring the innocuous slip of iron curled around my ankle. "I have. Mariam, Llewyn, and Deryn should be able to locate me anywhere in the sector with this and portal directly to me."

The three forsworn nodded in agreement. "We're receiving your location," Deryn confirmed.

Re-equipping my boot, I rose to my feet and began casting. "Then everything is in order," I said, heading toward the door. "I'll keep in touch, but don't expect to hear from me in a few hours yet."

"Stay safe, Michael," Shael called after me.

You have cast vanish. You are <u>invisible</u>. Duration: 5 minutes.

"You, too," I replied over my shoulder, and opening the door, slipped out of the Roost.

The safe zone was exactly as it had been ten days ago: deserted.

Standing in the middle of the empty street and invisible to any would-be observers, I turned around in a slow circle and took in the surroundings.

The village was unoccupied; there was no question of that. The nearby log cabins were in the same state of disrepair I'd observed days ago, and no whisper of sound broke the quiet. Even the forest bordering the village's northern side looked empty—it's nearest reaches, anyway.

Lifting my gaze, I took in the horizon. The sun had only just begun to peek over the valley's eastern mountain range—the day was yet young— and no clouds marred the sky. Smoke did, though. Trails of gray rose up from multiple spots in the forest, creating ugly blotches that hung in the sky like portents of doom.

Or of war.

Narrowing my eyes, I tried to get a fix on the largest and most pervasive gray cloud. By my best reckoning, the spot in question was at least a two-hour hike northward, about halfway to the center of the valley. *The fighting there is ongoing,* I surmised. *If I hurry, I can still arrive in time to learn something.*

Decision made, I set off at a jog.

✳   ✳   ✳

Ten minutes later, I was in the forest proper and, despite the circumstances, felt my spirits rise. There was something unaccountably soothing about the ocean of green enveloping me. Tall redwood and oak trees arched high overhead, birds chirped softly, worms wriggled in the soil beneath, and the underbrush rustled ceaselessly. Everywhere I looked, in fact, life thrived, and of its own accord, a smile slipped onto my face.

Sector 12,560 made for a stark contrast to Sanctum, and I could only hope Elise and the others managed to transform the barren wasteland that was our new home into something resembling my pleasant surroundings—and they *were* pleasant despite the war raging in its midst.

Ghost would've loved it here, I thought, feeling a brush of sadness at her absence. No doubt she would have nagged me incessantly until I caved and allowed her to manifest. I chuckled to myself.

Perhaps, it's a good thing she's not here, then.

A sharp cry from farther north pulled me from my thoughts. It was followed by another from the east, and a third from the west.

Players.

Three separate parties, and by the sounds of it, they were on the hunt. The smile slipped off my face as hard-bitten caution reasserted itself. I'd come a long way since I'd last been in the valley, but it would not do to underestimate my fellow players, especially not those embroiled in a deadly war.

Dropping into a crouch, I took a minute to prepare myself.

I had time. None of the three parties was in mindsight or physical sight range yet, and I was fairly certain it was not me they were hunting. Even so, I didn't expect the unknown players to be anything but hostile if they discovered me.

This was a war zone, after all, and everyone was an enemy until proven otherwise.

Drawing psi, I began casting. I was already hidden in the shadows, but now it was time to see to my buffs.

You have cast engine of war, increasing your Strength, Constitution, and Dexterity by +20 ranks for 30 minutes.

You have cast vanish and trigger-cast quick mend.

Next, I checked my weapons. Faithful rested in my right sheath, and a stygian sword in my left. Since I'd left behind my most valuable equipment, my gear was definitely lacking. Still, what I lacked in gear, I more than made up for in abilities. If the incoming players somehow uncovered me, they would discover, not a sheep, but an angry wolf.

Craning my neck upward, I scanned the nearby trees, searching for a perch from which to observe proceedings. The oak tree five yards to my right seemed the perfect candidate, and I wasted no time equipping my climbing claws to scale its broad trunk.

Twenty seconds was all it took to get into position.

High up in the oak tree, nestled in its branches, wrapped in shadow, and buffed with vanish, I was nigh undetectable. Bending my head downward, I turned my attention back to the forest floor.

It was time to find out what all the fuss was about.

✳ ✳ ✳

It did not take long for the first group of players to emerge into sight range. As they did, their analyze data unfolded in my mind.

The target is Tanmir, a level 179 elven nightrunner. She bears a Mark of Greater Dark and a Mark of Ishita.

The target is Keven, a level 211 human warlock. She bears a Mark of Supreme Dark and a Mark of Erebus.

The target is Tuver, a level 190 half-giant hammerguard. He bears a Mark of Supreme Dark and a Mark of Tartar.

The target is ...

...

The information on the first three players set me back on my perch. To say I was surprised was an understatement.

What in hells is a Tartan legionnaire doing in the company of the Awakened Dead?

Tuver wasn't the only Tartan soldier in the approaching group, either. There were two others who bore Tartar's Mark, and four more who, while unMarked by the Power, also sported the insignia of a raging bull on their shoulder patches.

The rest of the ragged company of twenty were all Darksworn, and more importantly, by dress and appearance, were adherents of Erebus and Ishita.

Damn. This makes no sense.

Tartar was supposed to be at war with the Awakened Dead's Powers, and in fact, had been so the last I'd heard. Given the three Powers' history in this sector, before today, I would have bet anything that it wouldn't ever change.

Yet, here was a group of Tartan and Awakened Dead soldiers in close proximity to each other and *not* fighting.

What was going on?

"We see you, you bastards!"

The cry came from the east, but no sooner did I turn my head in that direction than a fireball sailed in from the north, and a split second after that, another shout rose from my left.

"There's no escaping us, darkspawn!"

My eyes narrowed as I worked out the implications. The Dark company could not be one of those I'd overheard earlier. They were a fourth group and, by all appearances, were being hotly pursued by the other three.

Who, and how large, the other companies were, I could not tell yet. They had still to come into view.

The Dark company rushed on. The incoming fireball—quickly dealt with by the trailing member of the group—barely slowed them at all. Gauging the course of the fleeing soldiers' flight, I realized their path was about to cross mine.

And indeed, the players passed directly beneath the tree I sheltered in. As they did so, Game messages unexpectedly unfurled in my mind.

Multiple hostile entities have failed to detect you.

You have passed a Perception check! Multiple farspeaker mental sendings detected.

Well, well.

Congratulating myself on my good fortune, I waited impatiently for the telepathic buzzing to resolve itself.

Eavesdropping on communication commencing...

"Where are we going?" I heard the half-giant Tuver ask hoarsely.

"To the safe zone," Keven wheezed in reply.

"That's your plan?" Tuver asked, sounding aghast.

"Why? Do you have a better one in mind?" the warlock retorted.

"I don't," Tuver shot back, *"but going there is—"*

Eavesdropping stopped. Telepathic link broken. The participants have passed out of range.

While I didn't get to hear the half-giant finish his thought, I was still delighted by the overheard snippet. I now knew where the players were heading, and I envisioned no problems with finding them anew if doing so became necessary.

Looking back over my shoulder, I watched the Darksworn disappear into the foliage to the south, then faced forward again. If I was right about what was going on, one or the other of the remaining groups should pass by shortly.

Making myself comfortable, I set myself to waiting.

✵   ✵   ✵

The next group of soldiers was not long in coming.

They emerged from the underbrush to the north in a wash of white. In stark contrast to the group before them, the newcomers were dressed in pristine uniforms embroidered in gold.

Lightsworn, I surmised.

Like the Dark company, the Light players were running flat out. But they were not fleeing. No, *these* were the hunters, and it showed in their predatory gazes and the naked anticipation in their faces. Letting my attention skip from Lightsworn to Lightsworn, I quickly parsed their player data.

The target is ...
The target is ...

...

Huh, interesting. Except for the foremost player, none of the other fifty Lightsworn were above level two hundred. Fixing my attention on that worthy, I inspected him anew.

The target is Jobe, a level 220 human inquisitor. He bears a Mark of Greater Light and a Mark of Muriel.

The picture was becoming clearer. But there were still two more groups—the ones to the east and west—whose identities were yet unknown.

They have to be Lightsworn too, I thought. Otherwise, there would be no reason for the Dark company to be fleeing—or the Light one to be so confident.

Had circumstances and a common enemy forced the Tartans and Awakened Dead to work together?

Perhaps, I thought. What was less clear, though, was how permanent or widespread the cooperation between the two Dark factions was.

My gaze fell on the approaching Lightsworn again. Fortuitously—or perhaps not—Jobe's company would not be passing under my perch, and for a moment, I contemplated repositioning so that I could overhear any telepathic conversations they might be engaged in. But only for a moment.

Too risky, I decided eventually, staying put.

I had no intention of becoming embroiled in the war between the Forces. My only 'must-do' objective in this sector was rescuing Saya. Everything else was superfluous.

Rustling leaves a few hundred yards to my left drew my attention. Peering in that direction, I saw another thirty Lightsworn emerge into view. They, too, were led by an elite.

More rustling. This time on my right.

Glancing around, I saw twenty more Lightsworn appear—also with an elite in charge.

That makes one hundred Light soldiers, three of whom are tier five players. Opposing them were a group of twenty Dark players that counted only one lowly elite among them.

No wonder the Dark company was fleeing so desperately.

But war was never fair. And the tables could quickly change. Today, it was the Dark that was disadvantaged. Tomorrow, it could just as easily be the Light.

So, feeling no sympathy for the outnumbered Dark soldiers, I watched impassively as the three Light companies continued their remorseless chase southward. In a few seconds, they would pass me by, and I would be free to continue my journey northward. While I waited, I ruminated over what I had learned.

Truthfully, it was not as much as I hoped.

As intrigued as I was by the Awakened Dead and Tartans' attitude to one another, it was the composition and deployment of Shadow's forces in the sector that I was most interested in. And I'd learned nothing of that.

Oh well, perhaps, I'll find out more when—

You have failed a magical resistance check.
Jobe has detected you! You are no longer hidden.

Chapter 603: The Fanatics of Light

"Minion of Shadow!" Jobe yelled. "Up in the trees. Get him!"

Multiple hostile entities have detected you.

Even in the midst of my surprise, I found myself wondering as to the Light elite's choice of words and why he had chosen to issue his warning aloud. *Not all of the Light players must have farspeaker bracelets equipped,* I decided.

As for how Jobe had sensed me... the answer to that mystery would have to wait.

I had multiple incomings. One hundred of them to be exact—and included amongst that number were both physical and ephemeral projectiles.

Anderman has cast fireblast.
Reki has shot a piercing arrow.
Oxtyn has launched a frost barrage.
Livicius is casting ...
Esterleen has ...

...

My expression grim, I watched the three distinct and separate volleys—one from the east, another from the west, and the last from the north—race toward me. It was overkill, of course. Any one barrage would be enough to kill me twice over.

If they landed.

Which, of course, they would not.

Focusing on the distant mindglow of a serline, I spun psi. It was time to retreat. The Light players may want a fight, but I didn't.

The casting finished in a rush, and rising smoothly to my feet, I stepped off the tree and into the aether.

Only to be unceremoniously yanked out again.

Spellcasting interrupted. You have failed to teleport.
Jobe has trigger-cast <u>imprisonment ward</u>. You have been imprisoned (unable to move farther than 20 yards in any direction from your current position). Duration: 5 minutes.

For a heartbeat, I didn't react. Then the precariousness of my situation intruded.

I was in freefall. Courtesy of my aborted shadow jump, I'd lost my perch on the tree branch. Worse yet, I still had an avalanche of spells and projectiles descending on my position.

"Goddamn," I muttered, spinning psi anew. I really didn't want to engage the Light players, but they were making that damnably difficult.

Halfway to the ground, my second spell completed, and this time, it went off without a hitch.

You have cast windborne.

I kept the windslide's design simple, and in an eyeblink I went from hurtling groundward to descending gracefully on a ramp of air. I reached solid ground without mishap, and spinning around in a circle, I took stock of the situation again.

At least a third of the incoming projectiles had changed trajectory to match my new position. *Seeking spells,* I thought bleakly. They were not the only things rushing toward me, though. Thirty of the Lightsworn were also converging on me. *Melee fighters.*

Hells.

I didn't have much time. Taking two quick steps to my left, I ducked into the shadow of a tall redwood and wrapped myself in darkness.

You have failed to hide.

A <u>heretic's unmasking</u> aura is present in the vicinity. This spell prevents any Dark and Shadow Marked players from concealing themselves while within the casting's area of effect.

I exhaled heavily.

I couldn't hide. I couldn't flee.

That left me with only one choice: to fight.

As much as I didn't want to become embroiled in a conflict with Muriel, it seemed her people were dead set on the idea. *So be it.*

Drawing my blades, I saw to my final preparations.

✻ ✻ ✻

You have cast load controller, gaining a 10-minute encumbrance aura that slows any armor-wearing foe within 5 yards by 50%.

You have cast wind daemon, multiplying your speed by 2x for 1 minute.

I was ready before the first spell began its final attack run. Motionless, I watched the ball of fire's approach. Five yards. Four. Three.

Now.

I dashed to the left. Unable to course correct in time, the fireball splashed harmlessly into empty ground.

You have evaded a homing fireball.

Next up was a volley of ice shards. Dropping into a roll, I ducked beneath the shrieking projectiles.

You have evaded 10 frost shards.

A shower of glittering stars rushed in from the left, a storm of arrows from the right, and an evil-looking pillar of blood from above. Knowing I wouldn't be able to avoid being struck altogether, I jumped back and straight into the star shower.

You have evaded a blood strike.
You have evaded an arrow storm.
You have evaded 4 of 20 blessed stars (repelled by void armor).
16 of 20 blessed stars have hit you.
Your void armor has reduced the damage incurred by 40%.
Void armor charge remaining: 84%. Your health has decreased to 76%.
Void thief triggered! Warning: you have reached the limit of your stolen spells. New spell not learned.

I emerged reeling from the light onslaught. Slivers of light clung to my armor like leeches, and in places, they'd burned clean through. But despite the blood dripping down my face and the pain wracking my limbs, I was only lightly impaired, if that.

Glancing up, I took stock. There was no time to celebrate, though.

The incoming volley of missiles was far from over—and this was only the Lightsworn's opening salvo. Surviving the encounter was by no means a certainty. Gritting my teeth, I pushed myself into motion again.

✻   ✻   ✻

Ducking, dancing, sliding, and generally using all twenty yards afforded to me by the imprisonment debuff in whatever manner I could, I wove an erratic path across the forest floor in an effort to evade as many of the incoming projectiles as possible.

Rays of frost shot by, missing me by mere inches, tongues of flame reached out with eager fingers, only to fall short, and arrow after arrow tried—unsuccessfully—to pin me in place.

But while I managed to evade the better part of the assault, even my daemon-gifted speed was not able to get me through unscathed.

You have evaded 23 hostile spells.
Your void armor has repelled 9 magical attacks!
Void armor charge remaining: 58%. Your health has decreased to 52%.

Glad that's over, I muttered, spinning to a stop. *Now where are—*

Maricella has critically hit you.
Quick mend triggered! Your health has been restored to 61%.
You have been knocked down, dazed (duration: 10 seconds), and stunned (duration: 5 seconds).

Ooof. The air escaped me in a rush, as a small but solid figure struck me in the midriff. Despite my assailant's diminutive size, though, she packed a punch, and I went sailing through the air.

I landed with an audible thump some ten yards away, and for five excruciating seconds was forced to lie listlessly, limbs and mind incapacitated.

You are no longer stunned.

I surged upward, or attempted to, anyway. With my head still ringing and my vision still blurry, the best I could manage was a shaky stumble upright.

What were my foes doing? And why hadn't they finished me off?

Someone from behind whistled in surprise. "Wow, Marce, he survived. Did you miss or what?"

Maricella—the gnomish fighter whose charge I'd the misfortune to be on the receiving end of and one of the Lightsworn's three elites—harrumphed loudly. "I don't miss," she declared.

"How'd he survive then?"

"Damn if I know," she grunted. "Should I hit him again?"

You are no longer dazed.

As my vision cleared, I saw that Maricella's question was directed at the tall, carefully groomed man standing next to her. His name was Jobe, and he was the one keeping me chained to the area.

The inquisitor's clothes were of the purest white and appeared to be cut from the finest of cloth. Maricella, by contrast, was covered in layers of unvarnished steel. In fact, she was wearing more armor than I'd seen on anyone, even a dwarf.

My gaze lingered a moment on the gnome. I'd underestimated her, I realized—and paid for it. Maricella's timing had been impeccable. She'd reached me just as the last of the Lightsworns' opening salvo had died.

I'd believed I would have more time to deal with the melee fighters, and as a result, I'd not given sufficient attention to their movements. In my defense, I'd been preoccupied with avoiding the missile storm, but that counted for naught now. The diminutive gnome had struck at me at the exact right moment, leaving me in my present predicament.

"No, I don't think you should," Jobe replied after deliberating on the question for a drawn-out moment. "We don't want to kill him just yet."

The two elites were standing about twenty-five yards away from me and outside the range of the imprisonment field—which fact explained their confidence. My gaze darting left and right, I took in the positioning of the rest of the Lightsworn. They, too, had ventured closer, leaving me at the center of a player-made circle that stretched nearly fifty yards in diameter.

They believe they have me trapped, I surmised.

And they did, but only up to a point.

"You want to question him?" the voice from behind asked, speaking up again.

Glancing over my shoulder, I identified him as the third Lightsworn elite—a ranger by the name of Elias.

"I do," Jobe said smoothly.

"Why?" Elias asked. "I doubt he knows anything of value."

"He is a Marauder," Jobe replied, unperturbed by his companion's skepticism. "Don't you want to know why they're back?"

"Who cares why they're back?" Elias sneered. "The Shadow is finished in this sector. Kill him and be done with it."

"We should continue this conversation," Maricella said, her gaze resting pointedly on me. "But privately."

Jobe nodded agreeably. "True." Raising his voice, he relayed his orders to the rest of the group. "Watch him. Make sure he doesn't try anything funny, and if he attempts to escape, stun him." Not waiting for a response, the inquisitor closed his eyes.

A half second later, Maricella and Elias followed suit, their faces also blanking as they turned their attention inward. The trio had obviously chosen to move the discussion to a farspeaker link—I hid a smile—which was not as secure as they believed.

Turning around, I strolled toward Elias.

"What do you think you're doing?" a Lightsworn demanded.

"Testing the limits of my cage," I replied easily. "Why? Are you going to stop me?"

The player's eyes narrowed to slits, but he refrained from responding. Ignoring him and the rest of the watching Lightsworn, I continued lazily on my way.

I kept my pace slow and deliberate, not wanting to spook my watchers. Nonetheless, I covered the distance quickly. But about four yards out from my target—as expected—I ran into an obstacle.

You are <u>imprisoned</u> and, until the debuff wears off, are constrained from venturing beyond this point.

Wincing, I rubbed the tip of my nose that felt as if it had run aground against something, and for all intents and purposes, it had—into an invisible wall that existed only for me.

A player chuckled. "Thought you were just going to walk through, did you?"

I shrugged. "It was worth a try," I replied without turning around to address him.

"Fool," he muttered.

Dropping into a crosse-legged stance, I yawned theatrically. "Nothing for it but to rest then. Be a good man, and wake me up when your bosses are done, would you?"

Not waiting for his reply, I closed my eyes and turned my attention to the undoubtedly more interesting conversation occurring a few yards away.

Eavesdropping successful!

"...might be Frey," Marciella said.

"It can't be," Elias insisted. *"I told you Shadow is finished in this sector. Between the Dark and ourselves, we've ground their army into dust. And it was a paltry one to begin with. There can't be more than a few score of them left in the sector."*

"Shadow isn't finished," Jobe disagreed. *"And you should stop saying so. You will only make the men needlessly complacent."*

"And don't forget, we've no confirmation that Frey is dead," Marciella pointed out.

"Bah, that witch has likely fled already," Elias scoffed. *"She's probably holed up in Shadow Keep as we speak!"*

"We don't know that," Marciella protested.

"But we can guess," Elias insisted. *"She always was a coward."*

"You're underestimating her again," Maricella said wearily. *"And don't forget whose envoy she is. The trickster's plans are never easy to decipher."*

"Scared, Marce?" Elias teased. *"I would never have believed it of—"*

"Enough," Jobe cut in. *"Maricella is right. We can't afford to take anything about the spy at face value. He might be Frey."* He paused. *"Or he might not. Either way, we can't trust whatever comes out of his mouth."*

"So, why bother trying to question him?" Elias demanded.

"Holding him for questioning was a mistake," Jobe conceded. *"You were right about that."*

"What do you want to do with him then?" Marciella asked.

"What we should have done in the first place," Jobe said grimly. *"Kill him."*

✳ ✳ ✳

Eavesdropping stopped. Telepathic link broken.

The moment I heard the inquisitor's pronouncement, I dropped out of the trio's farspeaker link. The situation had just gone from bad to worse, and it was clear I wasn't going to be able to bluff my way out.

My eyes snapping open, I shot to my feet and backpedalled back to the centre of my 'cell.' The wary gazes of the hundred or so watching Lightsworn tracked me the entire way, but I ignored them. They would figure out what I was about soon enough.

"Decal," I called, knowing I didn't have much time.

"I'm here," he replied instantly, his voice reverberating through my mind.

"Have you been following what's going on?"

"Yes, I can see everything you do as long as you are not actively blocking me."

"Good. It's time to work."

"Excellent. My targets?"

"The three elites." I pointed to Jobe, who'd just opened his eyes. *"Starting with him."*

"Now?" the simulacrum asked eagerly.

"Now," I confirmed, drawing psi in readiness.

A frown marred the inquisitor's face. Did he sense something amiss?

"What's he been up to?" Jobe asked of no one in particular. He meant me, of course.

"Walking. Sitting," a player replied. He shrugged. "Nothing untoward."

Jobe nodded slowly, but he didn't look convinced. "Do it, Marce," he ordered, turning to the gnome. "Kill—"

Decal has cast astral project.

Jobe broke off, his expression freezing, as the astral construct dove into his dreamscape. What was going on in the inquisitor's mind, I couldn't tell, nor did I have the time to find out. There were too many threats in the 'real' for me to dare attempt splitting my attention, and besides, from the looks of it, my simulacrum seemed to have things well in hand.

"Decal?" Elias asked loudly, his face a mask of confusion. "Who's that?"

Ignoring the ranger's question, Maricella laid a hand on the still-frozen inquisitor and shook him worriedly. "Jobe? You alright?"

The inquisitor did not respond.

"What's wrong with him?" a player asked.

It took the gnome less than a heartbeat to figure it out. "He's under attack." She spun to face me. "Who's helping you?" she demanded.

Smiling, I folded my arms across my chest and said nothing.

"Attention outwards," Elias snapped, catching on. "Watch the trees! Our quarry has allies in the woods."

I chuckled softly, but under the clatter of weapons and shouted orders, it went unheard as fully half the Lightsworn whirled around in search of my 'allies.'

That still left fifty-odd players—including Maricella—watching me, though.

All of them were studying me with deadly intensity and waiting for the least sign of provocation. But I remained at ease and with my arms folded. I had no intention of attacking the Lightsworn.

Not physically, anyway.

You have cast mass puppet.

Psi leaped from my mind and into the players arrayed on my right and, with the tenacity of a group of hungry honey badgers, delved into their minds. Surprisingly, though, many of my intended victims rebuffed my attempts at subversion.

You have charmed 5 of 20 targets for 30 seconds.

15 targets are protected by psi shields and are immune to mental manipulation.

Only five, I thought, bemoaning the spell's lack of success. Still, five were better than none. "*Attack,*" I ordered my new minions, not bothering to allocate them specific targets. Drawing psi anew, I prepared my next spell.

"He's a telepath," Maricella yelled, somehow divining what I'd done. "Warriors, charge. Kill him now!"

Adhering to her own command, the gnome dashed into the invisible circle holding me prisoner, her small form a blur as she rushed across the intervening space.

Maricella has cast pummeling charge.

But I'd learned from my previous mistake, and this time the fighter did not catch me flatfooted.

You have cast windborne.
You have evaded Maricella's attack.

Spiraling aloft on a ramp of air—and safely out of the reach of the gnome and the other fighters who'd join her in the circle—I continued casting.

"Bastard!" Maricella yelled, her heavy boots digging huge tuffs in the forest floor as she screeched to a halt and spun around to glare at me impotently. "Archers, mages—get him down!" she roared.

But there was no need for them to do that. My second spell had completed. Releasing it, I dove off my windslide and into the midst of the warriors who had so helpfully put themselves within reach of my swords.

You have cast slaysight.
You have paralyzed 6 of 10 targets for 60 seconds.

Slaysight proved more effective than mass puppet—that, or the warriors' defenses were less capable than those of the mages and archers. Unfortunately, though, Maricella was one of the fighters who proved immune. Still, I had enough other hapless targets to slay.

Landing lightly on my feet, I whipped out faithful and plunged it straight into the back of the closest paralyzed player—an orcish fighter whose fists looked large enough to crush me in a single blow.

You have cast piercing strike.
You have backstabbed your target for 10x more damage!

Unfortunately for the orc, despite his no doubt prodigious strength, his defenses were lacking, and faithful cut through his armor as easily as a knife through butter to bury itself in his heart.

You have killed Zengosh with a fatal blow.

Yanking out the steel blade, I danced two steps forward and stabbed a spearman moving too slowly in the chest.

You have killed Alrick with a fatal blow.

Spying another paralyzed victim nearby, I spun around on the heel of my right foot and drew a line of red across the throat of the senseless fighter.

You have killed Hiroshi with a fatal blow.

Three dead in as many seconds.

By now, I expected my foes to be deep in shock. Nothing about the second half of our battle was going the way they expected.

Almost as if she'd had the same thought, Maricella half-screamed, half-cried, "Whoreson!"

Glancing over my shoulder, I caught a glimpse of the gnome. She was trying to close the distance to me, but there were too many other players in the way, and I judged it would take her at least a few more seconds to reach me.

"Elias, you fool!" she yelled in frustration. "Don't just stand there gaping, kill him!"

But the other Lightsworn elite was also powerless to act. The warriors surrounding me were not just targets to kill; they were my shield too, and in their midst, I was largely obscured from the ranger's view.

Besides, Elias and the others outside the circle weren't exactly standing around doing nothing. Many were still frantically scanning the woods for my phantom allies or trying—albeit unsuccessfully—to restrain my five bespelled minions without killing them.

A broadsword flashed down.

Bending one knee, I ducked beneath the whistling blade, then riposted with faithful. But the half-giant who'd launched the attack was equal to my counter, and he fended it off with ease.

I backed away. More warriors were converging on me—and quickly.

They'd rallied behind Maricella's call, and I knew it wouldn't be long before I was overwhelmed. *Time to reposition.* Before I did that, though, I had a parting gift for my foes.

You have manifested 4 sentient shurikens.

The ethereal blades coalesced around me, momentarily startling the closest warriors. They'd get over the fright soon enough, but I didn't intend to give them that time. *"Kill,"* I ordered, directing the rapidly spinning psi constructs toward the four still-paralyzed players.

Rising swiftly into the air, the astral projectiles whizzed toward their targets. Not bothering to watch the mayhem that was about to ensue, I whirled around and shadow jumped.

✳ ✳ ✳

You have teleported into Maricella's shadow.

The spell executed flawlessly, and it was not hard to figure out why. This time around, I had not attempted to leave Jobe's imprisonment field which, unfortunately, was still active. Instead, I'd deliberately kept my jump short, teleporting to a target inside my 'cell'—this being Maricella.

I emerged from the aether behind the gnomish fighter and with my blades already angling forward in attack.

Maricella, though, was alive to the danger. Spinning around faster than I could've managed in all that armor, she brought up her own weapon in response.

Maricella has blocked your attacks. You have failed to injure your target.

A toothy smile spread across the Lightsworn's face. "Fool," she taunted. "You should've run."

My eyes fixed on the wickedly spiked maul she toyed with in her hands, I deigned to reply. A moment later, as if in reward for my restraint, another Game message flashed for attention.

Maricella has failed a physical resistance check!
As a result of your encumbrance aura, she has become <u>overburdened</u> (speed reduced by 30%).

Emotion ran riot across the gnome's face. Anger followed consternation, but only a heartbeat later, another emotion replaced it: fear. Maricella knew as well as I that being slowed was a death knell.

The Lightsworn was too stubborn to accede gracefully to the inevitable, though, and with a wordless howl, she lashed out, sending her maul rippling through the air in a vicious arc.

But the attack was many times too slow.

Sliding to the left, I ducked past the descending mace and sent my own sword racing forward.

I never got to complete the maneuver.

Halfway through, I spotted a shadow flit over me. How the unseen attacker had snuck up on me, I had no idea, but he was far too close already. Knowing I had no choice, I let my sword arm drop and flung myself farther left.

Tosh has failed to backstab you.
Maricella has fallen out of range of your encumbrance aura. She is no longer <u>overburdened</u>.

Rolling across the forest floor, I bounced back to my feet a safe distance away from the newcomer, Tosh, and Maricella. Spinning around, I faced the pair again.

The gnome—with the feverish ardor of one who'd cheated death—was advancing once more, as was Tosh, who to my surprise was a tier four rogue. That he'd managed to escape notice this long was impressive, and despite his low level, I eyed him with nearly as much concern as I did Maricella.

Unfortunately, I didn't have as much time to spare examining the pair as I'd like. Around the corner of my eye, I spotted *another* two players closing in fast from the left.

Hells.

Perhaps the gnome had been right, perhaps I *should've* fled to the outskirts of the circle. But there was nothing like cutting off the head of the snake to demoralize the enemy. Sadly, though, I'd failed to accomplish what I'd set out to do, and now I was in a pretty predicament.

I definitely didn't want to trade blows with the Lightsworn elite while I had three other assailants bearing down on me. Which meant there was only one thing to do.

Whirling around, I raced away.

"Stop him!" Maricella yelled. "He's running!"

But I wasn't running, or not only. I was also drawing mana.

Your sentient shurikens have killed 6 players.
You have evaded 78 hostile attacks and sustained injuries from 16 other attacks.
Quick mend triggered! Your health has been restored to 87%.

I spent the next minute of the battle dodging players and projectiles, all while waiting for my mana to finish weaving the casting I prepared.

I was not entirely successful, of course, and I felt the bite of more than one blade and spell as I ran rings around the warriors in the imprisonment field. But with quick mend keeping me hale, I was no worse for wear by the time my spell was ready.

Coming to a momentary stop, I surveyed the battlefield. In a bid to intercept me, the warriors inside the fifty-yard circle had spread out. Their confidence had grown as I failed to kill more of their number. My shurikens, which had managed to score six kills early on, had since been neutralized.

The Lightsworn had adapted surprisingly fast to the psi constructs and had raised an array of defenses to protect themselves. But while I found the shurikens' ineffectiveness somewhat disappointing, it did not trouble me unduly. By keeping the enemy distracted, they still served a purpose.

More concerning was the lack of news from Decal.

The inquisitor Jobe hadn't shifted position once, and he remained as slack-jawed as ever, which I took to mean my simulacrum's assault on his dreamscape was ongoing. Still, I found it worrying that Decal hadn't managed to overrun the Lightsworn elite's defenses yet.

It doesn't matter that he hasn't, I told myself, firmly squashing my doubts. *As long as Jobe remains inactive, whatever Decal is doing is working.*

My gaze skipped to Maricella—the next biggest threat on the battlefield. She would be the epicenter of the magic I intended to unleash. I'd failed to kill her earlier, but this time around I was sure things would go differently.

Right, let's be about it.

Stepping into the aether, I shadow jumped.

You have teleported into Maricella's shadow.

Like before, the gnome sensed my arrival immediately. "Finally decided to stop running, eh?" she jeered as she spun around.

"I have," I replied equably. "But not for the reason you think." Not waiting for her response, I let Adriel's stolen tier six spell manifest.

You have cast noxious vapors.

Trails of black smoke spewed out of my mouth and, before the startled gnome could react, enveloped her in their dark embrace.

Maricella has failed a magical resistance check.

She is <u>rotting</u> (health decaying at 10% per second). Duration: 5 seconds. Note, each subsequent touch from the vapors will increase the duration of the spell's debuff.

The Lightsworn staggered back, sputtering furiously as she tried to expel the deadly toxin, but it was too late for that. Nor was Maricella the only one affected.

The black smoke had not stopped gushing from my mouth, and now it hung all around me, a dark cloud that enshrouded me and everyone else close by.

Tosh is <u>rotting</u>.
Zuriyla is <u>rotting</u>.
Gen'Tal is <u>rotting</u>.
...

Spells splashed down on me from afar—as the mages attempted to stop my casting. I didn't care, though. I was sure my void armor was equal to the task of dealing with them.

Weathering the magical storm, I kept channeling, letting the black cloud around me grow and grow.

✳   ✳   ✳

20 players have died from noxious vapors.

Maricella is near death. Second wind triggered. Debuffs removed. Her health has started regenerating at a rate of 1% per second (duration: 30 seconds).

Decal has killed Jobe. You are no longer <u>imprisoned</u> or <u>unmasked</u>.

Decal has returned to <u>guard</u> your dreamscape.

Yet again, the gnomish fighter managed to escape death.

But in the wake of the second piece of news, I paid her survival scant heed. Jobe was dead, and I was free to flee—not that I intended to do so anymore. The damage was already done, and if Muriel learned my identity, she would undoubtedly bear a grudge.

"That took you long enough," I murmured to Decal as I drew psi. Now that I could exit my cell, it was time to take the fight to the archers and spellcasters.

"Apologies," he replied. *"The inquisitor's mental defenses were quite elaborate."* A pause. *"Who do you wish me to target next?"*

"Elias," I replied without hesitation.

"On it."

Decal has cast astral project.

Almost the same instant the simulacrum left my mind, I disappeared from sight.

You have cast vanish. You are <u>invisible</u>. Duration: 5 minutes.

Multiple hostile entities have failed to detect you.

I smiled at the cries of consternation that rose from the watching mages and archers as they lost their target. *Now, I was ready.*

Drawing more psi, I skipped through the aether to my next target.

✳   ✳   ✳

Despite the demise of the warriors in the circle, there were still more than seventy-odd Lightsworn players alive. Their numbers counted for naught, though, especially with them not being able to stop me from dictating the terms of the rest of the encounter.

Moving unseen between my foes, I picked them off one by one using a combination of shatter, charm, backstab, and paralyze. And a mere fifteen minutes later, the battle was over.

All the Lightsworn were dead, or nearly all.

Two still remained. Tosh, the tier four rogue whom I had deliberately not killed, and Maricella, who, remarkably, was still clinging to life.

Sheathing my swords, I approached the pair. Tosh was silent and mute, paralyzed by slaysight, while Maricella writhed on the ground, coughing and sputtering. She'd ingested a significant quantity of noxious fumes, and despite her valiant efforts at recovery, still hovered at death's door.

I knelt beside the gnome. I admired her tenacity, and it almost made me want to give her a quick end, but there was too much at stake, and I could ill-afford to show her mercy.

"Decal," I whispered, *"can you keep the rogue incapacitated while I deal with the gnome?"*

"Certainly, Michael," he replied. *"I'll put him to sleep."* Not needing further instruction, the construct streamed out of my mind and into Tosh's dreamscape.

Decal has <u>slept</u> Tosh. Duration: infinite. The debuff will remain in effect as long as the source spell is being channeled.

Satisfied that I would get no trouble from the rogue's quarter, I turned back to the gnome and laid an arm on her shoulder. "Relax," I urged.

Drawn by the sound of my voice, Maricella's gaze snapped in my direction, but her eyes were too unfocused and pain-wracked to focus. "What—? Who are..."

"This will all be over soon," I murmured, and reaching inside me, awoke ancient memories.

You have cast enslave.

My blood came alive as the spell took shape, its glorious song filling my ears and Maricella's while it sought to bind us together in unshakeable ties. Midway through the blood casting, though, a Game alert dropped into my mind.

Hostile Mark detected.

Maricella is a follower of the Light Power, Muriel.
Attempting to override her Pact-bound allegiance...

...

...

The Game alert caught me by surprise, not because of what it had to say—I'd known already that Maricella was bound to Muriel—but because of what it implied.

If I was reading the Adjudicator's words correctly, sworn players were harder to blood-bind. That meant...

You have failed to sever Maricella's Pacts or disable them for the duration of the blood spell. Enslave failed. As a result, your target has suffered critical damage.
Maricella has died.

I rocked back on my heels, cursing softly, as my supposition proved correct. Pact-bound players *were* harder to bind. Not only that, on failure, it seemed enslave inflicted massive damage to its target.

Oh well, at least I—

I broke off as another Game message flashed through my mind.

You have passed a mental resistance check.
Your meddling has gone unnoticed by Muriel. She has not been alerted to your attempted subversion of her follower Pact with Maricella.

My lips twisted sourly. It appeared the stakes when it came to followers were even higher than I'd previously suspected. I'd half had it in mind to blood-bind Loken's envoy once I found her and to learn everything I could about the trickster that way.

I would *not* be attempting that now.

But speaking of Loken's envoy...

I now knew her name: Frey.

As undesired as the encounter with the Lightsworn had been, it had yielded that important nugget of information. She had to be the one of whom the three Lightsworn elites had spoken.

I'd learned other things too. Whether or not Shadow's forces were truly done in this sector, it seemed clear they'd incurred significant losses— enough so to perhaps weaken whatever trap Frey had planned for me. That was the hope, anyway.

It was also clear that approaching the Light or Dark factions under any sort of guise would not go down well. Both factions were already too wary of Frey's tricks not to rigorously examine any visitors. And while I was fairly confident my wolven heritage would pass close scrutiny, I was less certain about how the doppelganger spell would hold up.

My gaze slid to Tosh. But I had other possibilities when it came to subterfuge. And there was more I yet needed to know about the sector. Blood-binding the rogue could help with both of those things. He, I was certain, was *not* Muriel's follower, and there was no reason why I should fail at dominating him.

Only one way to find out, isn't there?

Awakening my blood again, I recast enslave.

* * *

You have successfully dominated Tosh, a level 196 human rogue. Duration: permanent until death.

Tosh is now tied to you by bonds of blood that are unbreakable as long as he lives. As your creature, Tosh is compelled to obey your every command, no matter how unreasonable or onerous. On death, the blood ties between you and him will be severed, restoring his autonomy and wiping his mind of all memories of his time under your spell.

Warning: you have cast enslave twice in one day and cannot recast it again today. The blood memory requires a full sleep cycle to recharge.

A wave of dizziness passed over me as the casting completed, and I almost fell atop the still-sleeping rogue. Catching myself, I rose shakily to my feet.

"Decal, release him," I instructed, projecting my voice into Tosh's mind.

"Done," the simulacrum replied, appearing in my own dreamscape a moment later.

Shifting impatiently, I waited for the enslaved rogue to wake up. It took him nearly a full minute to do so, and when he did, his eyes were predictably clouded with confusion.

"Get up," I ordered.

Tosh complied immediately, which I noted only increased his bewilderment.

"Your questions can wait for later," I said before he could speak. "Right now, I need you to loot the bodies."

The rogue's gaze drifted to the corpses littering the glade. "Why?"

"To recover their gear before more Lightsworn reinforcements show up," I replied, thinking he must still be confused. "I'm sure someone must have used their farspeaker bracelet to scream for help at some point."

Tosh nodded slowly. "Elias would have, I'm sure. But that's not why I asked my question."

I cocked my head to the side. "Why did you then?"

He shrugged. "Because their gear and—" he gestured to himself—"and my own is nearly worthless. This is a warzone, and standing orders from command are for only basic gear to be worn at all times."

I grimaced. "That's... disappointing." But the order made sense. In fact, it was one I myself was following. Why wear your best gear and risk losing it in some random ambush? "Alright, check their equipment anyway, but only collect whatever you deem valuable."

Not protesting further, Tosh turned about and did as I bade.

While he did so, I turned my own attention inward to the waiting Game alerts. Before we moved on, I had a few chores of my own to finish.

Chapter 606: Enthralled, Charmed, and Beguiled

You and Ghost have reached level 285!

I grimaced on reading the first message from the Adjudicator. I'd gained three levels from killing the Lightsworn, and while that might have sounded like a lot, it was not, not when you considered the odds I'd faced—one hundred foes, three of whom had been full elites.

I sighed.

It was the level discrepancy to blame, of course. I'd grown too powerful for ordinary players to overcome, even if I was not quite ready to face player-Powers yet. Soon, I expected, I would stop gaining levels from killing tier four—and perhaps even tier five—foes altogether.

How I would level consistently then was an open question. But that was a problem for another day. Dismissing the alert, I focused on the next Game message.

Your light armor has reached rank 19, your sneaking rank 25, your telepathy rank 24, your channeling rank 24, your elemental absorption rank 13, and your null force rank 10.

I grunted in satisfaction, feeling a bit better about the battle now. My skills, at least, had progressed nicely. Especially noteworthy were the advances to my void skills. I'd repelled more than a few spells during the battle—most of which I'd barely noticed at the time—and it had paid off.

If nothing else, I thought sourly, *fighting in the valley should at least see my magic resistances grow appreciably.*

Yet, it was not the improvements to my void skills that interested me the most. No, that honor went to my sneaking. It had finally reached tier six. Which meant both vanish and backstab were ready for upgrade.

Unfortunately, though, I didn't have enough Dexterity slots to advance one, much less both abilities.

Still, it made the decision of how to spend my new attribute points easier. Reaching out to the Adjudicator, I conveyed my decision.

Your Dexterity has increased to rank 148. Available ability slots: 7.

This reminds me...

I'd not improved either mass puppet or windborne before the encounter with the Lightsworn, thinking I would have enough time to do so before my next battle, but as it turned out, I hadn't.

It was time to rectify that error.

Reaching into my backpack, I retrieved two of the upgrade gems I'd retained for just this purpose. Closing my fist around the first, I willed my intent to the Adjudicator.

Ability gem activated.

Creating ability tome...

...

You have acquired a tier V windborne ability tome.

I sighed, disappointed by the lack of variants on offer. Still, I hardly had any reason to complain. Windborne had proved time and again to be an effective tool, and I expected its tier five version to be no different. Opening the newly acquired tome, I absorbed its contents.

You have upgraded your windborne ability to <u>windsurfer</u>. Some follow the ocean currents in pursuit of extraordinary waves to ride. Windsurfers do likewise and are often found roaming the skies in search of powerful thermals.
The fifth tier of this ability allows you to create a portable windslide. The ramp of air will manifest beneath your feet and is freely movable in any direction in the air. It will remain manifested for 30 seconds and is capable of propelling you through the air at 3x your normal movement speed. In the event that you enter a naturally occurring thermal, the timer on your windslide spell will reset and will not count down until you exit the thermal again.

Despite myself, I felt my eyes widening in shock.
I knew elite spells were significantly more powerful than lower-tiered ones, and as a result, I'd been expecting a big improvement in windborne's functionality. However, I'd not anticipated such a fundamental change in the spell's dynamics.
The new ability—windsurfer—would quite literally allow me to soar like a bird. I glanced upward at the wide-open sky. If I found a thermal, I could spend hours airborne. Better yet, with vanish, I could do so while hidden from the sight of those below.
Hells, if this isn't a powerful scouting tool, I don't know what is.
Still smiling, I picked up the next upgrade gem, eager now to find out what improving charm had in store for me.

Ability gem activated.
Creating ability tome...

...

Tome creation halted.
There are 2 elite variants available for the charm ability.

My grin broadened. Some options, finally! Almost rubbing my hand in glee, I waited to see the choices on offer.
More text scrolled through my sight.

Variant 1: <u>enthralling circle</u>. This variant modifies the base spell, transforming it from a targeted ability to a channeled aura that charms any hostile that approaches too closely.
Variant 2: <u>overpowered charm</u>. This variant increases the max permissible affected targets to 40 and the spell's duration to 1 minute.
Variant 3: <u>beguiling shield</u>. This variant modifies the base spell, transforming it into an activated piercing spell. While the shield is active,

hostiles who attack you directly will be beguiled (charmed but not controllable) for 3 seconds and will automatically attack other hostiles in the vicinity.

Choose your tier 5 charm ability tome now.

My excitement vanished. It was not that the options on offer were not good. Quite the opposite.

I wanted *all* three, or failing that, two at least. I bit my lip. How was I supposed to choose only one? But wishing things were otherwise would not make them so.

Sighing anew, I set myself to working through what was sure to be a difficult decision.

Enthralling circle sounded like it worked in a similar fashion to the cold sphere spell I'd stolen from the frost ent in Draven's Reach, making it a good counter against melee foes. The spell would prevent unshielded hostiles from attacking up close, thereby ensuring I couldn't be overwhelmed by numbers alone.

Definitely useful.

Overpowered charm was... just that, overpowered. It would function in exactly the same manner as my existing mass puppet spell, except it would influence twice as many targets and last twice as long. *Also useful.*

Beguiling shield was the most unusual variant, and on first glance, seemed the weakest option. A three-second charm that didn't give me direct control of my charmed victims? That didn't seem like a spell worth thirty attribute slots.

But then again... beguiling shield would work against any foe who attacked me, melee *or* ranged. And crucially, it was a piercing spell too. The first such that I would own—assuming I chose the ability, of course.

Like Farren's darkness bolt, beguile would penetrate my foes' own shields. And that meant even mages would not be safe from its touch. This made beguiling shield superior to rapture, and after a moment's further thought, I ruled out the first variant from consideration.

But, of course, there were downsides to beguiling shield, too. For one, the spell functioned in a more passive fashion than overpowered charm. If my foes refused to attack me directly, beguile would simply not work. And secondly, if I were dispelled, I would lose whatever protections the spell afforded me.

Still, overpowered charm was not perfect either. Mind shields were a simple, if effective, counter to charming, and in the past, had caused me no end of trouble.

Then, too, there was slaysight to consider.

It had not escaped my attention that the number of targets the Class ability affected had significantly increased since tier one. I expected it to do so again at the next upgrade, and eventually, I foresaw it becoming my primary crowd control ability. And in the end, the difference between paralyzing twenty targets and charming forty was not so great that I couldn't do without the latter.

And that meant...

Breathing in deeply, I reviewed my thinking one more time.

But I could find no fault with my reasoning. Exhaling, I reluctantly concluded my choice was the right one: it was time to let go of charm in favor of beguile. While I much rather have both overpowered charm and beguiling shield, if I were forced to choose, beguiling shield was the better option.

It was no easy decision, though.

Charm was the very first spell I'd learned in the Game, and sentimental considerations notwithstanding, I'd come to depend on it heavily. There was no denying that charm's usefulness had been waning, though—and would wane further as I pitted myself against more powerful foes, all of whom I could expect to have strong mind shields.

Beguiling shield is the right choice, I thought, and with another heartfelt sigh, willed my decision to the Game.

You have acquired a tier 5 beguiling shield ability tome.

You have upgraded your mass puppet ability to <u>beguiling shield</u>.

To most of the uninitiated, charming and beguilement are the same thing. They are not. Charmed subjects are leashed to their host and cannot act without orders from them. But, with beguilement, no connection is forged between the victim and host. Instead, the beguiled will retain their innate initiative and will act as they see fit to protect and aid their beguiler.

In other words, beguilement does not leash a subject's will; rather, it 'convinces' them to transfer their loyalty to the beguiler. As such, a beguiled spell's touch is generally subtler and more difficult to pinpoint than a charmed one. And this is why many beguilement spells are able to pierce a target's mental shields, whereas charms spells cannot.

Beguiling shield is an elite tier ability that will surround you in a psionic shield. However, the spell is not a shield in the conventional sense, and it will not repel your foes' attacks. Instead, it will trace any direct-targeted attacks made against you back to the source and will trigger-cast <u>beguile</u> against them. This ability is an activated spell that will last for 5 minutes or until the psi empowering it has been consumed. Its activation time is slow, it consumes psi, and it can be upgraded.

Note, beguile, itself, is a piercing spell that will bypass shields and magical wards of tier 4 and lower. It is as effective against hidden foes as it is against those in plain sight. In the event that a target fails to resist its effects, they will become <u>beguiled</u> for 3 seconds.

You have 4 of 220 Mind ability slots remaining.

Your simulacrum's accessible telepathic abilities have been altered.
Decal can now cast <u>beguile</u>.
Decal can no longer cast <u>charm</u>.

I rocked back on my heels, reading and re-reading the avalanche of information the Adjudicator had just dumped on me, but there was nothing untoward in what the Game had to say.

Beguile functioned exactly as I expected, and any non-elite who attacked me while it was active was in for a nasty shock. I surveyed the battlefield anew. Dealing with a player-company like the one I'd just defeated had just become child's play.

Nodding in grim satisfaction, I beckoned Tosh to join me. The rogue appeared to have finished his looting and was waiting for me. "Let's go," I said.

"Where to?" he asked complacently.

"West," I replied. "And along the way, you can fill me in on everything you know about the war and how things stand in this sector."

Tosh had a lot to say.

Some of what he had to share was no more than I expected, the rest, though... the rest, I found fascinating.

It turned out that neither Maricella, Elias, nor Jobe was Sworn, despite all three being elites. They were followers only—their Marks were proof enough of that—which explained why I'd received no alerts from the Adjudicator informing me of Muriel's ire when they had died.

What Tosh had to say about Muriel was interesting, too. She appeared to be a significant player in the Game, and was at least a major Power, if not a supreme one—Tosh wasn't too clear on that point. It also explained, I supposed, why the three elites were mere followers and not Sworn. A Power of Muriel's caliber no doubt commanded dozens, if not hundreds, of elite players.

Jobe himself was an inquisitor, and his magic worked especially well against those aligned with the opposing Forces of Dark and Shadow. It was how he'd unmasked me in the first place.

I'd thought I was being clever by forging my Marks and imprinting a Mark of Greater Shadow on my spirit signature, but according to Tosh, that was why I'd been revealed. No minion of Shadow or Dark could hide from the inquisitor's gaze.

That in itself was another interesting tidbit of information and further validated what I knew of the doppelganger ability. It proved— conclusively—that Marks forged through it were more than skin-deep, and hostile spells would react to them as if they were real.

Tosh went on to confirm the name of Loken's envoy. It was Frey, and like the three elites had said, rumors of her death were unverified. Tosh suspected she was still alive, as apparently did many Light players. In search of the truth, the Lightsworn commanders had sent more than one scouting expedition to the wyvern caves in the west, but what they had discovered, Tosh didn't know.

The disposition of the armies in the sector was another curiosity. Before this, I would have bet on Dark winning the war, but by all accounts, they were losing—and decisively, too.

Despite all the marital strength commanded by the Tartan Legions, despite the Awakened Dead being entrenched in the adjoining dungeon, and despite Tartar and Ishita's people both arriving in sector 12,560 before Muriel's, they were losing.

And the primary reason for that was numbers.

Muriel had brought a host many times larger than the combined forces of Loken, Tartar, and the Awakened Dead. Now, her forces controlled the southern, eastern, and central regions of the valley. It was only over the western mountains—with the wyvern caves—and the northern ranges— where the dungeon entrance was located—that she did not hold sway.

The goblin tribes in the sector had been wiped out. Every other non-player force and minor faction had met the same fate. Now, only Muriel, Tartar, the Awakened Dead, and Loken contested the sector—and whether the trickster was still in a position to do so was questionable.

In fact, Muriel's hold over the sector was so complete that she could claim the safe zone tomorrow if she wanted to. There was no one and nothing in the sector that could stop her from doing so.

But the same could not be said for forces *outside* of the sector.

Which was the primary reason Muriel had not moved to claim the sector just yet.

The Light Power was wary of a trap—either of Tartar's making or Loken's. If she repositioned her armies around the safe zone, she feared coming under a two-pronged assault launched from outside the safe zone by the existing forces in the sector, and from within by a newly arrived army from elsewhere.

Certainly, Tartar and Loken were both powerful enough that if they so desired, they could field an army larger than the one Muriel already commanded in the sector. The Light Power knew this as well as anyone, which was why she was refusing to take the bait—if bait it was—and move prematurely against the safe zone.

Her plan—as far as a lowly player like Tosh understood it, anyway—was to ignore the safe zone until such time as she had full control over the sector.

And that was not proving easy.

Muriel's numbers counted for little in the twisting, narrow tunnels which had formerly been home to the wyvern Besina, and which now, presumably, was the refuge of Shadow.

The situation in the north was likewise complicated. While the Awakened Dead were a comparatively minor faction, they had an unassailable sector—Erebus' dungeon—at their backs to continually draw on for resources and manpower. And if that wasn't enough, their fortifications around the dungeon nether portal had been recently reinforced by the Tartans.

Something I'd never imagined happening.

But it seemed that the mixed force of Awakened Dead and Tartans I'd observed fleeing earlier was not an aberration as I'd hoped. Instead, they were a true reflection of the shifting alliances in the sector.

"And you're *certain* Tartar has permanently allied himself with Erebus?" I asked Tosh for the second time. "It's not just a temporary joining of convenience?"

"I am," he replied. "Or at least Muriel's Sworn are. They have told us so repeatedly."

I pursed my lips. That was the problem with questioning a rank-and-file soldier. No matter how convinced I was of Tosh's honesty, I couldn't be sure what he was being told was the truth—and not just a self-serving version of it.

But try as I might, I could see no reason for Muriel to lie to her own people about this. "Have you seen any evidence of—"

I broke off at a distant howl from the north.

Flicking up my hand, I signaled Tosh to halt. The two of us were traversing the forest by treetop. It was safer than traveling across the forest floor, and the Lightsworn rogue was agile enough to manage the feat. Still and quiet, I listened intently.

The howl was not repeated.

Nor did my mindsight pick out any gathering of players—small or large—in the vicinity. The howl was just a howl, an ordinary forest sound. Judging it safe to continue, I gestured Tosh onward, and we resumed our journey west.

"Why would Tartar bind himself to Erebus through a Pact?" I murmured, more to myself than Tosh. That was what he had supposedly done, according to the rogue.

"The Awakened Dead must have offered something too valuable to refuse in exchange," Tosh replied, thinking the question was directed at him.

"And what might that be?" I muttered, not expecting an answer this time either.

The spectrum of possibilities was too vast to speculate on. The real question, though, was what did a Power who'd been around for millennia need so badly that he was willing to tie himself to a faction he reviled to get?

"Some sort of chalice," Tosh replied matter-of-factly.

I stopped dead. "A chalice?" I repeated, turning around fully to stare at the rogue across the tree branch we strode. "You didn't mention a chalice before."

He shrugged. "You didn't ask."

I closed my eyes for a second, striving for patience. It was not Tosh's fault, not exactly. He was not an ally in truth but had been forced into the role, and that, unfortunately, came with some downsides. While I might easily compel him to answer my questions, getting Tosh to volunteer potentially useful information was not as straightforward.

"Tell me about the chalice," I ordered.

The rogue shrugged again. "I don't know much about it except that the Awakened Dead have it, it's been promised to Tartar, and Muriel wants it. We've been told to keep an eye out for the thing or any couriers that may be carrying it."

"Muriel thinks the chalice is here? In this sector?"

"Yes."

I frowned. "Assuming this chalice *is* the reason Tartar lowered himself to dealing with the Awakened Dead, why would Erebus bring it here? To a warzone of all places."

"I don't know."

"Of course, you don't," I muttered.

Tosh opened his mouth to reply, but I waved aside his burgeoning protest before he could get the words out. "Describe the chalice to me."

"It's small, made of blood red crystals, and supposedly deadly to the touch."

My frown deepened. I'd not been sure at first—the coincidence seemed a bit too fantastical—but now I had to wonder if the chalice Tosh spoke of was not the same one Loken wanted me to steal from the Power Paya. Certainly, the rogue's descriptions seemed consistent with the one I'd received from Morin all those months ago when Loken had first tasked me with retrieving the artifact.

"What do you mean by 'deadly to the touch'?" I asked softly.

"Just that. We were given strict orders not to attempt handling the chalice. Word amongst the rank and file is that the enchantments protecting the artifact are strong enough to kill at a touch."

This, too, tallied with information I had on Loken's chalice. The trickster had called it a Force artifact, and according to him, no Lightsworn or Shadowsworn could hold it. "So what were you supposed to do with the chalice after finding it?"

"Summon Muriel's Sworn immediately." Pulling out a small device from his pocket, Tosh held it up. "With this. I took it from Jobe's body."

I glanced at the object in his hand. It looked like one of the remote triggers I used with my traps and had a small stud on the top. Reaching out with my will, I called up the device's Game data.

The target is a: <u>stone of calling</u>. It is a rank 4 item that, on activation, alerts the linked caster and allows them to scry your location. It requires a minimum Magic of 16 to use.

I held out my arm. "I'll take that."

Obligingly, Tosh handed the item over.

"Thank you," I murmured, stowing it away. "Now tell me, what does the chalice do?"

"No idea."

I grunted, annoyed if unsurprised, by his ignorance. I'd been tasked to steal the thing and still knew damnably little about it. "Were you given any other information?"

Tosh shook his head.

That, too, was not unexpected. Sighing, I sank down to straddle the branch and rested my head against the tree's trunk while I considered what I'd just learned.

The chalice Tosh spoke of and the chalice I'd been tasked to retrieve had to be one and the same—which made it leverage. Loken wanted it. Tartar did too. And now it appeared Muriel had an interest in the thing as well.

If *I* got my hands on it...

Opening my eyes, I stared at the rogue who was watching me with undisguised curiosity. "Have you heard of a Power called Paya?" I asked.

Tosh's brows crinkled, puzzled by the apparent non-sequitur. "Yes, she's one of the Powers in the Awakened Dead faction, isn't she?"

"That's right. What do you know about her?"

"Uhm..." He scratched his head. "Not much. She arrived in the sector about six weeks ago, but according to the scouts' reports I remember seeing, she doesn't command a significant force."

So, Paya was in the sector as well. That stood to reason if the chalice was here. But wait... My eyes narrowed as something else Tosh had said caught my attention.

"You said Paya arrived six weeks ago," I said slowly. "Are you sure about that?"

"Six weeks or thereabouts," he temporized. "I couldn't tell you the precise day if that's what you're asking."

I waved away his qualification. "I don't need the exact date. When did the hostilities resume between the Dark and Light?"

Tosh stared at me.

Seeing his blank look, I rephrased, "I mean, when did the war begin in earnest?"

"Oh. Also, six weeks ago."

"Final question: when did Tartar ally himself with the Awakened Dead?"

"I can't say for certain, but it was announced shortly after the war began." He paused. "You see some significance to all of this?"

"Yes, I do," I whispered. Bowing my head, I reviewed the timeline.

Erebus buys Tartar's alliance with the chalice. They agree to do the exchange in sector 12,560. Paya arrives with the artifact. Muriel gets wind of the alliance and, fearful of what it may portend, attacks. After which, the alliance is announced to the troops.

I frowned. The chronology... fit. As far as Tosh's tale went, anyway, but there were more pieces to this puzzle.

Roughly five weeks ago, in a move that smacked of desperation, was *also* when Frey had abducted Saya. Initially, I'd thought it was the war that had caused Loken's envoy to act so, but now I had cause to rethink.

Why get me involved?

Realistically speaking, there was little I could do to stop a war between foes as powerful as Tartar and Muriel. And in hindsight, I realized I should have figured that out sooner.

It wasn't the war that had pushed Frey to act.

It was the chalice.

The very same chalice that Loken appeared intent on keeping out of the Dark's hands. What would the trickster do if he learned it was being given over to a Power as strong as Tartar?

Answer: whatever it took to prevent it from happening.

Up to and including kidnapping Saya.

I exhaled heavily as the implications sank in. I'd come into the valley, assuming that whatever was going on, Loken was not involved. Indeed, I'd been working on the principle that neither the trickster nor his envoy would do anything overly rash because they still needed me to steal the chalice.

But if the chalice was already in play... all bets were off.

Isn't that just peachy, I thought blackly as I realized my relatively simple plan to infiltrate Frey's base, find Saya, and get out was no longer viable.

Now, I had to assume Loken himself was present in said base. And if that was true, there was no way I was going to penetrate it undetected.

Damn. Damn and damn. What in hells do I do now?

Not get ahead of yourself for one. Breathing in deeply, I set aside my worries for the future and, returning to my timeline, reordered the sequence into something that made more sense.

One: Paya arrives in the sector with the chalice.

Why would she do that? Well, perhaps the Awakened Dead had finally learned how to make use of it and were intending on employing it against their enemies.

Two: Muriel's people find out about the artifact and attack.

Three: Staring annihilation in the face, the Awakened Dead turn to Tartar for help, promising him the chalice in exchange.

Four: The Dark Powers strike an alliance.

Five: Learning that the chalice is about to fall in Tartar's hands, Frey gets desperate and tries to force me to act.

I nodded slowly. The new chronology fitted events even better and made clear what the key to the puzzle was: the chalice.

Obviously, I would have to get my hands on it.

And before Loken, Tartar, or Muriel could do so. Then I would have all the leverage I needed to secure Saya's release.

I opened my eyes. I knew what I needed to do now.

I had to steal the chalice, that was certain.

But how I went about it... that bit was far from clear. And before I jumped down another rabbit hole, I knew I had to speak to Ceruvax.

He was the only one of my allies who had intimated knowing something about the thing. When we'd first discussed the mysterious artifact in Draven's Reach, the old wolf had refused to share what he knew. I smiled grimly. But I was sure once he heard Tosh's tale, he would see things differently.

Closing my eyes, I reached out through my farspeaker bracelet to the Roost. *"Old Wolf?"* I called, deliberately not using Ceruvax's actual name. The chances that someone was listening in were slim to none, but why take the chance?

"He hasn't arrived yet, Michael," Shael replied over the same communication link. A pause. *"And won't for another two days."*

"Damn," I muttered softly. I'd known that, of course, but caught up in the latest developments, the now-inconvenient timing of Ceruvax's arrival had slipped my mind. Thinking quickly, I came to a decision. *"One of you will have to carry a message back to him."*

"We can do that," the bard assured me. *"Has something happened?"*

"Yes, something has," I replied bluntly. *"But I don't want to get into it over the farspeaker bracelet. We'll talk more when I return to the Roost."*

"Understood," Shael replied.

"I'll take the message," Mariam offered.

"Thank you," I murmured. *"Tell the Old Wolf to forget the experiments with the nagas. I want him here as soon as he is done with the twins."* I hesitated, then added. *"It's urgent."*

"Got it," the forsworn replied. *"Leaving now."* A moment later, I sensed her exit the farspeaker link. No doubt, she'd already teleported back to Sanctum.

"We have some news of our own to share," Llewyn added before I could disconnect myself.

"What news?" I asked in surprise.

"The village has gotten busy since your departure," Shael reported. *"Your doing, I suppose?"*

I thought of the soldiers who'd planned on taking shelter in the safe zone. The bard had to mean them. *"Not really. The visitors you're referring to... are they, by any chance, a company of twenty Dark players?"*

"Twenty?" Deryn repeated dubiously. *"They sounded like a lot more than that."*

"They did," Shael agreed. *"And still do. We can hear them in the streets, but we haven't left the Roost to investigate."*

"And you shouldn't," I said, drumming my fingers along my thigh as I thought. *"How many players do you reckon there are?"*

"A hundred maybe?" Deryn suggested.

"More," Shael contradicted. *"They're searching the safe zone, one building at a time, but, of course, they can't enter any building they don't own, so we should be fine."*

Urgh. The only conclusion that I could reach from Shael's report was that Muriel's people had sent reinforcements. And by the sounds of it, they'd already traced the fleeing Dark soldiers to their refuge and were combing the safe zone for them.

Did I also have hunters on my trail?

My face tightened in grim realization. If I was not already being pursued, I was sure I would be once Maricella, Jobe, and the others from the defeated Light company revived in the safe zone.

I had two options, then.

One, portal back to the Roost, and out of harm's way, to wait out Ceruvax's arrival there. But even after receiving my message, the old wolf would not be able to leave Sanctum immediately. The twins' awakening would keep him busy for the rest of the day, and the earliest I could expect him to arrive was tonight.

But I saw no reason to waste an entire day doing nothing.

That left option two: continuing my exploration of the sector. Heading west to the wyvern caves no longer made sense, though. I couldn't risk getting entangled with Loken or his envoy until I'd spoken to Ceruvax. That left venturing farther north, traveling beyond the Lightsworn's fortified line of camps until I reached the Dark stronghold at the dungeon portal.

If Paya and the chalice were anywhere in this sector, it would be there. And while I had no intention of actually trying to steal the thing until I heard what Ceruvax had to say, there was no reason not to scout out the terrain first.

Opening my eyes, I let my gaze settle on Tosh. "Tell me everything you know about the defenses the Dark have erected around their base. And while you're at it, describe the Light's fortifications too."

✻   ✻   ✻

Tosh spoke at length. And not all of what he had to share was common knowledge. The blood-bound player was a rogue, and like most rogues, had a knack for ferreting out secrets—especially the secrets of places you might want to break in or out of.

After digesting everything he had to say about the Lightsworn and Darksworn's defenses, only one word came to mind when describing them: formidable. The spells protecting the Forcesworn's camps were far beyond anything I'd seen in even the Devil Rider's castle in the Eastern Marches.

Thankfully, though, they were not on par with Nexus' defenses.

Because while it appeared that Paya and a few other minor Powers were present in the sector, neither Muriel nor Tartar themselves were in attendance. That would have been a significant escalation in hostilities that neither side wanted at this stage. Practically, all this meant was that, at worst, I'd be facing tier eight wards.

And bypassing such wards was... doable. Attempting to do so would not be easy, and not without risk, but still doable.

Rising to my feet, I oriented myself northward. "Let's go," I ordered Tosh.

The rogue followed willingly enough, but the change in direction did not escape him. "I thought we were heading west?"

"Not anymore, we're not," I replied. "Now, we're heading north."

"Why?" he asked curiously.

"I want to see the Dark's stronghold with my own eyes."

Tosh stopped. "We'll never make it. The whole region is crawling with Light soldiers and scouts."

Smiling, I glanced over my shoulder at him. "That's what I have you for."

"Why don't we use a portal?" Tosh persisted.

I shook my head. "You know why."

Since sector 12,560 was still unclaimed, there was nothing stopping me from creating a portal to somewhere farther north than I'd already been to—like, for instance, the former camp of the Red Rats.

But doing so would neither be wise nor safe.

Players had ways of detecting a portal's opening. Not only that, they could also ward an area, stopping anyone from portaling into or out of it—just like the Riders had done in the Eastern Marches. And a war such as the one being fought in sector 12,560 was as much about warding and counter-warding to restrict the enemy's movements as it was about numbers.

All that meant, as time-consuming as it was, traveling on foot was the safest way to traverse the sector.

The rogue grunted, unimpressed by my response. "Using a portal will be safer than trying to sneak through the Light's lines wearing a Shadow Mark. Jobe isn't Muriel's only inquisitor, you know."

"A good point," I murmured. I'd been planning on changing my disguise later, when we got closer to our destination, but perhaps it was better to see to it now. Closing my eyes, I began casting.

You have transformed your form into that of Flynn, a level 212 human windwalker. You have changed your spirit signature to bear a Mark of Greater Light. Duration: infinite.

"Better?" I asked when I was done.

Tosh eyed my new skin warily. "How'd you do that?"

"Irrelevant," I replied easily. "The more important question is: will my disguise withstand scrutiny by the Lightsworn?"

The rogue frowned. "I assume that, however you did that, you used a spell?"

I nodded.

"Then the casting likely won't survive passage through the wards surrounding the camps. But... " He pursed his lips in thought. "It *should* be good enough to get us past any patrols we encounter."

"Excellent. And you have all the right passcodes for those, right?"

Tosh nodded, hesitated fractionally, then added, "But you do realize that sooner or later someone is going to realize my body is missing from the mess you left back in that glade?"

I cocked my head to the side. "Why should they? As you said, I left things a bloody mess. Perhaps your disappearance will go unnoticed."

The rogue shook his head grimly. "It won't."

I didn't question his conviction a second time. "Alright, how long do you think we have until your people realize you're missing?"

"I'll give it sixteen hours at most. By then, Elias would have resurrected, and the first thing he'll do is take stock of his command."

"Hmm. And what will Elias do then?"

"Report it up the chain," Tosh replied immediately. "After which, all the passcodes will be changed, and a sector-wide alert will be issued for my capture and questioning."

I grimaced. For Tosh to be so certain of Elias' reaction could only mean it was established procedure. And that meant... "I take it this happened before?"

"More than once," Tosh answered unhappily, "which is why command is so pedantic about locating missing soldiers. They don't want a repeat of previous... episodes."

"Well, then, I guess we're on the clock then." Thinking for a moment, I estimated how much time had passed since the battle with the Lightsworn.

It can't have been more than three hours ago.

That left us thirteen hours. Thirteen hours in which we had to pierce the Light cordon in the sector and reach the Dark stronghold at the valley's northern rim. *Very doable,* I thought.

Assuming we didn't run into any problems, of course.

Swinging about again, I jumped lightly onto the adjacent tree. "Let's go," I called to Tosh. "Time's a-wastin."

✳ ✳ ✳

The journey north began pleasantly enough.

With the Lightsworn rogue following close on my heels, we dashed from tree to tree, never alighting on the forest floor, and passed unnoticed by the surrounding wildlife. The Light patrols were similarly unenlightened as to our passage.

Using Tosh's knowledge of their routes—and my own mindsight when the rogue's knowledge fell short—I deftly wove a path through the roving squad of players. And for the first few hours, that was easy enough to do.

But as the day waned and afternoon approached, things changed.

In the intervening time, the Lightsworn patrols had thickened considerably, forcing Tosh and me to slow our advance to a crawl to avoid detection.

Multiple hostile entities have failed to detect you.

Multiple hostile entities have failed to detect you.

...

...

"It would be better to proceed openly from here on," Tosh said quietly.

I nodded grimly. No doubt, the rogue was receiving the same notices I was. And if the Game alerts and the increased patrols were anything to go by, we were approaching the Lightsworn camps.

The so-called Cordon of Light.

Muriel's people had not squandered the advantage their numbers had given them. They'd started their campaign in the sector by erecting a series of camps that stretched the breadth of the valley—from the western mountain range to the eastern one—and as they had pushed the Darksworn farther north, they had tightened their cordon, keeping the Dark players boxed in.

Now, the cordon was a series of ten heavily fortified camps arranged in a half circle around the Awakened Dead's dungeon portal. And the area between them was thick with patrols.

It was not the patrols that had spurred Tosh's comment, though.

I was confident my own stealth—and his too, perhaps—was good enough to avoid physical detection. We could sneak past the patrols if we had to. However, it was not just the patrols we had to worry about. According to Tosh, detection wards were strung across the entire stretch of open forest separating the camps. And how we would fare against them... was another matter entirely.

Time to find out what we're up against.

Raising my right hand, I rubbed it across the side of my helm and looked upon the forest with new eyes.

You have activated a sorcerer's coif.
You have detected multiple hostile spells!

Luminous lines of magic exploded into sight. They stretched from east to west, crisscrossing the area ahead in a crazy pattern that would make evasion difficult, if not impossible. Narrowing my gaze, I studied some of the individual spell weaves.

The target is the tier 6 ward spell: <u>the all-seeing eye of Light</u>.
The target is the tier 5 ward spell: <u>entangling vine</u>.
The target is the tier 6 ward spell: <u>inverted life sense</u>.

I sighed. Tosh had been wrong, I realized. *Or at least not wholly right.* The Cordon of Light was awash with more wards than the rogue knew about. The ones I could see were bad enough, but how many more were there that were beyond the ability of the sorcerer's coif to unmask?

The helm only revealed wards up to tier six, after all. But with Powers at play in the sector, I couldn't discount the possibility of even higher tiered wards covering the region.

The question now, though, was what to do.

Proceed or retreat.

Which was the wiser course?

In the end, I decided to advance.

It was a risk, yes, but I had Tosh and his passcodes, and at best, they would only be valid for another eight hours. Once the Lightsworn changed them, there was no guarantee I would be able to blood-bind another Tosh or even have the time to do so.

No, now was likely my best—and perhaps only—opportunity to investigate the Dark encampment. There was no point wasting it.

"You're right," I replied in belated response to Tosh's earlier question. "The time for hiding is done." Swinging off the branch, I dropped lightly onto the ground and let the shadows wrapped around me unravel.

You are no longer hidden.

Tosh followed suit, and a moment later, the pair of us stood in plain sight on the forest floor.

"You know the plan," I told him softly. "Lead the way."

Wordlessly, the rogue brushed past me, striding north. Following on his heels, I did my best to appear nonchalant. It would not be long now before—

"Halt!"

Tosh and I stilled as a Lightsworn patrol, ten strong, emerged from the underbrush to the west. Moving with practiced ease, they enveloped us in a half-circle. Tosh and I stayed motionless, doing nothing to deter them. Stepping forward, and with his hand resting casually on the pommel of his sword, the sergeant in charge eyed us carefully.

But there was nothing about our appearance to warrant suspicion. Like Tosh, I was dressed in white garments—one of the rogue's spare uniforms—and with my Marks altered, I was just another Lightsworn. Truly, there was no reason for the sergeant to be concerned.

No reason at all.

Keep telling yourself that, I told myself as the seconds ticked by and the patrol's silent regard continued unabated.

"State your names, ranks, and camp of origin," the sergeant barked finally.

I didn't shift nor show any outward sign, but internally I felt my tension dissipate. My disguise had just passed its first test.

"Tosh and Flynn," my companion replied, speaking up for both of us as we agreed he would earlier. "We're senior scouts from Camp Kappa."

Which was true enough, as far as it applied to the enslaved rogue, anyway.

"And today's passcodes?" the sergeant demanded, his demeanor still unbending.

Tosh rattled off a series of meaningless phrases and numbers.

I could tell immediately he'd gotten them right, as the sergeant's stance eased. "Right you are," he said affably. "So, what are you fellows doing out here all alone?"

Tosh shrugged. "Scouting. We've just come from down south."

There was nothing unusual about scouts travelling alone or in pairs, and the rogue's response should pass unremarked—which it did.

"Huh," the sergeant grunted. "Why are you this far west then? You're nowhere near Kappa."

"Oh, we're not headed back to camp yet," Tosh replied easily. "The mission's not over." He gestured vaguely northward. "After the stunt the Darksworn pulled last night, the higher-ups want answers. They want to know how the bastards got as far as they did."

The sergeant's head swung from south to north. "You're retracing their steps?" he guessed.

Tosh nodded. "That's right."

The Darksworn that both the sergeant and the rogue were alluding to was the same group I'd run across this morning. According to Tosh, they had been attempting to sneak into one of the Light camps and had slipped past multiple defensive layers before eventually being detected. They were not the first Darksworn company to try a stealth attack, nor were they likely to be the last, but Muriel's people insisted on investigating every attempted 'incursion.'

The sergeant's gaze flickered to me. "What about you? Nothing to add?"

"Nope," I replied lazily, not bothering to expand.

The sergeant frowned.

Tosh edged closer to the Lightsworn officer. "He's a specialist," he explained in a voice too low for the rest of the squad to overhear. "A sniffer. Don't irk him. Command doesn't want the Dark to get wind of what he can do, but it's quite something, let me tell you."

Nodding sagely, the sergeant stepped back. "Alright, I think we've delayed you lads long enough. Off you go."

Inclining our heads in thanks, Tosh and I slipped past the patrol as they parted to let us through.

We were on our way.

✳ ✳ ✳

Tosh and I were stopped thrice more.

Each encounter went roughly the same way as the first, and we passed unhindered every time. The wards, too, did not unduly trouble us despite my earlier concerns.

Perhaps the cordon was absent of any tier seven wards, or perhaps my doppelganger disguise was proof enough against them. Or perhaps the wards were only designed to stop anyone sneaking past the patrols. Whatever the case, we made it through the Cordon of Light unimpeded.

"We've made it," Tosh pronounced, coming to a stop about a mile out from the cordon, and well out of range of its patrols. "So, what now?"

Not answering immediately, I glanced over the rogue's shoulder at the northern mountain range peeking over the treetops. It was about another mile to their lower slopes, and soon, I expected we'd run into more patrols.

Those, though, would be crewed by Darksworn.

My gaze flickered back to Tosh. "Have you been this way before?"

He nodded. "A few times."

"And have you been to the Dark's base?"

"Only once."

I cocked my head to the side. "How far did you get?"

"Not very close," he admitted. "I reached the foot of the mountain but had to withdraw thereafter. There were no trees to provide cover, and the place was thick with spells."

I nodded slowly. "I want you to try again."

Tosh frowned. "You want me to scout the Dark's base, you mean?"

"Yes."

"How far do you want me to go?"

"All the way."

The rogue blinked. "I'll never make it."

I nodded gravely. "I know. But I want you to try nevertheless."

Tosh stared at me blankly. I'd just issued him a death sentence, one he was powerless to refute.

The sad truth was that I couldn't afford to let the rogue live.

Sooner or later, Elias and Jobe would figure out Tosh was missing, and then the Lightsworn would try tracking him in earnest. I couldn't let them take him alive, not while he was still enslaved and retained all his memories of me. I *could* always release the rogue from his blood-binding—wiping his memories in the process—but I knew if I did that, his first instinct would be to attack me.

That left only one other option: killing the rogue.

And if I was going to do that, I wanted to at least make sure his death was a useful one.

"Alright," Tosh said placidly. "When do I start?"

"Now."

✷   ✷   ✷

You have transformed your form into that of Raster, a level 203 human stalker. You have changed your spirit signature to bear a Mark of Greater Dark. Duration: infinite.

You have cast vanish. You are <u>invisible</u>. Duration: 5 minutes.

Tosh is hidden.

Cloaked in shadow, the Lightsworn rogue crept northward while I followed silently in his wake.

A Darksworn patrol appeared from the east.

Tosh froze. I did too.

Multiple hostile entities have failed to detect you.

Motionless, and from vantage points separated by a few dozen yards, we observed the newcomers. The Dark squad was twice as large as one of the Lightsworn patrols. We had scarce time to study them further, though.

Rushing swiftly through the forest, the players vanished from sight after a mere few seconds.

My brows crinkled.

I was no expert on patrols, but I would not term what the passing squad was doing as 'patrolling.' They had not even paused to scan the surroundings!

Tosh inched forward again. His patient shadow, I followed silently along.

A second patrol emerged from the west.

This one was as large as the previous one and moved with more caution than their predecessors—far more caution, actually. Their eyes darting furtively from tree to tree, the players huddled together as if fearful of attack.

I frowned.

The Darksworn exuded none of the confidence the Light players did—which was to be expected from a faction beset and besieged. Still, their demeanor appeared a trifle *too* scared.

The squad disappeared into the foliage on our right, cutting short my musings.

Tosh resumed moving. As did I.

A few minutes later, another patrol crossed our paths.

And they, too, seemed ill at ease. This squad was composed entirely of tartans and had the raging bull of Tartar displayed prominently on their shoulder patches. Yet, the players in question displayed little of the discipline I'd come to associate with the legion.

Their formation was ragged, their faces were unkempt, and worse yet, their gear appeared poorly tended.

My frown deepened. Three Dark squads. And all three in some state of disarray. It could not be coincidence.

It almost was as if the Darksworn's morale had been shattered. They seemed to believe death lurked around every corner and appeared ready to break at the slightest provocation. But from what Tosh had told me, the Lightsworn *weren't* on the cusp of victory.

So, what did the Dark players know that I didn't?

I was no closer to the answer, though, when the patrol passed and Tosh started up again.

Absently, I resumed my own steps. But my mind was less on the surroundings now, and more on what I would find farther north at the Darksworn encampment.

Somehow, I didn't think it would be anything like what I expected.

✳ ✳ ✳

An hour later, Tosh and I reached the treeline.

The valley's northern mountain range stretched before us, its tall peaks and rocky slopes in resplendent display under the afternoon sun.

I paid little heed to the scenery, though. Instead, my gaze fixed on the aberration midway on the mountainside—the Dark encampment. A haze surrounded it, a haze created by the multitude of spells layered around the region, and which made it hard to pick out any details.

The Dark encampment still stood, I could tell that much. And despite the ragged appearance of the patrols we'd run across, there was nothing to suggest the Darksworn base was in a state of disrepair.

Quite the contrary, in fact.

The defenses the Awakened Dead and Tartans had erected around the nether portal were the most formidable I'd yet seen in the Game. Getting in seemed an impossibility.

Tosh crept forward.

My gaze darted in the rogue's direction. I didn't try to stop him, but nor did I follow in his wake again. Nestled in the branches of an oak, I watched intently as Tosh inched out of the forest and onto the naked slopes of the mountain.

There were no patrols in sight, but that didn't mean there weren't any hiding close by beneath a ward.

Tosh advanced one step. Two. Five. Ten. He passed through the first ward I spotted, then the second, and still no alarm triggered.

Multiple hostile entities have failed to detect your blood-bound minion.

Pursing my lips, I whistled in silent appreciation of the rogue's skill. *Perhaps I've misjudged him. Perhaps he'll—*

An implosion ward has triggered.
Your blood-bound minion has failed a magical resistance check.

With no warning and no fanfare, the rogue crumpled, his bones caving in and his skin shrinking into nothingness in a matter of mere seconds.

Tosh has died.

Chapter 610: A Tricky Task

I closed my eyes, feeling the aching sting of bitterness in my mouth as I stared at the glistening pool of blood that was all that remained of Tosh.

That could've been me, I thought unhappily. I hadn't even sensed the ward that had killed the rogue. This fact, coupled with the quickness of his death, meant only one thing.

The ward had been tier seven. Or higher.

Conclusive proof that there were Powers in the Dark encampment. *I wonder which—*

Movement on the mountainside.

Breaking off from my musings, I watched a thin column of players rush down from the Dark encampment. Marching swiftly and with purpose, the hundred-strong tartan company drew to a halt around Tosh's remains.

That was fast, I thought. The players in view were nothing like the bedraggled Dark soldiers I'd observed earlier. Their uniforms were crisp, their armor gleamed in the sun, and their eyes were hard and keen.

A figure separated itself from the rest. The man in question was grim-faced, had close-cropped hair, and a trim beard. He was dressed in full plate mail that had seen better days but nevertheless still sparkled in the sun. I recognized him, of course.

It was Captain Talon. A split second later, the Game confirmed this, feeding me his analyze data.

The target is Talon, a level 295 human sentinel. He bears a Mark of Supreme Dark and a Mark of Tartar.

Talon jerked upright, his head, previously bent downward to study the pooling blood, whipping around to scan the trees.

For all that I was invisible, I held myself rigidly still. I'd not forgotten the shrewd captain, nor his uncanny perceptiveness. He'd either felt my analyze or sensed something else amiss.

"Captain?" a lieutenant called softly. "Is something wrong?"

"I thought I..." Talon shook his head slowly. "Never mind, I was mistaken." Turning back to the remains, he kneeled beside it, showing no sign of squeamishness. "What do we have here?"

The lieutenant—a player by the name of Kassandra—shrugged. "Nothing mysterious. Just a dead Lightsworn scout."

Talon frowned. "Are you sure? Lysinder's people know better than to venture this deep into our territory. What prompted this one to risk our wards?"

Kassandra shrugged again. "Who knows or cares?"

Raising his head, the captain threw her a reproachful look. "I do."

The lieutenant ducked her head apologetically. "Sorry. It's only one scout. It can't mean anything."

Talon glanced over his shoulder to scan the treeline again. "Are we sure about that?" he asked softly.

Kassandra frowned. "Captain?"

Talon, his face deep in thought, did not immediately reply.

While the captain formulated his response, I pondered over something else: the lack of farspeaker bracelets. Come to think of it, I'd not witnessed any of the legionnaires except for Tuver—and he'd been in a squad of Awakened Dead—using a communication device. Talon hadn't used them during my first visit to the valley, nor had Tartar's guards seemed to employ them during my audience with the Dark Power in Nexus. Was it a deliberate choice?

I was no nearer to the answer, though, when Talon rose to his feet. My attention jumped back to the captain. His face had cleared. *He's come to a decision*, I thought.

"Divide the company into ten squads," Talon ordered. "I want them to search the vicinity."

The lieutenant pursed her lips. "You think there are more scouts nearby?"

"Maybe."

"But we already have patrols out," she protested. "If someone was out there, they would've—"

Talon's face darkened. "Patrols? That's not what I'd call them. Those soldiers have been scarred by their time in the dungeon, and right now, they're too scared of their own shadows to be of much use."

"But still, they aren't—"

"Do it, Kass."

The lieutenant sighed. "As you wish, Captain." Swinging around, she called over the sergeants standing nearby and rattled off a series of commands. Doing her bidding, the sergeants divided the company as instructed and, in short order, led the ten squads into the forest.

Which left only Kassandra and Talon on the mountainside.

"What now?" the lieutenant asked.

"We wait," the captain replied grimly, his eyes darting over the treeline anew.

✻　✻　✻

Multiple hostile entities have failed to detect you.
Multiple hostile entities have failed to detect you.

...

...

I didn't move or retreat.

Captain Talon might have faith his men would be able to uncover me, but I didn't. So, renewing my buffs, I stayed where I was and kept watch. Just like the good captain was doing.

While I did, I reflected on the little I'd overheard. Lysinder, I knew already from Tosh, was Muriel's envoy and in overall command of the Lightsworn forces in the sector. The bit about the ragged patrols and the dungeon had been interesting, but I didn't know enough of what was going on to decide what to make of it.

In the end, I realized I'd gleaned little of value, but that was not to say there wasn't more to be learned. I just had to be patient. Talon and the lieutenant had not yet retreated to their encampment, and until they left, I wouldn't either.

Fixing my gaze on the silent pair on the mountainside, I waited.

After thirty minutes of fruitless searching, the squads returned to the mountainside empty-handed. "Nothing?" Kassandra asked.

"Nothing," a sergeant confirmed. "No footprints or tracks either." He gestured toward the blood-soaked ground. "Not for that one or any other."

Kassandra's brows crinkled. "You sure about that?"

The grizzled sergeant nodded. "The scouts are certain."

The lieutenant threw up her hands. "Then how did *he* get here?" she asked, meaning Tosh. "He didn't portal in, we know that much. Did he fly? Or do you think he—"

"He travelled by treetop," Talon interjected.

"Treetop?" Kassandra asked. "Is that possible?"

"Of course," Talon replied. "It requires some nimble footwork, certainly. But it can be done."

"Hmm," Kassandra mused, not sounding convinced. "So, what do we do now?"

"We head back to base," Talon replied, before turning to the sergeant. "Get the men ready."

"Yessir," the sergeant said, snapping off a salute and hurrying off.

Kassandra edged closer to Talon. "Are we not going to renew the ward?" she asked in a low voice. The whispered words were obviously not meant to carry farther than the captain, but my sharp ears caught them, anyway.

Talon grimaced. "We can't. It was one of Paya's," he replied just as softly.

"Oh. Damn." Kassandra's lips twisted. "Have the Awakened Dead not freed her yet?"

"No. The chalice still has her in its grip. It's all they can do to keep her confined in the dungeon." He shook his head. "The damn fool. I don't know what prompted her to such idiocy."

"Desperation, perhaps?" she offered.

"Maybe."

"Well, whatever it was, it has left us in a pickle," the lieutenant reflected. "Tartar is not going to budge. And Erebus' bunch are next to useless. We're caught between a rock and a hard place."

Talon laughed bleakly. "An astute assessment, Kass. But we're not going to solve the problem standing around here. Come, the men are ready. Let's head back."

✳ ✳ ✳

I watched the tartan company march off, a thoughtful frown on my face. This time around, I'd gained far more insight into events in the valley than earlier, and no matter how cryptic-sounding some of the captain and his lieutenant's utterances had been, three things were immediately clear.

One: Paya was in Erebus' dungeon.

Two: so was the chalice.

Three: Paya had already used the thing.

On the heels of this realization, a message from the Adjudicator unfurled in my mind.

Your task: <u>Heist in the Dark</u> has been updated. You have learned that the Awakened Dead Power, Paya, has already employed the chalice Loken requested you to steal. You have failed the task's primary objective (securing the chalice before it can be used).

Ah well, I thought as I digested the contents of the Game alert. *It was to be expected.*

Loken had required me to acquire the chalice before anyone could employ it, and I'd quite obviously failed to do that. Nor was I truly as sanguine about matters as I was trying to be.

The stakes had just been raised again—and considerably.

Not only was the chalice in play, but any consideration or leeway I could have expected from Loken as a result of the open task had just gone up in flames. There was nothing to stop him from killing Saya now—nor me, for that matter. Still, I was surprised I hadn't failed the task altogether.

That's only a technicality, though. It means nothing. Once Loken learns the—

Another Game alert flashed for attention.

Your task: <u>Heist in the Dark</u> has been updated. New objectives available!

My mouth dropped open in shock. *What—?*

The task giver has chosen to revise the original task. New objective: present yourself to Loken at the Shadow Keep in Nexus within 24 hours and give him a full accounting of your findings.

Stupid, stupid, stupid! I thought, cursing myself.

It had not occurred to me to wonder what would happen if I failed a task—or any of its objectives, for that matter—but of course, the Game had taken it upon itself to inform the task owner. And this time around, that was *not* the Adjudicator, as was the case with most of my tasks.

In this instance, it was Loken.

The trickster had directly bequeathed me the task to steal the chalice. I'd thought nothing of it at the time, because tasks were not binding. Yet, accepting a task was not without consequences—as I had just found out.

Hells, I thought, swallowing unhappily as the full implications of the message sank in.

Loken appeared to be taking a direct hand in events. He had to be, given the wording of the new objective. It didn't matter anymore if Frey had been the one who had originally orchestrated Saya's kidnapping. It was clear who was in charge now.

Loken.

Worse yet, if the trickster hadn't been aware that I was in sector 12,560 before this, he now was. And while the new objective made no mention of Saya, I clearly read the 'or else.'

If I didn't meet Loken as instructed, I was certain Saya would not live to see another day.

And I couldn't let that happen.

CHAPTER 611: PRIORITIES AND DEADLINES

It wasn't all bad news.

Yes, Loken's involvement complicated things inordinately, but there was some good news mixed in with all the bad.

Loken wasn't in sector 12,560.

At least not according to the task, he wasn't. How far I could trust the task description remained to be seen, but it gave me an opening. *Twenty-four hours,* I mused. It wasn't a lot of time, and it didn't leave me many viable options.

The simplest course would be to present myself at the Shadow Keep. But going to Loken with cap in hand was beyond foolish. I would *not* be doing that.

Alternatively, I could try stealing the chalice and using it as leverage—as I'd so recently resolved. But given what I'd just learned, getting inside Erebus' dungeon was not going to be easy. And that was only the first part of what I would have to do.

Assuming I could get into the Darksworn's base—which was not a given—I would then have to sneak or bluff my way past whatever other checkpoints Captain Talon had erected around the nether portal at its center—knowing the man, I was sure he wouldn't just be relying on the camp's outer wards to shield the dungeon—enter Erebus' domain, find the chalice, and deal with the Power holding it. All in twenty-four hours or less.

No, I decided. *Too many unknowns. Too complicated.*

That left only my original plan: rescuing Saya myself.

But with one additional wrinkle, namely, my new time limit. I had to extract her from Loken's people in twenty-four hours. How feasible this would be, I didn't know yet. Still, if recovering Saya proved beyond me, I could always retreat or call for help. This was not something I would be able to do in Erebus' dungeon.

Option three it is.

Glancing up, I studied the sky through the trees. It was still bright, and night wouldn't fall for a few hours yet. If I hurried, I could reach the wyvern caves by nightfall. The perfect time for an infiltration attempt.

But I'd already used blood puppet twice today, and I also had to check in with my allies. I grimaced. Returning to the Roost first made more sense. I couldn't afford any further missteps, and it was better if I suffered a delay now than to find myself wanting later on.

Rising to my feet, I retreated silently into the forest depths.

✱ ✱ ✱

I didn't travel far, just about a mile. That put me squarely in the no-man's-land between the Light Cordon and the Dark encampment—the perfect place to teleport out.

Retrieving a portal scroll from my backpack, I channeled mana into it. I had no doubt the Light and Dark players would sense the portal. Hells, I wouldn't put it past them to be able to trace the ley line I was forming all the way to its exit. But neither of those things would help them.

I would be long gone from the portal before anyone thought to investigate, and besides, my destination was innocuous enough.

Portal scroll consumed.
You have opened a greater portal within sector 12,560.

The luminous gateway snapped open and, masked by vanish and wrapped in shadow, I crept through.

You have entered a safe zone.

Leaving the leafy greenness of the forest, I emerged onto the dusty streets of the valley's only settlement—and its capital, too, I supposed. Concealed as I was, I wasn't all that worried about being spotted. Still, out of a surfeit of caution, I'd chosen a dimly lit alley as my exit point.

And the sounds carrying to my ears made me glad that I had.

The village, it seemed, was no longer as empty as it had been when I'd left. Letting the weaves of the portal behind me unravel, I padded silently to the mouth of the alley and peered out.

Like I'd half-expected after Shael's report, the village was crawling with players. Judging by their attire, most were Lightsworn. *Muriel's people.*

But it was not only Light players I spotted. There were dozens of Darksworn, too. I frowned, momentarily baffled by their presence. Then I realized they were resurrectees. More than ten hours had passed since the forest hunt I'd witnessed this morning, and by now, everyone except the elites would have been reborn.

My glance shifted to the right. Most of the players were congregated around a drab-looking warehouse—which made sense given that the building in question housed the safe zone's rebirth well.

I looked to the left. The Roost lay that way. Getting to it would be simple enough, but... my eyes drifted right again.

Despite my resolve not to get involved in the factional war in the valley, the conflict between the Light and Dark bore further investigation, especially since Loken's mysterious chalice seemed to be central to the hostilities. Any further information I could glean on it and the players involved could make all the difference later on.

My decision made, I slipped out of the alley and turned right down the street. *This won't take long,* I thought.

✳ ✳ ✳

The warehouse was even more full than the streets, and judging by the raised voices, catcalls, and angry shouts arising from within, all was not tranquil at the well.

Cloaked by vanish, I brushed past the players crowding the entrance and slipped unseen into the building. The inside of the warehouse was nothing much to behold. A bare open space of hard-packed ground, the only notable structure was the rebirth well itself.

Even as I watched, a player spawned.

Her face contorted from the remembered pain of dying, she gasped for air as she surged out of the water. Immediately, two players—both Darksworn from their Marks—rushed toward her.

And just as quickly, four Lightsworn moved to block them. Not in any obvious fashion, and certainly not in a manner the Adjudicator could deem hostile. Still, somehow, the four managed to put themselves between the newly resurrected player in newbie clothes and the two approaching her.

"Get out of our way, you fools!"

"Eh? Stop shoving me or I'll report you!"

"This is stupid, light whoreson! You can't stop us from getting to her."

"I don't know what you're talking about."

"And who are you calling a whoreson, darkspawn?"

Sighing, I turned away from the burgeoning confrontation at the rebirth well. What was going on there amounted to little more than childish games, and I was clearly not going to learn anything of value from those involved.

Craning my neck from left to right, I scanned the rest of the room. Nearly everyone I could see was below rank twenty. There was not a single elite amongst—

Wait.

My gaze latched onto the tall, still form of a half-orc. Feet spread and arms folded across his chest, he watched the proceedings with an impassive face. It was the orc's stillness that first caught my eye, but it was his familiarity that held my attention.

I *knew* him.

It was Ultack. Letting my gaze rest on the green-skinned giant, I waited for his analyze data to unfold in my mind.

The target is Ultack, a level 203 half-orc juggernaut. He bears a Mark of Greater Dark and a Mark of Tartar.

A huge double-bladed axe was strapped across Ultack's back, and two smaller axes—throwing blades, I thought—lay sheathed at his hip. Reinforced leather armor covered him from the neck down, but his arms had been left bare, proudly displaying the half-orc's bulging muscles and tartan tattoos.

He's come a long way from the lost recruit I met in the woods, I thought. But then again, so had I.

While Ultack wasn't exactly richly dressed, his player level and commanding stance were evidence enough of his stature amongst the Darksworn. And if that wasn't enough, the posse of lesser players standing watchful guard around the half-orc reinforced Ultack's importance.

He's a tartan officer now. Perhaps even a senior one.

I pursed my lips while I debated approaching the half-orc. Although I wore the form of an elite Dark player, Ultack would undoubtedly be suspicious of my advances—doubly so considering that identity swapping seemed to be a favorite pastime of Shadow's envoy, Frey.

But then again, we were in a safe zone, so even if Ultack was suspicious of my motives and true identity, there was no reason for him to feel threatened. And most crucially, given some of our shared history, he had the means of verifying that I was who I said I was—regardless of what my face looked like.

Ultack could be just the conduit I need to establish contact with Captain Talon.

Why I would need such was still unclear, even in my own mind, but right now, Talon was the one who controlled access to Erebus' dungeon.

Which was where the chalice was.

And one way or the other, despite whether or not I rescued Saya in the next twenty-four hours, my instincts were screaming at me that the chalice was important.

I would need to steal it.

If only to keep it out of Loken, Muriel, and Tartar's hands. As badly as the Powers wanted it, the thing had to be powerful, whether as a bargaining chip or as an artifact in its own right. And as strange as it sounded, locked away in a dungeon with 'only' a single minor Power for guard, the chalice was likely as vulnerable as it was ever going to be.

Right, that's decided. Stealing the chalice is priority number two. My gaze locked on Ultack, I slipped forward into the crowd. *Now, let's see if I can't lay down some of the groundwork to do that.*

I reached the half-orc's side without incident, deftly slipping past the escort of players surrounding him. At the last second, Ultack must have sensed something because his gaze shifted in my direction. He reacted no further, though. But then again, I was still hidden from sight.

Standing still in front of the taller player, I let the spells concealing me dissipate.

You are no longer hidden.

"What!"

"Who—?"

"How'd he get there!"

Predictably, my sudden appearance startled the nearby Darksworn, and more than one set hands to weapons or jerked into motion. Thankfully, though, they all remembered where we were in time and aborted any misguided attempt to shove, pull, or skewer me through.

I paid Ultack's escorts no heed. Keeping my gaze locked on the half-orc, I folded my arms across my chest, mimicking his stance.

Ultack's eyes tightened fractionally. "Who are you?" he asked softly, and not 'how did you do that?' even though I was sure that question had to be paramount in his mind.

I smiled. "An old acquaintance."

The half-orc did not frown, though I could sense he wanted to. "I don't know anyone named Raster."

Waving negligently, I dismissed his comment. "Raster is an alias only." I gestured to myself. "And this body? It's not my true form either."

"Minion of Shadow," someone hissed from behind.

"Shape changer!" another accused.

"It's Frey," a third growled.

Ultack didn't turn to acknowledge his people's comments any more than I did, yet there was no question he'd heard them. "What does the trickster want now?" he rasped.

I rolled my eyes. "If I were Loken's envoy, would I so blithely announce myself?"

The half-orc opened his mouth.

I held up my hand. "Wait. Don't answer that." Retrieving a small coin-like object from my pocket, I tossed it casually in the air before me. "Would Frey have this?"

Ultack's eyes narrowed as he analyzed the token of Tartar in my hand. Captain Talon had given it to me during my first visit to the valley, and from time to time, the soulbound artifact still proved useful.

"No, she would not," the half-orc pronounced. "But that you carry Tartar's token does not make you trustworthy. Nor does it mean that what you say is anything but lies and half-truths."

"You're right," I agreed affably. "Still, I promise I can prove my identity if you give me a chance. As for the veracity of my words... that you will have to judge for yourself after you learn who I am."

For a drawn-out moment, Ultack said nothing. I could tell he was chewing over my words, though. "Go on," he said at last.

I shook my head. "Not here. Too many eyes." For all that we'd been speaking softly, I knew our standoff had drawn more than one curious gaze. "Let's go somewhere more private."

Raising his chin, the half-orc scanned the room before coming to the same conclusion. Not bothering to signify his agreement, he spun around and headed for the exit. "Follow," he called over his shoulder.

And follow I did.

✳   ✳   ✳

Ultack led me to the tartan barracks sitting on the western end of the village. It was the very same building where I'd first met Captain Talon all those many months ago. In the intervening time, the structure had been significantly upgraded, but for all that, the barracks still reeked of emptiness.

"It looks different," I mused quietly, taking in the dust-covered furniture, cold hearth, and molding carpets.

Ultack closed the door behind us, firmly shutting out his gaggle of unhappy bodyguards. "You've been here before?" he asked, shooting me a glance.

"Yes." I tilted my head to the side, reflecting on the long-ago visit. "Actually, it was you who escorted me here."

The half-orc's brows drew down, clearly not sharing the same recollection.

"You and Cecilia," I added in the hope of jogging his memory.

Ultack's frown deepened. "Now, there is a name I haven't heard in a while."

"What happened to her?" I asked curiously.

"To my apprentice, you mean? She's dead," he pronounced. "One of the war's many victims."

"Oh." I paused. "But Cecilia was never your apprentice, you know—at least not while we were acquainted. She was your commander."

"That right?" Ultack asked in a flat monotone.

I nodded. Obviously, the half-orc was testing me. "It is. She never liked me either." I smiled. "Not even after I saved your hides from that rhomodillo."

A glint appeared in Ultack's eyes. *At last,* I thought.

"Michael...?" he asked slowly.

My smile widened. "You remember me."

Ultack grunted noncommittally. "Captain Talon will be pleased to hear you are back."

I laughed. "For how long are you going to keep testing me, Ultack? The last time we met, Talon promised to kill me if he ever saw me again."

The half-orc evinced no surprise. Clearly, he'd been aware of this fact. "What ability tomes did Cecilia and I deliver to you in the woods?" he asked abruptly.

I scratched my head, thinking. "Backstab, analyze, and... lesser imitate, I think?"

The half-orc snorted. "Close enough. It *is* you."

"Of course it is," I replied with a grin.

"What's with the face?" Ultack asked.

I shrugged. "I am a hunted man. Traveling incognito is necessary."

Ultack shook his head. "I should have realized how far down the path of deceit you'd delve after you had us buy you that imitate spellbook." He eyed me contemplatively. "You know that Tartar does not like deception players. And neither does Captain Talon."

"I *do* know."

"Yet, you are still here," he observed. "Speaking to me. Tartar's sworn follower. Why?"

I shrugged again. "Tartar might not find me as disagreeable as you think. I visited him in Nexus, you know."

Ultack's eyes widened. "And you came out of that encounter alive?"

I chuckled. "I did, surprisingly enough."

Ultack rubbed his chin. "You still have not told me why you are here," he pointed out.

My smile faded. "I have a favor to ask."

Ultack sighed. "I like you, Michael." He bared his teeth in an orcish smile. "I did since the first moment we met. But there is no denying you play your own game. The last time you were in the sector, things did not go well for the Dark."

"They didn't go badly either," I protested.

He shrugged. "Perhaps. But I cannot be doing you any favors without Captain Talon's say-so."

"Which is precisely the favor I need."

Ultack's brows crinkled. "What?"

"I need you to carry a message to the good captain."

"What message?"

"Tell Talon I am back in the sector and want to talk."

Ultack scratched his head. "That's it? That's all you want me to tell him?"

I nodded.

"Anyone could carry that message for you. Why bother approaching me?"

"Because only you could verify my identity. Only you can say with confidence that I am truly who I say I am, regardless of what face I wear."

Ultack grunted dismissively. "The captain knows you well enough to do that himself."

My lips quirked upward. "Talon threatened to kill me if I ever set foot in the sector again, remember? I would rather not risk that happening."

"Hmm..." Ultack rubbed his chin while he considered my request. "Why do you wish to speak to the captain?"

I shook my head. "I can't tell you that."

"Can't or won't?"

"Won't," I said firmly.

He eyed me suspiciously. "This is another of your convoluted plots, isn't it? A game you're playing."

I didn't deny the accusation. "It is, but I assure you neither Tartar, Talon, nor you are the targets."

He sighed. "I won't be your pawn, Michael."

"Nor am I asking you to be," I objected. "It's just a simple message I need you to carry. What harm is there in that?"

"Yes. What harm?" he muttered rhetorically. "But with you there's no telling."

"I promise you, Ultack, I mean you—"

Jerking forward with a swiftness belied by his size, Ultack placed his face inches from mine. "Are you a minion of Shadow?" he demanded.

I laughed involuntarily, caught off guard by the question. "What?"

"Answer me," Ultack growled, his mask of affability finally disappearing. "Are you one of Loken's?"

"No," I replied steadfastly, not backing away.

"Don't lie to me," he ground out harshly. "The trickster's minions only entered this sector after you intervened in matters. That cannot be a coincidence."

"So did the Light," I replied evenly. "Are you suggesting I serve Muriel, too?"

"Stop being cryptic," he snapped. "Tell me the truth. Who do you follow?"

"No one."

"No one?" Ultack laughed hollowly. "Impossible."

"It's true," I retorted, unfazed by his scorn.

"Bah," Ultack scoffed. "No one climbs as far in the Game as you clearly have without binding themself to a Power."

I raised my chin challengingly. "Yet I have. Not easily, admittedly. And not without being hounded by more than one Power. But I've clung on to my independence nevertheless." I folded my arms across my chest. "Disbelieve me if you wish, Ultack, but the truth is I serve no power greater than my own."

The half-orc stared at me for a drawn-out moment, weighing my words. "Alright..." he pronounced finally. "Say, I believe you. Why then, would you—a man with no master, supposedly—enter a sector contested by *three* of the Game's greatest Powers?"

"Well, when you put it like that," I said lightly, "it does seem a trifle foolish, doesn't—"

"Enough games," Ultack spat. "If you want my help, you will tell me why you are here."

I exhaled heavily. "I am here because of Loken."

Ultack's eyes bored into mine, and I could almost see the conclusions forming in his mind.

"It's not what you are thinking," I said firmly to ward off further accusations. "Like I told you before, I do not serve Loken, but... I do have business with him."

"What business?" Ultack demanded.

"I have a bone to pick with his envoy—Frey."

Ultack's glare intensified. I stared back mutely, letting the half-orc measure the truth of my words.

Finally satisfied with whatever he saw in my gaze, Ultack straightened. "Go on," he ordered. "Explain."

I said nothing for the moment. I'd not come into this meeting with any intention of explaining myself or why I was in the sector, but I suspected that if I didn't allay the half-orc's suspicions, he'd walk away without a second thought. "Do you know Saya?"

Ultack blinked, confused by the abrupt change in the conversation's direction. "The tavernkeeper?"

I nodded. "Yes. Her. She's one of mine."

"One of yours?" The half-orc shook his head. "I'm not following."

"Before leaving the sector, I bought the tavern from Benadean," I explained. "Saya was running it for me."

"I see. But that still doesn't tell me why—"

"Frey has kidnapped Saya," I said, cutting him off. "To get to me."

Ultack stared at me. "Why would Loken's envoy want to 'get' at you?" he asked slowly.

I shifted uncomfortably. "This is not my first trip back to the valley."

The half-orc's stare grew harder. "You've been here before? When?"

"The Marauders, remember them?" I asked, purposefully avoiding the question.

If Ultack noticed the evasion, he chose to ignore it. "Those fools," he muttered. "Of course, I remember them." He eyed me speculatively. "I also recall your tavernkeeper having some sort of problem with them."

I nodded. "Yes, they were trying to squeeze the tavern out of business and to force Saya—or me, rather—to sell. I came back to... rectify matters."

Ultack tilted his head to the side. "How?"

I smiled grimly. "By killing them all." I paused, then added with seeming reluctance, "And by striking a deal with Frey to ensure their faction never returned to the valley."

Ultack closed his eyes. Praying for patience?

"Then you deliberately entangled yourself with the trickster," he surmised.

"Yes," I replied forthrightly. What the half-orc didn't know was that by that point, I was already squarely in Loken's sights with no chance of escaping. That, though, was not a truth he needed to be enlightened on.

"And now," Ultack went on, "the price has come due."

I shrugged. "In a way, yes."

The half-orc opened his eyes. "So, what? You want Captain Talon's help now? The legions already have their hands full with the Light. We cannot go—"

I shook my head. "You mistake me. I don't want or need the legions' help. Frey is my problem. I will deal with her on my own."

"Then what *do* you want?" he asked, sounding exasperated.

"Only a meeting with Captain Talon."

Ultack sniffed disdainfully. "Now, that I find hard to—"

I cut him off. "I only mentioned Frey and Saya because you insisted on knowing my reasons for being in the sector. What I have to say to the captain has nothing to do with either of them."

Ultack studied me carefully, but this time around, he chose not to voice any doubts he might harbor. "Alright," he said finally.

I straightened. "You will speak to Talon?"

"Yes, I will pass on your request for a meeting." He sighed heavily. "Whether the Captain chooses to heed your request is another matter entirely."

"Of course," I murmured. "And thank you."

"You're welcome." He waved his hand dismissively. "Now get out of here before one of my guards attempts something foolish."

CHAPTER 613: THE BOTTOMLESS CUP

After leaving the tartan barracks, I hurried through the village, head bent and deep in thought. As much as it pained me, I'd not been completely honest with Ultack. But I had no other choice. He was a follower of Tartar, and there was no way he would knowingly betray the Dark Power or Captain Talon.

And I harbored no doubts. Both Talon and Ultack would perceive what I sought to do as a betrayal. If I stole the chalice, neither would look kindly on me again. Hells, as important as the artifact appeared to be to Tartar, I suspected showing any interest in the thing would guarantee Talon doing his utmost to keep me away from it.

Which was why I'd deliberately made no mention of the chalice.

It was better Ultack believed all I wanted was to speak to Talon. My true objective, though, was getting into the Dark's base.

I was betting that Talon would be as suspicious as Ultack about my motives, for which reason he would insist on speaking in person. And the most obvious place for us to meet?

The Dark encampment.

A location I would accept with every appearance of reluctance.

But the truth was, I didn't really have anything to say to Talon. Once I was inside his base, though... past all those layers of who-knew-how-many tier seven and eight wards—wards, I had little hope of penetrating on my own—then I gave myself better than even odds of reaching the nether portal to Erebus' dungeon.

And from there, the chalice was a step away.

Or so I hoped.

But the chalice was tomorrow's problem. Today, I had to rescue Saya.

Looking up, I spotted the Roost in the distance. Fading from sight using vanish, I cut straight toward it but didn't bother trying the former tavern's front door. It would be much better if no one realized the place was no longer vacant. Scaling the sides of the building nimbly, I climbed onto the roof.

"Shael?" I called, perched on a wooden truss.

"Michael? Where are you?"

"On the roof of the Roost. Open the trapdoor."

"What are you— never mind, I'm coming."

*   *   *

A few minutes later, I entered the Roost's common room—a room occupied not just by the four I expected, but by one other.

"Ceruvax!"

The old wolf inclined his head in greeting. "Michael. I came as soon as I could. I heard you needed me?"

Nodding curtly, I seated myself at the same table the other four were arrayed around. "I do."

"What's happened?" Shael asked, leaning forward in his chair.

"Too much," I murmured, "but we'll get to all that in a bit." I turned back to Ceruvax. "First, I need to know: how did the twins' awakening go? Did they succeed?"

The old envoy bared his teeth. "They did. Both Terence and Teresa have acquired their first blood memories."

"That's good." That was not the end of the matter, though, as Ceruvax well knew. "And?"

"*And* they have also become anointed scions of Lion." He shrugged. "You worry too much. I told you they would gain the trait. The Adjudicator will not allow any player to awaken their blood without also binding them to a bloodline."

"So, you said," I murmured, relieved. I'd been worried, as Ceruvax had just rightfully pointed out, that the twins would not become true scions of Lion—putting the legacy of Lion at risk.

Thanks to Atiras' Trials, Nyra, Ceruvax, and I were all scions of Wolf. When we eventually passed on, our spirits would feed the next generation of Wolves. Without the same sort of Trials to undergo, I'd feared Teresa and Terence would not become anointed. But thankfully, my fear had been unfounded, and they had gained the anointed scion trait.

Just like I had.

Still, I had to know the exact phrasing the Adjudicator had used. "Give me the details," I instructed. "Recite the description of the trait the twins received—word for word."

Ceruvax sighed. Nonetheless, he did as I asked. Recalling the twins' own words to him, the old wolf repeated them verbatim.

You have gained the trait: <u>anointed scion</u>. This trait irrevocably binds you to Lion. Your Mark of Lesser Light has been stricken from your spirit signature.

"That was the alert Teresa received," Ceruvax said in a more normal tone. "Terence's Game message was exactly the same."

"...irrevocably binds you to Lion," I repeated, with a huge grin. "Lion— not *House* Lion."

It was an important distinction.

When I'd become a scion, the Adjudicator had bound me to 'House Wolf.' Yet, the Game had changed the wording when it came to the twins.

Ceruvax nodded. "It seems you haven't completely broken things," he muttered.

The old wolf was referring to my goal of founding one House, of course. Needless to say, the task further complicated matters, and I'd been afraid that, given the twins' support of my ambitions, it would affect the pair's awakening.

Intent mattered in the Game, after all—as I well knew from my own experiences—and I'd been concerned that the Adjudicator would perceive the twins' willingness to abandon the concept of a 'House Lion' as them reneging on their ties to Lion.

But he had not done so. Which could only mean one thing.

It was not necessary for scions to bind themselves to a House, only to a bloodline.

"It's proof," I said, with supreme satisfaction.

"It is," Ceruvax agreed heavily—and obviously none too thrilled by the prospect. "Bloodlines are *not* synonymous with Houses."

I nodded. This had been my supposition all along, based on everything I'd learned from Adriel. Bloodlines and Houses *may* have been one and the same thing in the past, but that was more the result of choice—the choice of the dead Primes. A House did not *have* to contain a single bloodline.

And now I knew that for a certainty.

By gathering multiple bloodlines under a single roof, I would not be destroying the ancients' way of life. Lion and Wolf anointed scions—and even Primes—could coexist in one House. "The new House can work," I murmured.

Ceruvax sighed again. "It can." He tipped his head in my direction. "But more importantly, that's two bloodlines you've now revived. Well done, Wolf Lord."

I brushed aside his words. By the time I was done, I hoped for the new House to contain far more bloodlines than that.

"So, which one is next?" Deryn asked brightly, unabashedly inserting himself into the conversation that the others—even Shael—had seen fit to stay out of.

I glanced in the forsworn's direction. "Death," I replied blandly.

"Whoo-hoo," he exclaimed, not at all nonplussed by my response. "That sounds ominous."

I chuckled. "Knowing Adriel, it probably is—but it is not us who should be worried." That honor fell to the new Powers. I turned back to Ceruvax. "Any other news from Sanctum to report?"

The old wolf shook his head. "Nothing particularly noteworthy. There has been no word back from Anriq and Farren nor the brotherhood, but it's early days yet."

"What about Sedgwick?"

"He hasn't reported back either," Ceruvax replied.

"Hmm. And the stygians? Any sightings yet?"

The old wolf shook his head. "None. We have both nether portals under guard, and Safyre is holding a company on standby just in case there is a fresh incursion."

"I see. So, things in Sanctum are about as well as can be expected," I surmised.

Ceruvax nodded. "Pretty much." He leaned forward. "Now, tell me what's going on here."

Inhaling deeply, I began my tale, laying out everything I'd learned over the course of the day.

✳ ✳ ✳

"Oh my," Mariam remarked when I was done. "That's quite the tale."

I nodded, my face grim.

"It's a lot to unpack," Shael added.

"It is," I agreed, "But we can disregard the war and the warring factions for now."

"That's a whole lot of players to ignore," Llewyn objected.

"That may be," I allowed, "but the war is neither here nor there. Remember, our objective is not to secure the sector; it is only to rescue Saya. And with Shadow's contingent in the far west of the valley and seemingly isolated from the conflict in the north, there is no need for us to trouble ourselves over the Light and Dark armies."

"Until it comes time to recover the chalice," Shael pointed out.

I shrugged. "I've yet to decide whether stealing the thing is a wise idea."

Deryn frowned. "But... but why did you approach the half-orc then?"

I smiled. "Just laying the groundwork should retrieving the artifact become necessary. But like I said, the chalice is only of secondary importance right now."

"You're wrong," Ceruvax said flatly.

I turned his way. The old wolf had been largely silent through my retelling of the day's escapades, and he'd said nothing since. "What am I wrong about?" I asked carefully.

"The chalice is more important than your gnomish friend," he said.

Seeing the stern expression on Ceruvax's face and the unyielding glint in his eyes, I had a premonition of where he was going with this.

"No," I refuted slowly. "It is not."

"You don't even know what the artifact is," he said gruffly.

I raised my chin. "Tell me, then. That is why I called you here, after all."

"Hmpf. I thought that might be the case." Bowing his head, Ceruvax took a moment to gather his thoughts. "This is not the first time I've heard mention of a powerful artifact in the form of a chalice." He raised his eyes to meet mine. "When you told me about it in Draven's Reach, I couldn't be certain that the chalice I'd heard of during the war and the one you spoke of were related."

"And now?" I asked.

He blew out a troubled breath. "And now I'm convinced they have to be one and the same."

I leaned forward. "Why?"

Ceruvax held up his hand for patience. "First, let me tell you what I know, then you can decide for yourself."

"Go on," I said, sitting back.

"During the height of the new Powers' rebellion, when the war was raging hottest, a rumor reached House Wolf—a rumor, only mind you, there was never any verifiable information—of a legendary Force artifact that had been discovered by one of the new Powers. The artifact was a Dark chalice and was supposedly unusable by any Lightsworn and Shadowsworn. Apparently, it could be filled with an endless quantity of whatever liquid the bearer desired. It could drink in an ocean. Or a thousand mana potions. A bottomless cup, if you will."

It was my turn to frown. "That sounds… nice but not all that powerful."

"Nor does it match the chalice Michael just described," Deryn put in. "And besides, why would Loken go to all the trouble of getting Michael to steal something like that?"

"Be patient," Ceruvax said grimly. "And maybe, just maybe, you'll learn the source of the trickster's interest." He turned back to me. "You're right, as far as Force artifacts go, the chalice isn't particularly powerful. It was not the chalice's properties themselves, though, but the use to which the Darksworn put the artifact that made it an object of indescribable evil."

"What use?" Shael asked softly.

For a long moment, Ceruvax didn't answer. "There were rumors of the Dark conducting black experiments with the chalice," he said eventually. "And of them filling it with the blood of dead scions." His eyes took on a bleak cast. "And live ones too."

"Yuck." Deryn shuddered. "Why would they do that?"

"To drink it, of course," Mariam said, her face paling.

"But why?" Deryn scratched his head. "I mean, I know the new Powers are evil, but they're not vampires. Why would they want to—"

"To steal the scions' blood memories," I interjected, more out of a desire to quieten the forsworn than any desire to enlighten him. My gaze stayed fixed on Ceruvax the entire time. "That's what they were trying to do, right?"

He nodded. "That was our supposition, too. But there was never any proof one way or the other—no evidence to support that the chalice actually existed or that was how the Dark was using it."

"Hells," I muttered, bowing my head. There might not be any proof, but the facts did seem to fit, sort of anyway. Ceruvax's tale explained why Loken was afraid of leaving the chalice in Dark hands, and why he couldn't use it himself.

It might even explain why he asked *me* to steal it.

The trickster could conceivably be trying to use the chalice to confirm if my own blood was awakened. How, I wasn't quite certain. However, it certainly sounded like a plot convoluted enough to be worthy of Loken.

Ceruvax's story didn't answer all the mysteries surrounding the chalice, though.

"Loken labeled the chalice sentient," I said. "In fact, he went to great lengths to get me to believe that the chalice could speak. Does that fit with your picture of the artifact?"

Ceruvax shrugged. "I've told you everything I know about the artifact. The rumors made no mention of the chalice being able to talk." He paused. "Such is possible, but sentient artifacts are extraordinarily rare."

"Hmm." I rubbed my chin, pondering his response.

"What about the control Captain Talon believes the chalice exerts over Paya?" Shael asked. "Do you know how it's doing that?"

"I do not," Ceruvax replied disappointingly.

"Is such a thing even possible?" Llewyn asked. "I mean for an item to control a player as strong as a Power. Do you know of *any* artifact that can do that?"

"I do not," Ceruvax repeated, looking equally disturbed.

I pursed my lips. It seemed clear there was an element of truth in all the dire warnings I'd heard about using the chalice. Loken had cautioned me against doing so, Tosh had been ordered by his superiors not to even handle the thing, and the conversation I'd overheard between Talon and Kassandra implied that Paya's current straits were a direct result of her drinking from it.

What was less obvious, though, was what exactly had happened to Paya. And how.

And to top it all off, it also seemed as if the chalice held the blood of at least one ancient. I still didn't know what I should make of this fact, but one thing appeared clear.

The chalice could not remain in Dark hands.

Scrutinizing my face, Ceruvax appeared to discern the direction of my thoughts. "You see now why we must recover the chalice?"

I sighed. "I do. Nonetheless, it is a task that must wait."

His eyes narrowed fractionally. "Then you still intend on going ahead with your rescue attempt?"

I nodded decisively. "I do." I rose to my feet. "And now that you are all caught up, and I've learned everything I need to about the chalice, it's time for me to go to bed."

Shael stared at me blankly. "To bed? But I thought—"

"Wake me up in eight hours. That's when I leave for Besina's caves." Not waiting for a response, I headed up the stairs and to my room.

CHAPTER 614: INTO THE VIPER'S NEST

60 DAYS LEFT FOR BROKERING PEACE IN SECTOR 12,560.
27 DAYS UNTIL SANCTUM BECOMES A YOUNG SECTOR.
13 HOURS UNTIL LOKEN'S DEADLINE EXPIRES.

I awoke to a soft tapping on the door. "Michael?"

"Shael?" Throwing off the covers, I sat up. "What time is it?"

"Just after midnight," he replied through the closed door. "The others are ready and waiting."

"Alright," I replied, stifling a yawn. "I'll be right down."

Hearing his steps recede, I turned my attention inward to the pair of Game alerts awaiting my attention.

You have slept 8 hours. Your stamina, mana, and psi reserves have been fully restored, and your blood memories have recharged.

Ghost's nether manipulation has reached rank 16.

I smiled after reading the second message. Ghost, at least, was putting her time in Sanctum to good use and had already raised her nether manipulation to tier four. At the rate she was advancing, it would take her another two days—at most—to learn the elite variant of mist-thin.

When she did, it was my hope that Ghost would not only be able to thin the nether infesting the sector, but she would also be able to destroy it altogether. And, at that point...

At that point, Sanctum's restoration would be well and truly underway. *Who knows,* I reflected, *if all goes well, perhaps one day we'll transform Sanctum into the oasis the valley had once been.*

The packs would then be able to roam free without fear of persecution. As would the scions of the bloodlines. But that day was not here yet, and until it arrived, my work was far from done.

Rising to my feet, I hurried downstairs to join the others.

* * *

"What's the plan?" Shael asked the moment I stepped into the Roost's common room.

I shrugged. "The same as before. I infiltrate Frey's base, find Saya, and get out."

Ceruvax frowned. He knew it would not be as simple as I was making out. "What about Loken?"

"I think there is a chance he is still in Nexus."

The old wolf's frown deepened. "That's a big gamble to take."

Sighing, I pulled out a chair and sat down. "What else would you have me do? Loken is either in Nexus, or he isn't. I could sit here dithering about it all day, but that is not going to get me any closer to rescuing Saya. The time has come to act."

Ceruvax's eyes tightened, but he did not voice an objection to my assertions. The truth was, there was no way for us to confirm Loken's whereabouts beforehand, not given the twenty-four-hour time limit, and the old wolf knew that as well as I did.

"What will you do if Loken is in Frey's base?" Shael asked quietly.

I glanced at him. "I don't know," I replied forthrightly.

I didn't have a plan for dealing with the trickster—and trying to come up with one would be futile. Ignoring the fact that Loken was a supreme Power, he was also as slippery as hell, and until I had more information, attempting to predict what he would do next and figuring out a counter was going to be impossible.

Deryn's eyes grew wide. "It could be a trap!"

"Oh, I suspect it is," I told him bluntly. "Hells, I'm counting on it." Because if it wasn't, there was no reason for Frey to keep Saya alive, and she was probably already dead.

"But you're still going to stick your head into that viper's nest?" Mariam asked, looking aghast. "Even if it is Loken himself who is laying the trap?"

"Yes," I replied simply.

"Why?" she asked, perplexed.

"The last time I crossed paths with any of Loken's people, I was a rank fifteen player," I reflected, not answering directly. "My level has nearly doubled since then, and in terms of raw power... I'm at least three times as strong, if not more."

"You think Loken is going to underestimate you," Shael guessed. "That's why you believe he might be in Nexus. You don't think he will see a need to pursue you himself."

"Yes," I admitted. "There is a halfway decent chance Loken believes that Frey is capable of handling me on her own."

"But there isn't," Llewyn observed.

"Oh, there definitely isn't," I murmured wolfishly.

"It's still a risk," Ceruvax said, rejoining the conversation.

"A *calculated* one," I stressed.

He nodded slowly. "Agreed."

✳ ✳ ✳

Before leaving the Roost, I saw to my preparations. First, and foremost, I changed my shape back to my own—with a few minor tweaks, of course.

Loken was not stupid, and neither was Frey. Assuming I was discovered—and I had to assume I would be at some point—neither the trickster nor his envoy would believe the intruder to be some random player.

They would know it was me.

In which case, it didn't make sense to reveal more of my abilities than strictly necessary, and if I could help it, I wanted to keep knowledge of my doppelganger ability secret.

You have transformed back to your original form, falsifying your level as that of a level 201 voidstalker, and concealing your Powerful Acolyte Mark. Duration: infinite.

My transformation complete, I swung back to the others.

"Ah, there you are," Shael remarked. "The Michael we all know and love. I almost forgot what you looked like, you know."

"Very funny," I replied, before turning to the others. "Well, what do you think? Will my 'disguise' hold up?"

"By the Powers," Mariam whispered, studying my 'new' face in fascination. This was the first time she—or any of the others, for that matter—had observed my transformation.

"There's nothing, *nothing*, to say he isn't a level two hundred voidstalker," Deryn murmured.

"It is uncanny," Llewyn agreed. "His analyze data is completely misleading."

"I guess that means I pass muster," I said lightly, and glanced at Ceruvax.

"You're ready?" he asked quietly.

I nodded. "I am. Go on, do it."

The old wolf clapped his hands, drawing the attention of the three forsworn. "Enough gawking. Let's get to work."

Letting them get to it, I closed my eyes and waited patiently while the four mages wrapped me in their spells.

✳   ✳   ✳

Ceruvax has cast healing wolf (doubling your health regeneration rate) and ancient's protection on you (+20% to all resistances).

Mariam has cast unforced (+10% force resistance) and warrior's boon on you (+10 to all physical attributes).

Llewyn has cast spellbreaker (+20% spell evasion) on you.

Deryn has cast mirrored armor (+15% damage reflection) on you.

A few minutes later, practically humming with energy, I opened my eyes. Ceruvax and I had chosen the buffs the others would lay on me with care, and they all worked to improve my already-impressive resistances in some way.

None of the spells would last long, though.

At best, I had twenty minutes before the first expired. But by then, they should have served their purpose. *Still, there's no time to dawdle,* I thought, turning back to Ceruvax.

Reading the intent on my face, the former envoy stepped back and opened a portal using the coordinates in the aetherstone I'd given him earlier.

My steps deliberate, I strode toward the luminous gateway. There was no need for further farewells. The others all knew the plan—and the dangers it entailed.

"Good hunting, Wolf Lord," Ceruvax said softly. "If you need us, we'll be here."

Nodding wordlessly, I disappeared into the portal.

✻　✻　✻

You have left a safe zone.

I emerged from Ceruvax's portal on the eastern slopes of the valley, and about as far as you could get in the sector from the conflict raging in the north and Frey's base in the west.

Turning about in a slow circle, I examined the immediate vicinity around me. It was empty and lifeless—which was nothing more than I'd expected. My current location was no more than a waypoint, after all.

I couldn't portal directly from the Roost to the Shadow's lair, of course. Assuming Loken's people tracked back the ley line I used, that would only needlessly endanger the former tavern.

But nor did I intend on traveling to Besina's caves on foot.

For one, I was too short on time to do that. And for another, doing so would still mean me spending hours penetrating whatever cunning defenses Frey had woven around her base's entrances and exits—some of which had no doubt been specifically spelled to trap me. So, instead, I would do the unexpected.

And portal directly into Besina's cave.

Given that Loken's envoy was relying on stealth to hide her forces from the other faction's armies, I was certain she would not have laid down any sort of null field around her base nor shielded it with a magical barrier. Such spells—in the middle of nowhere—would have stuck out like a sore thumb, shouting out the location of the base to all who were keen to find it.

And without a null field or shield, Frey wouldn't be able to stop me from portaling into her base.

That was not to say Loken's people would not have ringed the area with other wards and protections. By portaling in, I would be blindly walking into them. Still, I was counting on my buffs, those of the others, and the strength of my void skills to negate the traps—taking a calculated risk.

Just like I'd told Ceruvax.

But that did not mean what I intended was without danger. Much would depend on how well Loken and Frey had anticipated my responses. *Will they expect me to—*

Reining in my freewheeling thoughts, I drew psi. Now was not the time to indulge in idle speculation. Weaving psi, I saw to my final preparations— setting my own buffs.

You have cast load controller, gaining a 10-minute encumbrance aura that slows any armor-wearing foe within 5 yards by 50%.

You have cast engine of war, increasing your Strength, Constitution, and Dexterity by +20 ranks for 30 minutes.

You have cast vanish and trigger-cast quick mend.

You have cast beguiling shield. While this shield remains in place, beguile will be trigger-cast against any foe that attacks you. Duration: 5 minutes.
You have cast wind daemon, multiplying your speed by 2x for 1 minute.

I exhaled heavily. I was finally ready, and all that was left was to open a portal to Besina's cave. Withdrawing a scroll from my backpack, I did just that.

Item consumed.
You have opened a greater portal within sector 12,560.

For just a split second, I stared at the glowing doorway. I'd reached the point of no return, and after this, there would be no turning back. But I'd known ever since entering the valley that this moment would arrive eventually, and I was ready as I could be.
Not hesitating further, I dove forward.

Transfer through portal commencing...
...
...

An invisible, well-nigh undetectable streak, I shot through the glowing doorway and into Besina's cave. Not knowing what I would be walking into, I'd deliberately forgone the slow, methodical approach. If an ambush awaited me, I'd undoubtedly spring it, but I was hoping my speed would also befuddle my ambushers and carry me past any lurking danger.

No ambush awaited, though.

Not of the kind I expected anyway. Instead, I rolled to a stop on the cavern's cold, hard floor, enclosed in soothing darkness and silence.

Huh, I thought, crouched down small. *That's unexpec—*

You have triggered a trap!
You have triggered a trap!
You have triggered 3 unknown wards! Alarm sounded, intruder repellent spells activated, and aether portals opened.

In an eyeblink, the stillness was shattered.

Shards of ice whipped through the cave. Flames billowed upward from beneath my feet. Missiles rained down from the stone ceiling. Strange purple cords of magic wrapped themselves around me. A siren blared in the distance. And from multiple points in the cave, the shadows coalesced into... things.

It was a veritable storm of magic.

And rightfully, it should have struck me dead. But the enemy had not reckoned with the strength of my protections.

You have evaded 3 magical attacks and repelled 5 hostile spells.
You have passed 2 magical resistance checks!
An unknown spell has failed to <u>reveal</u> you.
An unknown spell has failed to afflict you with the debuff <u>mark target</u>.
A shadow blizzard has hit you, inflicting force damage (damage reduced by 55% due to void armor and other buffs).
An inferno has hit you, inflicting fire damage (damage reduced by 85% due to void armor and other buffs).

6 level 210 shadow hounds have been summoned.
Multiple hostile entities have failed to detect you!

Looks like I spoke too soon, I thought wryly, and rose to my feet, ignoring the shadow, ice, and fire biting at me. My void armor was doing a good job of minimizing the damage they were attempting to inflict. And besides, there were far greater threats to focus on.

Like the six hounds, for instance.

They weren't the only threats, nor the most pressing, though. The shadow creatures had been called forth at six different positions in the cavern—chosen randomly as far as I could tell.

The closest was still a few dozen yards distant and, more importantly, couldn't see me. Oh, the hounds knew where I was—the exploded traps made that abundantly clear—but they had no obvious target upon which to focus their ire, for which reason, they were stalking toward me and not charging. And that gave me time.

Dealing with the beasts can wait, I decided, and turned about in a slow circle.

Repositioning quickly was vital, but so was understanding the threat landscape. Raising my left hand to rub at the side of my head, I simultaneously reached into the ring on my right hand with my mind.

You have activated a sorcerer's coif, gaining the buff, <u>ward-sensing</u> (tier 6).
You have activated a true-seer's ring, gaining the buff, <u>true-seeing</u> (tier 5).

I was not yet done. My senses could be sharpened further. Unfurling my mindsight, I wove stamina and cast.

Mindsight activated.
You have cast trap detect, gaining the buff, <u>spotter</u> (tier 4).

Ordinarily, my baseline perception was nothing to scoff at. Now, though, it was something else entirely.

Buffed by mindsight, trap detect, ward-sensing, true-seeing, and my allies' spells... well, let's just say, I expected little to escape my attention.

Which was why I evinced no surprise when a flood of Game alerts scrolled through my mind as I looked upon the cave with 'new' eyes.

You have detected a hostile spell!
You have spotted a trap!
You have detected a hostile spell!
You have spotted a trap!
...

...

Everywhere I looked, a haze of red occluded my vision. I didn't focus on any of the individual traps or wards, though. For now, knowing that they existed was enough. Peering past the telltale markers, I examined the rest of my surroundings.

I was in Besina's cave—the same one the wyvern mother had used as her den and sleeping chamber. It was also the very same place where she had held Saya prisoner. But right away, I could tell Saya was nowhere in the vicinity.

Not that I had expected Frey to be holding the gnome here.

I'd chosen this cavern as my entry point because of its size and openness. As large as the cavern was, it was nearly impossible to ward completely and provided plenty of room to maneuver.

Something I would need to do soon.

Because while the cavern was presently empty—well, empty if you discounted the six summoned shadow creatures advancing on me—the alarm was still blaring somewhere in the cave network, and I could only assume that wherever Frey was, she was marshaling her forces to deal with my incursion.

And when the Shadow's minions arrived, I needed to be ready to deal with them.

Alright, let's get to it.

Unsheathing my stygian sword with my left hand, I unclipped a small glass bottle from my bomber's belt with my other hand. The cavern floor was a literal minefield at the moment. My entrance alone had set off two traps and three wards, and unfortunately, I didn't have time to disarm or to dance around any of those that remained.

Which left me with only one option, really.

Triggering everything.

Hefting the bomb in my hand, I flung it forward.

You have ignited a firebomb.
2 traps triggered. 1 ward activated. 1 shadow hound unaffected.

Flames mushroomed upward from the cave floor, this time of my own making, and the result when it came to Frey's defenses was everything I could have hoped for.

Delicate trap mechanisms broke, and spell weaves frayed. The traps and wards didn't simply fizzle out, though. Instead, they detonated—but thankfully, that happened with me nowhere near the target area.

Unfortunately, my bomb was less effective against the shadow summoning.

While I had struck one of the beasts dead center, the impact did not give the creature pause, and it kept advancing. More interesting yet, the triggered wards and traps had *also* not impaired the hound.

Hmm... are they magic immune?

My lips thinned into a grim line. Dealing with the summoned creatures with purely physical weaponry was going to be more time-consuming than I wanted, and I still had the other wards and traps to deal with.

Time to speed this up.

Unclipping another handful of bombs from my belt, I flung them far and wide, paying scant heed to where the tiny glass bottles landed. As long as it was nowhere close, that was fine by me.

Then I did so again and again. And again...

You have ignited 3 ice bombs. 3 traps triggered. 6 wards activated.
You have ignited 4 acid bombs. 5 traps triggered. 3 wards activated.
You have ignited 3 firebomb. 2 traps triggered. 5 wards activated.

...

...

* * *

I didn't stop throwing bombs until my belt was empty.

By then, the cavern had been transformed into a mishmash of billowing smoke, raging fires, melting ice, drifting poison clouds, and spent magic. None of it bothered the shadow hounds, though, and they reached me unscathed.

Six hostile entities have failed to detect you!

But despite being almost within touching distance, none of the shadow beasts were able to pinpoint my location—no matter how hard they sniffed or how many random swipes they took at seemingly empty air.

"Decal," I called, carefully sidestepping past a swishing tail.

"*What do you need?*" he asked instantly.

"*Put these puppies to sleep.*"

A pause. "*I can't.*"

I frowned. "*Why not?*"

"*I've tried already, but their dreamscapes... they're empty,*" he said.

"Well, that's inconvenient." The words were muttered in rote only, though. That Decal couldn't do what I asked was less concerning than what it implied. My brows furrowing deeper, I tried to make sense of what the astral simulacrum had just said.

"*The shadow hounds are alive; I can feel it,*" I said slowly. "*So, when you say their dreamscapes are empty, you mean... they lack self-will?*"

"*Correct,*" he replied, confirming my suspicions. "*Someone is piloting the creatures remotely.*"

"*Someone like Loken's envoy?*"

I sensed his mental shrug. "*That would be my guess, too. I can try tracing the mental link binding the hounds back to the controller.*" Another pause. "*It will take time, though.*"

But time was what I didn't have. "*Don't bother,*" I said. "*I'll deal with the beasts myself. Keep an eye on the rest of the cavern. If anyone else enters—*"

"*I'll make sure they don't interfere,*" he promised.

"Good." Drawing my second blade, I waded into battle.

✳ ✳ ✳

The hounds were huge beasts, and over and above their magic immunity, they also had high physical evasion courtesy of their shadowy natures.

There were also six of them.

Still, the beasts did not unduly trouble me. Because, for all their impressive defenses, try as they might, the hounds could not see me. Using my invisibility, windsurfer, and shadow jump to good effect, I stayed out of range of the beasts' paws and jaws while striking at their flanks.

Duck. Swipe. Blink.

That was more or less my routine. Over and over, I repeated the same combination, repositioning only when it became necessary and doing my best to keep up the tempo of my attacks. Thanks to the bombs I'd thrown earlier, at least half the traps and wards in the cavern had been cleared, but that still left as many active, so of necessity, I restricted my maneuvering to areas I knew to be safe.

I was also conscious of both the passing time and the fact that whoever was controlling my foes was likely getting a blow-by-blow account of the battle. It was for this reason as much as anything else that I refrained from using my more... exotic abilities.

If Frey was watching, I didn't want her to realize my true strength until it was too late.

A level 210 shadow hound has died.

It took almost a full minute, but eventually, I slew the first shadow beast. And soon after that, I killed two more.

But that was all I had time for.

"Michael," Decal called out in warning. *"Disengage. Now!"*

I didn't question the terse instruction. Breaking off my assault, I shot aloft to the cavern ceiling using windsurfer. From there, I surveyed the cavern anew.

I saw no one, though.

Checking my mindsight, I saw that it, too, was empty. But Decal was not wrong. There was something... something that had caught his attention, and now that I was not embroiled in battle, it caught mine too.

Straining my senses, I picked up a faint tickle of noise at the very edge of my hearing. It was the sound of footsteps—far away, and a single set only, but approaching rapidly. There was more. The ground was also shuddering, quivering slightly at the impact of each footfall.

Whatever was approaching it was both fast and heavy.

And invisible to my mindsight.

"Hells," I muttered, having the sick feeling that things were about to get complicated.

Much more complicated.

Staying aloft at the stone ceiling, I scanned the outer edges of the cavern. Two things had become apparent: one, Frey had indeed been expecting me and had prepared accordingly. And two, she had chosen to fend me off indirectly. In the few minutes since my arrival, no player had made an appearance, and by this point, I was fairly certain none would.

Whether that was deliberate strategy on Shadow's part or happenstance, I wasn't sure, but whatever the case, it was damn inconvenient to my own plans. I'd been hoping to ambush the ambushers, turning the hunters into the hunted, and gaining the upper hand. But now... given the lack of enemy players in the cavern, I no longer had any reason to hang about.

And that meant it was time to pick out my escape routes.

One of the many reasons I'd chosen to enter Frey's base through Besina's sleeping chamber was because the cavern was a central hub of the tunnel network riddling the valley's western mountains. During my prior visit to the cave, I'd noticed no shortage of exits leading away from it. And while many of them appeared to have been closed off since, I still counted four different tunnels leading away from the huge cavern.

Three of which began to close even as I watched.

Emerging out of hidden pockets in the top of the openings, three heavy stone slabs slammed downward with a resounding thud.

"*Damn,*" I cursed, my eyes skipping to the remaining exit—the west one. It was, of course, the same one my still-unseen enemy was approaching.

An iron dome has been activated.

The area under effect had been sealed off from the rest of the sector, preventing the formation of any ley lines and cutting off all communication and connections with the outside world.

I sighed. I couldn't see the iron dome that the Adjudicator had so graciously just informed me about, but if I had to guess, I'd say it enclosed the entirety of Frey's base.

It was the final part of the envoy's trap, of course—at least I hoped it was the final part—and it did not catch me unawares. I'd been expecting Frey to seal off her base at some point.

I was only surprised that it had taken her this long to do it. But delayed or not, the newly-manifested iron dome reduced my options further. I could neither portal out nor call on Ceruvax or the others for help. I could still shadow jump, but given the dearth of available targets, that was less useful than it sounded.

Which has to be by design.

Frey—or Loken's strategy—was becoming clearer. More foes meant more targets for me to charm or maneuver around. That was why no players had rushed into the cavern. If Frey had guessed it was me who had tripped up her defenses, she would know I could turn her own people against her, even if she didn't realize the full extent of my new abilities.

My mouth twisted sourly. It was a clever ploy, but only time would tell if Frey had chosen the right tack. In the interim, I still had an approaching threat to deal with.

My eyes drifted back to the last cavern opening. I had only two options left. Meet the approaching foe outside or meet it here in the cavern.

I didn't fancy option one. I wanted as much space to maneuver as possible, and the tunnel beyond would likely not give me that.

But the cavern wasn't exactly an ideal battlefield either. Given the traps littering it and the three shadow hounds pacing below, if I stayed where I was, I would have to simultaneously contend with four foes and multiple unseen hazards.

Not to mention that if the final cavern opening did close at some point, which I was sure it would, then getting out of the cavern could prove... problematic.

It's no choice at all then.

Sheathing my blades, I rushed for the exit, well aware that I was racing from one ambush to another.

The only question that remained was what form the new one would take.

✳ ✳ ✳

The west stone door to Besina's sleeping chamber slammed shut behind me, dashing any hopes of retreat I may have harbored, while in front of me, the tunnel yawned wide, inviting me into its depths.

Interestingly enough, the moment the door sealed, I lost all awareness of the shadow hounds beyond. That meant either the creatures had been unsummoned the moment I left or... the cavern was psionically shielded. *Curious.*

But the sleeping chamber was behind me and of little import. Of more concern was the tunnel before me. Slowing my steps, I studied the terrain ahead.

About six feet wide and eight feet tall, the tunnel was little different from others I'd traversed on my earlier visits to the area. The sides were rough-hewn rock with plenty of handholds, and the roof, while not high, still afforded me some opportunity to maneuver.

More importantly, though, I spied no traps.

Nor, unfortunately, any side tunnels.

The only way forward was straight ahead—and directly into the arms of whatever was responsible for the heavy footfalls. *I still have vanish, though,* I thought. *Maybe I'll be able to hide from it.*

I snorted in derision. There was little chance of that. If Frey had planned for my charm and teleport abilities, she would sure as hell have a counter ready for my stealth. It didn't matter, though. One way or the other, I would defeat what awaited me. Dropping into a crouch, I advanced down the passage.

It did not take long for my foe to appear.

Barreling out of the far end of the tunnel, a silver form emerged from the darkness. Man-sized and man-shaped, it was clearly nothing natural. *A construct?* I wondered. Lacking any garments at all, the creature was formed entirely of a supine metal that glistened eerily in the darkness. It was bipedal, too—mostly anyhow—with two arms, two legs, and a single massive eye that was the only thing about it *not* silver.

Filling nearly the entirety of the construct's face, the eye was its only facial feature. More ominously, dancing rays of blood red shot out of the oversized orb to pierce the darkness.

Alrighty, I muttered. My foe's appearance was daunting enough, but I needed to learn what else I could of it while I had the chance. It would take the creature another thirty seconds or to reach me, I judged.

Reaching out with my will, I inspected it anew.

The target is Nemea, a level 282 adamantine golem.

Golems are yet a third type of construct, and as with all constructs, they are not born but made. Like simulacrums, they are permanent creations, but whereas a simulacrum mirrors their host, a golem does not. A golem's shape and form are only limited by the skill of their maker and the materials at their disposal, and as such, their prowess and abilities vary widely.

I sighed unhappily. Nemea was nearly my own level. On top of that, its body appeared to be made of solid metal—and not ordinary steel either. Adamantine was not a metal I'd run across yet, but I knew from my discussion with my allies that it was exceedingly rare and prized for both its hardness and spell resistance.

My swords were not going to damage the golem. Nor were my stolen spells.

Then there was Nemea's blood-red eye. I was sure as could be that the orb in question had been enchanted with true-seeing. There would be no hiding from its gaze.

And finally, there was the golem's speed. For all the creature's heavy footfalls, it was no behemoth. Nemea might not be as light as I was, but judging from how rapidly it was approaching, the damn thing was nearly as fast.

I sighed again. Studying my foe, I had no doubt it had been crafted specifically to combat me. Still, I had a few tricks Frey and Loken didn't know about.

"*Decal,*" I called softly.

"*Yes, Michael?*"

"*Tell me about the golem's dreamscape.*"

A pause, then, "*It bears a striking resemblance to those of the shadow hounds.*"

"*I can't say I'm surprised,*" I murmured in reply. "*Then, the golem lacks self-will?*"

"*It does,*" Decal confirmed. "*The creature is being remotely controlled. You won't be able to charm, blind, sleep, or otherwise strike at it with telepathy.*"

"Huh. What about its link with its controller? Can you sever it?"

"I can try," Decal opined. *"But the same restrictions I mentioned earlier apply. I will need time."*

Unbending from my crouch, I drew my blades. Only a few dozen yards separated me and Nemea now. *"Do it. I'll buy you the time you need."*

"As you wish," he replied. Streaming out of my mind, the construct seeped into my foe's dreamscape.

Decal has cast astral project.

The golem hurtled onward, oblivious, and I felt my momentary tension dissipate. Clearly, the creature—or its controller, rather—had not received the Game message I had.

Perhaps that was because Frey, or whoever else was piloting Nemea, lacked the necessary Perception to sense the mental intrusion, or maybe it was because they were simply too far away.

Whatever the case, Decal's intrusion had gone undetected.

Which was all to the good. Now the simulacrum could go about his work unhindered.

Banishing further thought of Decal, I focused fully on the onrushing golem. The first of the searching beams extending outwards from its eye was about to touch me. Staying unflinchingly still, I let that happen.

Horus' all-seeing eye has found you. You are <u>revealed</u> (exposed and unable to hide). Duration: 1 minute.
You are no longer hidden.

Just as I thought, I had a second to think before the golem itself rocked to a halt before me. Swinging its arms backward, it brought them rushing forward.

Nemea has resisted affliction by the debuff, <u>load controller</u> (immune).

I paid the Game alert no heed. Nor did I stay to meet the telegraphed attack. Dropping low, I rolled out of the way. Whirling around, the golem attempted a roundhouse kick.

It missed. By barely inches.

Hopping back to my feet, I riposted with one of my blades. Nemea didn't even bother blocking. Ignoring the incoming sword entirely, it attacked anew.

You have struck Nemea. 100% damage blocked (adamantine golems are immune to slashing damage).

Urgh. The resulting failure was no more than I expected. Still, being proved right didn't make me feel any better about the situation. Retracting my blade, I dodged the golem's next attack.

And the one after that.

And the one after that.

Hells, I thought, backing away. *This thing is fast.* Nemea charged forward, unwilling to allow me any respite.

And relentless.

Raising my blades, I dove back into the fight.

Chapter 617: The Hand Behind the Curtain

I lost track of time in the ensuing exchange.

The golem rained down blow after blow. And blow after blow, I dodged. I fought wholly defensively, my only goal to give Decal the time he needed.

The entire time, the stone door to Besina's cave did not open, nor did any other consciousnesses enter the range of my mindsight. Whatever the outcome of the battle, it seemed it was destined to be determined solely by Nemea, me, and Decal.

For the most part, the golem fought in the opposite manner I did—with unrestrained aggression. While it lacked swords, its hands were weapons enough. And except for its all-seeing eye and uncanny speed—which was nearly a match for my own—Nemea demonstrated no other capabilities.

Not that it needed them.

It was doing well enough already. Everything I had tried to hurt the creature—from Adriel's stolen noxious vapors spell to my own sentient shurikens—had failed. But conversely, the golem had not managed to land any blows on me either.

It was a stalemate that couldn't—and didn't—last.

Inevitably, I misstepped, and instead of delivering me safely from an incoming attack, an ill-timed lunge put me squarely in the path of my foe's sweeping arm.

Nemea has critically injured you!
You have failed a physical resistance check! Your ribs have shattered. Your health is at 53% and dropping.

The blow landed with an audible crunch.

Bones broke, my ribs caved in, and I went flying through the air to crash into an unoffending stone wall. The air in my lungs escaped in a rush, and I slumped bonelessly to the ground. But before the damage could become life-threatening, my defenses kicked in.

First quick mend triggered. Your health has been restored to 99%.

I gasped as my lungs reinflated.

The golem stomped closer, and I scrambled to my feet, ready to throw myself out of the way again. But this time, much to my surprise, no attack was immediately forthcoming.

"You've gotten faster," Nemea remarked, its voice echoing hollowly as it spoke from a non-existent mouth. "But not fast enough."

I knew that voice. "Frey," I muttered.

In response, the golem swiped at me again—almost lazily—but my broken ribs had already healed, and I easily avoided the attempted blow.

"So, you've learned my identity," Frey said conversationally, lashing out anew, this time with Nemea's left leg.

"I've learned a lot more than that," I retorted from between gritted teeth as I jumped away.

"But not nearly enough," Frey sneered.

Before I could respond, the golem launched another blistering assault. The attack, though, did not stop Frey from talking.

"If you *had*," the envoy continued, her voice displaying no sign of strain, "you would not have come here. As you can see, I've prepared for your arrival."

Obviously, wherever Frey was, she was not really inside the golem.

"Your preparations... are somewhat... lacking," I rejoined. Of necessity, the words escaped me in jerky half-statements as I ducked, dived, and sidestepped Nemea's attacks, thereby robbing them of any actual meaning—a fact which did not escape Frey.

"We'll see," she laughed.

A pause followed, both in Nemea's attacks and the envoy's speech. By this point, it seemed pretty clear that Frey was the one controlling the golem, and the pause could only mean the envoy was taking a moment to reassess her options or that something else had distracted her. Not squandering the opportunity, I began backing away.

Nemea didn't let me. Launching itself forward from a standing start, it resumed its assault.

"Afraid I'll get away?" I jeered.

"No," Frey replied easily, "but I don't fancy chasing you through the tunnels either."

Then why did you let me escape Besina's sleeping chamber? I wondered. I held my tongue, though, keeping the thought to myself.

"I'll admit your chosen point of entry caught me by surprise," Frey went on, her own thoughts clearly also dwelling on the wyvern's den. "After everything Loken told me about you, I was expecting a more nuanced approach."

"What can I say," I said, dodging the golem's swinging arms, "sometimes simple is better."

"Simple is *never* better," Frey rejoined. "But it did take me longer than I anticipated to bring my pet to bear. I must thank you for staying put for its arrival."

She meant the golem. "Why the pet? Afraid to face me yourself?" I taunted.

Frey chuckled. "Afraid? No. But why risk myself when this way is so much better?" Bringing its hands down from up high abruptly, Nemea attempted to smash me into pulp.

I was alive to the danger, though, and before the creature was halfway through its swing, I floated away on a current of air, leaving it to strike at nothing more than empty ground.

"Now, if only you would stay still," Frey muttered in an undertone I wasn't sure I was meant to hear.

I grunted. "What's your end game here? To kill me?"

"Oh yes. Definitely that. Slowly, if I can help it."

"Loken will not—"

"Oh no, you don't get to play that game this time," Frey said, cutting me off. "*This* time, I have the trickster's own blessing."

She did? Dread curdled in me. Somehow, I didn't think Frey was lying. "Then all this was nothing more than a trap? Your note was a lie, and Saya is dead?"

"Not at all," Frey replied, sending the golem barreling toward me again. "The trade we offered you was a legitimate one. But everything changed when you refused my master's task. You should not have shunned Loken's invite, you know. What you *should* have done is gone to Shadow Keep like he asked."

Not responding immediately, I threw myself out of the way of the charging golem. Frey's ploy was glaringly obvious. She was trying to use the conversation to distract me into making another misstep. The safer course, I knew, would be to shut up and let her ramble on, but I couldn't do that. The opportunity to learn something of value was too good to pass up.

"Tell me straight," I said as I regained my feet, "is Saya alive?"

A smug laugh was my only response.

My lips tightened. "Tell me, or I really will make your pet chase me through the tunnels."

"Ha! It is too fast for you to outrun."

"Who said anything about running?" I countered. "I can fly out of its reach anytime I want—and we both know it."

Momentary silence. Even the attacks stopped. "Why don't you then?" she asked eventually.

I shrugged from the safety of five feet away. "Because I plan on killing it." Which was nothing more than the simple truth.

"Killing it? A rank twenty-eight adamantine golem? You must be mad!"

"It's not the first time someone has accused me of being such," I replied unconcerned.

"Never mind the how, why?" Frey asked, sounding both curious and fascinated.

"Because it would inconvenience you," I said. "Creating that pet must have cost you a pretty penny."

Frey laughed—a little hollowly, I thought. "You have no idea."

"I gather you had it crafted specifically to combat me. How did you manage to acquire so much adamantine?"

"With great difficulty." Her voice firming, she added, "But the cost and effort were worth it. Your bravado means nothing. You stand no chance of defeating my pet. By coming here, you signed your own death warrant."

I smiled grimly. "We'll see."

"Yes, we shall," she agreed. "If you could hurt Nemea, you would have done so already. Nothing you do will—"

Decal has severed the connection between an adamantine golem and its master.
Nemea has been destroyed.
You and Ghost have reached level 287!
Your dodging has reached rank 24, and your insight rank 27.

Frey's voice cut off abruptly, and a moment later, the golem fell down face-first.

I chuckled softly. "You were saying?"

There was no response, of course.

✳ ✳ ✳

Before moving off, I took the time to study the dead golem—not that dead was the right word; 'lifeless' or 'unanimated' were perhaps more appropriate.

Kneeling down, I ran my hand lightly across the fallen creature. There was not a scratch on it. "Remarkable," I murmured.

"It truly was," Decal said from the depths of my mind.

"Good work slaying it," I replied. *"Did you learn anything in the process?"*

"I did," Decal answered. *"Nemea is exactly what the Adjudicator described— a construct. One without any mind of its own. It was wholly dependent on its controller for direction."*

"Who we now know to be Frey," I observed.

"Yes. Once I broke the link between them, the creature fell as you saw."

"Hmm. 'Broke the link…' that's all you did?"

"It is."

"What's stopping Frey from reinitiating control over the thing then?"

A pause. *"My guess? Nothing."*

I sighed. *"Damn. That's what I thought."*

"I doubt she can do it from afar, though," Decal offered. *"Given how complex the connection was, I suspect she has to be in physical contact with Nemea to reconstitute it."* The simulacrum thought for a moment longer. *"I also think it will take her time to do that—as long as it took you to create me, if not longer."*

I rose to my feet. *"You're probably right. But that doesn't change how Frey's likely to respond."* I kicked the golem. *"Even inert, this thing is too valuable to leave lying around. She'll try to recover it."*

"You think she might come herself?" Decal asked curiously.

"Maybe, or—"

I broke off at the grinding sound of rock on rock coming from behind me. Turning around, I saw the stone door to Besina's chamber inching upward.

"—or she might just send more of her minions," I finished.

✳ ✳ ✳

I didn't run.

The adamantine golem, I suspected, had been Frey's ace. I doubted that whatever else she sent against me would be nearly as effective. So, there was no reason to flee. But that did not mean there was no reason for caution.

So, while waiting for my next foes to arrive, I drew stamina and psi and recast my buffs.

You have trigger-cast quick mend.

You have cast load controller, engine of war, vanish, beguiling shield, and wind daemon.

The stone door was opening glacially slow, but eventually it reached three feet in height, and three four-footed creatures crawled out. The moment they were through, the door slammed shut anew.

Three shadow hounds? I wondered. That's *what Frey is sending against me?*

The trio were the survivors of my earlier skirmish in Besina's sleeping chamber and likely the closest reinforcements Frey had, but still... I'd been expecting to be facing a more substantial force.

Oh well.

Drawing my blades, I waited for the onrushing hounds to arrive.

But three shadow creatures drew up about a dozen yards short of the golem. "What did you do?" the central hound demanded in Frey's voice.

Huh, fancy that. She's controlling them the same way.

I didn't respond, though. The envoy knew the hounds could not kill me — hells, they couldn't even pierce my stealth—which meant their only purpose was to delay me until the real reinforcements arrived.

And if I could help it, I wasn't going to let that happen. Stalking forward, I advanced on the hounds.

"Tell me!" Frey screeched. "How did you—"

Blocking out the envoy's voice, I set about slaying the hounds.

CHAPTER 618: DICTATING TERMS

You have killed 3 level 210 shadow hounds.
You and Ghost have reached level 288!

Dispatching the last three shadow hounds went much faster than killing the first three. Mostly, because I had more room to maneuver. Then, too, this time around, I fought more aggressively and took more chances, both of which I could afford to do since I now had a clearer picture of what Frey could—and couldn't—throw against me.

Throughout the skirmish, Frey didn't stop pestering me with questions about Nemea's death. I studiously ignored her, though, suspecting my silence would annoy her more.

"Decal, keep watch," I ordered tersely once the last hound died.

Sensing his silent acknowledgment, I turned my attention back to the golem. I needed to destroy the thing, but I had no idea how to go about that, and I was achingly aware that I didn't have much time to come up with a solution.

Moving the thing seemed next to impossible. I had already tried, but despite all my tugging and pulling, it had barely budged. I could always shapeshift. As tough as the golem's body had proved to be, I doubted it would be fully immune to an elder wolf's teeth and claws. But I'd resisted the temptation to transform thus far, and I wasn't about to do so now. If Loken learned I could shift into a wolf, there would be no hiding what I was from him.

So, if I am unable to destroy it, and if I can't move it, that only leaves one thing.

Using Nemea as bait.

Frey had not given up on the golem, of course. She would send more of her minions to recover it. And that in turn left me with a rare opportunity to dictate the terms of the forthcoming encounters and prepare the battlefield in advance.

My gaze drifted to the stone door to Besina's chamber. It had not stirred since opening earlier, and while I didn't think Frey's people would come from that direction, it was still one possible approach that needed to be warded.

The golem itself would also need to be trapped, of course. My head swung in the other direction—toward the tunnel the creature had emerged from— the ground there would also need to be prepared.

I best get started then.

Bending my head, I ran my fingers along the blue rune on my wristband, activating its enchantment.

You have removed 5 trap-making crystals from your trapper's wristband. Remaining trap-making crystals: 295 of 300.

Working swiftly, I fastened the crystals onto the left side of the golem's neck.

You have connected 3 lightning elements to a motion cone and status key. A tier 4 trap has been successfully configured, concealed, and turned dormant.

I rose to my feet. *One trap down, fifty-nine more to go.*

* * *

I rushed through the configuration of the traps, knowing that more of the enemy could appear at any time. Hurrying from spot to spot, I placed twenty traps on or around the golem, another twenty at the stone door, and the last set in the tunnel's western approach.

Much to my surprise, I finished my work uninterrupted.

59 dormant tier 4 traps have been successfully configured.
Remaining trap-making crystals: 0 of 300.

The final trap configured, I raised my head and peered down the tunnel. There was still no sign of movement or anything else to suggest I had visitors incoming.

I frowned. Had I just wasted my traps? Was Frey not going to attempt recovering the golem?

But it was still too early to conclude that.

Rising to my feet, I strode down the passage. I had done all I could to prepare the battlefield. Now, it was time to explore.

* * *

The tunnel continued uninterrupted for about three hundred yards, curving enough that I soon lost sight of the entrance to Besina's sleeping chamber. I traversed the distance in silence and with my ears straining to catch the least hint of noise. I heard nothing, though, and eventually reached another cavern. Crouched low and wrapped in shadows, I surveyed the new chamber.

The cavern was small, barely ten yards in diameter. But despite its size, it still housed three other exits, two on the northern side and one on the southern end. All three passages were as dark and silent as one I'd just come through, though.

Hmm, what now? I wondered. I could keep exploring, sneaking down one of the tunnels. But doing that, I risked missing anyone coming from the other two.

Better to wait here, I decided.

Raising my head, I scanned the roof of the chamber. While the cavern itself was small, the ceiling was high and had plenty of tiny crevices.

I can hide there.

Weaving psi, I floated up to the roof of the cavern on a ramp of air and squeezed into the largest-looking nook.

It was tight, no doubt about it, but curling up small, I managed to fit in all my limbs and fully conceal myself. Hiding in such a mundane manner might be overkill, but then again, it might not. The golem's eye had pierced my stealth, and I had to assume whoever or whatever Frey sent against me next would be able to do so as well.

Now, to wait and see what appears. Closing my eyes, I began meditating.

❋   ❋   ❋

You have restored 100% of your psi reserves.

It was a full ten minutes later when the silence was finally broken. A subdued buzzing—so faint I almost failed to mark it—reached my ears from the southern tunnel mouth.

You have passed a Perception check and have detected the presence of a hidden hostile entity.

I had my first visitor.

And by the sounds of it, it was mechanical in nature. *Another construct,* I thought.

The construct did not appear in my mindsight, nor in my physical line of sight either. Squeezed up as I was in the crevice, I could see almost nothing of the floor below and had to be content with tracking the thing by sound alone. Barely breathing, I waited to see what the construct would do.

The buzzing did not grow louder.

But its location shifted.

The construct was on the move, I concluded. First, it circled to the right, then the left—checking the cavern and, presumably, searching for me.

A hostile entity has failed to detect you.
A hostile entity has failed to detect you.

...

The construct took its time.

Moving laboriously slow, it roved over every inch of the cavern floor, but somewhat shortsightedly, it failed to check the ceiling. Perhaps it couldn't. Whatever the case, when the construct finally drew to a halt, it had naught to show for its efforts.

Hmm. What will it do next, I wonder. Would it head towards Besina's sleeping chamber or down one of the other tunnels? Staying as still as I could, I waited to see what happened.

A crimson beam cut through the darkness.

Horus' all-seeing eye has failed to find you. You are still hidden.

I sighed. The new red light playing across the roof of the ceiling bore a striking resemblance to Nemea's. I had guessed right, it seemed. Frey had other minions capable of piercing my stealth, and while the creature in question had not found me, it would have if not for the crevice sheltering me.

Well, there is nothing for it but to wait.

A tense five minutes followed. The red beam continued to dance along the ceiling, but by then, the construct had surely scanned as much as it could of the cavern's roof.

I frowned. *Why isn't it moving on? It can't suspect—*

I broke off as a faint scuffing carried to my ears. Hardly daring to breathe, I listened intently.

And heard further whispers of noise.

The clink of metal on stone, the brush of cloth against rock, and beneath it all, the muffled sounds of soft leather shoes moving nearly soundlessly across the cavern floor.

You have passed a Perception check and have detected the presence of 10 hidden hostile entities.

My lips curled up in a snarl. The unknown construct was no longer alone. A large party, following in its wake, had entered the cavern. Players, would be my guess, and rogues at that.

Their consciousnesses were sealed, hidden from my mindsight, and their stealth was good enough that it had taken me this long to detect them.

Damnit, I cursed. The protections and makeup of the party below were clearly not happenstance. Frey had obviously taken great care in selecting the team below and had ensured they were well-equipped to combat my abilities. Still, the envoy had not accounted for *all* my abilities.

A fact which became evident as a different sort of buzzing—one not grounded in the physical—filled the aether.

You have passed a Perception check! Multiple farspeaker mental sendings detected.

Smiling tightly, I added myself to the telepathic link without a second thought.

Eavesdropping on communication commencing...

"It's clear," a feminine voice whispered.

"You're sure, Delia?" asked a deeper, gruffer voice—*male,* I thought.

"Yeah, Argus has uncovered nothing," Delia replied.

"What do we do now, Brunak?" a third asked. *"There are three tunnels leading away from here. Do we split up?"*

"Of course not," Delia snorted. *"There is only one Argus."*

"And only one Delia," Brunak—the gruff speaker—added wryly. *"Splitting up is not an option."*

"Then how do we clear the rest of the tunnels?" the third voice whined.

"Hmm," Brunak mused. *"We wait."*

"Wait?" Delia asked in a surprised tone. *"What for?"*

"For the rest of the group," Brunak said. *"Once they've secured this chamber, we can move on."*

"You think they'll be able to detect the intruder on their own?" Delia asked dubiously.

"No," Brunak answered. *"But they* will *be able to erect shields to seal off the other tunnels until we're ready to clear them."*

"Uhm, what if he breaks through the mages' shields while we're away?" speaker three asked.

"Then they'll fend him off," Brunak replied nonchalantly.

"You're sure?" speaker three persisted. *"Didn't this guy just kill Frey's golem?"*

"Supposedly killed," Brunak muttered in an undertone.

"I heard that!"

I knew that voice. It was Frey's.

You have passed a mental resistance check! Frey has failed to detect your mental intrusion.

"Sorry, boss," Brunak muttered contritely. *"I didn't think you were on the link."*

"That's no excuse," Frey said primly. *"Now, report. Why haven't you reached Nemea yet?"*

"It's Argus," Delia replied in Brunak's place. *"Clearing the tunnels with it is taking a lot longer than we expected."*

"We don't need it either, boss," speaker three said, joining the conversation. *"You should let us clear the tunnels on our own."*

"No," Frey said flatly. *"I told you the intruder's stealth is superior to anything you are capable of detecting. Don't underestimate him."*

"But—"

"The topic is closed," Frey said firmly.

Silence followed, which, while not exactly agreeable in nature, evinced the obedience the envoy desired.

"Delia," Frey continued a moment later, *"how are you managing with Argus?"*

"Controlling him is not easy," she admitted, *"but I'm coping."*

"You'll learn," Frey said. *"It gets easier with time."* She turned her attention to the party leader. *"Where is your team now?"*

"Hub Twenty-four," Brunak replied.

"Good. Then, you're almost there," Frey said. *"Be extra careful from here on out."*

"We will," Brunak promised. *"I want to wait for the main group before moving out."*

"Hmm. Yes. Do that. Report back when you have secured Nemea."

"Yes, boss."

"Then, I'll hear from you later," Frey said and dropped out of the farspeaker link.

Chapter 619: Advanced Party

Eavesdropping stopped.

Safely ensconced in the nook, I pondered the overheard conversation. Only seconds had passed since the players had stopped talking. It was clear to me now that, despite the undoubted setbacks Frey had suffered, neither she nor her people were panicked.

Somehow, I was going to have to change that.

And the best way to do so was by killing the party below—and the one that followed. Could I manage the feat, though?

Only one way to find out.

Moving with exquisite care, I began the slow and torturous process of extricating myself from the crevice—all without making a sound.

I knew I couldn't allow the rogues' party to reach Nemea. The Perception of Brunak and his fellows might not be sufficient to pierce my stealth, but I was fairly certain the rogues were no slouches when it came to setting and uncovering traps. If I let them, they would spoil the ambush I'd set up at the golem.

Which was why I had to kill them *before* they reached the thing.

Even if it meant revealing myself.

The red beam from the construct—or Argus as the rogues had called it—was still playing along the roof and walls of the cavern, but if I timed it right, I could gain the precious few seconds I needed to get out of the crevice before the enemy reacted.

"*Decal,*" I called, rousing my simulacrum, as I gathered myself at the crevice's entrance.

"*Yes, Michael?*"

"*The moment a target drops into our line of sight, attack. Don't wait for my say-so.*"

"*Any target? You don't want me to focus on the construct?*"

"*No, I don't,*" I said firmly. "*This fight will be all about speed, and severing the construct's connection will take too long.*" I paused. "*Besides, I don't think Frey is piloting this one. Delia is the controller. I suspect once we kill her, 'Argus' will no longer be a problem.*"

"*Got it.*"

"*Good. Then be ready.*" Turning my attention downward, I waited. The rogues had gone silent, neither moving nor talking over the farspeaker link. Eyes fixed on the nook's narrow opening, I watched for the appearance of the construct's crimson gaze.

When it passed, I would have to move.

My buffs were cast, and my swords were loosened in their sheaths. I still had no idea of the level of the foes I'd be facing, but I didn't have the luxury of time. The rogues would have to be killed fast and dirty.

Crimson light flashed bright in front of me.

Horus' all-seeing eye has failed to find you. You are still hidden.

Drawing psi, I readied myself.

The beam slipped past, and I flung myself forward and into open air.

The maneuver was neither elegant nor quiet, and though they made no betraying sounds, I sensed the rogues' attention snap upward, searching for me—which was no more than I was doing.

I, though, succeeded where they failed.

Multiple hostile entities have failed to detect you.

You have passed a Perception check and have detected 11 hidden hostile entities. Analyze triggered.

The instant I became aware of the players, their analyze data flashed through my mind.

The target is Brunak, a level 220 dwarven scoundrel.

The target is Delia, a level 201 human shadow puppeteer.

The target is Luran, a level 210 elven night blade.

The target is Orwin, a level 193 sword singer.

The target is...

The target is...

Decal has cast astral project.

I entered freefall. The drop was a short one, though, and I barely had time to draw my swords before I thudded down in the rogues' midst.

A blade snapped out, blindly searching for me.

I contorted my body, letting it pass by unanswered—or at least, unanswered by my own blades. The psionic shroud protecting me was not as forgiving.

Beguiling shield triggered.

You have beguiled Luran, a level 210 elven night blade, for 3 seconds.

Almost as soon as the psi spell wrapped itself around Luran's mind, the elf's second sword snapped out. But this time, I was not the target. And this time, the target was found wholly wanting.

Your minion has killed Tekan with a fatal blow.

The rogues converging on me reversed course, their shock palpable. Their reaction was instinctive, brought on as much by Luran's seeming-betrayal as by Tekan's quick death. Blades lowered, the rogues stared aghast at their former comrade, who was even now searching for another target.

Drawing psi, I advanced, ready to press the advantage. But I'd barely taken a step when Argus' evil red gaze fell upon me.

Horus' all-seeing eye has found you. You are no longer hidden.

Grimacing unhappily, I glanced left to where the construct stood. It was no adamantine golem that was for sure. While its shape and form were the same as Nemea's, its composition was different.

The adamantine golem had been solid and compact. Argus was neither. Made of grey-white smoke, this construct was even more ethereal than the shadow hounds had been. Reaching out with my will, I inspected the creature.

The target is Argus, a level 200 mist golem.

Like the name implies, mist golems are created from nothing more substantial than trails of dense white air. Lacking true physical form, they cannot be harmed by mundane weapons, nor do they deal any physical damage. Beware, though, mist golems are the perfect vessel for magical abilities and can quickly annihilate an unprepared foe.

Ugh, I thought. *Another golem.* Hopefully, though, this one would be easier to destroy than Nemea had been.

"There he is," Brunak roared, recollecting himself as I was unmasked. "Take him out!"

"But from afar," Delia cautioned. "He has some sort of charm aura around him."

Luran is no longer beguiled.

On the hunt for a fresh victim, Luran rocked to a halt. "Tekan?" he gasped, his gaze skipping from the nearby corpse to the bloodied sword in his hand. "What happened?"

No one bothered answering. Too focused on me to worry about their fellow's confusion, the other rogues were swapping out swords, daggers, and axes for crossbows and grenades.

For a split second longer, I continued my own advance, then thinking better of it, I backed away, swords raised warily. The rogues noticed. Brunak's eyes glinted, and Delia's lips drew upward in a smirk.

Unbothered by the enemy's sudden confidence, I held psi in readiness and waited.

Delia flung a grenade. Brunak threw an axe. Two other rogues released daggers, and three of the remaining four fired bolts from their crossbows.

But not everyone attacked.

Luran, still looking lost, stood apart. Argus, with his controller preoccupied, sat idle. And the last rogue looked to be fighting himself—Decal's doing, I thought.

I watched the incoming projectiles intently, holding my position until the last possible second.

Then blinked away.

You have evaded 8 attacks.
Beguiling shield triggered.
5 of 8 targets have failed a mental resistance check. You have beguiled 5 hostile players.
You have teleported into Delia's shadow.

Beguiling shield triggered just as I'd expected, and thanks to it, my foes were in complete disarray. Appearing behind Delia, I raised my blades, ready to deal death.

What I had not bargained on, however, was some of the rogues' attacks following me through the aether.

An unknown hostile has trigger-cast retarget.
An unknown hostile has trigger-cast retarget.
...

Four projectiles blinked into existence behind me. Startled, I froze for a split second. Then, recovering, I swung around to block the incoming attacks.

It was far too late, though, and one after the other, axe, dagger, and crossbow bolts rammed home into my torso.

Brunak has critically injured you!
First quick mend triggered.
Orwin has injured you! Inzameen and Hola have injured you!
Second quick mend triggered.
Your health has been restored to 63%.

I staggered backward—dazed, but only momentarily. Recovering, I ripped out the dagger and two bolts buried in my torso—the throwing axe had already fallen out—and refocused on my target.

One of the beguiled victims, Delia, was facing the other way and attacking someone else. The other rogues, too embattled by their fellows, weren't paying me any attention either.

The chaos wouldn't last, though.

I had to put what little time I had left to good effect. Lunging forward, I buried both my swords in Delia's broad back.

You have killed Delia with a fatal blow.
You have severed the connection between a mist golem and its master.
Argus has been destroyed.
Decal has killed Badger, a level 183 human assassin.
Brunak, Orwin, Hola, and Yez are no longer beguiled.

I smiled grimly. *Four down. Seven to go.*

✴   ✴   ✴

The cavern stayed a frozen tableau for a drawn-out moment after my foes' ensorcellment faded. I could tell Brunak and the others were at a loss about what to do. Attacking me seemed foolish—but so did running.

A faint buzzing sounded in my ears.

So, they've gone for option three: calling for help.

Dashing forward, I closed the distance to Brunak. The buzzing was emanating from him, and I could only imagine he was on the farspeaker link with Frey, crying for help.

I couldn't stop him from alerting the envoy, but I could make sure he didn't have time to share the details of what was unfolding.

Drawing up in front of the dwarf, I raised my blades. Brunak brought his axe up in guard position but didn't attack.

Huh, so it's going to be like that.

Feinting left first, I lunged from the right. Brunak wasn't fooled and swung around anticlockwise to face me. But the second maneuver was as much of a bluff as the first, and instead of attacking, I stepped into the aether—and out again behind the dwarf.

You have teleported into Brunak's shadow.

The dwarf's shoulders stiffened; he knew what was coming but had no chance to stop it. Chopping down with both my blades, I buried them through either side of the shorter player's neck.

You have killed Brunak with a fatal blow.

Five down.
Of the enemy elites, only Luran remained, and I turned my attention to him next. The elven night blade no longer looked confused. He knew what had been done to him, and by whom. A snarl fixed on his face, the elf rushed to meet me.
Just how exactly Luran intended to attack me, I had no idea, but with my blades lowered, I waited calmly to meet him.
The other rogues, meanwhile, had withdrawn to the far end of the cavern, muttering amongst themselves. The telepathic buzzing from earlier had stopped, so it was a good bet none of the five were able to communicate with Frey, for which reason I was content to leave them to Decal for now. The simulacrum, I sensed, had already slipped into his next victim's mind.
Six yards from me, Laran split into four.
Images, I thought.
Not breaking stride, the four Lurans moved to surround me. I let them.
A blade flashed in from the right. Another slashed down from the front. And near simultaneously, a third thrust forward from the rear.
None of the swords made contact.
Rising upward on a current of air, I evaded all three attacks.

Beguiling shield triggered.
You have failed to beguile 3 of 3 attackers (targets lack mind to affect).

The Game alerts were not unexpected. Still airborne, I kept my gaze fixed on the fourth Laran—the only one who had *not* attacked. He had to be the real thing.
Perhaps sensing what I was about, the four Larans converged on one another. But I was not deceived. My gaze fixed on my chosen target, I shadow jumped.

You have teleported into Laran's shadow.

I emerged behind the elf, swords held high and falling fast.
Laran tried to dodge, but I'd caught him flatfooted and with nowhere to run. His fate was already sealed, and a heartbeat later, my blades tasted flesh.

You have critically injured Laran.
You have critically injured Laran.
Laran has died.

The images vanished, and once more, silence descended upon the cavern. This time, the stink of fear was unmistakable. And it only ratcheted up a notch further as another player inexplicably collapsed.

Decal has killed Yez, a level 190 gnomish rogue.

Seven down.

A grim smile pasted on my face, I advanced on the remaining four players. They looked about ready to break, but I didn't want that, so I drew to a halt, and funnily enough, that caused them to calm.

As if they don't already know, I can close the distance in an eyeblink.

But panic could spur all sorts of weird responses in people, so I didn't question their reaction. And right now, the four were more akin to terrified prey than right-thinking players.

"*Decal,*" I murmured, taking advantage of the momentary pause, "*paralyze the one on the left. I need him for questioning.*"

"*As you wish, Michael,*" the simulacrum responded.

Blades at the rest, I waited patiently.

"H-hey man, will you let us go?" one of the four asked shrilly. "We're only doing what we've—"

Decal has paralyzed Orwin.

The Game alert was my signal to act. Not waiting for the rogue to finish, I rushed through the aether and slipped a sword through his chest. Retracting the blade almost before it pierced all the way through, I pivoted on my left heel, slashed downward once, and then lunged forward.

You have killed Hola.
You have killed Inzameen.
You have killed Jennice.

My maneuver completed, I spun to a stop. It was done. The rogue party had been decimated. And best of all, I now had a prisoner to interrogate.

Chapter 620: Second Team

You and Ghost have reached level 289!

I didn't attempt looting the dead—time was once again in short supply.

Brunak had been in communication with Frey long enough to tell her of the ambush. What the envoy would do with the information was uncertain, but I had to assume she would hurry the second response force along. Still, before attending to the rogue Decal held paralyzed, I spared a moment to inspect the farspeaker bracelets worn by Brunak and the other elites.

The target is a brushed silver bracelet from the Valley Command set. This item may only be worn by members of the Seekers of Discord faction. Likewise, only faction members may discern its properties.

Unsurprisingly, the device was unusable. Like my own bracelet, it was faction-locked. Still, the time spent inspecting the item had not gone entirely to waste. I'd learned something, even if the value of what I'd learned was somewhat questionable.

"Seekers of Discord," I murmured. So that was the name of Loken's faction—not that knowing so was of much help in divining the trickster's goals.

Why seek discord? To root it out?

Or to further it?

I shook my head. Like Loken himself, there appeared to be nothing straightforward about his faction. Identifying its members and figuring out what their motives were was not going to be easy.

Well, at least I have another name to pursue now, I thought, straightening.

Glancing to my right, I saw Decal's chosen target, Orwin, standing immobile and staring unseeing off into empty air. The opening from which the rogues had emerged was only a little further right and still dark. There was nothing to indicate the second party was close, but they had to be.

Did I have enough time to dominate Orwin?

Hells, if I know. But I couldn't let the opportunity slip by.

Striding over to the rogue, I slapped my hand onto his frozen shoulder. *"Keep watch,"* I murmured to Decal and awakened my blood.

✳ ✳ ✳

You have cast enslave.

You have successfully dominated Orwin, a level 193 sword singer. Duration: permanent until death.

The blood spell went off without a hitch, which while not a surprise, was still a relief. I'd deliberately not attempted to question any of the rogue elites. The last thing I wanted was for Loken to sense my meddling like Muriel almost had when I'd attempted the same thing on Maricella.

More importantly, though, I completed the spell before Frey's second team arrived. *Right, let's do this.* Shaking the rogue, I awoke him.

"Wha—? Where am—"

"Quiet," I ordered.

Orwin subsided.

"Good. I'll ask the questions. You will listen and only speak when spoken to. Your answers will be short and to the point. Clear?"

"Yes."

"Excellent. Now tell me about the main group. How big is it?"

"Ninety strong," Orwin replied.

"Ninety," I muttered. That was a lot of players to contend with, and I had to assume at least a few were elites. "What's their makeup?"

"Sixty mages. Thirty warriors."

"How many elites?"

"Nine."

Huh. So, one in ten. There were fewer elites than I expected, but more than I could afford to take lightly. Still, with the traps I'd set around the adamantine golem, dealing with the main party would not be impossible.

It was time to move the conversation on, though. "Where is Saya?"

Orwin's face scrunched up in confusion. "Who?"

My lips tightened. "The gnomish prisoner. The bait Frey used to lure me here."

"Ah. She is being held up top."

I exhaled sharply. Here it was at last. Confirmation that Saya was alive. *Then this has not all been in vain.*

I turned back to Orwin. "Up top, where? And how do I get there? Be specific."

The rogue raised his hand, his finger pointing straight up. "Up there. On the mountainside. To the left of the plateau that tops this cliff, you will find a game trail. Follow it. It will curve around the westernmost peak in the range and lead you straight to our camp. The gnome is there."

I frowned. Saya, it seemed, was not in the tunnels at all. Nor was Frey's base as I'd been assuming all along. And that meant...

This entire complex was conceived as a trap.

One meant to draw me in and hold me. And I had just dived in. Straight into the goddamn center. *Now, mustn't that have tied Frey in stitches,* I thought with a grimace. I had erred—badly, it seemed. But done was done. And now, I had to get out.

"How do I escape?" I asked Orwin.

"You can't. Not while the iron dome is up."

The iron dome. *Of course.* The jaws of the trap. I'd sensed it going up earlier but had not paid much heed. Now, I wondered if that had been a mistake. "What exactly is an iron dome?" I asked tersely.

"It's a construct of magic and steel designed to prevent anyone from entering or exiting the tunnels."

I frowned. "Magic *and* steel. What do you mean by that?"

"The backbone of the dome is a network of magically conductive steel rods laid in each and every tunnel. When the iron dome is turned on and mana is channeled through the rods, they form a containment field strong enough to deny even a Power access." Orwin paused. "As long as the dome is up, nothing is getting in or out of these tunnels."

My eyes narrowed. "That must need a powerful group of mages to maintain. Where are they?"

The rogue shook his head. "No mages are required. The iron dome is powered through its own mana well, which is stored in the selfsame artifact used to control it."

"An artifact?" I asked sharply. "What sort of—"

A dull rumbling rose in the distance, interrupting me.

"*Michael...*" Decal whispered.

"*I hear it,*" I replied. Cocking my head to the side, I listened intently for a moment.

The sound I was hearing was the tread of many feet—ninety would be my guess—walking swiftly, but not running, in my direction. The second team was about to make their entrance.

Almost out of time, I swung back to Orwin. "Quickly. The iron dome artifact. Where is it?"

The rogue stared at me blankly for a second. "You don't know?"

Fighting back the urge to shake him, I growled instead. "I don't. Otherwise, I wouldn't be asking."

Silently, Orwin raised his arm to point down a tunnel. "It's that way."

For a moment, I didn't understand, then comprehension dawned. "Besina's sleeping chamber?" I murmured, my eyes widening.

The rogue shook his head. "I don't know who that is."

"The wyvern mother's den," I corrected. "Is that where the artifact is?"

Orwin gave a clipped nod. "Yes. It's called a keystone." He bit his lip. "We thought you knew since... well, you know."

I nodded. "Since that's where I entered." My lips twitched upward in a smile. It seemed like I hadn't made a complete muck of things after all. The traps in the sleeping chamber made sense now, as did the blocked-off entrances, and the stone door that had sealed behind me.

The march of boots sounded again, reminding me of the onrushing enemy. My gaze flitted back to Orwin. "Sorry," I murmured.

"For what?" he asked curiously.

"This." Drawing back my blade, I plunged it deep into his torso.

You have killed Orwin.

✱　✱　✱

Leaving Orwin's lifeless body where it fell, I re-inserted myself in my hidey-hole. There was no reason for the incoming players to suspect Orwin had died anything but an ordinary death or that I had interrogated him first.

And that was a card I wanted to play to my advantage.

Tucked into the elevated nook once more, I stilled my breathing and waited. This time, though, I positioned myself better and made sure to retain some visibility of the cavern floor. Doing so was a risk, but after the

218

earlier conversation I'd overheard, I deemed it unlikely the main group would be accompanied by any all-seeing golems.

Multiple hostile entities have failed to detect you.

The Game message and the tramp of marching feet announced the arrival of the second team as its foremost elements spilled into the cavern below. Running my gaze over the group, I let their analyze data seep into my mind.

The chamber's size was not sufficient to house all ninety members of the second team, of course, but it was certainly big enough for the group's elites.

All nine of whom were presently gathered below.

So, Orwin was right about the second team's composition, I mused as I studied the nine players intently. Three were warriors, four were mages, while the last two were some sort of rogue hybrids. The lowest elite was level two hundred and ten, and the highest was nearly at envoy rank. *A not inconsiderable force,* I surmised.

No one else entered the chamber, from which I gathered the rest of the party had been instructed to wait while the elites investigated.

And investigate the nine did, and with admirable thoroughness, too.

The warriors turned over every corpse, inspecting their wounds minutely, the rogue-hybrids walked the perimeter of the chamber, their intent gazes darting into every nook and cranny, while the mages stood still in the center, muttering under their breath.

You have passed multiple magical resistance checks!
Multiple hostile entities have failed to detect you.

But despite their diligence, the Seekers of Discord elites' efforts were without reward, and I went undetected. And it was not long after that that another expected Game message dropped into my mind.

You have passed a Perception check! Multiple farspeaker mental sendings detected.
Eavesdropping on communication commencing...

"... seems pretty obvious what happened," an elite said. Her name was Amelia, and as a level two hundred and thirty sorceress, she was the highest ranked mage in the group.

"Oh? And what's that?" an elite warrior by the name of Piku asked. He was the highest leveled of the Discord players, and presumably, their leader, too.

Tanakh, one of the rogue-hybrids, shrugged. *"They were ambushed. Plain and simple."*

Piku glanced at him. *"How, though? Delia had Argus with her."*

Tanakh snorted. *"The golems can only detect what they can see. A smart player—and our quarry certainly seems that—would have had no trouble evading Argus' gaze long enough to spring his ambush. Speed and skill would have carried him the rest of the way, though."* The rogue gestured to the corpses scattered about. *"And the end result is this."*

"I told you we were depending on the golems too much," an elite by the name of Woodweaver opined.

Piku threw him a reproachful look. *"Those were Frey's orders, and you should know better than to—"*

"What about my orders?" Frey demanded, joining the conversation abruptly.

"We've completed them," Piku said, changing track smoothly. *"We've reached Hub Twenty-four and secured it."*

If Frey had overheard Woodweaver's incipient dissent, she chose to ignore it. *"What have you learnt?"* she asked.

"Brunak's party was slaughtered," Piku reported bluntly.

"No survivors?" Frey asked.

"None," Piku confirmed.

Momentary silence, then, *"How were they killed?"*

Piku glanced at Tanakh, who nodded minutely. *"By one man using bladed weapons,"* the steel-clad orc replied.

"Loken warned me not to underestimate him," Frey remarked. *"It seems like I didn't take his lessons well enough to heart."*

Piku didn't venture to comment on Frey's musings. *"What should we do now?"*

"Proceed to Nemea," Frey ordered, her tone all business once more. *"Once you have him safely in hand, contact me again."*

"You don't want us to split up and search the tunnels?" Amelia asked, sounding surprised.

"That's the last thing I want you to do," Frey rejoined.

"But we'll find him quicker that way," Amelia protested.

"Time is on our side," Frey said confidently. *"With the iron dome up, there is no way our quarry is escaping."* A pause. *"And I've made enough mistakes already. I won't compound them further by splitting your forces. Now go. And contact me when you're there."*

Eavesdropping stopped.

It took almost five minutes for the nine elites and the column of players that followed on their heels to file out of the cavern.

I waited patiently throughout.

My targets were doing exactly what I wanted them to, and while I would have preferred them to hurry along a bit more, I was content enough with the way things were proceeding.

After the last player exited the chamber, I dropped silently to the floor and, crouched on my haunches, waited.

Nothing and no one sprang out at me.

If the overheard conversation was all an elaborate trap, it was not in this cavern that Frey intended to launch her ambush. Rising into a half-crouch, I padded after the disappearing column.

Discipline was strong amongst the Discord players, but not so strong that I didn't overhear the disgruntled murmurs of the rank-and-file. It appeared that few, if any of them, were happy with the way Frey's hunt was turning out.

If only they knew what fate awaits them.

Finally, the enemy column came to a stop. Peering past the rearmost players, I saw that Piku and the other elites had reached the downed golem. Unfortunately, though, I was too far away to eavesdrop on their farspeaker conversation.

Hmm... now what? I wondered.

My foes were perfectly positioned for me to spring my own ambush. It was clear from the way they were arrayed that none of them had sensed my dormant traps, and it would only be the work of seconds to activate the devices and wreak chaos amongst the enemy.

But I did not do so.

The truth was my plans had altered in the wake of Orwin's information.

I could go ahead and kill Frey's second team—easily, too, I thought—but that would get me no closer to the artifact controlling the iron dome. And getting to the keystone had to be my first priority. It took precedence even over killing Frey.

Speaking of the envoy, it seemed certain she was stuck in the tunnel complex with me and the rest of her people. Given what Orwin and the Game had said about the iron dome, there was no way she was controlling it from outside. Dealing with Frey would have to wait for later, though, as would killing the second team.

First, I had to get back into the wyvern mother's den.

And the best way to do that—well, the only way, actually—was to convince Frey and her people to open the stone door for me.

Maybe they'll attempt to take the adamantine golem through.

That was the hope, anyway.

But I couldn't depend on hope. I needed to hear what the nine up ahead were discussing—and presumably, saying to Frey—so that I could push them to act in the manner I desired. How to do that, I didn't quite know yet, but I was certain I would once I was equipped with the right information.

Right, that decides it. I have to get closer.

Narrowing my eyes, I studied the column of players ahead. Trying to bluff my way through eighty-odd players who were already on edge was too risky, but sneaking past...

That *was* possible.

Especially if I didn't enter the enemy column and stayed on its fringes. With a plan of sorts, I rose to my feet and headed to the left tunnel sidewall. Bracing my back against it, I began sidling forward silently.

Here goes...

✳ ✳ ✳

Multiple hostile entities have failed to detect you.
Multiple hostile entities have failed to detect you.

...

Five minutes later, I was already halfway to my objective.

All along the enemy column, there was a narrow gap between it and the tunnel wall, one large enough to swing a sword or thrust a spear.

And for me to sneak through.

Doing so was not easy, and at times I passed close enough to smell the sweat under the passing players' armpits and to hear the rapid beats of their hearts. Without vanish, what I attempted would have been entirely impossible. But *with* vanish even the harshest of the hovering magelights was unable to reveal me.

Throughout my slow and cautious approach, I kept my gaze fixed on the Discord elites ahead. Their discussion was as silent as my footsteps, but animated, nonetheless. Arms were raised, eyes were rolled, and beards were tugged. What was spurring such histrionics, I had no idea. Still, I was grateful for it.

They just need to keep talking for a little longer, and I'll be in range. Then, I can—

You have passed a Perception check! Farspeaker mental sendings detected.

What?

As yet, I was too far from the nine elites for it to be them that the Game message pertained to. And that meant...

Someone else was using a farspeaker device. Someone close.

Freezing in place, I turned my gaze on the nearby players. The enemy column was only two man-wide, a smart decision as it gave each player enough room to maneuver should they be threatened.

But that same decision also narrowed down my choice of likely suspects.

It has to be one these six, I thought, eyeing the players in question. All six were warriors, but only one was not conversing with her fellows. That one, a player that analyze identified as Hailie, was staring straight ahead.

Just like I had been a few seconds ago.

My eyes narrowing, I scrutinized Hallie intently.

There was nothing remarkable about the woman. Her green-painted leather armor was inexpensive, the swords at her hip were just as unnoteworthy, and at rank eighteen, she was low levelled enough to be no threat on the battlefield.

But in light of the Game alert, Hailie's very normalness only piqued my interest further.

The faint telepathic buzzing sounded again, and already suspecting what I would hear, I let it resolve further.

You have passed a Mind check. Eavesdropping on communication commencing...

You have passed a mental resistance check! Your mental intrusion has gone undetected.

A moment later, the buzzing resolved itself into words which I listened in on shamelessly.

"*...will take forever,*" Amelia was saying.

"*I agree,*" Piku replied. "*It's better if we go through Hub Sixteen.*"

For a moment, I stopped listening. The little overheard snippet was enough to confirm my suspicions—and that was that Hailie was a spy.

Or Frey herself.

It would be just like Loken's envoy to travel incognito with her own people and to use them as cover to strike at me from hiding once I revealed myself.

On the other hand, it was *also* possible that either the Light or Dark faction had stolen a page out of Frey's own playbook and planted a doppelganger in Shadow's midst. Admittedly, though, this scenario was less likely. Loken would have taken precautions against traitors. And given his history, those precautions were likely to be potent.

So, I mused, steadfastly not looking at Hailie again on the off chance her Perception was high enough to sense my regard, *what do I do now?*

Kill the not-Hailie? Or wait to see what the nine Discord elites did?

Before I could decide, though, a new voice entered the farspeaker conversation, and I bent my attention toward it again.

"*Enough dithering,*" Frey ordered. "*Move out now.*"

"*But which way should we—*" Piku began.

"*I don't care. Pick a direction and go,*" Frey rasped. "*If our quarry wasn't already there, your incessant jabbering has probably drawn his interest. If you don't move soon, he will hit you before you do.*"

"*Hit us?*" Tanakh asked, sounding startled. "*But there are ninety of us and only one of him. Trying to take us out would be foolish!*"

"*You would think that, wouldn't you?*" Frey asked, somewhat grimly. "*But you would be wrong. Have you forgotten our quarry defeated Nemea? Or that he came here alone in the first place? This is not a player who shies from risk.*"

Up ahead, I saw the nine elites shuffle uncomfortably. Hailie, though, did not react to the envoy's words. But that did not mean as much as I wanted it to...

"Alright," Pike pronounced, *"you heard Frey. Let's get a move on."* He swung to face another armored warrior. *"Dres, call up your squad. They can carry Nemea."*

"Use Troy's squad instead," Frey interjected.

"Troy's?" a surprised Piku asked. *"But they're in the middle of the column and farther away."*

"Just use them," Frey snapped in asperity.

"Yes, ma'am," Piku replied, not protesting further. *"Troy, you heard the boss. Summon your people."*

The elite in question swung around and, raising his hand, signaled in the direction of the column. A moment later, to no surprise to me, 'Hailie's' squad began moving forward.

That clinches it, I thought. *Hailie is Frey.*

✳   ✳   ✳

My plans were once again in disarray. But this time, I didn't mind. Loken's envoy—Frey herself—was within reach of my swords. The urge to strike *now*, while she remained blissfully unaware of my presence, was great.

But I contained myself.

Because of course, not only was Frey within striking distance, she also stood on the edge of a minefield, and by her own orders was moving farther into it—into the very epicenter of the traps I'd prepared.

When she was within touching distance of the adamantine golem, then would be the time to act.

Turning away from the envoy, I took stock of my own position. I, too, was within the dormant minefield, and obviously that was far from ideal. My gaze fixed on Hailie, I began backpedaling, retreating back the way I'd come.

Hailie-Frey reached the adamantine golem before I managed to get clear of the enemy column, but that was alright—I had already passed the last of my traps. *This is far enough,* I decided.

Drawing to a halt, I watched proceedings unfold up ahead.

Troy was gesticulating at his squad and, complying with his orders, Hailie and her fellows gathered around Nemea and heaved. It took three tries, but eventually, the nine players, working in tandem, managed to lift the construct off the ground.

Hailie—by design, I suspected—had placed herself at the golem's head and had her hands wrapped around his neck. I smiled. That only put her more at risk.

"Move," Troy barked.

Hailie's squad took a step in my direction. Then another. And another. They were obviously struggling. Still, they were managing with the burden they bore, and it wouldn't be long before they achieved a workable rhythm.

The time to act had come.

Reaching into my pocket, I removed a pair of remote triggers and, without delaying further, pressed down on both.

You have activated 20 tier 4 traps with a status key.
You have activated 20 tier 4 traps with a status key.
40 tier 4 traps are no longer dormant.
Hailie has spotted a trap!
Hailie has spotted a trap!
...
...

Ahead, I saw Frey's limbs freeze and her mouth open to cry out in warning. But it was too late for that—far too late.

A hostile entity has triggered a trap!
A hostile entity has triggered a trap!
...
...

A hostile entity has triggered a trap!
A hostile entity has triggered a trap!
…

…

The tunnel flashed white, turning brighter than the noonday sun for an instant as a hundred and twenty jagged bolts of lightning forked quickly into existence one after the other.

All nine elites were struck. Most were hit more than once, some more than a dozen times. The mages among them had their shields up already, but that didn't count for much in the wake of the concentrated lightning storm.

Elites died.
And lower leveled players, too.
Like wheat under a scythe, they fell in rapid succession.

Piku has died.
Tanakh has died.
…

…

26 hostile entities have died.
You have critically injured Hailie!
You have critically injured Hailie!

Hailie-Frey also suffered the storm's wrath, and she, too, was brought low—but then something entirely unexpected happened.

Hailie has died.
The doppelganger spell surrounding Hailie has been forcibly dispelled, revealing her true form as that of Frey.

Frey's deathwish ability has triggered!
A deathwish ability is a trigger-cast spell that manifests in the split-second between death and the spirit fleeing.
Frey has cast <u>shadowy renewal</u>, reconstituting her spirit in the nearest friendly construct.
Frey has transformed into a level 290 adamantine golem.

My mouth dropped open in horror. I'd been hoping—no, I'd been *expecting*—to kill Frey. Instead, I'd only compounded my problems. Not only had I not prevented the adamantine golem from becoming a threat again, but my actions had resulted in reviving it in the worst possible way.

With Frey in direct control.

Hells.

For all intents and purposes, Frey *was* now the golem.

"Deathwish," I murmured, shaking my head in renewed disbelief. It was an exceedingly rare ability, and in all my time in the Game, I'd only encountered one foe with it—the swarm viper from Draven's Reach. That creature had been hellishly hard to kill.

Frey, I suspected, would be even harder to slay.

At the tortured scream of metal on metal, my attention snapped back to the present.

The adamantine golem was rising to its—her—feet.

"He's here," Frey roared. "Find him!" In time with her words, a searchlight shot out from the golem's blood-red eye.

Wrenching my gaze away from the envoy, I took in the rest of the force—or rather its remnants. As much as a third of the group had been decimated by the lightning storm. And as was to be expected, chaos ruled supreme amongst those that remained.

Frey's roar had captured the attention of all the Discord players still standing, but they remained at a loss of how to go about fulfilling her orders. My vanish was still active, and short of a player running accidentally into me, none of them were going to find me.

The golem's Horus eye, on the other hand... there would be no avoiding that.

I can't stay here, I realized. The time had come to retreat and regroup.

But golem-Frey still had a sizable force under her command, and before I fled, I needed to do something about that. Reaching into my pockets again, I drew out another remote trigger.

I'd activated only forty of the sixty traps I'd set earlier—those near the stone door and those around the golem itself—thinking they would be enough to deal with Hailie-Frey. And while I had been right about that, the outcome was not what I desired. In any case, my westernmost traps were still unused.

And now there was no reason to save them. Pressing down on the remote in my hand, I brought the last of my traps to life.

You have activated 20 tier 4 traps with a status key.

The reaction was immediate. About a dozen yards from me, the array of hidden motion cones shattered, releasing their deadly enchantments.

A hostile entity has triggered a trap!
A hostile entity has triggered a trap!

...

...

For a second time, the tunnel flashed bright white—much to the dismay of my foes. Fresh mayhem ensued, and more players fell.

But not enough did. Not nearly enough.

19 hostile entities have died.

"Goddamnit," I muttered. My traps had left the Discord company dazed and reeling, but too many of them remained alive for me to withdraw just yet. Drawing my swords, I swung around to face the closest squad. Nearly all of its survivors were still befuddled, blinded, or injured by the lightning that had ripped through their ranks, but they wouldn't stay that way for long.

Blurring forward, I attacked.

Chopping down with the sword in my right hand, I sliced through a ranger's armor. Lunging forward on my left leg, I sent the point of my other blade driving through a warrior's shield and straight into his throat. Swinging around, I hacked into a third player, then, somersaulting backward, killed two more.

5 hostile entities have died.

Better, I thought grimly.

Out of the corner of my eye, I spotted a metallic flash.

The golem was racing forward. She was over fifty yards away, but closing the distance fast. Even amongst the hue and cries of the distraught company, Frey had not missed the demise of the five players, and it would not be long before—

Horus' all-seeing eye has found you. You are <u>revealed</u> (exposed and unable to hide). Duration: 1 minute.
You are no longer hidden.

Well, that was always going to happen, I thought, undaunted. Still, Frey had uncovered me quicker than I'd anticipated, and now I was exposed.

Time for the grand finale.

Releasing the weaves of the spell I held ready, I spewed plumes of black smoke out of my mouth.

You have cast noxious vapors.

Adriel's stolen spell was only the first part of my planned two-stage maneuver, though. Delving into the ring on my right hand, I drew forth the spell stored within.

Mage's surprise activated. Spellhold casting released.
You have trigger-cast furious storm.

Lightning manifested again and, joining the spreading vapors, wreaked more havoc on the enemy. The twin spells had no effect on the onrushing golem, of course, but for the shell-shocked players, it proved too much.

Beset by lightning for the third time in less than a minute and fresh horror in the form of the black smoke, the Discord company broke, its morale shattered. Swords and staffs were dropped as players took flight. Some ran unseeing past me, others huddled small against the stone door on the other end. One and all, though, they ignored the rallying cries of the remaining elites and Frey's angry orders.

Smiling in grim victory, I swung about to face the furious golem. Only a dozen yards separated us now. *That's damnably close.* Feigning a lack of concern I most certainly did not feel, I bowed mockingly to Frey.

"You little bastard!" the envoy roared. "I will rend you from limb to limb for this!"

Eight yards.

"Not today, you won't," I retorted.

Six yards.

Drawing psi, I fixed my mindsight on one of the fleeing players that had hurtled past earlier.

Four yards. Three. Two.

At the very last moment, I shadow jumped away and left Frey to grasp impotently at nothing but empty air.

✻　✻　✻

You have teleported into Ameford's shadow.

I emerged from the aether primed to kill.

Sending my right sword darting out, I dispatched the hapless player who had facilitated my escape even before he realized I was there. Then, I was off—almost before the corpse hit the ground.

Dashing down the tunnel in the opposite direction from Frey and her remaining minions, I skidded into Hub Twenty-four. Barely pausing for breath, I picked an exit at random and careened down it, too.

For now, my only concern was to put as much distance between me and the Discord company as possible. Frey would not give up on the chase, I was sure. But now, she had far fewer minions to call upon, and finding me would be that much harder.

Even with the golem's Horus eye.

Speaking of...

Right on cue, a Game message unfurled in my mind.

You are no longer <u>revealed</u> and may hide once more.

About time, I groused. Drawing stamina, I recast vanish and faded into the shadows again.

You are <u>invisible</u>. Duration: 5 minutes.

I was safe, or about as safe as I could be locked inside an underground complex with Loken's envoy. Slowing my steps, I glanced over my shoulder. The tunnel behind me was dark and silent. I'd outrun pursuit.

But for now, that was good enough.

Drawing to a halt, I rested the back of my head against one of the tunnel's sidewalls and, for the next few seconds, just concentrated on breathing.

Once my heart stopped pounding and my breathing slowed, I called up the waiting Game messages and reviewed the outcome of my ambush.

20 players have died from noxious vapors and furious storm.
You and Ghost have reached level 290!
Your shortswords has reached rank 25, your telekinesis rank 22, and your thieving rank 19.

Despite my best efforts, things had gone from bad to worse. Saya wasn't in the underground complex. This didn't even appear to be the Shadow's main base. Instead, Frey had configured the area as one big trap.

In which I was now stuck.

With her and twenty-odd other players.

My lips turned up in a wry grin. *Well, it could be worse.*

"How?" Decal asked, his mindvoice brimming with curiosity as he intruded on my thoughts.

I chuckled softly. *"Well, we could still be facing Frey, the golem, and the full company of a hundred Discord players."*

Decal ignored my poor attempt at humor. *"You didn't use me in the ambush,"* he stated instead. *"Why not?"*

"I was going to," I admitted. *"But then, Frey resurrected herself in the golem, and everything changed."* The smile slipped off my face. *"Right now, you are my best hope for defeating the golem. Frey cannot find out about you until it's too late."*

I sensed his agreement.

"What are you going to do now?" he asked.

I shrugged. *"The only thing I can—figure out a way into Besina's sleeping chamber and turn off the iron dome."*

"Good luck," Decal replied before fading back into the depths of my mind.

Alone in my head once more, my thoughts turned to Loken's envoy again. Thus far, Frey had demonstrated a wide variety of abilities. During our first encounter, she had laid a compulsion on the dire wolves. Her being able to do that meant she was a powerful telepath. She had also, on multiple occasions, transformed herself, making her skilled at deception, as well. Then, there was her ability to pilot constructs from afar and even inhabit one.

I shook my head. I didn't know what Class all that added up to, but it was clear in my mind that Frey was a skilled and powerful caster.

Yet...

She had cast no spells in our most recent encounter. This, despite her very obvious rage and my needling. And now that I had a moment to think over the matter, I realized it was probably because she couldn't. Courtesy of her golem body, the envoy had likely lost access to her magic.

In a last gasp effort to stave off death, Fey had displaced her spirit— in a manner not altogether different from the one used by the possessed in Draven's Reach. The possessed had been limited by the nature of their new bodies in what they could do.

I suspected the same held true for Frey. For all that Frey's deathwish had saved her and made her immune to damage, it had *also* robbed her of her most powerful offensive abilities. It would take the expertise of someone like Adriel to confirm my suspicions, but I didn't think I was wrong.

I smiled. *So as bad as the situation is, it's not all bad.*

CHAPTER 623: MOVE AND COUNTERMOVE

I needed to take down the iron dome.

To do that, I needed to get into Besina's sleeping chamber, which in turn meant looting Hailie-Frey's corpse. Whatever device Frey had been using to open and close the stone doors, she had surely kept it on her person—former person, rather.

Hailie's body was likely being guarded, though. And by golem-Frey herself. So, before I went investigating, I needed to make sure I was properly prepared.

The first thing I had to do was to invest my newly acquired attribute points. I'd accumulated a whole eleven since the night's ventures had begun—a tidy sum by any measure. Reaching out to the Adjudicator, I willed my intent to the Game.

Your Dexterity has increased to rank 159. Available ability slots: 18.

Eighteen ability slots were enough to improve another of my Dexterity abilities, but I was not carrying any ability tomes or gems on me, and doing so would have to wait for later. Still, the extra Dexterity would undoubtedly come in handy in the interim.

Next, I renewed my buffs. They wouldn't be of much use against the golem, but there were still twenty other players out there, a few of them elites, too.

Finally, ready, I swung around and headed back the way I'd come.

*　　*　　*

Hub Twenty-four was empty and free of traps—I knew this because I'd painstakingly checked every inch of it before moving on—on the other hand, the tunnel leading to the wyvern mother's den was occupied.

Cloaked in shadow and perched on a rock just outside the range of the golem's eye, I studied the three figures guarding the stone door at the end of the tunnel. The first was golem-Frey herself, and the other two were the elites, Troy and Amelia. As evidenced by the corpses on the ground, six of the elites had perished in the triple lightning storms.

Where is the ninth, though?

Pursing my lips, I scanned the tunnel anew, but I still failed to spot any sign of the last elite survivor. She wasn't the only one missing, either. In total, twenty players had survived my ambushes, most of whom had panicked and scattered. They could be anywhere in the tunnel complex by now. But 'most' was not all, and in the split-second before retreating, I'd noticed other players taking refuge by the stone door.

So, where had they gone in the interim?

Until I had an answer to the mystery, I could not act. After my repeated ambushes, Frey and her people would be doubly wary, and perhaps even had an ambush of their own prepared. An abundance of caution was called for.

Looks like there is nothing for it but to wait.

Sighing, I made myself as comfortable as I could on my perch and set about doing just that.

✳   ✳   ✳

Ten minutes passed, then another, and still the trio at the stone door did nothing. Frey spent the entire time pacing up and down, muttering to herself. The two elites threw her sidelong looks but said nothing.

Not out loud, anyway.

From the glances the pair exchanged, it was clear they were chatting over their farspeaker link. Interestingly enough, Frey did not retrieve Hailie's bracelet and re-equip it, which I took to mean that she couldn't. Given the glaring absence of any weapons or armor on the golem's body, it was likely the construct wasn't able to use any player equipment.

That was just supposition, of course, but the speculation helped pass the time.

It was boredom, too, that eventually prompted me to inspect the golem anew. The Adjudicator's response, though, was far from enlightening.

The target is Frey, a level 290 adamantine golem.

Nothing in the Game message even suggested at Frey's true nature—that she was a player and Loken's envoy to boot. Nor was there any hint either that the analyze information returned was fabricated.

It was proof enough—if I needed it—that Frey's deception was high enough to defeat my insight.

On a more positive note, Frey appeared oblivious to my probe. Whether that was because she was in a golem body or because my own deception was greater than *her* insight, I didn't know. Whatever the case, I was grateful, and with no other choice than to be content with the Adjudicator's response, I resisted conducting further probes and got back to simply waiting.

All in all, it wasn't the most interesting of stakeouts.

Five minutes later, though, I was glad I'd embarked on it.

Footsteps rang out at my rear—precise, firm, and doing nothing to conceal themselves. A moment later, both elites swung around to face the tunnel.

"What is it?" Frey asked, this being the first words she'd spoken to the pair since I'd begun my watch.

"Jerika is back," Troy replied.

"Is she alone?" Frey rasped.

Amelia hesitated a moment—while she checked with Jerika over the farspeaker link, I thought— before replying, "Yes, she has Camira, Olivie, and Dreadmoon with her."

"Only three?" Frey growled. "How damnably far did the others run?"

Wisely, Amelia and Troy treated the question as rhetorical.

Multiple hostile entities have failed to detect you.

Peering over my shoulder, I spotted the four Discord players being spoken of. Jerika—the ninth elite—had her chin up, but the three players shuffling in her wake were trying to look anywhere except at the golem. Their sheepish expressions and demeanor weren't helping Frey's mood any.

"Where did you find them?" the envoy demanded as the three passed by without so much as a glance in my direction.

Jerika's eyes darted to the trio shifting uncomfortably behind her before answering. "In Hub Fourteen."

Frey's golem-face was incapable of expression, but I thought I could sense a frown in her voice as she asked, "What were they doing there?"

"Hiding," Jerika muttered low enough under her breath that Frey wouldn't hear. "Regrouping," she added in a louder voice.

Frey didn't dispute the obvious lie. "Did you verify their identities?"

"I have," Jerika confirmed.

Frey glanced at Troy. "Give them their orders and see them in place," she instructed before turning back to Jerika. "What about the others?"

"Do we need them, really?" Jerika asked doubtfully. "We can—"

"Find them," Frey interjected.

"But—"

"Now."

Jerika exhaled heavily. "As you wish, boss." Spinning around, she retreated back down the corridor.

I watched the elite leave through narrowed eyes. I was tempted to follow immediately on her heels, but I was more curious to see what was going to happen to the luckless trio.

Swinging around, I turned my attention back to the players gathered by the stone door. Frey had started pacing again, Amelia was intoning the words of a spell under her breath, and Troy was talking sternly to the trio, berating them for deserting earlier—and from the sounds of it, he was just getting started.

How long is this going to take? I wondered unhappily.

I still intended on trailing after Jerika. I wouldn't be able to do that, though, if Troy went on for much longer. *Can't he just—*

Amelia has cast <u>prickly barrier of interference</u>.

In an eyeblink, an opaque wall of white sprang into being between me and the Discord players, cutting them out of view. I couldn't even hear Troy's harangue any longer or see any of their mindglows anymore.

"Decal," I murmured, *"can you see the dreamscapes of the six players by the stone door?"*

A pause. *"No, Michael."*

I pursed my lips. *"Not even Frey's?"*

"Not even the golem's," he confirmed.

I sighed. It didn't look like I was going to get my wish and find out what Frey intended for the trio. I could always stay and wait for Amelia's barrier to go back down, and then try to figure out what had happened, but that didn't seem like the particularly smart thing to do.

Not when I had a more promising lead so close.

Rising into a half-crouch, I turned about and followed silently after the disappearing Jerika.

✳ ✳ ✳

A hostile entity has failed to detect you.

I caught up to Jerika before she left Hub Twenty-four. The elite was not hurrying, nor did she appear particularly worried about what the darkness concealed.

Which fact immediately put me on guard.

Jerika might be an elite, but I had just slaughtered nearly eighty of her fellows. That alone warranted a modicum of caution.

So, why wasn't she afraid?

I already knew Jerika's level and Class, but just to be certain, I reached out with my will and inspected her anew.

The target is Jerika, a level 203 human shadow seer. She bears a Mark of Supreme Shadow.

I learned nothing new from my latest analyze attempt. I had little idea what the shadow seer Class entailed. At a guess, it was a mystic or cleric Class of some sort.

Interestingly enough, Jerika did not bear a Mark of Loken. But then again, only half of the Discord elites I'd analyzed so far had borne the trickster's Mark, so I couldn't read much into the fact. More frustrating, though, I didn't know the source of Jerika's brazen confidence.

What made her feel safe walking the tunnels alone?

Was she a decoy?

A trap?

I couldn't see how, but that didn't mean she wasn't. I sighed, somewhat at a loss of how to proceed. The nebulous, half-formed plan in my mind called for me to enslave the elite, but did I dare make the attempt if she was something other than what I expected?

What choice did I have, though?

If I didn't subvert Jerika, my only other option was conducting a frontal assault on golem-Frey, Troy, Amelia, and however many other players they had concealed near the stone door. And that would *still* leave the mysterious Jerika unattended to at my back. Which was an even worse option.

Better if I deal with her now, while she is alone, I decided. *And if she has some sort of surprise in store for me, best I find out now what that is.*

With this in mind, I drew my blades and stalked closer.

I didn't launch my assault immediately.

For one, Jerika was still too close to Frey and the others for my liking, and for another, I wanted to spend some time observing the elite.

But even after scrutinizing the Discord player for a full ten minutes and padding in her wake as she wandered seemingly aimlessly through the tunnels, I spotted nothing else amiss about Jerika's demeanor. At one point, I even drew close enough to plunge my blade through her exposed back.

To no noticeable effect.

Perhaps, she is always this confident, I thought sourly.

It didn't matter. I'd waited long enough, and delaying further would serve no purpose. The time to act had come. Dashing forward, I raised the blade in my right hand and, pommel first, struck Jerika on the back of the head.

Or tried to.

Jerika has trigger-cast <u>ethereal form</u>, shifting out of phase with the real plane. While ethereal, Jerika cannot be harmed, but neither can she pass through solid objects, interact with items, or perform any harmful actions.

Your target has evaded your attack.

As pommel met flesh, flesh vanished.

And before my eyes, Jerika turned ethereal, her form becoming hazy and translucent. Borne on by momentum, my sword and arm passed harmlessly through the once-solid player.

Jerika jerked to a halt and spun around.

A hostile entity has failed to detect you.

"Who's there?" the shadow seer demanded, her voice only a touch unsteady.

Still unsettled by the spectacular failure of my attack, I said nothing.

"There's no point hiding," Jerika crowed, her voice growing more confident, "you can't hurt me, you know."

I swallowed unhappily. That much appeared all too apparent, but I wasn't quite ready to concede the point. *"Decal, I need you to—"*

"I'm sorry, Michael, I cannot."

I paused. *"You haven't even heard my request yet,"* I said mildly.

"True enough," he admitted. *"But I can guess what it is easily enough. I can see the person before you—but only through your own eyes. To my own sight, she is invisible, and her dreamscape, if it exists, is hidden. It is as if she doesn't have one at all. There's nothing I can do to her."*

"I see," I muttered. If even Decal couldn't act against Jerika, then she was truly protected from harm in her current form.

So, what do I do now?

"Come on, show yourself!" the elite shouted, her voice growing more strident.

Seeing no harm in granting her demand, I did as she asked. At the very least, it should buy me time to figure out a way around the elite's spell.

You have dispelled vanish. You are no longer hidden

Sheathing my sword and in full view once more, I bowed mockingly before the Discord elite. "You called?"

Her translucent eyes glittering, Jerika studied me avidly. "So. You are he."

"He?" I asked, raising one eyebrow.

"Frey's nemesis. The one she is hunting so obsessively."

"Yes, that would be me."

"Why does she want you so badly?"

I shrugged. "Your guess is as good as mine."

Jerika's ghostly face scrunched up. "Don't take me for a fool. You must know!"

I shrugged again. "But I don't. On the other hand, I do know why *I* am here."

"Ah, yes. The gnome."

I kept my face studiedly neutral. "You know where Saya is?"

It was Jerika's turn to shrug. "Perhaps," she replied noncommittally.

My lips turned down fractionally. Jerika appeared in no hurry to leave, but neither did she seem about to let anything slip, and anyway, I already knew where Saya was. "That's an interesting spell," I observed, changing the subject.

"It is, isn't it?" Jerika agreed cheerfully.

"How long can you keep it going?"

"Forever," Jerika replied smugly.

I very much doubted that. The spell was either single-cast, meaning it had a finite duration, or a channeled variant, in which case it would require a constant supply of mana to maintain. "What's your end game here?"

"*My* end game? What's yours?" Jerika retorted. "Your attack failed, and as you can see, there's nothing you can do to harm me now. So, why don't you run along?"

I shook my head. "No, I don't think so."

"No?" Jerika repeated, confounded.

"No," I repeated. Drawing psi, I cast.

You have manifested 4 sentient shurikens.

Jerika's eyes slipped from me to the astral projections hovering nearby. "Those can't hurt me," she said with a snort of disdain.

"Not now, they can't." I smiled. "But once your spell lapses, things will go differently, I promise."

Jerika shifted uncomfortably. My confidence was unsettling her, I could tell. Still, she didn't back down.

"By then, I will be long gone and back in Frey's company," she retorted.

"You won't," I disagreed.

"And why's that?"

"Because I'll stop you."

She laughed. "And how are you going to do that? I thought we already established you can't hurt me."

I grinned. "Oh, I don't need to hurt you to stop you. All I need to do is stand in your way."

Jerika's brows drew down. "That's preposterous! How is that—"

Not waiting for her to finish, I swung about and retraced my steps to a narrow stretch of corridor. Turning around anew, I widened my stance and spread my arms. "Let's see you pass now," I challenged.

Jerika stared at me for a drawn-out moment before understanding dawned.

"Uh-huh," I said, seeing the light of recognition in her eyes. "You forgot we're in an underground complex. And how was it that the Game described your ability?" I paused for effect. "That's right, you can't pass through solid objects. Well, guess what? *I* am a solid object, and you aren't getting past me."

Jerika scowled. "There are tunnels aplenty. Try to block this one, and I'll only find another way through."

"No, you won't." Drawing, psi, I stepped into the aether and out again, behind Jerika. "Because I am faster than you. Wherever you go, I'll be there to stop you."

The elite spun around, her eyes narrowing.

Folding my arms across my chest, I jerked my chin in the direction of the spot I just vacated. "Go on, make a dash for it. See how far you get."

Jerika glowered at me but didn't take me up on my offer.

I smiled, but there was nothing pleasant about my expression. "This has just turned into a waiting game, and believe me, I am better at it than you are. When you lose, and you *will* lose—" I gestured to the shurikens—"they'll be ready to pounce."

✳ ✳ ✳

Jerika didn't take me at my word.

She tried to flee, first one way, then the other. Both times, I didn't even have to use shadow jump to get in her way. That was not the end of the matter, though. The shadow seer tried anew—and failed anew. Then tried again, and again, and again...

Eventually, Jerika attempted something different. Hurtling one way down the tunnel, she waited until I moved to block her before spinning around and slipping back into the real.

Jerika is no longer ethereal.

The transition was seamless. One moment, the elite was translucent; the next, she wasn't. Then, drawing the dagger sheathed her hip, Jerika whipped her right arm forward, striking at where she knew I would appear.

And appear there I did.

But if the shadow seer was hoping to catch me off-guard, she failed. Like I told her earlier, I was faster than her. Then, too, I was expecting her to try such a maneuver—or something very much like it—for some time now.

Swaying out of the way of the arcing blade, I backhanded the elite with my left hand, while simultaneously striking her hard in the stomach with the flat of my sword.

The twin blows left Jerika dazed and staggering. Before she could recover, I lunged forward and ripped the farspeaker bracelet off her right arm—because of course, the elite's next instinct would likely be to cry for help.

"Wha—?" Jerika stuttered, staring down at her arm in confusion.

I didn't bother explaining. Raising my sword again, I brought the pommel whipping down on the back of her head.

This time around, no trigger-cast spell manifested to save Jerika, and she crumpled into an unconscious heap without protest.

✳ ✳ ✳

Before Jerika could regain consciousness, I cast enslave.

You have successfully dominated Jerika, a level 203 human shadow seer. Duration: permanent until death. Warning: you have cast enslave twice in one day and cannot recast it again today.

Much to my relief, the blood spell went through easily and finished without incident. Sitting down cross-legged beside the prone player, I prodded her with my sword. It was finally time for me to get some answers, and I wasn't about to wait until Jerika awoke naturally.

Finally, the elite stirred. "What did you do to me?" she groaned as she sat up gingerly.

"Readjusted your priorities," I replied carelessly.

Jerika blinked blearily. "What does that—"

"Quiet," I ordered, holding up a hand.

The elite's mouth closed with an audible snap.

"Good. Now, tell me what Frey is planning."

"I don't know," Jerika replied.

I sighed in disappointment. "Do you at least know what she did with the three players you took back?"

Jerika didn't question my knowledge of her recent movements. "She sent them into the wyvern's den."

I frowned. "Why would she do that?"

"I don't know."

"Right," I muttered. "And what about the other players you find? Does she intend on doing the same with them?"

"Yes."

I rubbed my chin considerately. The tidbit of information Jerika had just provided offered some interesting possibilities, but there was more I needed to learn before my plans could take shape.

"I can understand why Frey sent you alone into the tunnels," I said, moving on, "but how does she expect you to verify the identity of the players you find?"

"The dark seer is a composite Class," the elite replied. "I am a diviner too."

"Ah." I tilted my head. "What do you see when you look at me?"

Jerika's face went blank for a moment, and I felt an interrogatory ripple wash over me. "Your name is Michael, and you are a level two hundred and one voidstalker."

My brows rose. "Is that all you see?"

She nodded, her own face curious. "Why, is there something I've missed?"

"No," I replied casually, not even willing to share the truth with the dominated player. I leaned forward. "Alright, now walk me through your orders. Step by step, and leave nothing out..."

✳   ✳   ✳

I questioned Jerika for another good twenty minutes, confirming what Orwin had told me and extracting everything the elite knew about Frey and her plans—which sadly did not amount to much.

I did learn Frey's Class, though.

The envoy was a shadow puppeteer, a rare Class that, according to Jerika, gave Frey the nearly unique ability to control living and inanimate objects from afar.

I'd already known as much, so the information was not as useful as I'd anticipated. More to the point, Jerika was also able to confirm my suspicions about the golem, which was that while housed in its body, Frey was unable to use any player items or even her own abilities.

I also learned that while the Discord players knew enough to be afraid of my telepathic abilities, Frey had *not* warned her people to be wary of imitators or of being dominated.

It was confirmation of sorts that, despite his varied and wide sources of information, neither Loken nor his envoy was aware of how far I had come in the Game. If either of them knew the truth—that I could wear any face or blood-bind nearly anyone—I was sure they would have taken greater care to see their people protected.

As it was, the measures Frey had put in place were cursory only and far from what was necessary to stop a specialized deceiver and blood-binder like myself. It was a flaw in the envoy's trap that I intended to ruthlessly exploit.

All in all, Jerika turned out to be a fount of useful information, leaving me quite pleased by my decision to pursue her. When I was done with my questions, I rose to my feet and gave the elite her final instructions.

"From this point on, you will resume following Frey's orders. You will do everything she has asked of you, exactly as you would have ordinarily, but with one caveat, and that is you will tell no one you encountered me or who I am. Nor will you interfere with any of my own actions. Understood?"

Jerika nodded. "Do I start now?"

"Yes," I replied, handing her the farspeaker bracelet I'd ripped from her earlier. "Pretend I am not even here."

Wordlessly re-equipping the item, the shadow seer swung around and resumed her interrupted journey down the tunnel.

✳ ✳ ✳

Slipping into the shadows, I trailed after Jerika.

My plans had solidified after interrogating the elite, and while they contained no small element of risk, I judged what I'd come up with to offer the best possible hope of escape.

It was too soon to tell if I would succeed, though, and rather than worry about all the things that might go wrong, I focused instead on the elite ahead.

For the next thirty minutes, Jerika skipped from tunnel to tunnel, searching each meticulously. The elite was not wandering aimlessly as I'd originally assumed, either. My questioning had revealed that she was scrying the tunnels as she went, tracking the fleeing players by some sort of magical spoor. It was how she had found the previous three players.

And it was also how she found the fourth.

"Terry, is that you?" Jerika called as she approached the newfound player. He was seated on the bare ground, with his back to a wall, and his head hanging between his knees—the very picture of misery.

Lifting his head, Terry stared at the approaching shadow. "Jer?"

"It's time to head back," Jerika said, drawing to a halt before the still-seated figure.

"Head back?" Terry asked doubtfully. "Is there even anything to head back to?"

"There is," Jerika said firmly. "I'm not sure if you noticed earlier, but Frey is with us now, as well—in person." She paused. "Kind of, anyway."

Terry either didn't hear the qualifier or chose to ignore it. "Frey," he shuddered. "By the Powers, that makes it even worse."

Jerika nodded sagely. "There will be consequences. You know Frey doesn't take desertion lightly, but you can't stay out here on your own forever."

"Why not?" Terry shot back.

I stopped listening. I'd heard all I needed to. Terry would serve my plans well enough. Shadow jumping forward, I buried my sword in his throat.

You have killed Terry with a fatal blow.

Chapter 625: A Purge of Iron and Steel

You have cast doppelganger, transforming your form into that of Terry, a level 190 human warrior. Duration: infinite.

A few minutes later, I was following in Jerika's footsteps as 'Terry.' My plan, of course, was not to fight Frey for access to Besina's sleeping chamber but to get her to unwittingly allow me in.

I'd employed similar tactics to penetrate the Riders' defenses in the Eastern Marches. Then, things had not turned out so well, but I hadn't had doppelganger to call upon that time, and this time around, I was all but certain there were no Watchers emplaced to trip me up.

As instructed, Jerika did not deviate from her orders and spent the next two hours collecting lost players. Just past the two-hour mark, though, a buzzing—heralding an incoming farspeaker message—sounded in my ears.

Holding up a hand, Jerika brought the column of eight players trailing in her wake to a halt as she paused to listen to whomever was speaking to her.

A moment later, she swung around. "That was Troy, people. We've been recalled. Time to head back."

"What about the others?" one of Jerika's lost sheep asked timidly.

The elite shrugged. "They'll keep for now. I'll gather them later."

"If there is a later," someone else groused.

Ignoring the muttered comment, Jerika marched forward, deliberately setting off at a demanding pace that discouraged further conversation.

In the middle of the trailing column, I exhaled carefully. *This is it,* I thought. *Time to find out how well my preparations will hold up.*

✳ ✳ ✳

We reached the stone door without incident.

"Took you long enough," Frey harrumphed as our small column drew to a halt before her and the other two elites.

Jerika shrugged. "They were scattered far and wide. Searching the tunnels takes time; there is no getting around that. I recovered as many as I could."

"But not everyone," Frey grumbled, her single golem-eye skipping down the line of players arrayed behind the shadow seer. I held my breath as her gaze passed over me, but when no outcry followed, I immediately relaxed. Like Jerika had said, Horus' red beam was designed for one thing only: uncovering stealthed players.

"Five are still missing," Jerika agreed, not disputing the envoy's observation. "I'll head immediately back out to find them."

"No, you won't," Frey contradicted.

In the act of turning away, Jerika paused. "I won't?"

Frey shook her head. "You won't. We've wasted enough time already. It's time to move things along."

"Does that mean you're ready to tell us what comes next?" Troy asked, perking up in interest.

Frey nodded. "I am. Raise your shield, Amelia."

Moving to comply, the mage quickly intoned the words of a spell under her breath.

Amelia has cast <u>prickly barrier of interference</u>.

You have entered a warded area that is immune to surveillance from without. No sights, sounds, scents, or magical signatures will cross over the prickly barrier. Additionally, anyone attempting to penetrate the barrier from outside will suffer physical and magical damage.

Ah, so that's what it does, I thought, studying the familiar wall of white that had sprung up behind me and the others. I noted in passing as well that it was just as opaque on this side as it had been on the other.

"Alright, boss," Troy said, turning back to Frey, "spit it out. How do we kill the bastard?"

"We purge the tunnels," the envoy replied simply.

Amelia frowned. "And by purge, you mean?"

"Scouring them with magic—lots and lots of magic. By the time the spell is done, there will be nothing left alive anywhere but the control room."

The three elites exchanged glances before Jerika asked cautiously, "How are we casting this spell?"

Frey laughed. "Through the iron dome, of course."

Amelia's eyes widened.

Frey nodded in response to the elite mage's look. "The iron dome is not just a shield. It's a weapon too. The steel rods laid in the tunnels can just as easily conduct destructive energy as they can generate a nullifying field."

"But-but... why didn't we purge the tunnels earlier?" a perplexed Troy asked. "*Before* the bastard slew so many of us?"

"Because we were in the tunnels ourselves then," Frey replied patiently. "You all were spread out around the perimeter watching for his entry."

"And instead, he entered right smack in the middle," Amelia muttered. "Through the control room itself."

Frey nodded. "That was unfortunate and turned all my plans on their head. But in any case, using the iron dome to kill our quarry was never the original intent." She paused. "In fact, I can scarce believe I am being forced to use it now."

Jerika cocked her head to the side. "Oh? Why's that?"

Frey was silent for so long, I didn't think she was going to answer, but then, with a shrug of her massive shoulders, she said, "Plan A was the traps set at the perimeter—which he bypassed." She gestured down at herself. "Plan B was the golem that he somehow disabled. Plan C was all of you. Plan D was me." She sighed. "Weaponizing the iron dome is my final contingency."

"And if it fails?" Jerika asked quietly.

"Then I face Loken's wrath," Frey observed morosely.

More silence followed.

"Who is this guy that Loken wants him dead so badly?" Troy asked finally.

"That," Frey said firmly, "is not a matter up for discussion."

The warrior ducked his head, accepting the rebuke.

"If you're going to use the iron dome, why do you need us?" one of the players behind me asked suddenly. "It's not that I'm not grateful for being saved from certain death, but why did you go through all that trouble of recalling us in the first place if you don't plan on using us?"

The three elites turned Frey's way, awaiting her answer.

"Oh, but I do plan on using you—all of you," Frey replied. "The iron dome's mana well needs to be topped up before it can be weaponized, and for obvious reasons, I can't be the one to do it anymore. You lot will have to see it restored."

"Then let's get inside and be about it," Troy said. Removing a small device from his pocket, he pressed down on it, causing the stone door behind him to rise.

Nodding in agreement, Frey strode over to her corpse and slung it negligently over one shoulder.

Amelia eyed the envoy. "What about the remaining bodies?"

"Leave them," Frey ordered.

Amelia threw her a reproachful look. "Piku and the others will want their stuff back."

Frey sighed. "Very well. Get the deserters to help carry the bodies in. But only the elites' corpses, mind. The rest can stay where they lie."

*　*　*

A body draped over my shoulders, I followed the other players into the wyvern's den—the so-called control room. No one tried to talk to me, for which fact I was grateful. If they had, I might have inadvertently slipped up and revealed myself. Because right then, my thoughts were full of one thing only: what Frey had revealed.

It was not the envoy's plans themselves that disturbed me. Rather, it was the extent to which she—and Loken, by extension—was willing to go to see me dead.

He has to know what I am. Or at the very least be deeply suspicious of the truth.

There was no other reason for a Power like Loken to go to such lengths to slay one player, after all. Equally worrying was that I couldn't see how killing me would help Loken any.

Yes, I would die.

But so what?

I had more than enough lives to spare and, when killed, would only resurrect in the safe zone. At which point I would flee as hard and fast as I could. Unless...

Unless the trickster also has a scheme in place for capturing the sector. One that he intends on triggering at the moment of my death. Taking control of the sector was the only way Loken could stop me from fleeing out of reach.

But even that did not make sense.

Loken's faction would need a minimum of twenty-four hours to claim the sector. I, on the other hand, only required sixteen hours to resurrect. The timing did not line up.

He must have something else in mind then. Something he hasn't told Frey. Or that she hasn't told her people.

As disturbing as all this speculation was, though, it didn't change my own plans and what needed to be done. Brushing aside my musings, I turned my attention outward again and refocused on my surroundings.

Ahead of me, Frey and the other elites had come to a stop, carelessly dropping the bodies they carried at their feet. I did the same with the one I held. I took care, though, to mark the position of Hailie-Frey's corpse. That was one body I wanted to loot if the opportunity presented itself.

Troy whistled appreciatively. "Phew, he really made a mess of the place."

Amelia snorted. "By blowing up *our* traps."

Troy shrugged. "Whatever works, right?"

Turning away from the elites' conversation, I studied the chamber for myself. Troy was right. I *had* made a mess. But considering the den was largely a barren space, if you ignored the lingering poison clouds and scorched boulders, the damage was only superficial.

I knew from the information I'd gleaned from Jerika that the only critical piece of equipment in the chamber was the artifact used to control and power the iron dome. It was safely tucked away in the left corner of the chamber, far away from all the damage I'd wreaked.

I spotted five other players in the selfsame corner. Unless I missed my guess, they were already hard at work empowering the device anew with mana.

"Troy, close the door," Frey ordered. "The rest of you come with me." Not waiting to see if we followed, the golem strode purposefully in the direction of the keystone.

No one immediately heeded the command. "What about the traps?" I heard one of the nearby players ask in a worried whisper.

"They've been turned dormant again," Amelia assured him. "Now stop dawdling and follow the boss."

Striding forward myself, I did just that.

✳ ✳ ✳

Now that I was in the wyvern's den once more, I was faced with a slew of options again. I could go after Frey, the artifact, or both.

Let's not get too ambitious now, I thought wryly.

"Jer, can you come over here for a second?" I called loudly, peering closely at the ground.

Amelia and Troy glanced curiously at me, but Jerika waved them on. "Go on. I'll see to this."

I stayed where I was, letting the distance between me and the rest of the column increase while I waited for the shadow seer.

"What is it?" she whispered as she strode up to my side.

"When I reach the keystone and give you the signal," I muttered loud enough for only her to hear, "I want you to kill the other two elites. Troy first. Then Amelia."

"As you wish," Jerika replied, her face expressionless.

"Good. That is all then."

Swinging back around, Jerika rejoined the column, with me trailing after.

"What was that all about?" I heard Troy ask.

"Nothing," Jerika replied. "He thought he saw something, but it was nothing."

"You sure?" Troy asked.

"I am."

"Alright then," he replied, letting the matter lie.

We reached the artifact in short order. Striding up the five players arrayed around it, Frey waved them aside. Then, turning around, she picked out four more from the column, seemingly at random. "You, you, you, and you, come here."

By chance, I was in the group selected.

"Place your hands on the keystone and channel mana into it," Frey instructed.

The other three players moved to comply, as did I. Drawing up to the artifact, I let my gaze linger on it for a moment. The keystone was crystalline in nature and of similar construction to the shield generator we were using to conceal Sanctum. That made it fragile.

And easily destroyed.

To make certain no surprises awaited me, I reached out with my will and inspected the device.

The target is the rank 7 artifact: the <u>Iron Dome Keystone</u>. This item may only be used by members of the Seekers of Discord faction. Likewise, only faction members may discern its properties.

"Go on," Frey growled, seeing me hesitate. "What are you waiting for?"

I could almost certainly touch the artifact, but I doubted I'd be able to channel any mana into it. It was time to put my plan into motion.

Glancing up, I met Jerika's gaze. The shadow seer was staring at me intently, waiting for my signal. Nodding fractionally, I gave her the go-ahead, then bent my head and lowered my hands in pretended compliance with Frey's orders.

As expected, a bellow of rage and anger tore through the cavern before I could make contact.

My head jerked up, as did those of the others nearby.

Jerika had plunged one of her daggers hilt-deep through Troy's neck. The elite warrior was still alive, but he wouldn't remain that way for much longer. Drawing her second dagger, the shadow seer whirled around to attack Amelia.

"Stop her!" Frey roared, even while moving to do so herself. She wasn't the only one. Overcoming their shock, half the remaining players rushed forward with their weapons raised.

I didn't join them.

This was my chance—the moment of maximum distraction. Palming a handful of bombs in my hands, I flung them at the keystone, then fled on a ramp of air.

A split second later, fresh explosions rocked the cavern.

You have cast windsurfer.
You have ignited 3 acid bombs and 3 fire bombs.
You have destroyed a tier 7 keystone!
Troy has died.
An iron dome has been deactivated.

For a moment, silence reigned. Then chaos ensued.

"The bastard is here!" someone cried.

"He's bewitched Jerika," another shouted.

"Find him!" Amelia shrieked.

Only Frey said and did nothing.

The destruction of the keystone seemed to have stunned her senseless. *She knows,* I thought, smiling tightly. *She knows whatever happens from here on out, she's lost.* There would be no recovering from this for her.

The envoy's trap was in tatters, her forces were decimated, and the iron dome was down, leaving me finally free to flee the underground complex.

And I planned on doing just that.

First, though, I had one last parting gift in store for Frey.

Chapter 626: A Parting Gift

Before I could enact the last part of my plan, I had to see myself safe. Letting the windslide beneath me dissipate, I dove into the shadows and disappeared from sight.

**You have cast vanish. You are <u>invisible</u>. Duration: 5 minutes.
Your minion has died.**

As I did, Jerika collapsed under the weight of the blades brought to bear against her. I felt no regret at the shadow seer's passing. She had served her purpose well, but there was no way she would survive what was coming.

None of the Discord players would.

"Where is he?" Frey rasped, finally seeming to shake off the debilitating dread that had gripped her. Whirling full circle, she scanned the cavern with Horus' eye.

But the moment when Frey could have stopped me had passed, and I was already out of her reach. Ignoring the revealing red beam playing along the cavern walls a few dozen yards away, I turned my attention to the rest of the Discord players.

Only Jerika and Troy had perished in the brief fray that had erupted, and now the remaining fourteen players were spreading out, searching the darkness like Frey was doing.

But they, too, had no hope of finding me.

"Come out, coward!" Amelia shouted suddenly. "Show yourself!"

"Yes," Frey hissed, stalking round and round in ever-widening circles. "Let's finish this."

I paid their taunts no heed. While I agreed with the elite and envoy that it was time to end matters, I would do it my way. Reaching into my backpack, I withdrew an item.

It was the stone of calling that Tosh had looted from Jobe.

Holding the object in my hand, I studied it for a long, drawn-out moment. It was a summoning device that, once activated, would act like a siren call for the Lightsworn.

There would be no turning back after I used the stone.

Muriel's people would portal in en masse within moments of it being activated. That they were as much my enemies as Loken's people were was irrelevant.

Sometimes, all it took to defeat one enemy was another.

Because the truth was that Muriel's people were the best hope I had for seeing golem-Frey dead. The only other options available to me were either sending Decal into Frey's dreamscape or transforming into an elder wolf and killing the envoy myself.

And I wanted to do neither of those things.

Knowledge of the simulacrum's existence and my shapeshift ability were cards I needed to hold in reserve until a rainy day. The wider Game—and Loken especially—could not be allowed to learn about them. And whatever happened next, it was unlikely Frey would die a final death today. What she learned, Loken would too.

So, really, when you looked at it that way, I had little choice in the matter. I *had* to use Muriel's people.

Decision made, I refocused on the item in my hand and willed it alive.

You have activated a stone of calling.

The deed done, I drew back my arm and flung the stone as far away as I could. It hit the ground with an audible clink, drawing the attention of the Discord players, and while they rushed toward it, I crept silently away in the opposite direction.

✳ ✳ ✳

It took all of five seconds for the Lightsworn to arrive.

First one, then two, then ten portals opened in the cavern. And out of each glittering gateway, Muriel's people poured out.

Of course, their attention immediately focused on golem-Frey. Not only was she the biggest and most visible threat in the chamber, but the adamantine golem itself was also extremely valuable.

Everyone would want to claim a bit of it for themselves.

Frey didn't fail to recognize the danger either. The instant the first Lightsworn appeared, she went from racing toward the flung summoning stone to a course nearly perpendicular. "Follow me," she cried, and obediently, the ragtag remains of her force did just that.

Watching the Discord players' flight, I was puzzled for a moment by the envoy's chosen trajectory. Then, I realized she was making for the closest stone door—which was not the same one we'd all entered mere minutes ago.

"Open it, Amelia," Frey yelled.

Doing as instructed, the mage elite gestured at the stone door, and it began to rise.

That Frey was intent on escape was obvious. Given how slowly the chamber's doors could open, though, I didn't think the envoy and her people would win free of the cavern.

But then something unexpected happened.

Change in state of spotted traps detected...
Amelia has activated an unknown number of dormant traps with a minefield controller.

A trap has been triggered!
A trap has been triggered!
...
8 Lightsworn players have died.

"Damn," I muttered as a new series of explosions rippled through the cavern. Somehow—I wasn't sure how—Amelia had rearmed all the traps in the control chamber in a single go. That, at least, was what I suspected she had done, but there was no way to tell for certain just yet.

I'd tucked myself deep in the shadows, and what I had considered a safe distance from both the hunters and hunted. Unfortunately, I'd not given due consideration to the dormant traps. And while I'd done my best during my previous visit to the chamber to destroy as much of the minefield as I could, none of my bombs had reached my current location in the cavern.

And now, who knew how many active traps surrounded me?

Hells, I cursed. *This could get complicated.* My thoughts turning to my own safety, I wove stamina and enhanced my sight as much as possible.

You have cast trap detect, gaining the buff, <u>spotter</u> (tier 4).

You have activated a true-seer's ring, gaining the buff, <u>true-seeing</u> (tier 5).

Alrighty, now let's see what I have to deal with. Craning my neck from left to right, I slowly inspected the immediate surroundings.

You have spotted a tier 4 trap!
You have spotted a tier 4 trap!

Two, I breathed. There were only two traps in close proximity to my current position. And better yet, both traps were more than three feet away.

I was in no immediate danger, I realized, relaxing fractionally.

Disarming the traps could wait for later. Right now, there were more important happenings in the cavern that I had to focus on. Making sure not to move more than strictly necessary, I turned my attention back to the unfolding battle.

There was not much to see, however.

Courtesy of the rearmed traps, Amelia had gained enough time to erect her prickly barrier of interference, and presently an opaque curtain of white hid the stone door Frey had been heading for—and presumably the fleeing Discord players, too. The Lightsworn were still advancing, but their advance had grown more cautious.

I sighed. More of Muriel's people were still streaming into the cavern, and it was only a matter of time before Amelia's barrier was taken down, but by then, I suspected, Frey and her people would be long gone—either by vanishing into the tunnels or escaping through a portal of their own.

And that meant Frey's capture and death were not a sure thing anymore.

I shrugged fatalistically. The fate of Loken's envoy was no longer my primary concern. My own escape was. Given how fast the Lightsworn were multiplying in the cavern, it would not be long before one of their commanders thought to sweep the area for hidden enemies. I couldn't be around when that happened.

But first...

Sweeping my gaze to the right, I focused on another of the cavern's stone doors—the one I had entered through. Hailie-Frey's corpse was still there, unattended to and forgotten. Could I get to it?

Perhaps.

I couldn't walk there. There were too many traps around for that. But if I used windsurfer, I could avoid the minefield. The only open question was whether the nearby Lightsworn would sense me.

It's worth the risk, I decided.

Frey was an envoy, and not just any envoy, but an envoy to one of the Game's most preeminent Powers. Her gear would be immensely valuable, if not perhaps as valuable as the adamantine golem itself. But there was no retrieving that monster.

Weaving psi, I summoned a windslide.

You have cast windsurfer.

The invisible ramp of air manifested beneath my feet, and at a thought, I willed it upward until I was elevated some thirty feet off the cavern floor. Hanging there for a moment, I waited to see if any of the hundred or so Lightsworn in the chamber had noticed the windslide's appearance or my new position.

But one and all, the Light players were focused on the northern end of the cavern, on the stone door through which the Discord players had just fled.

Deeming it safe enough, I sent the windslide gliding through the air and towards my target.

✳   ✳   ✳

I reached Frey's corpse without mishap.

Lowering my airborne conveyance to the ground, I disembarked quickly and without fear of triggering any traps. I'd already cleared this section of the minefield during my initial incursion, and I was confident the ground was safe.

But I could not count on the Lightsworn preoccupation with the north stone door lasting much longer, and that meant there wasn't enough time to properly loot the corpse. So, instead, I removed the locator beacon I'd gotten from the forsworn and stuffed it in one of the corpse's pockets.

Then, I shoved the entire body in the deepest crevice I could find in the hopes that it would stay undiscovered until I returned to reclaim it.

My last chore in the cavern done, I finally bent my thoughts to getting out.

The easiest approach would be to open a portal, but there would be disguising its appearance or emergence point, either, and I didn't want anyone—Lightsworn or otherwise—tracking me.

There was one other alternative.

The very first time I'd entered Besina's sleeping chamber, I had done so by creeping through an entryway on the east side. A cave mouth leading up to the cliff face had been close by.

There was a chance—a slim one, perhaps—that the exit in question had not been walled over. I would need to get the east stone door opened first, though. Glancing in the direction of Troy's body, I spotted the door controller he'd used earlier still clutched in his cold hands. *Opening the door should be easy enough using that.*

Padding over to the corpse, I picked up the controller and pressed down on all four studs along its length.

In response, the west, south, and east stone doors began opening. What was happening with the north door, I couldn't tell. Amelia's barrier was still up.

But it was the Lightsworn response that interested me more.

The simultaneous opening of the three doors gave them pause, and I could almost sense their sudden and intense fear that they'd walked into a trap. That was not the case, of course, but they didn't know that.

So, instead of pushing out and investigating the anomaly, the Lightsworn's formations retracted and closed ranks, leaving me free to glide around the cavern on my windslide and exit the east door with no one the wiser.

Chapter 627: Meet the Jailors

The cave mouth was exactly as I remembered it.

Better yet, it was unguarded. Creeping up to its edge, I peered out. Below me, the cliff on which the entrance perched fell away sharply. Above me, the stars and moon still shone bright. Dawn was still a few hours away, which suited me perfectly.

The clifftop itself wasn't far, less than three away. Unlike the last time I'd been this way, I wouldn't need to scramble aloft this time. Summoning a windslide anew, I let a current of air carry me upward.

I alighted several feet past the edge under an empty sky and barren landscape. *Right, now to find Saya.*

Orienting myself according to Orwin's directions, I set off westwards.

✱ ✱ ✱

It took me a few hours to make the trip.

During that time, I saw no one nor spotted anything to make me suspicious, but just in case, I stayed cloaked the entire time. I also spent a good deal of the trip updating Shael and Ceruvax. The pair had been worried by my long silence and had questions aplenty, all of which I did my best to answer.

As I rounded the peak of which Orwin had spoken, though, I shut down the farspeaker link and bent all my attention on the surroundings. I couldn't afford any distractions. Not now, not when I was so close to my objective.

Shortly, the Discord base came into sight.

Although calling it a base was a bit much. It was more properly a camp. A small one.

Stretched out flat along the ground on an adjacent slope, I studied the still-distant camp.

In a shallow ravine, next to a dry riverbed, five tents had been pitched in a circle. This was about the extent of the camp's infrastructure. A campfire blazed merrily in the cleared space between the tents, and seated around it were three familiar figures.

Bornholm.

Tantor.

Morin.

My lips tightened at the sight of the trio. It could be no accident that these particular three were here—my gaze slid to the small cage resting at the far side of the fire—guarding what, by all appearances, was Saya's prison cell.

The gnome herself was clearly visible through the bars of the steel cage she was locked inside. But unlike the trio seated around the fire, she was sleeping.

Glancing left and right, I took in as much of the surroundings as I could see, but even so, I failed to spot any signs of a trap or anyone else. Frey, in particular, was nowhere to be seen.

It was not as if I was expecting the envoy to be here, though.

I didn't know the golem's fate yet. She might be dead already. Or she might not.

But the only way she could have beaten me to this camp was by portaling in—and Frey would not have done that, because the Lightsworn would have simply tracked her portal and followed her through.

And that was the last thing Loken's envoy would want.

Frey wasn't the only danger around, though, and looks could be deceiving.

Drawing on my stamina and psi, I scrutinized the scene anew. Only this time, I used mindsight, trap detect, and true-seeing to study the area.

They reported the same thing: no wards except those around Saya's cell, no traps of any kind, and no one else around but the four already clearly visible at the fire. I was still not satisfied, though.

Reaching out with my will, I inspected each of the four carefully.

The target is Morin, a level 208 shadow druid and painted human. She bears a Mark of Supreme Shadow and a Mark of Loken.

The target is Tantor, a level 203 phantom sorcerer. He bears a Mark of Greater Shadow and a Mark of Loken.

The target is Bornholm, a level 206 gray berserker. He bears a Mark of Major Shadow and a Mark of Loken.

The target is Saya, a gnomish tavernkeeper. She bears Marks of Lesser Dark, Lesser Light, and Lesser Shadow. Her health and energy pools are at 100%, and she is currently suffering under the debuff: <u>displaced</u>. In her present state, Saya is immune to all damage and may not communicate or interact with anyone outside her prison cell.

Morin, Tantor, and Bornholm's analyze data were no more than I expected. Saya's, on the other hand, was more disturbing. That the cage of steel enclosing her was also warded was clear, but what was the need for the debuff?

Was it to keep Saya from talking to her captors or them from speaking to her?

It's hard to say, I thought, biting my lip in frustration.

The tableau ahead was clearly of Loken's making and designed to convey a message—but an ambiguous one. Because, of course, with Loken, what other kind was there?

The scene could be a naked threat: *Look. See. I can turn even your friends against you.* Or it could be a signal that Loken was open to negotiation. Or maybe, its only purpose was to confuse.

The real question, though, was what did I do next?

Did I approach the camp openly? Or did I slay the 'guards' from the shadows?

But no, I couldn't do that.

Not to ones I once deemed friends—even if they no longer thought of themselves as such.

And that there is likely Loken's real purpose with this little scene: to make me hesitate.

But even knowing as much, I knew I had no choice. Sighing, I rose to my feet. It was time to reacquaint myself with my former comrades and to find out exactly how much of a kinship they still felt with me.

✻　✻　✻

You have transformed back to your original form, falsifying your level as that of a level 203 voidstalker, and concealing your Powerful Acolyte Mark. Duration: infinite.

You have cast vanish. You are <u>invisible</u>. Duration: 5 minutes.

I approached the Discord camp stealthed and invisible. I tripped no wards on the way in, nor did the three players sitting at the fire react in any visible way to my approach.

Ten yards from the campfire, still cloaked, I drew to a halt. None of the three looked up. They weren't talking, eating, or doing anything other than sitting, but it was obvious from their serious expressions and alert gazes that they were awake.

"What brings you all three the way out here?" I asked mildly, using ventro to disguise my location.

The trio's reaction was immediate.

Bornholm spun around, axe in hand. Morin flew to her feet, vines snaking out of her staff, and Tantor wove mana.

But the trio lacked a target for their ire.

Three entities have failed to detect you. You remain hidden.

"Who's there?" Morin demanded, addressing a spot to my right—the direction from which my voice had emerged.

"What? Don't you recognize the voice?" I asked, letting my words project from the opposite direction.

The trio exchanged glances, then Tantor ventured cautiously, "Michael?"

"The one and only," I replied with false cheer.

"It can't be," Bornholm muttered. "She wouldn't, would she?"

The dwarf's question wasn't addressed to me, though. It was to Morin that he looked for an answer.

The painted woman closed her eyes in momentary pain. "She would, if she deemed it necessary," she replied, the strain in her voice undisguised.

"Who are we talking about?" I asked lightly.

The three exchanged glances anew, but this time no one ventured to answer.

"It wouldn't be Frey, would it?" I asked.

None of the three answered, but from their startled expressions I could tell I'd guessed right.

"You know... her?" Tantor asked carefully.

"We've met a time or two." I chuckled. "I'm afraid our last meeting didn't end well for her."

Morin's face whitened, Bornholm groaned, and even Tantor looked pained. "Please don't tell me you mean what I think you do by that?" the elf whispered.

"I'm afraid you're going to be disappointed then. Frey's dead. Or she was anyway. Now, she's stuck in a golem's body."

No confusion or disbelief marred the three's faces at my response. They clearly believed me. It was equally clear, too, that they knew enough of the envoy's abilities to understand what I meant.

"That's why she hasn't been answering," Bornholm muttered.

Morin laid a restraining hand on the dwarf's shoulders. "Don't say any more," she warned. Turning around to where she thought I was, she asked, "Will you show yourself, Michael?"

"I am not sure," I replied flippantly. "Can I trust you?"

Despite the manner in which I'd asked the question, Morin gave my request serious consideration. "Yes," she replied gravely. "You can. We won't attack unless you do."

I pondered her response for a second, then nodded. "Alright," I replied, and let the shadows around me unravel. "Let's talk then."

✳   ✳   ✳

You are no longer hidden.

True to her word, Morin and the others did not attack. They did, however, cast a whole battery of revealing and detection spells on me, all of which I allowed and staunchly bore.

As powerful as some of their spells were, though, none of them came close to revealing my true level or any of my many secrets.

"Are you quite done yet?" I asked finally.

Tantor nodded. "We are." He turned to Morin. "He is who and what he claims to be."

The painted woman sighed. "I almost wished he weren't. That would make all of this easier." Before anyone could respond to that bleak statement, she gestured me to an empty spot by the fire. "Will you sit, Michael?"

Almost, I declined, then nodded sharply. "After you."

The others seated themselves, then I did so as well. As I took my assigned place, I stole a glance at Saya. She'd remained sleeping for the entirety of my conversation with the trio and had not stirred once. Her inactivity worried me, but now was not the time to address the matter.

"So, will you answer my question now?" I asked, turning back to Morin.

"Which one?" she asked quietly.

"Why are you three here?" I asked.

"Ah. It's... complicated."

I smiled humorlessly. "I'm sure it is, but I'd like to hear your answer anyway."

Morin shook her head. "It's not that I don't want to answer. I can't."

I stared at her for a moment, then glanced at Bornholm. The dwarf had always been less able to hide his thoughts than the others, but his forlorn expression, I gathered Morin was not lying.

I sighed. "I take it then, that Frey forbade you from answering my questions?"

"Not *your* questions," Bornholm blurted out before Morin could respond.

"Bornholm," Tantor growled in warning.

"What?" the dwarf growled back. "She ordered us not to reveal any details about our mission. She *did not* forbid us from answering any questions at all!"

Tantor rolled his eyes. "You know what—"

Morin slashed her hand downwards. "Let him speak, Tantor."

The elf threw her a startled look. "But—"

"But nothing," Morin said, cutting him off again. "Frey played us false. We'll stick to the letter of her instructions, not the spirit of them."

The elf subsided. "Alright, but you know she won't let this go unanswered."

Morin shrugged complacently. "I do, and we'll deal with the fallout later." She swung back to Bornholm. "Speak."

The dwarf didn't need further encouragement. "Like I was saying," he said, addressing me intently, "we weren't given any instructions about *you* at all, just the mission."

My eyes narrowed. Bornholm was skirting around the issue, as were the others, but from what they had said—and had not said—I gathered Frey had failed to mention that their mission involved me.

"I see," I murmured. "I take it then that none of you knew I was the one who was going to show up?"

Tantor's face remained studiedly neutral, but both Morin and Bornholm shook their heads. "We didn't," the dwarf confirmed verbally.

Sitting back, I rubbed my chin thoughtfully. "Do you know who your prisoner is?"

"No," Bornholm answered before anyone could stop him.

Given everything I'd just learned, his answer didn't surprise me. "Then, you'll be interested to learn her name is Saya."

Both Morin and Bornholm's faces remained blank, but Tantor couldn't refrain from wincing. "The one you told us about when we met back in Nexus?" the elf asked.

"The very same," I murmured.

"I remember now!" Bornholm exclaimed. "You rescued her from a wyvern, didn't you?"

I nodded solemnly.

He frowned. "Wasn't that all supposed to have occurred somewhere near here?"

I pointed downward. "In the very tunnels beneath our feet."

Morin paled again. Tantor, too, was looking queasy. Both of them were beginning to connect the dots.

Bornholm's frown deepened. "Why would Frey—" he began.

Laying a hand on his arm, Morin stopped him. "Tell us more, Michael," she said quietly.

Obligingly, I did. "Saya is not just someone I rescued. She is also in my employ and runs the tavern I own in this sector's safe zone. Some time ago, she was kidnapped." I paused. "I now know it was Frey who was responsible."

Bornholm's face grew red. "Why would she do that?"

I shrugged. "I'm not quite sure. But it's clear that Frey is using Saya as a pawn in her vendetta against me." I held each of their gazes in turn. "Which brings us to why I am here today."

"You're here to rescue your companion," Tantor observed quietly.

I inclined my head in his direction. "And you've been ordered to stop me."

No one said anything, which I took to mean I'd guessed their mission correctly. I, too, stayed quiet, and the tension mounted, deepening with every passing moment of silence.

Once again, it fell to Bornholm to shatter it.

"Damnable hells, lad! We didn't know," he cried out.

"I believe you," I said softly

Morin exhaled heavily. "But it doesn't change matters, does it?"

I shook my head sadly. "I have to rescue Saya. And you have to try and stop me."

Tantor shuddered. "We must follow our orders." He paused. "Or else risk becoming forsworn."

At great cost, I stayed quiet. The three were Loken's followers, and as much as I wanted to tell them they were wrong about what they thought being a forsworn meant, I didn't dare.

"You will not back down?" Morin asked solemnly.

I shook my head. "Will you?"

"We cannot," she replied.

I nodded. "Then I'm afraid our truce is at an end." I held her gaze. "Agreed?"

She nodded unhappily. "Agreed."

I didn't hesitate. I didn't dither. I attacked.

I moved against Tantor first.

As a mage, he was a significant threat, and besides, he had become complacent enough during our conversation that he'd lowered his shield, leaving him achingly vulnerable.

You have teleported into Tantor's shadow.

Emerging from the aether, I loomed over the still-seated elf. I drew my sword in a flash, and before Bornholm and Morin could do more than rise from their seats, I brought the pommel crashing down on the back of Tantor's head.

I didn't pull the blow, but struck hard enough to crack bone, causing Tantor to slump unconscious.

You have critically injured Tantor.

"Michael!" Bornholm cried. "What are—"

I didn't let him finish. Taking Bornholm down physically would take too long. The dwarf's thick armor was all but impregnable to my swords. His mental defenses, on the other hand... those, I knew from past experiences, were somewhat lacking.

Which is why I struck at him with my mind and not my blades.

You have cast slaysight (shatter).
Bornholm has failed a mental resistance check!
You have weakened your target's mental defenses by 50% for 60 seconds.
Morin's sticky vines have struck you. You are <u>entangled</u> (immobilized). Duration: 60 seconds.

Long, vicious threads of living vegetation wrapped around my legs, torso, arms, neck, and head, trapping me so tightly in place I could scarcely move an inch. Thankfully, though, my sight was not completely blocked by the vines, and I could still see Bornholm.

Deciding to ignore the vines for now, I drew psi again and fashioned a second spell.

"No, lad! Don't do this," Bornholm pleaded. He had still not drawn his warhammer. Nostalgia, it seemed, was staying his hand as it was not Morin's. But while I was grateful for the sentiment, I couldn't afford to go lightly on the dwarf.

My casting completed, and I released it against Bornholm without delay.

You have shattered Bornholm's mental defenses! Remaining duration: 58 seconds.
Morin has cast venomous thorns.

A trio of poison darts rammed into my rear. Morin was not holding back much—if at all. Still, I continued to ignore her as I swamped Bornholm's mind with a third and final casting.

"Please stop—"

You have induced Bornholm to sleep for 60 seconds.

"—thhh..." The dwarf's words ran aground as he fell face forward onto the ground.

Morin has begun a divine summoning!

Light swirled at the edges of my vision, and I could only imagine it was coming from the portal the druid was opening somewhere behind me. But now that I could finally focus my attention on Morin, I realized the druid herself was outside my line of sight. I couldn't even move my head enough to see her; her vines held me too tightly.

But I don't need to see Morin to attack her, I thought. Drawing psi, I cast anew.

You have manifested 4 sentient shurikens.

The moment the ethereal blades coalesced around me, I ordered them to attack, and from the muttered oath emanating from behind, I guessed their appearance had caught Morin off guard.

Morin has evaded a shuriken's attack.
Morin has blocked a shuriken's attack.
Your shuriken has injured Morin.
Your shuriken has injured Morin.
Morin's spellcasting has been interrupted! Divine summoning failed.

I smiled in grim satisfaction. No more spells thudded into my rear, which I took to mean the druid had her hands full battling the four shurikens. Leaving her to it, I turned my attention to the vines holding me fast.

Escaping their grasp, though, was not going to be easy.

My blades were out of reach. One had fallen to the ground when the vines had entrapped my hands, the other was still in its sheath. Worse yet, none of the spells I had at my beck were suitable for hacking through vegetation.

Damnation, how am I going to get out of this?

Maybe shadow jumping will work, I thought. Drawing psi, I teleported anew, this time using the unconscious dwarf for a target.

You have teleported into Bornholm's shadow.

The spell worked, and I stepped out of the aether beside Bornholm. But I was not the only thing that emerged from the aether. The vines followed me through—leaving me just as trapped and immobilized as before.

Urgh.

There was only one other thing I could think of trying. Drawing psi again, I summoned a windslide.

You have cast windsurfer.

The ramp of air appeared beneath my feet, and obedient to my will, it levitated me aloft. The windslide could do nothing to free me from Morin's vines, of course. But crucially, it could turn me around.

Flying on the ramp of air, I ordered it to cut a small arc through the sky.

A heartbeat passed, then another, then Morin came into view. I smiled. Like Bornholm and Tantor, the druid's mindglow was shielded, but now that I could see her, I could assault her mental defenses.

You have cast slaysight (shatter).
You have reduced Morin's mental defenses to 80%!

My smile broadened. I had the druid now, and it was only a matter of time before she, too, fell, like the others.

✳   ✳   ✳

You have induced Morin to sleep for 60 seconds.
You have knocked Morin, Tantor, and Bornholm unconscious. Duration: 5 minutes.

Morin eventually succumbed to my psi attacks the same way Bornholm had.

After she fell, I waited for the vines around me to dissipate, then retrieved my sword and beat all three players senseless with it.

Unfortunately, I had no way to keep any spellcaster—much less elite ones—from using their magic while they were awake. So, instead, I relied on a more brute-force approach.

I struck each of my former companions on the back of the head—repeatedly in the case of Bornholm—and used analyze to query the state of their debuffs. Only when I was certain each would remain out for at least five minutes did I let them be.

Admittedly, my handiwork left Morin, Tantor, and Bornholm quite battered, but I consoled myself that it was better than the alternative—which was sending all three to their deaths.

My captives secure, I finally gave Saya my attention.

She had not stirred once during the ruckus, making me certain that whatever else the displaced debuff was doing to her, it was also stopping her from being aware of what was transpiring outside her cell.

Stalking forward, I walked a slow circle around the gnome's cage. Except for the magic running up and down its steel bars, the cage looked ordinary enough. Even a closer inspection of the contraption with analyze failed to reveal much.

The target is an enchanted <u>steel prison cell</u>. The enchantment around this item subjects all occupants to the debuff, <u>displaced</u>, which prevents them from interacting with the outside world in any manner whatsoever.

On the face of it, Frey's choice of prison cell for Saya seemed quite strange. But then again, Saya was only a civilian, and the magic she had access to was limited and purely non-combative in nature.

A prison did not need to be all that secure to hold her.

And this one appeared to be doing a good enough job already.

At least it makes the job of freeing her easier, I thought, eyeing the mundane iron lock holding the door to the cage shut. I'd already inspected the thing for traps, but there were none.

With a shrug of my shoulders, I raised the pommel of my sword and struck at the lock.

The single blow was enough to shatter the contraption.

Still not quite able to believe how easy this final step had been, I carefully swung back the cell door. At its slow creak, the prisoner within finally stirred.

Saya is no longer displaced.

Rising to her elbows, the gnome rubbed blearily at her eyes and, for the first time, got a good look at me. "Michael?" she asked half-disbelievingly.

I smiled. "In the flesh." Leaning down, I stretched out an arm. "Here, take my hand."

Her eyes still wide with wonder, Saya did as I bade and rose gingerly to her feet.

"Oh my," she murmured as I helped her out of the cage. "I can't believe it. You actually found me!"

"It took longer than it should have," I apologized contritely, "but in my—"

Saya held up a hand. "Stop, Michael. None of that matters. What does matter is that you're here now." Dashing forward, the smaller player hugged my legs tightly. "Thank you."

"You're welcome," I replied with a contented grin.

Stepping back, Saya peered around me at the three bodies stretched out along the ground. "And who are they?"

"Your jailors," I replied, not bothering to turn around myself.

"Oh. Are they dead?"

I shook my head. "No, just knocked out."

Saya's brows creased. "Are you sure? That one looks like he is stirring."

"What?" Spinning around, I rushed over to check on the trio. A quick analyze, though, was all it took to ascertain the three would remain unconscious for at least another two minutes.

"You must've been mistaken," I said, still bent over the prone players. "These three are well and truly comatose. But just to be certain, perhaps I'll hit them all again. That way, there'll be no chance of any of them waking up while we make our escape."

"Oh, I'd rather you didn't, my boy."

I stilled. I knew that voice.

And it was not Saya's.

Whirling around, I found not the gnome standing behind me but Loken.

The damnable trickster himself.

CHAPTER 629: THE ART OF DECEPTION

My face grew several shades lighter. "Loken?" I whispered.

The trickster's painted black lips spread in a broad smile. Loken was in what I'd come to think of as his jester incarnation, whom I'd first met while in Erebus' dungeon. "In the flesh," he replied, parroting my earlier words to Saya.

Speaking of...

"*You* were the one in the cage?" I asked, nearly choking on the question. "You were...?"

"Saya," he finished for me. "That's right. But only for a day." The trickster's face took on a forlorn cast. "I really don't have time for protracted performances anymore." The sadness disappeared from Loken's gaze, and the next moment, he was bright-eyed, bushy-tailed, and rubbing his hands in glee. "I must say, though, I haven't had this much fun in ages. I will treasure your expressions forever!"

My mouth worked soundlessly. My mind was still playing catch-up, and the only thing I could truly make sense of in the moment was that I hadn't rescued Saya. "Where's Saya?" I demanded.

Loken pouted. "What? Am I not good enough for you?"

My eyes grew hot. The Power was toying with me, and for no more reason than it pleased him to do so!

Or perhaps not.

Perhaps Loken was deliberately trying to provoke me. But if that was the case, I didn't want to give the bastard the satisfaction of seeing me angry.

I took a calming breath. "You still haven't answered my question. Where. Is. Saya."

Loken's eyes glittered, and I could sense the question needled him. His next words, though, were as cold and unemotional as iron. "Dead."

I didn't believe him. "You're lying."

"I'm not," he fired back.

He had to be. Saya couldn't be dead. If she were, none of this made any sense. But how was I going to get Loken to admit the truth?

"Now, if we can move on to more important matters?" the trickster asked blithely.

I stared hard at him, ignoring the question, and of their own volition, my fingers began flexing. They ached to hold something—like a sword—but even amidst my burgeoning anger, I knew that attempting to draw a blade was beyond foolish.

"Oh, for crying out!" Loken exclaimed, seemingly already bored by my reaction. "I'll swear by my words if that will help."

Before I could think of a suitable response to this, he closed his eyes and reached out to the Game.

"As the Adjudicator is my witness," Loken intoned a second later, "I swear to you that the gnome Saya is dead." His eyes snapped back open. "There. Do you believe me now?"

I opened my mouth, a retort ready on my lips, but before I could speak, a Game message unfurled in my mind.

The Power Loken has sealed a Pact attesting to the death of the gnome Saya of sector 12,560.
Your task: <u>Rescue the lost Pup</u>! has been updated. You have received indisputable proof that Saya is dead. Revised objective: punish the one responsible for her death.

I squeezed my eyes shut, struggling to come to terms with what Loken had just said. Even the incontrovertible proof of a sealed Pact was almost not enough to convince me.

But I would not—could not—deceive myself. As harsh as the truth was, I had to face it head-on.

Saya was dead.

It was confirmed. And now, I would have to live with that fact. As I would have to with the fact that I had put the lives of everyone who had depended on me at risk for nothing. Safyre, Ceruvax, and the others had been right. I should not have embarked on this venture.

I had gambled and lost. Saya was dead. And now I was at Loken's mercy. *The only thing left to try is to keep him from realizing how much that is the case.*

I opened my eyes. "By whose hand?" I asked in a whisper.

"Frey's," Loken replied carelessly, "but it was by my order."

I nodded wordlessly, too dulled by grief to feel even a flicker of anger at his response. "Why?" I asked simply.

"Why what?" Loken asked with lively interest. "Why did I do it? Why did I choose her? Or why did I make you believe she was alive?"

"All of the above," I replied, refusing to be drawn into another of Loken's games.

My response surprised a chuckle from him. "Well, let's take it from the top then, shall we?" Raising his right hand airily, Loken began ticking off points on his fingers. "I did it to teach you a lesson. I chose Saya because she was important to you. And I let you believe she was alive because I know how you do so love a good rescue operation—" he laughed, seemingly amused by his own wit—"and because I needed to draw you out."

"Why?" I asked in a monotone again.

Loken rolled his eyes. "Come, my boy. You're going to have to put a tad more effort into your questions than that."

"Why did you need to draw me out?" I asked, ignoring his amused expression.

"Ah, finally, an interesting one!" He leaned forward with pretended seriousness. "It's because I *know*, you see."

"Know what?"

"What you are, *wolfling*," Loken replied, answering in kind.

The trickster's answer did not surprise me as much as I expected, and I realized that ever since he'd told me about Saya, I'd been anticipating something like this. Loken would not have ordered a drastic a measure as having Saya killed—all simply to teach me a 'lesson'—if he didn't have a strong inkling of the truth.

He knows I've awakened my Wolf blood.

Loken cocked his head to the side. "What? No pretended outrage? No tiresome denials?"

I shrugged. "Why bother? You appear to know everything already."

"Well, I wouldn't go *that* far," Loken replied. If he was thrown by my uncharacteristically dull responses, he was doing a good job of hiding it. "I know a lot already, but not everything." The trickster's eyes grew cold. "Not yet anyway."

I nodded, as unfazed by the sudden, cruel glint in his gaze as I had been by his earlier words. "So, that's why I am here—to be interrogated."

"Exactly," Loken said, beaming with pretended pride.

Things were as bad as I thought, then. "There's one thing I don't get, though."

"Only one?" Loken quipped.

"Well, perhaps more than one," I replied evenly.

My disinterested tone was not subterfuge. The news of Saya's death seemed to have drained the emotion out of me, and even though I knew I should be scared—trembling even—in the face of Loken's revelations, I couldn't seem to work up enough effort to care.

Is that Loken's doing, too? I wondered idly. Was the trickster subverting my thoughts?

"*He isn't,*" Decal murmured in response to the unvoiced thought. "*I would sense if he was meddling with your mind.*"

"*Are you sure?*"

"Yes," Decal replied confidently. "*Loken may be a supreme Power, but your mind is my fortress. His touch will not go unrecognized here.*"

"*I see.*" Then what explanation was there for my unusual passivity?

"*What you're experiencing is grief and shock,*" Decal said, volunteering information again.

That sounded about right. I hesitated, then asked, "*Can you tamp it down?*"

"*I can. Are you sure you want me to do so?*"

"*Yes.*"

"*As you wish.*"

A hand waved in front of my face. "Hello? Michael? Are you still with me?"

I turned my focus outwards again. "If your intent all along was to capture me," I observed, continuing on as if I had not just spent a half-minute staring off into space, "why was Frey trying so hard to kill me?"

Loken peered at me strangely for a beat, but he didn't ask about my protracted spell of silence. "*Where* she was trying to kill you answers the why."

I waited for him to go on, but when he didn't, I added in objection, "That makes no sense."

Loken smiled. "That's because your understanding of the iron dome's enchantments is somewhat lacking. The dome was not only designed to stop outgoing and incoming communications, it is also meant to prevent the passage of spirit entities—including dead ones. If you had died while the dome was still up, your spirit would have remained trapped inside the complex until it could be collected and transported to a... more suitable sector."

I stared at him. "You mean one under your control."

"Like I said—a suitable sector," Loken murmured.

I snorted but let the matter lie. "And what about this camp? Why the elaborate charade here?" I glanced at the three prone players behind me. Tantor, Morin, and Bornholm should have awoken by now. That they were still unconscious could only mean Loken was keeping them forcibly asleep. "And why bring *them* here?"

"Why else except for my amusement?" Loken laughed.

I glared at him.

"What? Don't believe me? Oh, alright then. I brought them here to distract you, to keep you from realizing the true game afoot. While you were busy questioning their reasons for being here, you weren't wondering about Saya's identity." His voice took on a lecturing tone. "Always remember, deceptions work best when they are subtle. Lean too hard on one and it will fail you. Layer your schemes and hide one within another. That's the surest route to success."

I didn't comment on the impromptu lecture, unwanted as it was. "Then, they didn't know about your plans?"

"They did not," Loken confirmed.

"I see," I muttered. "But why the charade in the first place?"

"Ah. Like I told you earlier, I don't know everything. In fact, it's only now that I've come to realize that all of this—" Loken spread his arms, encompassing the camp and the tunnels underfoot in the gesture—"was unnecessary."

"Oh?"

Loken wagged a finger under my nose. "You, my boy, are hiding more than one secret."

I said nothing.

"I haven't uncovered all of them, but I will," he promised. Spinning around, Loken retreated a few steps. "But to the point, do you know what I learned today?"

Once more, I stayed silent.

Undaunted, Loken went on, "Today, I learned that you're a Power just like me. Well, perhaps not like me. After all, you're still only an acolyte. But the important thing is you *are* a Power. I knew it the moment you first set foot in the camp." He threw me a knowing look. "And you know what that means, don't you, Michael?" Not waiting for my answer, he continued his monologue, "It means I don't have to use proxies like Frey to deal with you. It means I can do this."

On the tail end of the Power's words, magic rippled out of him and straight at me.

There was no avoiding it, and even if I somehow managed the feat, I suspected the end result would be the same.

Loken has cast Shadow's clammy fist. You are <u>shadow-struck</u>. Duration: infinite.

CHAPTER 630: A GAME OF QUESTIONS

I couldn't move. I couldn't even so much as twitch a muscle.

My legs, hands, fingers, and even my eyes were locked immobile. I could still breathe, think, hear, and see. But I couldn't do much else. My abilities were locked down. My items were disabled. And my void armor had been rendered useless.

I was helpless. And Loken's prisoner.

I'd known this was coming almost from the first moment Loken had appeared. But I'd know equally as well that there would be no escaping the trickster—not now, not while I bore a Power Mark.

So, I'd done the only thing I could and eked out as much information from Loken as the Power had been willing to share. If I survived past today, perhaps I would one day get a chance to use it against him.

Without another word or further explanation, Loken stepped out of my line of sight, leaving me to stare at nothing but the empty mountainside. I could still hear him, though. He was moving light-footedly somewhere behind me and, at a guess, was reviving his three fallen followers.

With little else to occupy me, I turned my attention to my one and only chance of escape. *"Decal, can you see Loken's dreamscape?"*

Palpable silence.

"No, Michael," he replied softly. *"I cannot. It's hidden in a manner beyond my ability to fathom."*

"Damn." I'd known I was grasping at straws with the request, but I'd had to ask anyway.

"I'm sorry," he added.

"Don't be. It's not your fault." It was my own.

✻ ✻ ✻

I wasn't sure how long Loken kept me waiting. It was long enough for the sky to begin brightening, but beyond that, I couldn't tell. At some point, someone—I thought it was Tantor—placed a soundproof box over me, depriving me of even more sensory input.

Then, the passage of time seemed to crawl even further. Left alone with my thoughts, I circled over everything Loken had said and not said.

The trickster knew I was a Wolf. He knew, too, that I was a Power, but he'd implied—and the facts supported him on this—that he'd only learned as much after I entered the camp. From this, I concluded Loken had analyzed me. It seemed the Shadow Power's insight was high enough for him to not only pierce the disguise I'd woven around myself, but to do so without me being alerted by the fact.

But beyond these few simple realizations, I did not know what else the trickster knew and did not know. I was certainly about to find out, though.

I had an interrogation coming; there could be no doubt about that.

And the questions Loken chose to ask would be as revealing as those he didn't. Less certain was what good the knowledge would do me. I had no hope of escape, and no clever stratagems to evade the trickster's probes. At this point, my fate was all but sealed.

But I would not stop fighting.

I would not stop resisting right up until the very end.

And besides, in the grand scheme of things, I was unimportant. What happened to me did not matter so long as Sanctum survived. If I could hide anything from Loken, it would have to be the location of the sector.

If I managed to keep that one little secret, then I would consider it a victory. Sighing, I let my worries fade away. They were too depressing to ponder over much longer.

"I'm sorry, Safyre," I whispered as my thoughts began to shut down. She couldn't hear me, of course, but I felt it was important to voice the apology to her—even if I was the only one around to hear it.

"I should have listened. I'm sorry I didn't."

✳   ✳   ✳

I awoke some time later.

Amazing as it seemed, I'd fallen asleep. What's more, I was no longer shadow-struck, and the box enclosing me—*coffin, more like it*—had been removed.

Rising from the prone position I'd been placed in, I took stock of my surroundings anew.

To my surprise, I realized I was still on the mountainside and in the selfsame camp in which I'd been captured.

"Were you expecting something different?"

I turned around at the familiar voice. "Yes, actually. I was expecting to be squirreled away in the deepest darkest dungeon you could find, one with torture implements close at hand."

Loken laughed. "None of that is necessary."

"No?"

"No. I can manage this without any of that."

That certainly sounded ominous. "But why here?" I asked, spreading my arms to encompass the camp.

The trickster shrugged. "It's close, it's convenient, and it's isolated.

I nodded, even if I didn't quite understand or believe his reasoning, and turned around in a slow circle. Not everything about the camp was the same as when I'd been placed in the box.

Morin, Tantor, and Bornholm were still around and sitting at the campfire once again, but Saya's steel cage had vanished. In its place, a shimmering dome of magic had been erected. The dome itself was many times bigger than the prison cell had been and in fact was large enough for me and Loken—both of whom were inside—to walk around freely.

I gestured upward. "What's that?"

"A null field, one keyed to you specifically," Loken replied, being more forthcoming than I expected. "You will not be able to exit the field, use any of your active abilities, or query the Adjudicator while inside the dome."

That explains the lack of Game messages.

Glancing down, I saw that I was dressed in what looked like newbie clothes. I'd been stripped of my swords and all my gear, as well. Even my soulbound items were nowhere in evidence. How Loken had managed that feat, I had no idea, but it was clear I wouldn't have access to them while in the null field.

"One can never be too careful," Loken replied in response to the unhappy look I gave him.

"I—"

I broke off as a soft voice surfaced in my mind. *"I'm still here, Michael."*

"Decal?" I murmured, feeling unaccountably grateful at his presence.

"Yes, it's me."

It was only by the dint of great effort that I didn't reach up with my hand and try to find the mindslayer's torc that should have been around my neck. I couldn't feel its comforting weight, which made Decal's voice in my mind all the more confounding.

"How?" I asked, perplexed. *"The torc—"*

"—is still equipped," he finished for me. *"Loken wasn't able to remove it, nor any of your other soulbound items, for that matter. He was able to conceal them from your senses, though."*

"I see." Loken would not have been able to analyze the mindslayer's torc either. Only I, as its true owner, could do that.

That must have frustrated him no end, I thought gleefully.

"What's so funny?" Loken asked, frowning.

I shrugged. "How dangerous you still consider me," I lied smoothly.

Loken's eyes narrowed fractionally at my answer, but he didn't respond.

I jerked my thumb in the direction of Morin, Tantor, and Bornholm. "What about them? Can they hear us?"

"No, Michael," Loken said solemnly. "No one from without can hear us inside here."

I sighed. I'd suspected as much. "So, what now?"

Loken strode closer. "Now, we begin the questioning."

*　　❋　　❋　　❋*

"What are you going to do to me?" I asked, striving not to sound nervous.

Loken shrugged. "Compel you to tell the truth."

"Are you not already doing that?" I asked, even though I knew from Decal he wasn't.

The trickster grinned unpleasantly. "Believe me, you will know when you're being compelled."

I licked suddenly dry lips. "And if I cooperate?"

"Then things will go easier, but I know you, Michael—perhaps better than you know yourself." He shook his head. "You will not cooperate."

"But if I do," I interjected quickly. "Will you answer some of my own questions?"

Loken smiled lopsidedly. "Still scheming, wolfling?"

I said nothing.

"Tell me, do you genuinely believe you will win free from here?"

"No," I answered truthfully.

"But you're still willing to roll the dice and play for keeps?"

"Yes. Always," I said stoutly.

Loken chuckled. "Ah, there's the Michael, I remember. So brazen and full of such promise. It's a pity you turned out so disappointing."

There was no good response to that, so I kept my mouth shut.

"Very well, I will play your game," Loken said indulgently. "But only so long as your answers are truthful and complete. Deal?"

"A question for a question?" I persisted.

"A question for a question," he agreed, his lips twitching in amusement. "Then we have a deal."

Loken wagged a finger at me. "But don't think to deceive me, boy. If I believe you're being evasive, the deal is off. Understood?"

I nodded. "And how will I know if you're being honest?"

He snorted. "Angling for a Pact, are we? The short answer is you won't. And no, I will form no Pact with you over this."

I didn't push the matter any further. I was in no position to win any concessions from the trickster, and I sensed I'd gained as much as he was willing to concede.

"Excellent, then," Loken said, slapping his hands together in anticipation. "Shall we begin?"

I nodded mutely.

"Good. First question." He leaned forward intently. "How did you become a Power?"

* * *

Loken's first question was a big one, and I didn't rush my answer.

Relating the bare minimum facts to the Power would be easy enough, but he'd warned me to be complete, and I couldn't afford to be perceived as hiding anything. At the same time, I didn't want to overshare.

But on the other hand, I *also* wanted to feed Loken with enough seemingly interesting information that he wasted his next question on inconsequential matters. It would be a fine line to tread, and I was not sure I would be able to do so.

Another problem, of course, was that I had no real endgame in mind. Right now, Loken held all the cards, and the only thing I could do was to play for time and hope inspiration struck at some point.

Inhaling carefully, I gave my answer. "I became a Power by slaying a stygian harbinger with the help of two lichs, both of whom were non-players and higher leveled than me at the time."

"Interesting," Loken replied, genuinely appearing to consider my answer so. "Are the two lichs you mentioned aligned with the Awakened Dead?"

This time, my answer came quicker. "No, definitely not. In fact, both consider themselves enemies of Erebus and his people." I paused. "That was two questions. My turn now."

Loken laughed in amusement but didn't contradict my statement. "Go ahead," he said, waving me on.

"Where is Frey now?" I asked promptly.

The question appeared to catch Loken off guard, and his eyes widened ever so slightly. "A strange first question," he murmured. "My envoy is still in the underground tunnels and at the present moment, is leading the Lightsworn on a merry chase." His gaze darted to mine. "Next question."

Loken was right. My question *had* been strange—from his perspective, anyway. But the game we played was rigged. I couldn't afford to ask the same big questions Loken did—the trickster would only lie if I did. So instead, my strategy was to question him on matters that, while still relevant, were on the periphery of what he considered important, in the hope that he would answer—and answer truthfully.

"Why are you not in Nexus?" I asked slowly. "You gave me a task to appear before you at the Shadow Keep, and tasks *cannot* be falsified. So, how is it that you are not there?"

Loken laughed, in apparent delight at the question. "Good one, my boy! But your question is flawed. You see, you are making assumptions—incorrect ones, it turns out."

"Oh?" I asked, eyeing him warily.

He nodded, his eyes shining brightly. "I *am* in Nexus." He paused. "And I am here, too."

"You're in two places at once? How—" I broke off, my eyes widening. "You've cloned yourself!" I breathed.

Loken didn't say anything, but he didn't need to. I was sure he was telling the truth. His answer fit too neatly to be anything but honest.

"My turn," Loken said laconically, drawing my attention. "What is your current Wolf Mark?"

My expression sobered. Loken's question was venturing into dangerous territory, and despite my earlier resolve, I was not sure I could—or even wanted—to answer him this time around.

But if I didn't... he'd simply wrench the answer from my mind.

"He might not be able to do that as easily as you think," Decal said quietly.

"Why do you say that?" I asked, feeling a sliver of hope.

"Your mental defenses are still active," the simulacrum replied. *"And don't forget, I am also here to guard your dreamscape. Loken will not have an easy time plucking the answers he desires from your mind."*

"That sounds... promising, but how certain are you that we'll be able to hold him off?"

"Not certain at all," Decal replied contritely. *"I'm sorry, Michael, but if it were anyone else, I could give you more assurance. As it is..."*

"This is Loken, we're talking about," I finished for him. *"I understand."* With a Power like Loken, there were never any guarantees. But Decal was right as well. I should not assume Loken could compel me as easily as he claimed. Then, too, unless things had gone more drastically wrong than I suspected, Loken should have no knowledge of the simulacrum in my mind.

He could be underestimating me.

It wouldn't be the first time someone did that, either.

"Are you quite done debating yourself?" Loken asked, intruding on my musings.

I glanced at him from under heavily lidded eyes. "I am."

"Well, alrighty then. Now answer the question. And no lying," he warned, noticing my tension.

I exhaled carefully. "I won't be answering. I am done with this game."

CHAPTER 631: DREAMS FULL OF POWER

A pregnant pause. Then, "Well, that was fast."

I shrugged.

Loken smiled, but there was an edge to the expression this time. "I told you you wouldn't cooperate."

"And it appears you were right as usual," I said complacently.

"I do so like being right," Loken murmured. His gaze darted my way again. "Are you sure you want to do things like this?"

I nodded.

"Then so be it," the Power pronounced, his tone hardening.

Bracing myself, I watched Loken carefully, but even so, I missed seeing him move.

One moment, the trickster was standing six feet away; the next, he was looming over me, with his hands glued to either side of my head. Before I could react, my head was wrenched back, and my gaze was pinned by Loken's.

"Your Wolf Mark," the trickster breathed, his tone low and mellow, and his eyes dark and mesmerizing. "Tell me what tier it is at."

But despite Loken's sudden hypnotic nature, I was not swayed. "No."

The trickster's lips tightened fractionally, but he didn't break off his stare. The next instant, his eyes grew larger, glittering like diamonds, and the contours of his face began to ripple in a fashion that was at one time both distributing and fascinating.

"Please, Michael," he pleaded. "Tell me."

"No."

"I must know," Loken begged, his voice growing more melodic.

"No."

"The Fate of the Forever Kingdom itself could be at stake," the Power implored, his features still changing in a manner I found more and more breathtaking.

"How?" I croaked, struggling to hold onto my resolve.

"The stygians, Michael. Have you forgotten the stygians?"

"Of course I haven't," I scoffed. "What about them?"

"They want you because of what you are."

He shouldn't know that, I thought, the haze he'd induced in my mind clearing oh-so-briefly for that single, succinct thought to penetrate. But the moment did not last, and the errant thought was swept away by Loken's mesmerizing demeanor before I could make more sense of it.

"They want you," Loken crooned. "But I can protect you. Tell me what I need to know and I will."

"Anything for—" I bit my lip hard, restoring sense to my scattered thoughts. "No, I cannot."

"Please, Michael," Loken beseeched, his voice trembling with the depths of his need.

"I... c-can't." I broke off. That wasn't the right answer, was it? I tried again. "Alright, I'll—"

"Hold on, Michael," Decal called, his voice shining bright in my mind like a silver beacon. In the wake of the simulacrum's words, the shadowy tentacles swamping my mind fled, and clarity returned.

"Get away from me, you bastard," I growled out aloud.

In an eyeblink, Loken's face shifted back to normal—or what passed for normal for the trickster, anyway—and he shoved me roughly aside. "Interesting," he mused, stalking around me in a tight circle.

"What is?" I panted as I slowly climbed back to my feet. Exhaustion sat heavily on me, and my legs felt like jelly. If I didn't know better, I would have sworn I'd just run a dozen miles or more.

"I almost had you," Loken reflected, more to himself than me. "But there at the end, it was almost as if—" his eyes narrowed—"something or someone interfered."

"All the more power to them," I murmured, pretending ignorance.

Loken's eyes darted to the side, and following his gaze, I saw Morin, Tantor, and Bornholm pressed up against the sides of the dome, eyes glued on the events unfolding inside.

Did Loken suspect one of them of interfering? My lips twitched. *Better that they shoulder the blame than Decal.*

The next moment, Loken spun around, seeming to dismiss the trio from consideration. "Let's try that again, shall we?"

I sighed. "Yes, please let's do," I said with false enthusiasm.

✳   ✳   ✳

Loken did not fare any better the second time around or the third. The fourth time, he did even worse, and by his fifth attempt, every single question he asked was met with a resolute and firm denial.

It was obvious that with every iteration of the Power's mental assault, my own defenses were adapting, growing more solid and impregnable with each attack, until eventually, Loken's compulsion spell failed to gain even a foothold in the recesses of my mind.

Observing the same results I did, the trickster's conclusion was no different from mine, and he finally stormed away in disgust.

"Your mind is a tougher nut to crack than many Powers I've met," he spat in a rare and uncharacteristic moment of frustration. "Where did you learn such strength?"

I grinned toothily. "Like I'd ever tell you."

Loken stared at me dispassionately. "Do not mistake this setback for anything other than what it is, wolfling. I've destroyed Primes stronger than you'll ever be. I will break you, too, I promise."

"Enough yapping then and get on with it," I muttered, no longer caring how much my words might anger Loken. He and I were done, and if by some miracle, I survived today, there would be nothing but lasting enmity between us.

Going down on my knees, I waited for Loken to clasp his hands to my head again, but to my surprise, he did not immediately do so. Instead, creating an opening in the dome, the Power waved through the trio watching avidly from outside.

"You three will need to hold him down for this next bit," Loken ordered when the trio shuffled in like recalcitrant children.

"Yes, Master," Morin acknowledged, her eyes downcast.

"Why, what are you going to do to him?" Bornholm asked gruffly.

Loken's gaze darted his way.

"Uh, master," he said, adding the honorific belatedly.

"I'm going to enter his mind, if that is alright with you," Loken explained acerbically. "And extract what I need that way."

The dwarf nodded in slow and careful consideration. "It is, so long as you don't hurt him."

It was a response that Loken did not find amusing in the least, but that had me chuckling.

"Lay him flat," the trickster snapped, not deigning to reply to the dwarf. He pointed at Morin. "You, hold down his legs." He waved irritably in Bornholm and Tantor's direction. "And you two, grab his hands."

I did not resist as the trio carried out their orders, and in short order, I was placed flat on my back and spread-eagled on the ground. I was not sure why Loken did not paralyze me himself with one of his spells, but whatever the Power was about to attempt seemed like it was going to be orders of magnitude more serious than the compulsion spell he'd tried earlier.

"Decal," I whispered, *"are you watching this?"*

"Yes, Michael, I am."

"I think... I think Loken is about to send a simulacrum into our mind."

"I think so, too," Decal agreed. *"Rest assured, I'm ready."*

"Good luck," I murmured. Turning my attention outward again, I was just in time to spot Loken getting into position. Placing himself above my head, the Power leaned down and placed his hands on either side of my face.

"What are you going to do?" I asked curiously.

Loken did not bother answering. Perhaps he was still irritated by Bornholm's questioning, or perhaps he was still frustrated by his earlier failures. Whatever the case, the trickster's face was unwontedly serious as he closed his eyes and began chanting.

I strained my ears to listen, but the words he intoned were so softly spoken that even my wolf-enhanced hearing was not able to make sense of them.

Well, nothing for it but to wait for him to begin then. Stilling my own thoughts, I held myself in readiness.

For the next minute, no one spoke, and other than for the soft drone of Loken's chant, the silence went unbroken.

Then the chanting stopped, Loken's head sagged, and his body grew still.

Whatever the Power had in store for me, it had begun.

                              *   *   *

It started with pain—agonizing, excruciating pain.

I clenched my jaw and gritted my teeth, but the pounding in my head grew and grew until, unable to help myself, I moaned pitifully.

"Lad? Lad?" Bornholm asked, shaking my hand roughly. "What's going on?"

But I did not have enough sense of mind left to answer him.

My eyes were wide open. I could see nothing, though. Nothing but painful white light. If I still had access to the Adjudicator, I knew damage messages would be scrolling through my mind in long, ceaseless lines. I was hurting—badly—and all the pain was concentrated in my head.

My thoughts turning inwards, I reached for my alter ego. *"Decal!"*

But the simulacrum did not respond. Either he was being wracked by the same agony, or something else had happened to him.

A line of wetness ran down my chin, then another, and another.

"His eyes are bleeding," Tantor whispered in a hushed tone.

"His nose too," Bornholm observed gruffly. "Is this supposed to be happening?"

"I don't know," Morin whispered softly.

"Should we heal him?" Tantor asked.

"I don't know the answer to that either," Morin said sadly.

"Look at the Master!" Bornholm blurted suddenly.

"What are you going on about—" Tantor broke off, then added in an almost awed tone, "By the Powers, Loken's bleeding too."

"By the seven hells," Bornholm muttered. "What is going on?"

But if anyone knew, they weren't saying.

                              *   *   *

An indeterminate time later, the pain receded and my eyes cleared, and though I was as weak as a newborn filly, I felt a beatific smile spread across my face at the sudden cessation of agony.

A weight sagged down across my face. It was Loken, his body nearly all dead weight. Someone—Morin, I thought—lifted him off.

"Is he breathing?" Tantor asked worriedly.

"Yes," Morin replied, "Barely, but he's breathing all the same."

"Did the healing not take?" Bornholm asked.

"No, not on either of them," Morin replied.

"Maybe we should lay Loken down beside Michael," Tantor suggested.

Morin shook her head. "We can't. The Master's hands are stuck fast to Michael's face. They won't come free."

"I'm fine," Loken said, speaking up suddenly. But from the wretched croak in voice, he was anything but.

"What's going on, Master?" Tantor asked worriedly.

"I'm in the wolfling's mind," Loken replied in a slurred tone.

"What wolfling?" a perplexed Bornholm asked.

"He means Michael," Morin explained.

"The transition has claimed a greater toll on me than I expected," Loken went on. "It will be up to you three to guard my body."

"You can count on us, Master," Tantor said grimly. "No harm will come to you while we live."

A tired smile lit one side of the trickster's face. "Thank you," Loken murmured. "What about Michael? How is he?"

A bearded face peered down on me. "His eyes are open," Bornholm reported. "But I am not sure if he is seeing anything. He isn't blinking."

"Has he said anything?" Loken asked.

Morin shook her head. "Not a word."

"Good. That must mean he is inside his head, preparing," Loken murmured. "It'll do him no good, though."

Morin and Tantor exchanged glances, but only Bornholm had the courage to ask, "What won't?"

Predictably, Loken ignored the question. "Keep vigilant and stay alert," he ordered the trio. "This shouldn't take too long."

Not waiting for their responses, Loken vanished—or rather, his mind did, leaving his body to sag listlessly once more. I knew where he had gone. Loken had stepped into my dreamscape.

And it was time I did too.

✳ ✳ ✳

I entered the dreamscape simply by closing my eyes in the real and willing myself into my mind. When I opened my eyes again, it was to find myself standing in the same forest where I'd first met Decal.

The place was not the same, though.

The forest was no longer pristine, and its beauty, what little remained of it, was marred. As many as a third of the tall, graceful trees had been hacked down, burned to cinders, or had simply withered into dried-out husks. The underbrush was either overgrown or entirely absent in spots. The sky itself was another scar on the landscape. Angry bolts of lightning rent the sky, and storm clouds hung thick over the trees.

"This is Loken's doing," I muttered.

"It is," Decal agreed, appearing next to me, *"but not the way you mean."*

"Meaning?" I demanded, swinging around to face him.

"Meaning Loken himself has come," Decal said.

I nodded. *"I know. I overheard him tell the—"*

"No, you don't know," Decal interjected. *"At least not fully."*

I stared at him. *"Explain then."*

"It is Loken-the-person—and not Loken-the-simulacrum—that has entered our dreamscape. Do you understand the difference? Loken-the-simulacrum is an offshoot of the real Loken, a self-contained portion of his mind. Loken-the-person is the entirety of what it means to be Loken. His full

consciousness." Decal held out his hands. *"And it is all here. In this dreamscape."*

"Impossible," I muttered, as the full implication of Decal's words sank in.

The simulacrum shook his head. *"I would have claimed so too before today, and I would have been just as wrong as you are."* He pointed out the many signs of the forest's destruction. *"All of that is not the result of any attack. It is merely the consequences of Loken coming here."*

"It's like trying to pour two cups' worth of water into a single cup," I murmured, finally understanding the source of the excruciating pain I'd experienced earlier. My body had not been designed to house two entire consciousnesses.

"Exactly," Decal agreed. *"Only in this case, the more apt analogy is that of trying to pour an entire jug of water into an already full cup."* He held my gaze. *"Loken's mind is that much larger than your own."*

I nodded mutely. He was correct. *"But this invasion is not without consequence for Loken either. He is suffering from it as much as I am."* I shook my head. *"Why do something so stupid?"*

Decal shrugged. *"Loken must be desperate for the information he seeks."*

"But why not send his simulacrum instead of—" I broke off, realization setting in. *"He* doesn't *have a simulacrum,"* I breathed.

"That's the only explanation that makes sense," Decal agreed, looking just as excited. *"And that means while Loken is here..."*

"...there's no one around to pilot his body," I finished for him.

The simulacrum and I stared at each other, both thinking the same thing. *"It can be done,"* Decal surmised.

'I agree." I swung around to stare into the forest's depths. *"Where is Loken now?"*

"Searching for the information he seeks." Decal smiled. *"But it is better concealed than the trickster realizes. It will take him longer to find than he expects."*

That gave me time. Turning about, I clasped Decal's hand. *"You'll keep him occupied?"* I asked.

"I'll run him ragged," he promised, *"and too busy to realize what you're doing back in the real."*

"Good man. Best of luck to you," I murmured in farewell. Then, without further ado, I willed myself back into the real.

I had work to do.

✳   ✳   ✳

Little had changed in the null field since I'd first closed my eyes.

Bornholm was still holding my right hand, and Tantor my left. Morin, though, had released my legs in favor of cradling Loken's head in her lap.

I couldn't trust Tantor, I knew—not with what I needed to ask of him. Morin, too, was suspect. Bornholm was the one I trusted the most. He was the one I needed to appeal to.

But how to do that while still keeping the others in the dark?

I have to draw Bornholm closer and get rid of one of the others, I decided.

Attempting to do so was going to be a risk, though. But there was no helping that. *Here goes.* Opening and closing my mouth like a fish, I smacked my lips loudly together.

"Hey, you see that?" Bornholm asked, noticing the movement immediately.

Both Morin and Tantor turned my way. "What's he doing?" the elf asked with a frown.

"No idea," Bornholm replied with a shake of his head.

Moving my lips again, I rattled off a series of nonsense words so softly no one could hear them clearly.

"He's trying to talk," Morin guessed.

Leaning forward, Bornholm placed his head near mine.

I repeated my mutterings, but still too softly for Bornholm to make sense of any of it.

The dwarf leaned closer, putting his right ear within inches of my mouth.

"Don't say anything and don't move," I said at a volume that was clearly audible to Bornholm.

I sensed the dwarf go rigid.

"What did he say?" Morin asked curiously. Clearly, she'd noticed some change in Bornholm's demeanor.

"Tell her you're not sure yet."

"Don't know yet," Bornholm repeated obligingly. "But I'll get it in a moment."

"Good," I whispered. "Now tell them I'm asking for water. Make sure Tantor is the one to fetch it. When he is gone, place a blade in my right hand."

The dwarf didn't move.

"Please, Bornholm," I pleaded. "You know me. And by now, you surely have learned more about Loken than you want to know. Who do you trust more? Who would you rather have as a friend? Me or him?"

Still, Bornholm did not move.

"I can hear him speaking," Tantor said. "What's he saying?"

There was no trace of suspicion in the elf's voice, but if Bornholm kept hesitating...

"He's asking for water," the dwarf said suddenly. "Will you get it? There's something else he is trying to say, but I haven't quite got it yet. I want to listen some more."

"I don't know," Tantor said doubtfully. "Loken ordered us not to—"

"Go, Tantor," Morin said. "It'll be fine. Michael is not going anywhere. Neither of them is."

"Oh, alright." Rising to his feet, the elf departed.

I held my breath, barely containing my relief.

Something cold and hard landed in the palm of my right hand. The hilt of a sword. I closed my fingers around it. "Thank you, Bornholm," I breathed. "I promise I'll not forget this."

The dwarf rushed to his feet suddenly, his gaze flying to a distant speck on the mountainside. "Hey, Morin, you see that?"

The druid glanced in the direction the dwarf pointed. "What?"

"Movement, I think," Bornholm growled.

Her expression growing alarmed, Morin focused more fully on the distant speck.

I smiled, impressed by Bornholm's improvisation. He'd performed his part admirably, going beyond what I'd asked of him. Now, it was time for me to do my own part.

Readying myself, I exhaled a slow, controlled breath.

Then I moved.

My body was weak. My arms were heavy. But my mind was sharp. And I had no little skill with a blade.

Even as my body failed to whip around in the manner I expected, I corrected and adjusted my movements on the fly.

Spying my sudden motion around the corner of her eye, Morin began turning around. My gaze fixed on Loken's slumped body, I ignored her.

Spotting the naked blade in my hand, Morin's eyes widened. A spell formed on her lips. But it was already too late.

Rolling almost into the druid's lap, I drove the point of my sword squarely through the base of Loken's skull and straight up into his brain.

Death claimed him instantly.

A null field has dissipated.
You have killed Loken, a level 512 supreme Power!
You and Ghost have reached level 305!
Your meditation and telepathy have reached rank 26.

More messages scrolled through my mind, but I paid them no heed. They could all keep for later. The important thing was that Loken was dead, my mind was free, and my secrets were safe—the most important ones, anyway.

But everything had changed today, too.

Loken might be dead, but he was far from defeated. The trickster would be back, and when he returned, the other Powers would learn the truth of who and what I was.

And then, the course of the Game would change forever.

✳   ✳   ✳

THE END.

Here ends Book 9 of the Grand Game.
Michael's adventures will continue in **The Mad God**.
Coming in 2026!

I hope you enjoyed the story! If you did, please leave a <u>review</u> and let other readers know what you think.
<u>Click here to leave a review</u>.

If you're enjoying the Grand Game, you might also want to check out my other series: **The Dragon Mage**. It follows our protagonist, Jamie Sinclair, and is set in another universe altogether.
Happy reading!
Tom Elliot.

MICHAEL AT THE END OF BOOK 9

<u>Player Profile: Michael</u>

Level: 305. Rank: 30. Current Health: 100%.
Species: Human. Lives Remaining: 4. Ghost's Lives Remaining: 4.
Active Pacts: 13 / 20.
True Marks: Powerful Acolyte.
True Marks (hidden): Worthy Adversary, Wolf Protector, Wolf Progenitor.
False Marks (fabricated): Lesser Shadow, Lesser Light, Lesser Dark.

<u>Faction Data: Forerunners</u>

Faction officers appointed: 7. **Sectors claimed:** 1 / 3 (+1 from Safyre).
Faction Leaders: Michael, Safyre.
Factional Traits: 1 (rift sense).
Governor of Sanctum: Safyre. **Active Buffs:** bastion of healing.

<u>Forerunner Officers</u>
Faction Custodian: Adriel.
Nether Expeditionary Force Leader: archlich, Farren.
Brotherhood Liaison: dwarven merchant, Sedgwick.
Reach Outpost Commander: nagian psi knight, Zekiel.
Guardian Outpost Commander: nagian werefox, Elise.
Home Guard Captain: nagian mage hunter, Lucius.
Vault Guard Captain: windknight, Keros.

<u>Forerunner Groups</u>
Nether Force: Anriq, Regus, and wolfmen.
Reach Outpost: 25 nagians, 1 company of Bane Wolves, 1 forsworn elite.
Guardian Outpost: 25 nagians, dire and arctic wolves, 1 forsworn elite.
Home Guard: 25 nagians, Adriel, 3 companies of Bane Wolves.
Vault Guard: 25 nagians, 5 forsworn rank 4 players.
Tower Dungeon Party: Nyra, Terence, and Teresa.
Support Team One: Shael, Ceruvax, and the forsworn elites: Mariam, Deryn, and Llewyn.

Players pledged: Nyra, Ceruvax, Terence, Teresa, Anriq, Shael, Keros, Sedgwick, +10 forsworn mages, Kartara, Senzo, Duskar, Cait, Fiona, Heglin.
Non-players pledged: Adriel, Pack of the Reach (500), Bane Wolves warband (2,000), arctic wolves (200), dire wolves (130), nagians (100).

<u>House Data</u>

Governing bloodline: Wolf.
Core Tenet: Just Retribution.
Second Tenet: Protector of the Ancients.
Third Tenet: Stygian Nemesis.
Affinities: Renegades, outcasts, and criminals.

Followers: 2 / 200 (Nyra and Ceruvax).

Active Buffs

** denotes boosts affected by items.*
Damage reduction (DR) (reduces damage incurred only):
Life: 20%. Death: 25%. Air: 65%. Earth: 65%. Fire: 65%. Water: 65%.
Shadow: 50%. Light: 50%. Dark: 50%. Nether: 120%. Physical: 62%*.

Resistances (RES) (negates damage and/or rebuffs spell effects):
Life: 10%. Death: 12.5%. Air: 32.5%. Earth: 32.5%. Fire: 52.5%*. Water:
32.5%. Shadow: 25%. Light: 25%. Dark: 25%. Nether: 80%*. Physical: 0%.
Mental: 25%*.

Ghost (DR / RES): Fire: 85% / 102.5%. Nether: 85% / 102.5%. Physical: 91%*
/ 42.5%. Mental: 25%*.

Stolen spells (0 / 3)

None.

Other Benefits derived from Items

Damage: +40% damage (faithful).
Abilities: perceive tier 6 spelled wards (sorcerer's coif), spellhold: furious
storm (mage's surprise), penetrate tier 5 illusions (true-seer ring).
Traits: none.
Skills: +5 ranks in thieving (scoundrel's wristband).

Attributes

Available: 31 points.
Strength: 48 (40)*. Constitution: 56 (44)*. Dexterity: 183 (159)*.
Perception: 132 (127)*. Mind: 228 (220)*. Magic: 106 (85)*. Faith: 20.

Classes

Available (Michael): 4 points. 0 ascendant points.
Available (Ghost): 4 points.

Primary-Secondary-Tertiary tri-blend: voidstalker (fabricated).
voidstealer XIV (hidden).
Ascendant Class: wolf lord (rank I, hidden), sire wolf (rank I, hidden).
Familiar: stygian pyre wolf XV (unique, hidden).

Traits

HFO: *denotes human-form-only benefits.*
WFO: *denotes wolf-form-only benefits.*

void heritage II (wolf, hidden): +4 Dexterity, +4 Strength, +8 Mind, +8
Perception, +12 Magic.
voidwalker II (wolf, hidden): improved senses in all conditions,
nethersight, immunity to blindness.

arctic wolf II (wolf, hidden): +10 Constitution, +4 Mind, +6 Strength.
were's bite II (wolf, hidden, ascendant): 0 to 30% chance of granting another player the were-trait.
sire's strain (wolf, hidden, ascendant): boosts your other wolf traits by +1 tier.
elder form II (wolf, hidden, ascendant): +20 to all attributes, shapeshift.

house elite (bloodline, hidden): bound to House Wolf, detect dormant wolf bloodline strains.
secret blood (bloodline, hidden): conceals the wolf blood of yourself, your followers, and your familiar.
blood puppet (bloodline, hidden): grants you the enslave ability.

beast tongue: can speak to beastkin.
Marked: can see spirit signatures.
inscrutable mind: +8 Mind.
mental focus IV: increases effectiveness of Mind skills by 40%.
intrepid explorer: logs all locations in first-discovered sectors, and safe zone location in any visited sector.
spell illiterate: cannot cast mana-based spells.
potion resistance II: potency of potions reduced by 2 ranks.
spirit talker: can speak to spirits.
bold blood: +1 attribute per level.
higher evolution II: can evolve your Class to ascendant rank 2.
commander (ascendant): can share bloodline traits or blood memories with your followers.
champion (ascendant): increases the strength of blood memories.
spirit familiar: can bind a willing spirit as your familiar.
mage-host: +10 Mind, +10 Magic.
slip-through-shadows*: 20% chance to evade aoe damage.
mentalist I: you can use your mindvoice to speak to non-telepaths.

spirit familiar (Ghost): mirrors player attributes and level, and shares ability slots with them.
psionic being (Ghost): retains telepathic skills and abilities from her former incarnation as a dire wolf.
free spirit (Ghost): can roam an unlimited distance from her host, but only within the same sector.
born again II (Ghost): grants your familiar 2 additional lives, will resurrect in spirit vessel.
pyreborn II (Ghost): +60% fire magic resistance and +60% fire damage.
voidborn II (Ghost): +60% nether resistance and +60% necrotic damage.

primal creature II (WFO, legendary): 18 feet long, +30% resistance, 3 attack types (physical, fire, poison).
regeneration II (WFO, legendary): health regeneration of +2% per second.

rift sense (factional trait): reveals the location and tier of all rifts in sector.

Available skill slots: 0.
light / hide armor (current: 197. Constitution, basic).

dodging (current: 245. Dexterity, basic).
sneaking (current: 259. Dexterity, basic).
shortswords / tooth and claw (current: 250. Dexterity & Strength (WFO), basic).
two weapon fighting (current: 228. Dexterity, advanced).
thieving (current: 193. Dexterity, basic).

chi (current: 213. Mind, advanced).
meditation (current: 262. Mind, basic).
telekinesis (current: 222. Mind, advanced).
telepathy (current: 261. Mind, advanced).

insight (current: 276. Perception, basic).
deception (current: 269. Perception, master).

channeling (current: 240. Magic, basic).
elemental absorption (current: 124. Magic, master).
null force (current: 92. Magic, master).
null life (current: 49. Magic, master).
null death (current: 55. Magic, master).
nether absorption (current: 247. Magic, master).

magma maw (Ghost) (current: 162. Magic, master).
stygian claws (Ghost) (current: 170. Strength, master).
ash armor (Ghost) (current: 176. Constitution, master).
telepathy (Ghost) (current: 143. Mind, advanced).
death magic (Ghost) (current: 147. Magic, advanced).
nether manipulation (Ghost) (current: 163. Magic, master).

Abilities

Constitution ability slots used: 15 / 44.
greater load controller (HFO) (15 Constitution, master, light armor).

Dexterity ability slots used: 141 / 159.
crippling blow (HFO) (Dexterity, basic, shortswords).
minor piercing strike (HFO) (5 Dexterity, advanced, shortswords).
deadly backstab (30 Dexterity, elite, sneaking).
superior trap disarm (HFO) (15 Dexterity, master, thieving).
superior lockpicking (HFO) (15 Dexterity, master, thieving).
greater set trap (HFO) (15 Dexterity, master, thieving).
wind daemon (30 Dexterity, elite, two weapon fighting).
vanish (30 Dexterity, elite, sneaking).

<u>Mind ability slots used:</u> **216 / 220.**
beguiling shield (30 Mind, elite, telepathy).
stunning slap (HFO) (Mind, basic, chi).
windsurfer (30 Mind, elite, telekinesis).
lesser engine of war (30 Mind, elite, chi).
sentient shurikens (HFO) (30 Mind, elite, telepathy).
shadow jump (30 Mind, elite, telekinesis).
greater quick mend (30 Mind, elite, chi).
impregnable mind (30 Mind, elite, meditation).
astral bite (Ghost) (5 Mind, advanced, telepathy).

<u>Perception ability slots used:</u> **126 / 127.**
powerful analyze (30 Perception, elite, insight).
greater trap detect (15 Perception, master, thieving).
conceal small weapon (HFO) (Perception, basic, deception).
mimic (HFO) (30 Perception, elite, deception).
superior ventro (5 Perception, advanced, deception).
doppelganger (45 Perception, grandmaster, deception).

<u>Magic ability slots used:</u> **20 / 85.**
superior draining bite (Ghost) (10 Magic, expert, death magic).
mist-thin (Ghost) (10 Magic, expert, nether manipulation).

<u>Strength ability slots used:</u> **32 / 40.**
charge (WFO) (1 Strength, basic, tooth and claw).
overpowering blow (WFO) (1 Strength, basic, tooth and claw).
ponderous steps (WFO) (30 Strength, elite, tooth and claw).

<u>Non-ascendant abilities:</u>
adept slaysight (hidden) (Class, elite, telepathy): paralyze, shatter, sleep, terrify, blind.
void thief extraordinaire (hidden) (Class, elite, any void skill and telepathy): 3x steal, siphon, negate, redirect on direct-damage, channeled, damage over time, aoe, wards).
awakened slayer (hidden) (Class, tier 7, telepathy, meditation): create an astral simulacrum (guard, project).
manifest (Ghost) (Class, master): explosive entry II, necrotic wake II.
diresight (Ghost) (Class, advanced, telepathy).
direshield (Ghost) (Class, expert, telepathy).

<u>Blood spells:</u>
enslave (hidden) (blood memory, greater): dominate 2 subjects per day.

<u>Ascendant abilities:</u>
shapeshift (hidden) (ascendant Class, legendary): twice per day, greater elder wolf.
lacerating bite (hidden) (WFO) (ascendant Class, epic, tooth and claw).
stunning paw (hidden) (WFO) (ascendant Class, legendary, tooth and claw).

fearsome aura (hidden) (WFO) (ascendant Class, legendary, telepathy).
portal master (ascendant, mythic).

Known Key Points

Kingdom Sector 1 (Nexus) safe zone.
Kingdom Sector 12,560 (wolves' valley) nether portal and safe zone.
Kingdom Sector 18,240 (Sanctum) nether portal 1 (guardian tower), nether portal 2 (Draven's reach), and safe zone.
Kingdom Sector 75,172 nether portal 1 (Draven's Reach) and safe zone.
Kingdom Sector 65,231 (Korg Minor) safe zone and nether portals to Korg Deep.
Kingdom Sector 65,232 (Korg Major) safe zone and nether portals from Korg Deep.
Kingdom Sector 45,104 (Brotherhood sector) safe zone.

Dungeon Sector 101 (scorching dunes) exit portal and safe zone.
Dungeon Sectors 102, 103, and 104 (haunted catacombs) exit portals and safe zones.
Dungeon Sector 105, 106, 107, 108, and 109 (guardian tower) exit portals.
Dungeon Sector 14,913 (candidate's dungeon) exit portal and safe zone.
Dungeon Sector 73,102 (Draven's Reach) one-way entrance portal, safe zone, and exit portal.

Nether Sector 30,199 nether portal 1 (dead), Rift-X (closed, tier 7), Rift-W (open, tier 3), Rift-Y (open, tier 5), Rift-Z (open, tier 6).

Aetherstone Bracelet Stored Points

sector 24,401 safe zone.

Netherstone Stored Point

sector 30,199 (Rift-X: somewhere in dunes).

Equipped (21 / 30 Game items)

Weapons (1 equipped)
faithful (+40% damage).

Armor & Clothes (9 equipped)
sorcerer's coif (perceive tier 6 wards).
ranger's kit (+24% damage reduction, 4 pieces).
bomber's belt (0 x acid bombs, 5 x smoke bombs, 0 x ice bombs, and 0 x fire bombs).
belt of the chameleon (8 x rank 4 nether protection crystals, 9 x rank 4 disease protection crystals, 6 scent concealment crystals, 5 x mental concealment crystals, 4 x rank 6 disease protection crystals, 2 x rank 5 poison protection crystals, 1 x rank 4 strength enhancement crystals, 0 x rank 4 dexterity enhancement crystals, and 2 x rank 4 magic enhancement crystals).

scoundrel's wristband (+5 ranks thieving, 0 / 300 trap-making crystals) (<u>triggers</u>: pressure plates, sound glasses, tripwires, motion pins, remote control, spell detector, psi detector. <u>elements</u>: lightning, poison clouds, fire, spring-coiled daggers, bear-trap clamps, small explosives, blots of darkness, ice, spiked-pit, hallucinogenic mist. <u>guides</u>: reflect, split, and funnel. <u>keys</u>: remote, timed, status.)
ranger's kit vest (16% damage reduction).

<u>**Rings & Accessories (10 equipped)**</u>
goliath's ring (+8 Strength).
acrobat's ring (+8 Dexterity).
sharpshooter's band (+4 Perception).
hale stone (+8 Constitution).
troll's talisman bracelet (+6% damage reduction).
mage's surprise (+10 Magic, spellhold: trigger-cast tier 5 spells).
simple potion bracelet (3 / 3 full heal potions).
true-seer ring (true-seeing: penetrate tier 5 illusions).
unmarked farspeaker bracelet (unmarked set, 1 of 6).
mindslayer's torc (+25 mental resistance, awakened slayer ability) (soulbound).

<u>**Other (1 equipped)**</u>
large bag of holding (200 slots).

<u>**Ghost (1 equipped)**</u>
Forerunner collar (council set, 2 of 30).

<u>**Backpack Contents**</u>

<u>Money</u>: 223 golds, 5 silvers, and 3 coppers.
10 x field rations.
2 x flasks of water.
2 x iron daggers.
1 x bedroll.
1 x coil of rope.
cat claws.
5 x full healing potions, 0 x minor heal potions, 2 x rank 4 cure poison, 1 x rank 6 cure disease potions.
17 x acid bombs, 20 x smoke bombs, 20 x ice bombs, and 17 x fire bombs.
small bag of hiding (tier 6 concealment ward).
a simple shovel.
1 x blue mages robes, 1 x black mages robes.
stygian shortsword, +3.
stygian shortsword.
15 x greater portal scrolls.
stone of calling (summon Muriel Sworn).

<u>**Upgrade Items**</u>

<u>Soulbound Items</u>
Tartan token.
Vivane token.
Kesh Emporium access card.
tavern bill of ownership.
BHG ID (junior member, 1 / 10 active jobs).
journeyman rogue's underworld token.
pioneer's compass (soulbound, attuned to safe zone).
unmarked chest key card (from Nicola).
Forerunner faction token (ID: 0001).

<u>Miscellaneous Loot</u>

None.

<u>Alchemy Stone Contents</u>

None.

<u>Bank Contents</u>

<u>Money</u>: 655 gold, 0 silvers, and 0 coppers.
2 x full healing potions.
2 x full mana potions.

<u>Tavern Money</u>: 300 gold, 0 silvers, and 0 coppers.

<u>Open Tasks</u>

Heist in the Dark (steal chalice from the Power, Paya).
A Perverted Trial (stop the Triumvirate abuse of the Combat Trial).
Brokering Peace (establish peace in sector 12,560 within 4 months).
Brotherhood Obligations (join the brotherhood on two nether expeditions).
Revive the Guardians (awaken Draven's brethren).
Locate the Lost Prime (find the hidden Prime).
Resurrecting Death (make Adriel a scion again).
Found a new House (persuade two non-Wolf Powers to join your House).
Rescue the lost Pup (punish the one responsible: Loken).
Campaign 30,199 (free sector 30,199 of the void).

<u>Open Pacts</u>

Deliver cynacilin. Status: pact obligations fulfilled. Blythe owes Jasiah a favor equivalent to the worth of sector 75,172.
Inner Council Pacts with Safyre, Anriq, Teresa, Terence, and Shael.
Guardian Tower Access Pact with Bacheus (deliver a tithe once a month for access).
Brotherhood Kingdom Chapter Pacts with Kartara and Senzo.
Brotherhood Nethersphere Chapter Pacts with Duskar and Cait.

<u>Feats Accomplished</u> (by book)

Solo your First Boss, Play the Game.
Novice Dungeoneer, Realize your Lineage.

Rift Defender, Pioneer of the Realms, Solo your First Dungeon.
(none).
Master Dungeoneer, The Bigger they Are, A Mighty Player.
Ascending to New Heights, Charging Headlong into Power, First of Many.
Apprentice Dungeoneer.
Solo a Power, Realm Explorer.
Mentalist, Rift Redeemers, Fell a Tree, The Road to Power, Ambitious.

<u>**Simulacrum Profile: Decal**</u>

Level: 305. Rank: 30. Current Health: 100%.
Species: construct. Lives Remaining: 1.
Fabricated Class: astral projection.
True Class: astral aspect of the Power Michael.
Damage reduction (DR): none.
Resistances (RES): 25% mental resistance.
<u>**Accessible Traits:**</u> inscrutable mind, mental focus IV, mentalist I.
<u>**Accessible Skills:**</u> telepathy.
<u>**Accessible Abilities:**</u> guard, project, shurikens, paralyze, shatter, sleep, terrify, blind, beguile.

BOOKS BY TOM ELLIOT

BY TOM ELLIOT

The Grand Game (<u>series page</u>)
Book 1: The Grand Game: <u>ebook</u> | <u>audiobook</u>
Book 2: Way of the Wolf: <u>ebook</u> | <u>audiobook</u>
Book 3: World Nexus: <u>ebook</u> | <u>audiobook</u>
Book 4: House Wolf: <u>ebook</u> | <u>audiobook</u>
Book 5: Wolf in the Void: <u>ebook</u> | <u>audiobook</u>
Book 6: A Scion's Duty: <u>ebook</u> | <u>audiobook</u>
Book 7: Ancient Debts: <u>ebook</u> | <u>audiobook</u>
Book 8: The Lost Reclaimed: <u>ebook</u> | <u>audiobook</u>
Book 9: Dreams of Power: <u>ebook</u> | audiobook (coming soon)
Book 10: The Mad God: <u>ebook</u> (coming soon)

The Grand Game Box Set (<u>series page</u>)
Book 1-3: Birth of a Player: <u>ebook</u>
Book 4-6: Rise of an Elite: <u>ebook</u>
Book 7-9: The Makings of Power: ebook (coming soon)

The Grand Game, Elana (<u>series page</u>)
Book 1: Empyrean's Rise: <u>ebook</u>
Book 2: Empyrean's Flight: <u>ebook</u>

Annals of the Runeguard (<u>series page</u>)
Book 1: Proving Grounds: <u>ebook</u> | <u>audiobook</u>
Book 2: Sector 52: ebook (coming soon)

BY ROHAN M. VIDER

The Dragon Mage Saga (<u>series page</u>)
Book 1: Overworld: <u>ebook</u> | <u>audiobook</u>
Book 2: Dungeons: <u>ebook</u> | <u>audiobook</u>
Book 3: Sanctuary: <u>ebook</u> | audiobook (coming soon)
Book 4: Sponsors: <u>ebook</u> (coming soon)

The Gods' Game (<u>series page</u>)
<u>Crota, the Gods' Game Volume I</u>
<u>The Labyrinth, the Gods' Game Volume II</u>
<u>Sovereign Rising, the Gods' Game Volume III</u>
<u>Sovereign, the Gods' Game, Volume IV</u>
<u>Sovereign's Choice, the Gods' Game Volume V</u>

AFTERWORD

Thank you for reading the Grand Game!

If you enjoyed the book, please consider leaving a review on amazon [click here]. I'm already at work on Michael's next adventure.

If you have any questions, comments, or want to support my writing, please feel free to contact me through my site, TomLitRPG.com or Discord.

Regards,
Tom
Support me on PATREON or join the conversation on DISCORD
Amazon Author page | Goodreads | Facebook | Reddit | Discord |

DEFINITIONS

Accord: old agreement between new Powers ceding control of Nexus to the Triumvirate.

Adjudicator: controller and arbitrator of the Grand Game.

alchemy stone: a device used to store alchemical components.

ancient: old Power.

anointed scion: a scion who has bound himself to a bloodline.

ascendancy: process of being a Power.

ascendant: descriptor often applied to Game aspects involving higher evolution.

ascendant undead: term the Adjudicator used to describe Stayne, meaning unknown.

blended Class: a combined Class.

blood awakening: the process of recalling blood memories.

blood infusion: the absorption of the essences from former scions.

blood memories: gifts from your forebears containing the power of the ancients themselves.

bi-blend: a combination of two melded Classes.

bloodline: reference to the ancient from which the player is a descendant.

breaking: refers to the breaking of the world, the fracturing of the Forever Kingdom into sectors, aether, and nether.

Circle: aka Ritual Combat Circle.

civilian player: a player without a class or combat abilities. Civilians do not have a player level.

class-unique skill: a skill that is unique to a Class and can only be acquired through a Class stone.

closed sector: a landmass that does not physically border another, making the area inaccessible except by portal.

composite spell: a multi-stage spell made up of two or more individual spells.

controlled sector: a sector owned by a faction. Ownership of a sector gives the faction's players increased privileges in the region.

Class: a defined path or vocation that gives a player access to specific skills.

Class evolution: the advancement of a Class, generally to a better-ranked one, due to particular traits, skills, or Marks acquired by the player.

Dark: one of the three Forces.

Darksworn: a player pledged to the Dark who values the self over the collective.

deathwish: An ability that is triggered in the instant between a creature being dealt fatal damage and the spirit fleeing the body.

Elite: a tier five player, i.e. someone above level two hundred.

ebonblade: soulbound weapons found in the Twilight Dungeon.

envoy: a trusted representative of a Power authorized to speak on their behalf.

Endless Dungeon: A section of the Nethersphere where dungeon mechanics are active.

Everborns: term used to describe players.

evolution: the advancement of a player's core characteristics.

factional trait: a trait possessed by all members of a particular faction.

familiar bond: a permanent spirit binding between a spellcasting player and a creature, allowing them the transfer of Game-gifted knowledge from host to familiar.

follower: a player that has pledged themself in a binding vow to a Force or Power.

Force: Light, Dark, Shadow. The building blocks of the cosmos and energy in its rawest form.

Forcesworn: Collective term referring to Darksworn, Lightsworn, and Shadowsworn players.

Forever Kingdom: the world of the Nethersphere and Kingdom.

forsworn: a sworn who has betrayed their Power.

Game: refers to the Grand Game.

gatekeepers: holders of ancient lore, guardians of the ancients' trials.

half-form: the in-between state where the player is in a mix of his two forms (man-form and beast-form).

House: House of the Ancient.

House of the Ancient: a grouping of followers pledged to one Prime.

Kingdoms: the collective name given to sectors located in the aether.

lycan: werewolf.

ley line: magic threads connecting nether sectors.

Light: one of the three Forces.

Lightsworn: a player sworn to the Light that champions the cause of the many, even to his own detriment.

marshmen: mysterious dwellers in the saltmarsh district.

meld: the process of combining multiple Classes into one.

mindglow: the visible signature of a mind as seen with mindsight.

neutral sector: a sector unowned and unclaimed by any faction or Force.

Nethersphere: collective name given to the sectors in the nether.

Netherspawn: stygian creatures.

nethersight: ability that allows stygian to see through free-floating nether.

new Power: one of the Powers that usurped the ancients.

oath breaker: one who has broken a Pact.

Pact: a binding enacted between a Power and player, overseen by the Adjudicator.

Power: an evolved player.

power word: a blood memory ability.

Prime: head of ancient bloodline. An ancient.

Prime Conclave: a gathering of Primes referred to by Kolath.

Primehood: the act of becoming a Prime.

rift: unstable portal from the nether. Ley line created by stygian seed.

scav: short for scavenger. A player who loots kills not his own.

scion: one bearing the blood of an ancient.

scion abilities: the abilities Michael had earned during the Wolf trials: astral blade, chi heal, mind shield, shadow blink.

seeking spell: spell that distinguishes friend from foe.

Shadowsworn: a player pledged to Shadow.

stolen spell: a spell acquired from another and cast using their skills and attributes.

soulbound: an item that remains with the player after death.

sworn: as in sworn servant. A sworn is a follower of a Power who has sufficiently deepened their binding Mark to benefit from the binding.

the real: reference to the physical realm.

trap-making crystal: crystal in trapper's wristband. Can be manifested as different trap components.

tratin: underwater sentient species with gills and blue scales.

trials of the ancients: tests created by the Primes for their successors.

tri-blend: a combination of three melded Classes.

trigger-cast: a spell held in readiness and invoked under specific conditions.

unsworn: not a sworn servant, and not bound to a Power.

upgrade gem: a game item used to advance an ability a single tier.

voids: informal term used to reference players who possess a void Class.

void Classes: a rare subset of Classes that specialize in damage reduction.

void's chosen: term by which the stygians address the stygian seeds.

void fathers: void trees.

Watcher: a Game artifact typically used to uncover deception players.

windslide: ramp of air formed by windborne spell.

were-trait: a trait carried by all were-players, fueling their ability to shapeshift.

weres: short for werewolves and other were-players.

wolfmen: hybrid species, non-player werewolves.

wolf trials: ancient trials created by Wolf Prime.

wolfkind: used interchangeably with wolfkin.

KEY CHARACTERS & FACTIONS

FACTIONS

Albion Bank: major non-aligned bank in the Forever Kingdom.
Awakened Dead: A Dark faction.
Axis of Evil: An alliance of Dark factions.
blackguards: Policing force in the Dark quarter.
dawn brigade: Policing force in the Light quarter.
Devil Riders: small Dark faction.
Forerunners: Michael's faction.
gray watch: Policing force in the Shadow quarter.
Mantises: A Dark faction of assassins.
Marauders: small Shadow faction.
Reaper Clan: small Dark faction.
Silent Blades: small Dark faction.
Shadow Coalition: A power bloc of Shadow, made up of like-minded Shadow Powers.
Tartan: the faction of Tartar, the god-emperor.
Tartan legion: the military forces of Tartar.
Triumvirate: A unique faction composed of Light, Dark, and Shadow that control Nexus.
Unity Council: the governing body of Light, made up of all Light-affiliated Powers.

GUARDIANS

Draven: centaur construct in Draven's Reach.
Kolath: mysterious construct in the Guardian Tower.

GUILDS AND NON-FACTIONS

Bane Wolves: mercenary band out of New Haven.
Bounty Hunters Guild (BHG): headquartered in the plague quarter, mercenaries.
Information Brokers: a gnomish organization in the plague quarter.
Pack of the Reach: wolfmen pack.
Kesh Emporium: merchant company owned by Kesh.
Stygian Brotherhood: headquartered in the plague quarter, experts in all-things-nether.

HOUSE WOLF

Atiras: Dead Prime Wolf.
Ceruvax: Former envoy of Atiras.

Michael's Aliases

Actus: level 101 human brawler.
Eccleston: level 192 half-elf phantom assassin (brotherhood alias).
Havick: level 187 human scout (old brotherhood alias).
Henry: level 132 human scout.
Jasiah: level 152 human duelist (Blades alias).
Taim: level 247 human explorer (New Haven alias).
Linx: level 230 elven blade dancer and disciple of Menaq.

Non-Players

Adriel: lich, Farren's sister.
Arden: Gnome information broker.
Algar: human captain, New Haven.
Avery: New Haven magister.
Castor: Possessed mage.
Cilia: First amongst the dark elves of New Haven.
Cyren: Gnome senior information broker.
Elron: dark elf marshal, New Haven.
Everard: dark elf master archer, bane wolf.
Farren: lich, Adriel's brother, new archlich.
Gamil: New Haven shopkeeper.
Lorn: Orc Chief in New Haven.
Loskin: Archlich.
Megtir: dwarven captain, bane wolf.
Minakawa: dark elf captain, New Haven.
Regus: court's security chief.
Sunfury: A phoenix.
Sienna: Human lord in New Haven.
Stormhammer: Dwarven Thane in New Haven.
Zorgulg: orc captain, bane wolf.

Players

Anriq: werewolf criminal.
Barac: crusader, male centaur.
Beorin: senior BHG member, dwarf.
Bornholm: Michael's companion from Erebus' dungeon, dwarf.
Cara: alias given to Kesh's agent in plague quarter by Michael.
Dathe: unknown werewolf player.
Devlin: Viviane's guard, unknown aquatic species.
Dinara: underworld den chief in Nexus.
Ent: guard outside emporium, armsmaster, giant.
Eyes: The BHG HQ doorkeeper, species unknown.
Frey: Loken's envoy.
Jasiah: duelist, human male.
Genmark: ward architect, gnome male.
Gintalush: mantis assassin, insectoid.

Hannah: BHG client liaison officer, human female.
Kartara: huntmistress at Stygian Brotherhood Chapterhouse.
Keros: forsworn and human windknight.
Kesh: master merchant, owner of the emporium, human woman.
Lake: guard outside emporium, berserker, giant.
Malikor: Mammon's envoy.
Michael: protagonist.
Misha: Marauder tracker, aka the Hound.
Moonshadow: aeromancer, male elf.
Morin: Michael's companion from Erebus' dungeon, the painted woman.
Nicola: under-dweller and underworld merchant, civilian.
Nyra: sniper, Michael's apprentice.
Orlon: Triumvirate knight-captain in the plague quarter, human.
Pitor: rank 15 warrior, Kalin sworn, human, Marauder sub-boss.
Richter: constable in Triumvirate citadel, human civilian.
Saya: apprentice alchemist, tavernkeeper in wolves' valley, gnome.
Shael: red minstrel, half-elf.
Simone: sharpshooter, half-elf female.
Stayne: Erebus' henchman.
Stonebeard: Triumvirate captain, dwarf.
Talon: the captain, Tartar's envoy.
Tantor: Michael's companion from Erebus' dungeon, high elf male.
Teg: Michael's escort in citadel, human.
Terence: human fighter, swordsman.
Teresa: human fighter, blade devotee.
Tevin: Marauder knight.
Toff: player outside haunted catacombs, ogre
Trion: Triumvirate holy knight, Herat sworn, human.
Trexton: herbalist in Triumvirate citadel, Simone's contact, dark elf.
Tyelin: Blythe's envoy.
Wengulax: mantis assassin, blade dancer, human.
Wilsh: Blackguard captain, human.
Yzark: Marauder boss.

POWERS

Arinna: Light Power.
Artem: Shadow Power. Goddess of nature.
Blythe: Dark Power, faction leader of the Silent Blades.
Erebus: Dark Power, leader of the Awakened Dead faction.
Herat: Light Power, member of the Triumvirate.
Ishita: Spider goddess, Dark Power, member of the Awakened Dead.
Loken: Shadow Power.
Kalin: Minor Shadow Power, faction leader of the Marauders.
Mai: Unknown Power and collector of artifacts.
Mammon: Dark Power, faction leader of the Devil Riders.
Menaq: Dark Power, leader of the Mantis faction.
Muriel: Light Power contesting Wolf Valley.
Mydas: Shadow Power, member of the Triumvirate.

Paya: Dark Power, junior member of the Awakened Dead ruling council.
Rampel: Dark Power, member of the Triumvirate.
Tartar: Dark Power, also known as the God-Emperor.
Viviane: Power owning the Albion Bank.

WOLFKIN

Aira: dire wolf dame.
Barak: dire wolf elder.
Cantur: half-mad wolf.
Duggar: dire wolf alpha.
Oursk: dire wolf sire.
Leta: dire wolf elder.
Monac: dire wolf elder and former alpha.
Moonstalker: Oursk's pup.
Shadetooth: Oursk's pup.
Snow: arctic wolf pack alpha.
Star: Snow's mate.
Stormdark: Oursk's pup.
Sulan: dire wolf healer.
Suva: dire wolf elder.

LOCATIONS

bounty hunters guild headquarters: in the plague quarter.
court of the dead: archlich's stronghold. Also court.
Dark quarter: eastern side of Nexus.
Eastern Marches: collection of open sectors that Draven's Reach exits onto.
global auction: auction in the safe zone.
guardian tower: public dungeon.
haunted catacombs: public dungeon.
highlands: arid northern grasslands and hills of the Eastern Marches.
information brokers office: in the plague quarter.
Kesh Emporium: merchant house in the safe zone.
Korg: collective name for the three sectors of Korg's Deep, Korg minor, Korg Major.
Light quarter: western side of Nexus.
lowlands: fertile southern lands of the Eastern Marches.
market square: square housing global auction.
New Haven: city in Draven's Reach.
plague quarter: southern side of Nexus.
saltmarsh district: area in the southeast of plague quarter.
scorching dune: public dungeon.
Shadow Keep: central castle in the Shadow quarter.
Shadow quarter: northern side of Nexus.
Sickening Ooze: dungeon in saltmarsh.
Sleepy Inn: Michael's tavern, aka Wyvern's Roost.
Southern Outpost: tavern in plague quarter.
Wanderer's Delight: hotel in the safe zone.